TO THE LIONS

CHUCK DRISKELL

To The Lions
ISBN 978-1492780069

Copyright © 2013 by Chuck Driskell
Published by Autobahn Books
Cover art by Nat Shane

First Edition: September 2013

autobahn
BOOKS

For Phillip Day, a great friend who truly cares.

Chapter One

Texas

GAGE HARTLINE thought he'd cleaned all of the blood from his hands. But he saw a little bit, right there, just underneath his fingernail. There wasn't supposed to be much to the contract job he'd finished that morning—but Gage, many years before, had learned to ignore the word "routine." Along with a team of other operators, he had been contracted to provide transport and security for a remote meeting in the hills of northern Mexico. During the meeting, however, as seems to occur in meetings of that sort, shots were fired. By the time the smoke cleared, and the rival faction had been dispatched, Gage was on a chopper, racing north, back over the border, holding both of his hands to his fellow operator's chest, providing a seal of life so the man could continue to breathe.

That had been this morning, just after dawn.

Thankfully, the man who'd been shot was going to live. In fact, according to the two doctors who had performed very private surgery on him, he'd been lucky. The bullet had missed his heart and spine. And, per the doctors, whoever had provided first aid for the bleeding and the sucking chest wound had most definitely saved the man's life.

Gage's hands twisted on the wheel as a feeling of positivity coursed through his body. Years before, he'd received intense battlefield medical training at the Army's Operational and Emergency Skills Course—the training had served him well on a number of occasions. Today's shooting victim wasn't the first to benefit from Gage's extensive training. While dealing with a shooting didn't typically constitute a good day for Gage Hartline, this day had been a success. The operator was alive and would recover fully.

Before taking his money and the prearranged rental car, the originator of the job had issued each of the operators a dire warning: "You're radioactive right now. Lay low."

And lay low Gage would but, according to his rumbling stomach, it was long past time to eat. He checked the mileage on the highway—13 more miles to flavor nirvana.

Behind the wheel of a silver, rental Chevy Impala, Gage motored to the north on Interstate 35, the air conditioner blowing cold white vapor at him in

1

an effort to counter the outside Texas heat. His destination was the Dallas/Fort Worth International Airport. He was more than halfway there, having watched the southern half of Texas float by as he cruised at 79 miles per hour.

From prior experience, Gage had planned a food and fuel stop in Waco. His reason for doing so was a transcendent Texas barbecue joint, named Rudy's, just off the interstate. Though Gage lived in North Carolina, a place that boasted of their famed brand of pork barbecue, Gage couldn't understand the regional rivalries and the constant bashing of the other barbecue styles.

He loved all of it.

Six minutes later, Gage exited the highway and parked between Rudy's and the adjacent gas station.

NEARLY FULL for only the second time in a week, Gage refilled his half-gallon cup with iced tea and sat back down to polish off the remainder of what had been a massive pile of succulent beef brisket. While he ate, he powered up his mobile phone, seeing a text from Colonel Hunter, the former leader of Gage's special operations team. Gage swallowed a mouthful of brisket and called the colonel.

"You alive?" Hunter asked without preamble.

"So it seems, sir. How are you?"

"Keeping the reaper at bay. Wily old bastard's gettin' closer every day." Hunter's tone turned serious. "How'd it go?"

"Went fine until daybreak. There was a little dustup at the tail end of the conference."

"Body bags?"

"None on our team. One guy had a hole in him, though. Supposedly no permanent damage, thank goodness."

"This world…"

"Yeah."

Hunter paused a moment before saying, "I need to run something else by you."

"Before you tell me, sir, just know that I really need to shut it down for a month or so."

"That's not like you."

"I realize that, but I need a little time to reset. I've been gone eighty percent of the time in the last six months. There are bills to pay. Dentists to be seen. Clothes to wash. I also need to call our friends in the Unit, too…do a little training. I just need to get caught up and feel my own pillow for a month." When referencing "the Unit," Gage was speaking of the 1st Special Forces Operational Detachment-Delta, most commonly known as Delta Force. Located on the populated area of Fort Bragg's western edge, Delta has access to some of the finest training grounds and methods in existence.

"I know you've been on constant red cycle, son." Hunter cleared his throat. "But understand, there's big green to be made on this one. *Big* green. Naturally the character you'd be working for is the unsavory sort." Hunter let that last part hang.

Gage thought about how little money he actually had. And, being nearly 44 years old, his body would likely start to fail him in the coming decade. He could use a nest egg. Then he truly could "shut it down" for a while—maybe for good.

"By big green, are you talking high five figures?"

"My intel says the potential is well into seven figures."

That made Gage pause a moment. "When are we talking about, sir?"

"As soon as possible."

"Clarify, please."

"You're back tomorrow?"

"Yes, sir. Due in Raleigh on the first flight."

"Then you'll need to leave tomorrow night."

"Shit," Gage breathed.

"Big green, son."

"Who's the originator?"

"I'll tell you that in person."

Gage stared down at his remaining brisket. Rudy's didn't serve their food on plates. When a person goes through the food line, they carry a wax paper-covered sturdy plastic crate, like soft drinks come stacked on. This allows Rudy's servers to pile the meat and sides on in pound quantities.

Although his belly was full, Gage really wanted to finish his brisket and accompanying cream corn and green chile stew. And he'd hoped to do so without the weight of a high-paying job on his mind. He asked Hunter when he needed an answer.

"Tomorrow'll be fine. Let's meet mid-morning out at Raeford. Talk it through over a greasy breakfast. Can you get there?"

"As long as American Airlines does their part."

"Fine."

Just as Gage was about to end the call, he heard a distant scream. He turned, seeing some other diners standing and pointing out the window.

"Gotta go, sir. See you around ten tomorrow." Gage hung up the phone and shoveled another bite of brisket in his mouth. He continued to watch the crowd at the window.

"Looks like more of 'em gang members," an older man with a classic Texas drawl commented. "Little peckers are ruinin' ever-thang 'round here."

"That boy ain't done nothin' to 'em neither," chimed in a heavyset woman.

Another piercing scream penetrated the restaurant, followed by yelled protests from the assembled crowd.

"Damn it," Gage breathed. He threw down his fork, took his buttery wedge of Texas toast, and stalked outside. It didn't take long to see what was going on. Across the parking lot, between the fuel islands of the gas station, four tough-looking post-teens had surrounded someone. The way they moved to block the person made it clear they weren't letting him pass.

And they were cackling like hyenas.

Bad situation.

Walk inside the gas station and tell the attendant. Then leave.

Gage licked his lips, glancing at the gas station. There was a line of people.

They were watching the scene. They should intervene. Call the cops, even.

Stick your head in, tell them to make the call, and leave.

He turned back to the group of toughs. They were bumping the person in the center with their chests.

Their curses were vicious.

They laughed.

They mocked.

Leave it, Gage.

"Stop bothering him!" was the yell from an unseen woman. "Can't you see he ain't looking for a fight?"

Ignoring the protestations of his inner voice, Gage took a bite of toast and edged toward the encounter.

As he neared the scene, the picture grew clearer. The man in the middle of the circle was probably only about sixteen years old. He had dark skin and a pair of thick glasses, and judging by his clothes and lack of musculature, it was obvious he wasn't the type to engage four violent gang members. He looked like the type of kid that should be on the debate team—not brawling at a gas station. Once it was clear that he wasn't getting past the group, he lowered his eyes in an unthreatening manner. He just stood there, not engaging his tormentors at all.

He was displaying patience. The kind of patience Gage Hartline did not possess.

Beyond the scene, at the gas pump, sat a battered old Buick with a Louisiana handicapped license plate and sticker. Outside the car was a woman of approximately fifty years of age. She was utilizing a walker and was on a cell phone, speaking frantically. She had to be the young man's mother and she was looking around, frantically telling the person on the phone anything she could to identify the gas station where they'd just filled up.

Gage's attention turned back to the punks surrounding the young man. They were probably a few years older than the young man they were mocking, maybe as old as mid-twenties. Covered in tattoos and adorned with numerous piercings, they all wore the same style sleeveless jacket, each with the same poorly-drawn logo pronouncing them as members of some piss-ant gang called the 5th Street Fiends.

When Gage had almost reached them, the woman on the phone yelled at the gang members that the police were on their way.

"Fuck the police, fuck you, and fuck your bitch-ass son," one of the punks yelled, high-fiving his buddies as he laughed at his own insult.

Then one of the punks began mimicking the young man. He put circled fingers over his eyes and began to walk in circles, saying "I'm a little bitch," over and over. This drew riotous laughter from his friends.

This wasn't a racial incident. There were all manner of skin tones involved. No, this was nothing more than cruelty. Sheer bullying.

Gage hated bullies.

He thought back to the warning he'd received this morning.

You're radioactive right now. Lay low.

You heard the man, Gage.

Lay low.

Lay low.

One of the punks smacked the young man in the back of the head, sending his glasses tumbling to the concrete.

Gage finished his toast and slipped the telescoping blackjack from his back pocket.

Wait for the cops, Gage.

5

The young man's mother screamed.

"Shut up, you fat old bitch!" one of the punks yelled. He turned and shoved the boy they were tormenting, sending him to his knees.

Rage ruled the evening.

Punk number one—short, tubby, and with a shaved head—was the first one to hit the deck. Gage struck him with his elbow just behind his right ear, turning him off like a light. If he'd had the luxury to pause and admire his handiwork, Gage would have seen two of the punk's front teeth break as his head smacked the oil-stained concrete.

But Gage was already on to punk number two, the biggest kid of the bunch. He was the one who had done the little mime job earlier. He'd turned, cursing Gage as he pulled his arm back for a punch. Before he had a chance to throw that punch, Gage's trusty spring-loaded blackjack smashed his nose, sending him down to the ground, squirming like an earthworm on hot asphalt. Not satisfied that the punk was out of commission, Gage smashed a straight left into his ear as he passed, momentarily silencing him.

The last two punks had backed well away. Gage grasped the young man who'd been the target of their insults, lifting him and nudging him toward his mom. Gage looked at her and told her to drive away.

When Gage turned back to the two punks still on their feet, his eyes went immediately to the gun being aimed at him. The punk aiming it, a ghostly white kid with a poorly-represented Eminem fantasy, held the gun "gangsta-style." It was a small, cheap revolver, probably a .32.

"You dead, mothafucka!" he yelled, pulling his lips back to his gums in some prehistoric effort to appear menacing.

His still-standing partner, a stick-figure tattooed punk, stood behind his gun-toting friend, sneering and saying, "Yeah, bitch, who's bad now?"

"The police are coming!" the mother yelled from Gage's right.

"Get in the car, ma'am," Gage said, keeping his eye on the gun. "Just drive away."

"Get on your knees, muthafucka!" the one with the gun said to Gage. His finger was all over the trigger.

Heart thudding, Gage chanced a fast glance to his left. The first punk was still down, facedown, teeth fragments shrouding his face. He wasn't moving or even twitching, making Gage briefly wonder if he'd killed him. The second one, the one with the gash across his broken nose, was sitting up but didn't seem to have any will to rejoin the fight. Turning back to the one with the gun, Gage pondered his options.

"I said get on your damned knees!" The punk took a few more steps in Gage's direction.

Keep coming, you little shit.

"Cap his ass, Slick. Burn that bitch down," the stick-figure friend urged.

Suddenly, sirens punctuated the night. Probably from years of conditioning, both punks whipped their head to the sound.

Bad for them. Good for Gage.

He lurched forward, leading with his right boot and catching Slick, the gun-toter, in his narrow chest. The .32 went off, shooting up and shattering a fluorescent light. The kick knocked the punk into his skinny friend as they both tumbled to the concrete.

Lurching forward, Gage kicked again, knocking the .32 from Slick's hand. Gage kicked a third time, connecting with the kid's jaw, snapping it like a dry cottonwood branch. As his motion continued, Gage brought the blackjack down on top of the fourth punk's rising head, sending him back to the ground.

After a fast scan of all threats, Gage pushed the .32 again with the side of his foot, sending it skittering under an adjacent car. He stood there in modified knife-fighter's position, the blackjack at the ready in his right hand. Three of the punks were awake but seemed to have no appetite to come off the deck for another dose of the former special operations soldier.

With the blackjack pulled back, ready to strike, Gage yelled his query to the conscious Fiends. "Why were you picking on that kid?"

The skinny one that had been dispatched last still retained a measure of piss and vinegar. From his downed position, he snarled and extended his middle finger as he said, "Blow me, *pendejo.*"

Conspicuous due to its flashing lights, a police car could be seen rocketing under the interstate bridge. This would all be over in less than a minute. Keeping his eyes on the other Fiends, Gage dropped the blackjack. He straddled the skinny Fiend and dug a fingernail into the soft skin behind the punk's ear. With his other hand, he gripped the Fiend's vulgar middle finger, bending it to a point of whiteness.

"Aiyee!" the punk screamed.

"Tell the kid and his mother that you're sorry!"

The Fiend continued to scream, but said nothing. With no time to spare, Gage snapped the Fiend's finger, immediately grabbing the one next to it.

"What do you say now?"

"No! No! Please!"

"Tell them!" Gage yelled, twisting and pulling the finger, simultaneously burrowing his fingernail into the soft skin behind his ear.

7

"I'm sorry!" the Fiend cried. "I'm sorry for what I did to your son!"

Screeching, the police car bumped over the curb and roared into the gas station.

Gage released the pressure but maintained control over the gang member.

"Stop!" roared the command over the police car's loudspeaker.

Somewhat mollified, Gage straightened, raising his hands above his head. With admirable efficiency, the police took control of the scene.

The first few minutes were utter chaos and went about the way Gage expected. Once the McLennan County sheriff's deputies had taken control of the situation, they began to attempt to determine what exactly had happened. Sitting alone in the air-conditioned police car, his hands cuffed firmly behind his back, Gage remained quiet. Though a tiny piece of him was angry that he'd let himself get pulled into such a situation, he didn't regret it one bit.

In fact, he'd rather enjoyed it. But Gage's primary concerns were with the young man and his mother.

Gage watched her, sitting over by the store portion of the gas station, tearfully explaining all that had happened to a trio of deputies. The deputies occasionally glanced at Gage.

Finally, after about a half-hour, a statuesque, ebony-skinned deputy wearing sergeant's stripes opened the rear door of the police car. He helped Gage out, leaving the cuffs on.

"You got I.D., pardner?"

"Yes, sir. In that rental car over there."

"Mind if I have a look in the car?"

"No, sir. But you're going to find something in there."

"What's that, pard?"

"My pack."

"What's in your pack?"

"A package of money."

"How much?"

"Fifteen grand, cash."

The sergeant arched his eyebrows. "Okay, pard, am I going to find anything else?"

Thankful they'd not brought their own weapons for the contract job, Gage said, "It's a rental and I haven't been through it, so I can't speak for anything other than what's in my pack."

Another deputy stood with Gage while the sergeant walked across the lot to Rudy's and went through the rental. He came back with the small dark pack, placing it at Gage's feet.

"Your I.D. in there?"

"Front pocket."

The sergeant retrieved the I.D. "Gage Nils Hartline of Hope Mills, North Carolina." He looked up. "Where's Hope Mills, pard?"

"Fayetteville," Gage said.

The sergeant, eyeing the I.D., began to walk away. Suddenly, he stopped, coming back, scrutinizing Gage. "When I call this driver's license in, what am I going to learn, Mister Hartline?"

"Nothing, sir. No record at all," Gage answered earnestly.

"What sorta job you do?"

"I'm a contractor."

"You currently employed?"

"No, sir."

"Well if you ain't employed, pard, where'd the wad of cash come from?"

"I did a side job."

"Where, and for whom?"

Gage took a moment before answering. "To be honest, I don't know *who* it was for, and I don't know exactly where we were. South of here, but that's all I know."

"Mexico?"

"It might have been, sir."

The sergeant was visibly displeased. He turned to the deputy next to Gage. "They already run the first two to the M.C.J.?"

"Yes, sir. The other two's over at the ambulances still gettin' 'valuated."

"Go over there and check on 'em, Murphy. If they don't need to be admitted, get 'em hauled up to the jail. I'll be along directly."

When the deputy had taken his leave, the statuesque sergeant removed a tin of Copenhagen, seating a massive pinch between his cheek and gum. He opened the front door of the patrol car, coming back with a Styrofoam cup and spitting into it. He lowered his voice, saying, "Mister Hartline, the Fiends might be skinny punks, but they're well acquainted with violence. And judging by the three witnesses I talked to, you ran through 'em like a twister through a slat barn."

Gage shrugged. "I had the drop on them."

"On two of 'em. Then, based on what I heard, you had a dime-store Rossi .32 aimed at you and still managed to extinguish two more gang-bangers."

"Pricks ruined my barbecue dinner."

The sergeant smiled with eyes only. "You were in Rudy's?"

"Finishing my meal. I had a few bites left." Gage shrugged again. "They pissed me off. That was the first good meal I'd had in a week."

The sergeant briefly glanced to the east. "Fayetteville's right there at Fort Bragg."

"Yes, sir."

"Home of the Airborne, Special Forces, Delta, and probably more retired and mothballed mercenaries than any place on this here planet earth."

Gage said nothing.

The statuesque sergeant grinned at Gage, the brown of the snuff marring an otherwise gleaming set of teeth. "I was infantry and a Ranger, ninety to ninety-five, Mister Hartline. Korea then Fort Campbell, Special Troops Battalion, in the hundred-and-first. Spent a good bit of time in Bosnia with all types of you boys from Bragg." He spat and took a step closer. "I suppose you don't wanna hang around and make statements, do you, pard?"

"I'm in a bit of a hurry, sir."

"Thought so." He turned Gage and un-cuffed him. "I'm gonna forget about the fifteen grand. Somehow I got a feelin' you ain't plannin' on filing that on your comin' taxes." The dark-skinned sergeant aimed his muscular arm to Interstate 35. "See that strip of asphalt right there?"

"Yes, sir."

"I want your butt on it. And, if you'll please high-tail it outta my county, Mister Hartline, I got all kinda stuff to do tonight. For starters, I gotta get the surveillance video and make sure my buddy in ops can obscure a rental car's license plate. Then I gotta go by my jail and make sure some of my friends on the wrong side of the bars know just what those four shits did here tonight. You with me?"

"In lock step," Gage replied.

"Then I gotta tell a prosecutor and maybe a judge that some white knight took down four of our local Fiends and didn't hang around long enough for us to collar him. They ain't gonna wanna believe me but, when I tell it, it's gonna sound like the truth."

"Thank you," Gage said.

The sergeant extended his hand, giving Gage's a powerful shake. "Good to meet you, Mister Hartline."

10

"You, too."

The sergeant handed Gage his telescoping blackjack. "Slip that back in your pocket."

Gage did.

"You still here?"

"Negative," Gage replied, lifting his pack and accepting his North Carolina driver's license. Rather than obey the sergeant and go straight to his car, he risked the man's ire as he walked to the side of the service station where the young man's mother was nervously smoking a cigarette, speaking to a female officer. Using her walker, the mother stood, bear-hugging Gage as if she'd known him her entire life. While she nearly broke Gage's neck with her hug, Gage was happy to see her son, sitting placidly on the curb, eating peanuts and drinking his soda. He appeared fine.

Gage chatted with the mother for a moment, learning that they'd come to Waco to visit Baylor University.

"We've never had a college graduate in our family," the mother said, eyes welling with tears as she looked over at her son.

"Is Baylor offering him a full-ride?" Gage asked.

"Not quite," she answered, worry in her eyes, her lip quivering. "But he's got a number of schools offering him quite a bit. He's worked so hard."

Gage sensed a greater need. He reached into his pack and removed a small portion of the money, leaving it in the bag. Then he placed the remainder of the money bundle in her hand. "This is for you and your son," he whispered. "Maybe it will be enough to put his tuition over the top, wherever he decides to go."

The mother was too stunned to react and Gage didn't wait around for a reply. He hurried back to his rental car, waving at the sergeant who was standing in the same spot, scowling at Gage. The Impala's tires squealed as Gage rocketed from the Waco gas station, aiming the GM product north toward the yet unseen bright lights of Dallas-Fort Worth, wondering if he could make it on the amount of fuel he still had remaining.

He was low on cash, too, he reflected. Good thing Colonel Hunter had another job lined up.

Big green. Life-changing green.

As Texas roared by, Gage Hartline settled back into the seat, giving a small salute as the sign told him he was leaving McLennan County.

Despite the deep laceration on his elbow, he'd enjoyed his brief time there.

Chapter Two

Barcelona, Spain

THE WEDDING took place among Barcelona's high society and, primarily because of his handsome appearance and impeccable wardrobe, Xavier Zambrano fit right in. Only the wedding director and the mortified mother of the bride wondered how Xavier got an invitation. But they didn't dare ask him. They knew better.

Since it was a semi-formal afternoon wedding, Xavier nearly stole the show with his fashionably-late entrance. His shoulder-length black hair shone, swept back majestically. His face, with a beard of short stubble, was deeply bronzed. Contrasting with his dark hair and tan skin, Xavier's white teeth sparkled as he flashed his dazzling, store-bought smile at the guests when he was shown to his requested position just behind the family of the groom. Xavier wore an immaculately-tailored, cream color linen suit. Rounding out his expensive wardrobe were supple, handmade Italian loafers and a dazzling Breitling diver's watch. He could have easily graced the cover of any Barcelonan fashion magazine.

Save for the tattoo of a smoking revolver on the left side of his neck.

Ahead of Xavier, escorted by one of the groomsmen, was a younger woman, Xavier's date, no more than twenty and sufficiently beautiful enough to demand every male guest's unwavering attention. She was tall and lithe, standing apart from the Spanish crowd due to her natural blonde hair and ice blue eyes. She wore an arresting pink dress that clung to every undulation of her nubile body. Though what she did, according to wedding etiquette, was quite rude, she beamed at the guests when she shooed them down the pew, affording her and Xavier two prime seats, at the center aisle and just behind the family of the groom.

The perturbed guests seemed ready to protest before noticing Xavier's neck tattoo. Upon seeing it, they hastily made room, forcing smiles as they did.

To Xavier, his date was of less consequence than the eight-thousand euro watch on his wrist. She was an accessory, who would be used for his personal amusement, and deviation, later in the evening or, if the mood struck him, at the reception a bit later. Seated, the procession beginning, his date allowed her hand to roam, squeezing Xavier before he gripped her wrist, moving her hand back to her own lap.

"Not in church," he whispered primly, straightening as wealthy young groomsmen—Spaniards educated in places like Cambridge, Heidelberg, and Yale—filed in, each murmuring some private joke to the groom as they passed by to take their predetermined spot.

As he would later at the reception, Xavier merrily made eyes with the other guests, as if this delightful ceremony warmed his tender heart. The truth was, deep inside Xavier, he desperately desired to belong. Raised in a hovel, he'd eventually learned how to associate among the affluent ruling class. Sure, he'd killed men with his bare hands. Yes, he'd watched as men were held down and forcibly sodomized as punishment for their actions. Xavier had even once bitten off a man's nose (though he'd used his original teeth, not the lovely new veneers that had cost him a small fortune.)

Even if Xavier didn't have the conspicuous tattoo; even with the dashing figure he cut in a crowd of dashing figures; and despite his massive German automobile and the model-worthy woman on his arm; if a discerning member of society were to study him closely, they would discover the flaws in mere minutes. Such scrutiny has occurred since the beginning of high society, to those who are into that sort of thing: a new member is welcomed to the country club, because they have the kind of wealth that's the first, and *most* important, membership requirement. Once a person is among society, however, some forgotten little detail can easily out them as a mere commoner. Maybe it's their spouse, or a shirttail relative they'd rather not claim. Or perhaps they wind up drunk at a social gathering, groping women in their nether regions. Sometimes it's simply cursing or displaying the lewd and lascivious behavior that separates mere mortals from the pillars of society.

And, somehow, though he did desire to belong, Xavier also enjoyed the slight disconnect that would often occur when he interfaced at societal events such as this. Older women in their late fifties, wearing sparkling sequin gowns that showed the tops of their tired, age-spotted bosoms, would spot him from afar, standing tall and proud, looking every bit the part of a famous actor from the distance. Xavier delighted in the fact that his mere presence probably made their hearts race, remembering their glory days as they took a quick, contemptuous glance at their white-haired husbands, droning on about tedious golf or dreary yachting. The older women, high on champagne and the glamour of the gathering, wanted to believe they had one last good affair in them, dreaming of having their suety legs wrapped around this dashingly dangerous man in the trappings of an exclusive hotel room.

When the older women approached him, Xavier relished in their reaction upon noticing the tattoo. Sometimes they were already speaking to

13

him when it caught their eyes. Most of the women turned tail upon seeing the tattoo, making some silly excuse to quickly evacuate. But some, the brave ones, lingered.

Xavier had had more than his share.

So, although a part of him desired to be a feted member of society, Xavier was comfortable enough to merely enjoy the whiff of society he received when at power-rich functions such as this wedding. And, two hours later at the exclusive *Paulau Nacional* reception, after dining on sumptuous lobster mated perfectly with rice pilaf, haricots verts, and highly acidic Picapoll wine from Catalonia, Xavier sent his date to mingle after he made eye contact with an associate. Summoning the man, Xavier hitched his head.

The associate placed his plate on a table, said something to his wife—she was at least twenty years his junior, and well-kept—then walked through the crowd and passed through the rear doors. Thirty seconds later Xavier followed, finding an ornate hall marked by high arches and lighted oil paintings. He could hear the nervous flicking of what sounded like a Zippo and, after thirty paces, found Amando standing in an alcove off to the right, staring at an interior garden through a floor-to-ceiling window.

"Smoking is not allowed in here," Xavier said, curling his lip at the vile cigarette. "You might draw unwanted attention."

Amando Segura, a short, cultured-looking man with gray hair and puffy bags under his eyes nodded obediently, taking a quick drag before pressing the cigarette into a large plant. "Were you invited?"

"I crashed the wedding just to see you, old friend."

"Bad news," Amando said quietly, brushing a few stray ashes from his blue suit.

As was his habit, Xavier combed both hands back through his mane of hair. He stared out into the gardens, pondering the "punishment" he might mete out if Amando's news irritated him.

"Did you hear me?" Amando demanded, cutting into Xavier's train of thought.

Xavier came back to the moment and smiled coldly at the man. "I fail to understand how a man in your position, who has had *no* success in regard to my proposal—that you readily *accepted*—finds himself annoyed at having to repeat himself."

"Please accept my apologies," Amando quickly replied. "I'm simply frustrated that what you've paid me to do hasn't come together."

A clock could be heard ticking as Xavier glared at the telecom executive. "I suppose '*hasn't come together*' is one way to put it. And your current analysis of the situation is?"

"Are you one hundred percent certain he was receiving the call while he was near the resort of—"

"He was near Cadaques, yes. And the time before, he was near Llafranc. And the time before that, Mataro. No question."

"Then there is only one answer, unless there's a technology available that I'm not aware of, and I seriously doubt that."

Xavier arched his eyebrows, tapping his loafer.

"As I've surmised before, Ernesto Navarro is using a satellite phone."

After running his tongue over his porcelain teeth, Xavier said, "A satellite phone."

"Indeed. He's not using a landline or a tower-operated wireless phone. If he were, we would match the words being spoken from the other end. We're able to do this with only a five second delay and, on each of the three occasions, we've had nothing close to a match nor have we received any cellular signal carrying that, or any type, of encrypted data."

"And what of the phones emanating from the prison?"

Amando shook his head. "Nothing there either. They're probably both sat-phones, and I want it noted that I already *told* you this after the previous two tries."

Though his birth Aragonese-Spanish was cob rough, Xavier had spent so much time in London over the past five years that he'd purposefully developed a West End London accent on the tails of his spoken Spanish. He felt it added to his sense of refinement and, though it wasn't his intention, made him seem less threatening.

But at stressful times like this, he struggled not to fall back into his birth accent, tripping on pauses in his speaking the way a determined stutterer does when trying to get out an uninterrupted phrase. He pulled an audible, whistling breath into his Roman nose and asked, "Have you any suggestions for intercepting a satellite phone?"

"No, Xavier. That technology is out of my sphere of influence."

Xavier eyed Amando through slits, hating every fiber of the executive's diminutive being. "Then our business is done. You failed me." He reached into his jacket pocket, removing the envelope containing 3,000 euro, proffering it. When Amando reached for it, Xavier allowed it to fall to the floor. Amando's body jerked as he reflexively started to reach for it before stopping, raising his distrustful eyes to Xavier.

"What?" Xavier asked with mock innocence. "Do you think I'm going to hurt you?"

"No, señor."

"Then get your money."

Amando bent to the envelope.

Using a half-strength soccer kick, Xavier caught Amando in the jaw, knocking him back on his rear end. The executive sat there for a moment, inventorying his face with both hands, working his jaw before he pulled a piece of a tooth from his mouth. Xavier watched as Amando then held his head down, concealing his face as his body began to shudder and sniffing sounds could be heard.

"Oh no," Xavier muttered, looking to the heavens and laughing. "You're crying? My God, man, how do you live with yourself?" More laughter. "One kick makes you weep like a woman? Actually, not even a woman. Just last week I watched a dainty little Austrian woman hold out against the working end of a cattle prod. They zapped her at least ten times and she never once cried." Xavier tilted his head in an admissive manner. "She talked, eventually, but never cried. Gained my respect."

"I'm sorry for crying but you scare me."

"Amando Segura, you're the only man on this earth, outside of *my* sphere of influence, who knows of my efforts to seek the man in question. Shall I verbalize what might happen if I hear tale of this escaping to other interested parties?"

"No, señor," Amando answered with a strong shake of his head.

"Are you certain?"

"I will never, ever breathe a word of this to anyone."

Xavier extended his hand to Amando, helping him up. "How's the jaw?"

"It pops when I open it," Amando said, his lip quivering.

"Well, I apologize for my temper."

Amando seemed surprised but pleased. "Thank you, señor."

Xavier retrieved the envelope and handed it to Amando.

"Is there anything else, señor?"

Cocking his eyebrow, Xavier asked, "The lady with you, she is your second wife?"

"Sí, señor."

"What happened to your first wife?"

"We divorced, señor."

"Ah," Xavier said with a nod. "It just didn't work out?"

Amando narrowed his eyes. "Sí, señor, something like that."

"I'd advise you not to lie when I ask you this." Xavier waited with an open face until Amando nodded. "That woman out there, your current wife…did you have sexual relations with her *while* you were still married to your first wife?" Xavier quickly spiked a finger into the air. "Don't lie, Amando, because I will know, and there *will* be further retribution."

Seeming aghast at the line of questioning, Amando nodded.

"Very good, Amando," Xavier said. "Well, since you failed me, since I didn't get what I wanted and, since I compensated you and, since…well, I'm just in the mood, I'd like you to step out there and tell your adulterous wife that I intend to make love to her."

Amando's lips parted but no sound emerged.

"I want her today. *Now.*"

"But…"

"Tell her that I want her to be naked," Xavier pointed to a decorative chaise covered in wine velvet, "on that couch, right there, in precisely ten minutes." Xavier tilted his chin upward and studied the small man.

"Señor, are you…are you serious?" Amando asked, attempting to smile.

"I never joke about making love."

"But…but she's my wife. I love her and how could I ever explain such—"

Xavier moved toe-to-toe, glaring down at the executive. "The same way you convinced me you would get me Navarro's exact position, you little *gusano*. The same way you convinced your first wife that there was no one else until you left her high and dry for that woman out there." Xavier's voice had risen but now he brought it back down. "You've taken twelve thousand euro from me, for shit, and the very least you can do is open your wife to me, so I can regain some measure of satisfaction."

Amando trembled for a moment before whirling and vomiting in the same planter he'd used to extinguish his cigarette. Gripping the heavy edges of the gilded planter, he turned, a string of saliva hanging from his pink lower lip.

Xavier clicked his Breitling. "You now have exactly nine minutes to make your impassioned pitch. And, when my timer runs out, she'd better be on that couch, naked and willing."

Motioning Amando up, Xavier said, "C'mon, Amando, that blue suit is actually quite nice and you're getting puke on it." Once Amando was standing, wavering, Xavier glanced at his watch. "You've already pissed away thirty more seconds. Oh, and if you start getting ideas that this is some silly fool's errand, and that I might forgive you if you fail to convince her, you'd be wrong. Along with your home on that pathetic little hill at Pedralbes, I know about your son, the *cerebrito*, zit-faced mathematician wannabe at Zaragoza…and your daughter, pre-med and promiscuous…in the event you didn't know...studying at the charming Universidad d'Oviedo." Xavier menacingly flashed his teeth. "If you do not come through, they'll be getting visits from me. And the daughter's visit with me will be lengthy, Amando, if you know what I mean."

Amando's expression couldn't have been more horrified if he was ordered to slice his own throat with a razor. With a glance at his watch, Xavier coolly pronounced that seven minutes remained. He called out to Amando when he reached the double doors. "Amando! When she's on the couch, I don't want her demurely covering herself." He lowered his chin. "*Ready*—and—*willing*."

With a resigned nod and tears on his cheeks, Amando disappeared.

Raeford, North Carolina

AT THAT same moment, 4,232 miles away, Gage Hartline, hungry again, tore into a late breakfast. Having already doused it with hot sauce, he forked an egg white omelet, briefly regretting his decision to go with the healthier version of the incredible, edible egg. Gage had flown in on the earliest flight out of Dallas/Fort Worth and arrived in Raleigh ninety minutes before. With only a tiny bag of salted peanuts in his stomach, he sped straight to the Fort Bragg area without eating.

The restaurant Colonel Hunter had suggested they meet at was known as PK's Grill & Pub. The small restaurant was unique because it was situated at the Raeford Parachute Center, one of the busiest skydiving drop zones in the world. Nestled a few miles from sprawling Fort Bragg, Raeford is a training center, and recreation spot, for many of the world's elite covert operatives. Gage had spent many, many days training here. Back during Gage's military training, Raeford Parachute Center had been owned by the venerable Gene Paul Thacker, a skydiving pioneer and legend who had recently passed away.

The world was less interesting without good ol' Gene Paul.

Despite all the military, anyone could visit Raeford and enjoy themselves by watching the bevy of skydivers. And one would never guess that a number of the jumpers are members of the Special Forces, Delta Force, and all manner of shadowy operations that have hatched from the world's nest of special operations.

Skydiving is an open, friendly community. At Raeford, it isn't at all uncommon to find a group skydive populated by civilians and military alike, their common bond being the hair-raising sport they all share.

Inside of three minutes, Gage finished his omelet and plain wheat toast, gulping down his water as Colonel Hunter ambled back over. Hunter had eaten before Gage had arrived and, just as Gage had sat down, Hunter was summoned to a quiet corner of the restaurant by a distinguished-looking older gentleman Gage didn't know.

"Know who that was?" Hunter asked, sitting back down and using a toothpick on his teeth.

Gage reached across the table, pointing to Colonel Hunter's two uneaten pieces of toast.

"Take 'em."

"Who is he?" Gage asked before devouring the first piece of toast.

"Name's Harwood. Was in Fifth Group in 'Nam. Had a helluva career. Back when I was tabbed to assemble our team, Harwood was in the running for the job. We'd jumped together before, out here actually, and also gone to a few schools together." Colonel Hunter stared out the window as a student flared high under canopy, tumbling to earth and performing a nice parachute-landing-fall. Hunter's voice became distant. "Man, I thought Harwood was gonna knife me the next time I saw him, judging by the way he looked at me."

"Jealous?"

"Bah," Hunter said, dismissing it. "You know how competitive it all was. Soon after, we got shipped off post, he went to the Pentagon, and that was the last I saw of him."

"And?" Gage said, searching the table but finding no more food.

"Got himself three stars up in D.C. He was just telling me about the paper war that went on after Crete."

Gage pulled in a breath through his nose at the mention of Crete. He'd been a member of a special team, commanded by Colonel Hunter, that had been designed to perform the blackest of missions. Once chosen, the members of the team had assumed new identities and could not be officially traced back to the United States. For a number of years the team had performed as designed—defusing potentially deadly situations around the world. It was not uncommon for them to kidnap, to destroy and to kill, all in the interest of the United States.

But one blazingly hot day in June, on the rocky island of Crete, changed all that. Two children had died that day, and with them died Colonel Hunter's team. The entire affair had been a regrettable accident, and truly not the team's fault.

But, as usual when politicians are involved, someone had to take the fall.

Although the government kept the team's existence quiet, the team was scuttled and each of its men censured. Colonel Hunter was ungraciously sent to his retirement. Gage, like most of the others on the team, floundered. Special operations were all he knew, and now he practiced his skill privately.

"You okay?" Hunter asked.

"Yeah," Gage said, shaking the memories of Crete from his head. After years of torturing himself, he'd learned to put it behind him.

"Anyway, Harwood fought like hell for us up there in D.C."

"You believe him?"

"Yeah, I do. He's a leathery old pecker…but, then again, so am I."

The two men shared a smile.

Colonel Hunter still looked like he could lead a platoon up a well-defended hill. In his early sixties now, he was tall and continued to wear his steely-gray hair well inside Army regulation standards. Hunter's icy blue eyes and Oklahoman accent fit perfectly with the man who men naturally wanted to follow. He'd been toying with a salt shaker before smacking it on the table.

"Get enough to eat?"

"I might have another omelet," Gage said. "While I decide, want to tell me about this job?"

Colonel Hunter glanced around. Several members of the Army's precision skydiving team, the Golden Knights, were reviewing a jump video in the corner. A few students, easily denoted by their hideous billowy jumpsuits, were up at the bar buying Gatorade. Otherwise, everyone else was outside enjoying the mild late spring morning, jumping, preparing to jump or watching the skydivers.

"Ever heard of Los Soldados?" Hunter asked Gage.

"The Soldiers?"

"It's a huge crime syndicate in Spain."

"No."

"Well…their boss wants to hire you."

Gage tilted his head. "Sir…"

"I know," Colonel Hunter said. "But, from what I was told by a person I trust implicitly, this fellow isn't *all* bad. And though I have no idea what he's wanting you to do, he's willing to pay you ten grand, plus expenses, just to come *listen* to him."

"Wow," Gage said, leaning back.

"Yeah."

"In Spain?"

"Yeah, Catalonia. That's the state Barcelona's in. Don't know where you'll meet, though. They were cagey about that but they did mention the Costa Brava."

"And this is all because you owe someone a favor?"

"Don't let that influence you. I simply said you were my best contact. The decision's yours and it won't bother me a bit if you don't go."

"Ten grand," Gage murmured. "No catches?"

"Nope. You can take his cash and walk if you want."

"Northeast Spain in May," Gage said, glancing outside.

How could Gage say no?

They discussed the proposal for a half hour, with Gage learning little else than he'd already been told. They walked outside just as Raeford's Super Twin Otter roared into the warm air with a full load.

"When was the last time you jumped?" Colonel Hunter asked.

"A while."

"Got time for a hop and pop? Get our knees in the breeze outta the Cessna, clear the cobwebs out?"

"Are you serious?"

"Do I joke?"

Gage chuckled then glanced at his watch. "You said he's paying my fare?"

"The itinerary they sent routes you from Fayetteville to Kennedy, then on to El Prat. Leaves around six this evening."

"Rain check on the jump," Gage said. "I need to do a wash, get a shower, and throw some things in a bag."

"I've got your cash, your ticket, and the phone number I was given, all back at the house."

"Just so we're clear, sir, I'll go and listen to him, but I'm not taking a job from some Spanish mobster."

"I know, son. Just take the man's money and enjoy a free trip." Hunter eyed Gage. "They told me they're sending someone to pick you up at El Prat."

"Meaning, you *told* them I was coming."

Hunter smiled with his eyes only. "Ten grand is ten grand. In fact, I've already got your money."

"I may have to run a little deception at El Prat. I don't like courtesy limos."

Hunter nodded his head knowingly. "Just call the man once you're in country."

"After this, sir, wait a few weeks before you do any more favors."

"At least you're flying business class," Hunter added.

Gage had been stepping into his truck but stopped. "You're kidding."

"Nope."

"This'll be the easiest job I ever turned down," Gage said just as a bevy of skydivers began to swoop in under canopy.

Gage Hartline had no idea of the temptation that awaited him in Spain.

Barcelona, Spain

BACK AT the gala wedding, Xavier chuckled contentedly after sending Amando back to his wife with the incredibly indecent proposal. Popping a mint into his mouth, he strode back into the main hall. Across the room, up on a platform, the bride and groom were embroiled in the ridiculous tradition of smearing cake on each other. Though he'd never been married, and would never entertain such a notion, Xavier briefly imagined what he might do if a girl smeared cake on him. Too cultured to mete out her punishment in public, he would handle things afterward, making sure she—

Is that Redon? he asked himself, interrupting his pointless train of thought.

Cortez Redon was the top *acusador* in the region of Catalonia—his position was similar to a state attorney in the United States, yet more powerful. A balding, petite man, Redon was outwardly pompous—yet Xavier knew that, behind closed doors, Redon was easily bought. In fact, they'd recently finished a transaction that had netted Redon a pile of money in return for his not pursuing a case involving one of Xavier's most productive smugglers. Redon's obese wife was talking to two other ladies as the acusador visibly slipped backward in the throng, no doubt trying to find more interesting company to speak with.

Xavier looked left, spotting Amando far across the ballroom, away from the crowd and near the bandstand, gesticulating as he made his urgent point to his wife. Feeling his arousal coming up, especially when the wife slapped Amando, twice, Xavier turned back to Redon the acusador, reading his lips. He'd settled in with a busty, striking young woman of no more than eighteen, telling her he'd "been noticing her all day", dazzling her with his embossed business card and fancy title, urging her to call him if she "ever needed anything at all." Xavier shook his head as he closed the distance.

"Acusador," Xavier said loudly, standing directly behind Redon.

Redon's neck and ears immediately reddened at the interruption. He turned, his brow line shooting up upon seeing Xavier. Gathering himself, cutting his eyes in both directions, he whispered, "What are you doing here?"

"Watching these two young lovers get married, acusador. Is that now a crime?"

"We shouldn't be seen talking," Redon hissed.

Xavier moved around Redon, smiling at the young woman. "Call the acusador soon, darling. He will do *anything* in his power to help you...so that you might help him." Xavier let his eyes focus on her juicy décolletage, repeating, "Anything."

The young woman's lips parted as she eyed Xavier dreamily, tilting her head to look at his Leones tattoo.

Disregarding her, Xavier turned to Redon.

"Your tastes haven't changed, I see."

"What do you want?"

Xavier glanced to the spot where Amando had been "speaking" to his wife. Only Amando was there now, glumly staring toward the rear of the grand hall. Xavier's brown eyes tracked across the parquet floor, seeing Amando's wife trudging to the rear concourse, mopping her eyes with a tissue.

Perfect.

Turning the other direction, Xavier spotted his Swedish date standing alone by the wine bar. She was looking at him, so he motioned three minutes and pointed to the rear doors. She nodded, winking at him before running her long tongue slowly over her upper lip. His exit now secure, he turned back to the corrupt government attorney.

"If you're uncomfortable speaking with me, Redon, please turn and watch the festivities while I ask you a question." Redon obeyed, standing close to Xavier. The newly wedded couple had made their way off the platform and were heading to the bandstand as slices of cake were being distributed to the guests. Xavier glanced at Redon to make sure he was paying attention. Though he had his eyes on the procession, he clearly was.

"Who that you know might have access to satellite data, in regard to satellite phones?"

Redon put on a broad smile when the emcee called all unmarried men and women to the stage for the tossing of the bouquet and garter. "I'm not sure I follow," he said naturally.

"Simply put, I want to know the exact location of someone I'm certain is using a satellite phone. I want a contact who can track the person down to the meter."

Redon began slowly walking with the crowd toward the stage. Numerous women formed a crescent around the bride, laughing and jockeying for position. "I'm not sure," Redon said casually. "But I've no doubt such a task would require," he cleared his throat audibly, "*tribute* to numerous people. It would be *muy caro*. What else can you tell me?"

"The person I seek is here in Spain. He's very careful. Just find out how it can be done and reach out to me as soon as possible." Without another word, Xavier turned and walked to the rear of the grand hall.

The leggy Swede awaited him, posing with one of her long legs jutting provocatively through the slit in her dress. Xavier closed the distance quickly, glancing back to see Amando, staring from across the room. With a fluttering finger wave Xavier led his date through the double doors, quietly shutting them and placing an index finger over his lips. His date silently questioned him and he made a motion for patience.

Guiding his date forward, keeping her on the carpet runner, Xavier walked on the hard floor, so that only his set of footsteps was audible. Column after column passed until the broad area with natural light was upon them.

There was a final corner concealing the scene.

What will we find around the corner? Xavier wondered, barely able to keep himself from laughing.

As they continued forward, they passed the corner and the decorative sofa came into view. Sitting on the sofa, leaning back, naked as the day she was born, was Amando Segura's wife. Her hands trembled beside her, as it seemed it was paining her not to cover herself.

Though he had a plan that he intended to stick to, Xavier couldn't help but feel his pulse rate spike. The wife was actually quite attractive in the nude and, judging by what he knew of the diminutive Amando, Xavier could think of no way he was coming close to pleasuring this wholesome woman twenty years his junior. While she didn't have the lean, hard body of his Swedish date, Amando's wife possessed a natural figure without excess weight. Her breasts were large and firm and, setting Xavier off, was a small hoop navel ring that told him she was possibly promiscuous and might have been secretly excited over this encounter.

But it was not to be. Xavier had created the entire ruse to humiliate Amando.

Feeling his date stiffen and gasp sharply at the ribald sight, Xavier eyed Amando's wife and said, "My dear, I'm not sure what you're doing but you really should get dressed. Someone might be offended by your nudity and I saw a number of children in there." Holding his date's arm, they continued on.

The Swede turned back as they walked, making a vulgar gesture at Amando's wife and saying, *"Hora!"* They passed through another set of double doors as Xavier surveyed the rooms.

At the very rear of the massive museum, Xavier led his date into a vacant choir chamber, taking her right there on a bench. The images of Amando's wife and the buxom young woman the acusador had been cajoling danced in his mind, fueling his lust.

Also flitting through his otherwise endorphin flooded brain were images of what would happen once he finally located his arch-nemesis, the cowardly Ernesto Navarro.

With the intensity of a rabid wolf, Xavier howled with pleasure upon his climax. His blissful wail was heard by nearly every remaining guest at the reception.

Chapter Three

El Prat Airport, Barcelona

During his first-ever trip while seated in business class, Gage learned that the exclusive front-of-the-aircraft seating afforded passengers a multitude of benefits. From the lie-flat seats to the constant service of food and booze, Gage could tell the airline had worked diligently to make sure that an average passenger who happened to be flying in the front would debark and immediately swear to never fly coach again. While he felt the service was a bit overdone, especially on an eastbound flight that traveled through the night, Gage could see why some people would opt to pay a severe multiple of the coach price just for the lie-flat seat alone.

Gage had performed memorization work during the first portion of the flight. Though he despised it—it elicited bad memories of high school biology exams—memorization was one of the most important preparations for his type of work. After memorizing phone numbers and names, he scanned images from Google Earth, studying each of the seaside cities and the restaurant he planned to use for the first meeting. Then he studied avenues of approach, of escape, and landmarks.

Satisfied that he had everything down pat, Gage eventually slept. Having no need for May's featured wine, an Italian Piemonte, he had shooed his flight attendant away three hours into the nine-hour flight, telling her to discontinue his service so he could get a little rest. Thankfully for Gage (and setting off a memory about another flight he'd once been on) there were no unruly passengers aboard this flight, and he could feel his mind slowing to a point where he eventually slumbered.

Though he'd have loved to have gotten six hours of sleep, he managed about four, sleeping fitfully despite all the features that had been provided to make him comfortable. It wasn't the airline's fault—he blamed himself. This was the first time he had traveled back to Europe since the business with the diaries, and Monika. Understandably, his nerves were slightly on edge. This time, however, his destination was not Germany or France. The 767 he was aboard had just parked at the Terminal 1 gate of Barcelona's sprawling El Prat airport.

Upon clearing customs with his counterfeit passport, Gage stepped to his flight's luggage carousel where he retrieved two large suitcases, already on the revolving belt, both wrapped in purple ribbons and appearing stuffed to the gills. He hoisted his carry-on onto the top of the two suitcases and made a pit stop at the restroom, donning a loud Hawaiian shirt from his suitcase. He shook out a droopy ball cap, tugging it down over his hair, then began the trek to the main terminal, purposefully walking adjacent to a garishly-dressed vacationing woman in her mid-fifties.

There were additional customs officers at the exit but they paid him no heed. With his showy clothing and large suitcases, Gage looked absolutely nothing like an arriving mercenary. He stepped into the throng outside the secure area, estimating that there were sixty people awaiting arriving passengers. To the right stood a row of drivers, each holding a sign. Gage noted the one holding the sign for "Harris," the name he was supposed to be traveling under.

Pressing forward through the crowd, staying next to the woman, Gage glanced left, seeing another man well behind the crowd. He was leaning against an advertisement-adorned column, his eyes narrowed as he studied each passenger coming through the door. Gage glimpsed the man's illuminated iPhone, held low and half-concealed. As Gage continued to walk, he angled behind the man. The man lifted the phone, mimicking the actions of a person typing a quick text or email. But he was checking the photo, and the photo was none other than Gage Hartline, almost certainly taken surreptitiously and, from what Gage could tell, at some point in the last year.

Believing he'd escaped both men's watchful eyes, Gage ambled on, lugging his two prop suitcases which happened to be stuffed with clothes from Goodwill's dollar rack. He angled right, descending a conveyor that took him to a lower level, to the taxi stand. On the lower, outdoor level, Gage donned dark sunglasses. He paused, appearing to stare up at the signage, but cut his eyes back to the ramp. He saw no one who appeared to be following him. Making an educated guess, he felt the driver and his partner were the only two who were waiting for him. They would have assumed he'd not checked any bags and, by this time, were probably beginning to panic since he hadn't appeared.

It was time to leave.

Since it was so early in the day, the taxi line was short. Gage told the attendant he wanted to be taken to the seaside resort of Lloret de Mar, drawing raised eyebrows from the man.

"Señor, that will be a very expensive fare. More than a hundred euro."

"It's okay," Gage said with the same stupid grin. "My company is paying for this whole trip. As long as I get a receipt, we'll let old man Humphries worry about it."

The attendant, who'd no doubt heard it all in the busy tourist destination, smiled disinterestedly at Gage's reply and scribbled "Lloret" on the taxi card. He deposited Gage's bags into the rear of the mini-van taxi and received a five-euro tip in return. As the taxi exited the airport into the morning traffic, the driver glanced at the taxi card and asked Gage where in Lloret he would like to be taken.

"Where the main entry road meets the beach," Gage answered in English, hearkening back twenty-two years. And despite the somewhat uncomfortable seat, he reclined and managed to nap for the entire hour-long trip, relieved that his first obstacles had been cleared.

Lloret de Mar, Spain

UPON HIS arrival in the seaside resort, and after paying the exorbitant cab fare with the expense money he'd been fronted, Gage checked into a second-row hotel, booking a modest room for the night for considerably less than what he'd paid for his ride from Barcelona. He took a shower, making the water very hot to ease his cramped muscles. The gash on Gage's elbow burned in the water, making Gage briefly wonder what had become of the four Fiends back in Waco.

From the few clothes he'd wedged into his pack, he donned cargo shorts and a t-shirt, an outfit that would blend in well in the inexpensive seaside town. Then Gage headed back outside. It was now nearly noon and the May sun baked the Mediterranean resort. The streets were quiet in the likely hung-over party town, with most of the foot traffic wearing the bored countenance of locals. Gage walked inland, following Avinguda del Rieral for about a kilometer until he saw the large hotel he'd noticed on the drive in. Its brass sign out front claimed four-star-S status—exactly what Gage needed.

After eyeing the main entrance for a moment, he entered the sprawling hotel complex through the side entry, at the spa and tennis courts. There, after practicing a bit of his rusty Spanish on the pert female attendant— enjoying her radiant smile and affected interaction—he threw one of the embroidered hotel courtesy towels over his shoulder and wended his way into the cavernous main lobby of the hotel, just any old guest coming back from a trip to the spa.

While Lloret de Mar is a bargain basement destination for much of Europe, it still commands incredible views and is situated ideally between Barcelona, the Pyrenees, and the French border. The nightlife is famously frenetic, especially during the summer months, as teens and twenty-somethings from all over Europe flock to the resort's energy and low prices.

Most of the hotels near the water, such as the one Gage had checked into, were quite inexpensive. This four-star-S hotel, however, catered to a different type of client. In the lobby he spotted the bright white clothing and freshly groomed lap dogs he'd seen during his last trek to Paris. And although he was wearing a common t-shirt and plain shorts, Gage put on an important air, laboring to add a German accent to his Spanish as he asked the concierge for a courtesy phone.

"Of course, sir," the concierge said, whipping a cordless phone from an unseen spot behind the counter.

Gage situated himself in a corner leather chair, dialing a long series of calling card numbers from memory, learning that he had only a few dollars' worth of time remaining.

I should recharge the phone card now, he thought. Upon glancing at his watch, short on time, he decided to do it afterward. He then dialed the phone number he'd been given, pulling in a breath as the phone rang.

"*Díme,*" commanded the person who picked up.

"May I please speak with El Jefe?" Gage asked, remembering the explicit instructions that he was not to use Navarro's name on the telephone.

"I know who this is." A pause. "Where are you?"

"What's important is that I'm calling El Jefe." Gage could hear what he guessed was Navarro's voice in the background, speaking in Catalan-accented Spanish. There were a few muffled sounds before a new voice could be heard on the line. The voice was odd-sounding, as if it were computer-generated.

"Is this Mister Harris?"

"It is."

"Mister Harris, my men awaited your arrival at the airport. Was there a problem?"

"No, señor. I suppose I didn't see them."

"But you made the flight?"

"Yes, and thank you for the business class seating. I've never enjoyed such comfort."

There was a pause. "I was expecting we would be meeting by this time."

"A meal works best for me. Meet me this evening at nine, in Tossa de Mar, in the pedestrian area. There's an Italian restaurant there called Il Dipinto. I'd prefer you be alone."

Despite the voice modulator, Gage could hear the tiniest note of indignation. "You will pardon me for saying, but when I pay a sizeable retainer and fund a person's travel, I'm not accustomed to being directed what to do and where to be."

"And you will please pardon me for my careful nature. Because, señor, this is the only way I will agree to meet you. If you do not agree with my request, you will not see or hear from me again."

"I cannot come alone, or to the place of your choosing. I have far too many enemies to hazard such a directive."

"Would you hire me, especially going through the channels you did, if you didn't trust me?"

Navarro's silence provided Gage his answer.

"Señor, the restaurant is in an alleyway. Bring one man and post him at the head of the alleyway. One man *only*. I will be alone and I have no intention of doing anything other than dining, and chatting, with you."

The modulator squelched as Navarro exhaled loudly into the phone. "Agreed. Nine this evening."

"I look forward to meeting you then."

Forgetting to recharge his calling card, Gage thumbed off the phone and handed it back to the concierge along with a crisp ten euro bill. He made his face contemplative, tapping the polished counter with his fingernail.

"Can I help you with something else, señor?"

Gage nodded, removing another ten from his pocket. "Would you be able to assist me in the hire of a small charter boat for an evening cruise?"

The concierge beamed as he consulted an old-fashioned Rolodex.

AFTER WALKING back to his own hotel, Gage napped until nearly 5:30 in the afternoon. When he awoke, aside from his lingering jet lag, Gage felt quite good. Following another shower, he dressed in his favorite khaki utility pants and a long-sleeved bush shirt. Smelling of soap and shampoo, Gage made his way out into the early evening and headed to the main strip, near where it intersected with the beachfront road, headed to a unique club he'd noticed earlier in the day.

Gage was betting on someone at the club having an item he needed.

The club was marked by a large neon sign displaying the outmoded hammer and sickle associated with the Soviet Union. The name of the club was Eastern Bloc, written using both the English and Cyrillic alphabets. The building loomed large on the main strip, covered in sheets of chrome and fronted by numerous velvet ropes that would later restrain the throng as they waited to enter. But at this early hour the club was deserted, save for a lone man inside the door. He had a shaved head, dual diamond earrings, and a hideous burgundy suit with gold piping for trim. Judging from a quick glance at the musculature under the gaudy suit, he appeared to be the type of fellow who could handle himself in conflict.

Feeling the want of caffeine, Gage seated himself at an adjacent street-side café, ordering an espresso and eating the semi-sweet cookie that came with it. All the while, he watched the man inside the doors of the club, studying his actions. Finished, Gage left five euro under the saucer and stepped to the velvet ropes of club Eastern Bloc.

Closing his eyes, Gage took a deep breath, momentarily unsure of this route of action.

You're unarmed, Gage. This is your easiest and quickest method of rectifying that.

"Shit," Gage whispered, wishing he didn't feel compelled to do this. He stepped to the glass door and knocked three times. The man in the burgundy suit turned, mouthing something Gage couldn't make out. It probably had to do with Eastern Bloc's opening time which, according to the Cyrillic-style letters on the door, wasn't until nine in the evening. The man went back to what he was doing behind the podium, involving paper tickets of some sort.

Gage eyed the cut of the man's suit closely. *Yep, two of them, right where I'd wear them, too.* Gage was guessing .40 calibers in chrome…or gold. He knocked again.

The beady blue eyes came up, showing a high level of irritation. Gage curled his finger. The man came to the door, eyes beaming lasers. There was the snap of a bolt. The door opened, bringing with it the residual smell of cologne, vodka, boiled cabbage and sweat.

"What do you want?" the man growled in English. Gage saw the glint of gold teeth and, from under the man's collar, the brief hinting escape of a jagged chest tattoo. The man was almost certainly what Gage thought he was.

"I was told to speak with you," Gage said in German.

"English or Russian," the man growled. Gage repeated the phrase in English, again using a German accent.

"Who told you speak with me?"

Gage swallowed and looked both ways. "Last night, here, the girl with brown hair. I don't know if she was Russian or Ukrainian. Anyway, she said to come by early and to only speak with Yuri about it. I've got all the money."

The Russian's face contorted. "Yuri? There no damn Yuri here. My name is Dmitry. And what money?"

31

Gage showed his palms and backed onto the sidewalk. "Okay, you know what, I'm nervous enough about buying this stuff from someone I don't know and I think she gave me some bad information. I'm really sorry for bothering you. I'll go elsewhere, cool?"

He turned and began to walk away, struggling not to grin. He heard the scrape of Dmitry's knock-off Gucci loafers on the sand-gritted sidewalk. Then Gage was whirled around by a strong hand.

"What you talking about?" the Russian asked, still gripping Gage's shoulders.

"You know…"

Dmitry gave Gage's shoulder a shake. "No, I don't know. Tell me."

Gage glanced around before leaning close to the Russian's ear and whispering, "The white pony."

"White pony?"

"C'mon man…y'know…coke."

"Cocaine?"

Gage shook his head, trying to pull back. "See…I knew it…this is a bad idea."

The Russian held firm. "*What* cocaine?"

"This is bad…so, so bad," Gage murmured to himself, clamping the bridge of his nose. "Look, man, my supplier fell through. Disappeared one day like a ghost. And when I explained it to the brown-haired girl last night, she told me she was certain Yuri could replace my guy."

Dmitry released Gage, assuming a look of innocence. "We don't sell drugs here."

"Hey, man, I understand." Gage looked up and down the sidewalk in desperation, as if he might find a cocaine supplier nearby. "It's just that this is going to be the first big weekend of the season…I guess I'll just tell my, you know, *merchants*…that they're going to have to go elsewhere."

The Russian's ring-adorned hand clamped down again. "*You* wholesale to dealers?"

"I really don't want to broadcast that."

The Russian's poker face evaporated as big money entered the picture. "Exactly how much product you look to buy?"

"You're not a cop, are you?" Gage asked. Dmitry's instantly contemptuous expression provided the answer. Gage glanced around again. "A 'key' would do me. But two would be even better. I can go as high as three…" Gage added a toadying smile, "*if* I get a quantity discount."

The Russian licked his lips as he processed this. "That is lot of money."

"You're telling me, pal. One kilo is going to run me twenty-three, maybe twenty-four." Gage was guessing at this amount based on a job he'd worked a few months back. Thankfully, the Russian didn't flinch. "And just imagine what I'm giving up on my end if they have to go elsewhere. Cut up and stepped on, I'm clearing quadruple my cost in Tossa and sometimes seven, eight times cost here in Lloret, especially when it's high season."

That got his wheels turning. This thug's thinking about rolling me for my cash. Okay, Dmitry, just take the bait.

"Come. You go inside club," Dmitry said, his voice softening somewhat.

"You know what?" Gage said, faking nervousness. "Let's just both walk away. I've got a bad vibe about this whole deal. I probably should drive down to Barcelona."

"No, no, no, my friend. Come inside. I get you good drink and I call my boss. We help each other, okay? Good friends."

"Are you sure?" Gage asked, still resisting.

"We help," the Russian insisted, flashing his humorless gold smile. "And we become good friends for long time. This good thing for all of us, yes?"

As Gage reached the threshold, he stopped. "Just so you know, I don't have the money with me."

The Russian peered back with a cloudy face. "Why you say?"

"Well, it's just that I've had a few bad experiences with…you know, with Russians. You might have some of your friends downstairs ready to beat me up."

The Russian laughed. "You watch too many German movies, *zalupa.* Come…it's just me and worker girls." He motioned in front of his chest, as if he were hefting melons. "You might see nice boobies, yes?"

"That never hurts," Gage replied.

He followed Dmitry down a flight of painted red stairs, again noting the cut of the man's jacket and the twin bulges under his arms. Harsh light blared from above, made worse by the walls' shiny red paint. At the bottom of the stairs, to the right, were thick double doors with the letters CCCP emblazoned diagonally in bright yellow. The Russian smiled reassuringly at Gage as Gage glanced up at a security camera. He wasn't concerned about the Russian turning him in to the police, but there was no point in having a video record of what he hoped to accomplish.

Not here. Wait a moment.

After entering a five-digit code on a keypad, the Russian pushed his way inside. Music was the first thing Gage noticed, playing at half the volume it would later, but plenty loud for Gage's taste—a throbbing modern beat of some sort. The club was very dark and looked like any nightclub does when it's without the swarms of people it's designed for. There were columns throughout, each surrounded by dancing platforms and yellow rails, large enough to hold one or two dancers. The left side of the room was elevated. The right side, several feet lower, claimed a long bar with a curving neon countertop running nearly the entire length of the club. The upper half had a small bar halfway back and that's where Dmitry gestured Gage to sit.

"You want drink?"

"A beer will do."

Dmitry stepped behind the bar and popped a beer, sliding it in front of Gage and pointing at it. "Baltika...bring on jet here just for club. You not find Baltika anywhere in Spain."

Gage pretended to sip the beer, tasting just a hint on his lips. "I feel like I'm in Moscow already."

The Russian roared laughter and came around the bar. "I be back five, ten minutes, yes? I make call about your kilos. Enjoy beer and..." He screamed a name Gage couldn't understand, afterward motioning with his hand. Gage turned to see light briefly spill in from the far side of the room as a lithe figure glided into the darkness. A woman. The Russian met her halfway across the club, harshly speaking to her as he went out the way she'd come in.

After he passed through the door, Gage watched as Dmitry stared back through the glass.

The stare was malevolent.

Gage turned his eyes to the woman. She stood still for a moment, then allowed a zip-up jacket to slide off her torso and fall to the floor, making her way to Gage in only a bikini and heels. Under the red lights of the bar, Gage quickly decided that stunning wasn't a powerful enough word to describe her.

She moved beside him, standing close but keeping her eyes averted. Gage couldn't help but notice her scent—it was one of summer, the way a freshly-tanned woman smells after a shower. Her eyes were still turned away, her beautiful face drawn.

She doesn't want to be here.

Gage studied her, drinking in the woman's full triangular face with wide cheekbones. Her eyes were large and were either blue or green—it was too dark to tell. Guessing she was in her early twenties, Gage instantly marked her as sad—probably exploited by her Russian club-owning masters. She began to speak to him but he couldn't understand.

"I can't understand you. Do you speak English or German?" he yelled over the music.

She focused on him. "English is okay."

"Whatever you were speaking didn't sound like Russian."

"Polish. I'm Justina." She said it with a silent "J", sounding like "Yoos-tina."

"Pleased to meet you, Justina," he replied, glancing to the door she'd entered from. "You thought I was Polish?"

"I wasn't really thinking," she replied.

"Are you here alone, Justina?"

"What's your name?" she asked, ignoring his question.

"My name is Gregor," he answered, using the German version of the false name he typically used. "So is it just you and him here?"

"No. The other girls are back there working," she curled her lip, "and *him*."

"You're a waitress?"

"And bartender. And janitor."

"Why are you here so early?"

Justina laughed, though it was more of a snort. "Are you kidding?"

"No."

"You do *not* live in Lloret." It wasn't a question.

"Just during the season."

"All the Russian clubs are like this one. The girls, we get here in the early afternoon. We do everything to run the club, yes? We clean. We stock bar. We prepare food. We take out the trash. We scrub the bathrooms. Then we must cross the street and lay in the tanning bed to stay tan. After that, we use shampoo and shower under the hose out back and make pretty in the mirrors and work until four in the morning. We have to remove our tops and show our tits after midnight so we can get grabbed by disgusting men. Then we go to the tiny house with all the bugs and mice, sleep six hours and repeat everything. We do this *seven* days a week."

"Your English is good."

"Language is not hard for me. Being here is, though."

Gage turned on the stool, screwing up his face. "Why don't you just leave?"

"Where do I go?" she asked, taking a step back. "I have no money. No education. They know all this when they come to Poland and hire us."

"Don't they pay you?"

"At the end of summer. While here they feed us bad food and clothe us in skimpy things. If we get very, very sick we might go to doctor. That is all."

Gage listened to her explanation without outward emotion—he couldn't afford it at the moment. "Hang in there," was all he said as he turned back to the bar, trying to put what she'd said out of his mind.

"You're not German," Justina said, moving around so he could see her. After her pronouncement, her full lips tilted upward.

"Excuse me?" he replied in perfect German.

"No. You're not German," she said with conviction. "I know this. Like I said, I am good at language."

Gage had studied several languages at the Defense Language Institute in Monterey, California, a government institution that claimed to be the finest training facility in the world. And even during his time living in Germany, no one had exposed him the way this Polish woman had just done.

"Why are you here?" she asked.

"Just doing some business with Dmitry."

"No."

"No?"

"You're up to something."

"It's just as I said."

She leaned closer. "Can you help me?"

"Excuse me?"

"I cannot stay here."

"Then leave."

"I can't just leave."

"Not sure what I can do to help."

Her hand gently touched his shoulder. "I can tell you're different than the men who come in here."

Gage turned to her. Her eyes glistened as she stared at him.

"I'm just a man."

"I need a man—a good one."

"Do you ask all men things like this?"

She appeared hurt. "No, I do not." Nibbled her bottom lip. "The last few days have been bad and…and I've got to leave."

"What happened?"

"Nothing happened. The changes are here," she said, tapping her temple. "The things I was able to put up with in the past years I cannot deal with anymore. Make sense?"

Gage nodded.

Before he could answer, light spilled into the room again as Dmitry the Russian reentered the main portion of the club. Gage watched him, seeing the Russian reflexively touch his pistols.

Gage turned back to Justina. "Do me a favor, okay?"

"Yes?"

"Go behind this bar and get me another beer."

"You haven't touched that one."

"Please," Gage said, placing his beer on the shelf beyond the bar.

Justina shrugged, moving away from Gage, making him briefly gloomy at the absence of her close presence. But, as pleasant as the five-minute interlude had been, it was time to finish this diversion and move on to the big meeting at Tossa de Mar.

Just as Justina ducked under the moveable bar hinge, the Russian stepped to the spot where she had just stood, again gripping Gage's shoulder in his irritating manner.

It was like replacing a bouquet of beautiful and fragrant flowers with a smelly turd.

"I have good news," Dmitry said majestically. "For twenty-six thousand euro per kilo, cash in your hand, we can—"

Gage's left hand struck like an angered cobra.

Using his entire body, he swiveled, his left hand whipping around like a bolo. But, instead of a fist, he held his palm flat with his thumb outstretched. The effect was similar to a karate chop, and it struck the Russian squarely in the throat, on his larynx. Predictably, shut down by his body's limbic system, Dmitry crumbled in a choking heap.

Gage pounced on him, straddling his torso as his hands shot inside the Russian's splayed suit jacket, spiriting away the matching pistols. As Dmitry lay choking, Gage gave the handguns a quick appraisal, realizing he hadn't been too far off in his original estimation. Star pistols, model SS in .380 ACP. .380 was not Gage's favorite caliber, not by a long shot, but it would do for now. Both pistols were finished in handsome Starvel nickel and outfitted with excellent grips. He jabbed one into his waistband while raking the slide on the other, ignoring the round that arced to the floor. Gage was far more concerned with the round that replaced it.

As the stunned Russian recovered his air, Gage aimed the freshly cocked pistol at him. "Do not move, *zalupa*—I will shoot you."

The Russian had been trying to get up but instead he lay back, gagging and coughing loudly.

Gage stood and backed away to the door. He kept the pistol trained on the Russian, subconsciously adjusting his hands on the pistol, familiarizing himself with its weight and feel. When he reached the door, the Russian rose to his elbows, screaming a torrent of curses and gesturing with his balled fist.

Gage opened the door with his rear end and the last thing he saw in club Eastern Bloc was Justina the Pole, eyeing him in shock. But, just as she had earlier when outing him as a non-German, the corners of her mouth turned upward.

She gave Gage a small wave.

Unable to move for a few seconds, Gage shared the gaze with Justina. Then he turned, ducking his head for the camera's sake, and ran up the stairs, exiting into the gloaming of the Spanish evening.

Chapter Four

While Gage had been to Lloret as a post-teen in the Army, he'd never been to neighboring Tossa de Mar. Now, seeing it from the water, with the lights twinkling against the backdrop of the reddish hills, the town overlooking a crescent beach, Gage made a mental note to come back someday. While the sun had fully set behind the hills, there was probably another hour of twilight left. Gage's two favorite hours of the day were morning and evening twilight, especially in the summer months, when the dusky conditions lingered on and on. He could see why movie directors called it the "magic hour," because of the richness and layers of depth the low light provided. And Tossa de Mar looked especially handsome during such a flattering hour, especially when viewed from the water. White buildings were the norm, interspersed with cheerily-colored buildings and the occasional rock outcropping. Above the small boat, towering over the water on its rocky promontory, was a Spanish castle, lit by strung lights, a beautiful painting.

As they trolled in a few feet of water, well inside the foot-high waves, Gage motioned to the small boat's pilot to beach the craft here. After one final thrust from the motor, it went silent before the sand could be heard gently scrubbing underneath the bow. Gage hopped off, not caring that his boots and pants legs were soaked. He paid the man his required seventy euro, adding in a generous tip, before turning the 22-footer back to sea and giving it a shove. As the motor burbled to life, the pilot turned, giving Gage a two-finger salute before he chopped through the small waves, headed back to his slip just north of Lloret.

With two Star SS pistols weighing down his already wet pants, Gage cinched his belt tighter and skirted the narrow sand of the promontory. A check of his Timex showed he was expected in ten more minutes. Without caution, because he was certain Navarro's man—*or men, if I'm correct*—wouldn't be expecting him to arrive by sea, he walked straight into Tossa de Mar, heading up a steep pedestrian street to the southwest of the restaurant.

Like most towns on the Costa Brava, Tossa was built directly onto the side of the rocky Catalonian hill. Having scrutinized and memorized the map on Google Earth, Gage was confident in his approach to the restaurant. The street he climbed was lined with shops and cafés, but too narrow for any large restaurants with outdoor seating. This was good. He was searching for a landmark, a fountain outside of a church and, after five hundred meters, found it. At that point he was to make his way into a narrow alley to his right. If Navarro had broken his promise and brought more than one man, and if his people had any sense at all, this was where the hidden men would be stationed.

Gage was no longer moving normally. His steps were each lifted and slowly lowered to the earth in front of him. A scraping sound was not desired at the moment. Before he turned the corner, he removed one of the Russian's Star SS pistols, gripping it in his right hand as he glanced at his Timex. It was now time for the meeting.

Ahead of Gage, at the end of the narrow alleyway, was a rusty railing that had once been painted black. Running with the railing, just as Gage had memorized, was a narrow alleyway that ran parallel to the street he'd just ascended.

Pistol extended, Gage made his way up the alleyway until, around a slight bend, he saw what he suspected. Standing behind a narrow copse of saplings was a man. He was wearing black slacks and a shimmering short-sleeved button down. His skin was light brown and, other than the large caliber pistol in his right hand by his leg, he might have passed as a worker in the alleyway having a smoke.

But Gage knew by his own pace count that where the man with the gun was standing was above the side street that housed the Italian restaurant Il Dipinto—his meeting place. The man's back was partially turned to Gage and, after a few more steps, Gage could hear the man murmuring. A few more steps and an angling to Gage's left showed a small hands-free device on the man's ear—a Bluetooth. He was obviously talking to someone posted elsewhere.

This was going to be delicate.

Deciding not to overthink it—because he was only ten feet away—Gage prowled forward. In a swift movement, he moved within a foot and pressed the Star into the small of the man's back as he controlled the man's right hand with his own right hand.

"Do not move," Gage said loudly enough to be heard on the Bluetooth device. "And whoever is on the other end of the line, don't you move either. I'm Señor Navarro's dinner companion. We *agreed* that he would post only one guard." The man in front of him stiffened but said nothing. Gage slid his hand downward. "Let's all be peaceful. Hand that over and I will lower my weapon." As he tugged on the large handgun, Gage could hear something being said through the Bluetooth device and, just afterward, the man released the gun.

Gage backed away and, in his rough Spanish, told the man to turn around by saying, *"Date la vuelta, por favor."*

The man was young and handsome, his face displaying a mixture of indignation and fear. Gage recognized him from earlier as the man from the airport who'd held a sign with Gage's pseudonym. Honoring what he'd promised, Gage held both pistols down to his side. *"Habla Inglés?"*

A nod.

"I'm not going to hurt you. But I told Señor Navarro he was to bring *only* one man. Where are the others?"

"Only one. Outside the restaurant on the main pedestrian avenue."

"Tell him we're coming down, and he's not to show any threat to me. *Comprende?"*

The man spoke into the Bluetooth, listened for a moment, then spoke again. He nodded.

"Very good," Gage said, stepping forward. He peered through the leaves of the saplings, seeing a man at the rear table, a white fedora resting on the table next to him. It was Navarro, don of Los Soldados, a man whose image was all over the Internet as the most powerful, and aged, mobster in Spain. In front of Navarro were a bottle of Pellegrino and a powder-blue box of Dunhill fine-cut cigarettes.

Lifting his eyes, Gage saw Navarro's other man at the mouth of the alleyway—the man from the airport who'd been eyeing Gage's picture on his phone. He was pacing, staring up to where Gage and the unarmed sentry stood.

It was a satisfying image.

Realizing his tedious precautions of the day were probably completely unnecessary, Gage didn't regret them at all. Over the previous eighteen months he'd gotten his sea legs again. And the very first lesson, especially when dealing with criminals, was to trust no one. Even men vouched for by Colonel Hunter. Gage couldn't afford to take any chances, like a bullet in his back while he dined.

He turned to the sentry. "Drop through here and go stand with your partner."

"My pistol?"

"I'll return it after I eat."

Flashing a childlike expression of remorse, the sentry slid through the railing and released to the ground. Gage watched as Navarro turned and frowned at his man. Gage pocketed both pistols, now carrying three in his pants.

Grasping the center bar, Gage followed suit and slid through the railing. He dropped in behind Navarro, holding up his weighted-down pants. Straightening, Gage realized a woman at an adjacent table had seen him and the sentry drop in from above. Startled, she touched a hand to her upper chest. Gage smiled at her and said, "Atajo," the Spanish word for shortcut.

He stepped to Navarro's table and sat without invitation. To his credit, Navarro showed no surprise other than an arched white eyebrow. Navarro used his thumbnail to slit the cellophane from his cigarettes, peeling away the foil and removing a single cigarette.

"Mister Harris," he said, inclining his head. "I truly appreciate your caution."

"You said you would only bring one sentry. Yet you went against your promise and posted an armed man hidden behind you."

"My sincere apologies. It was not done out of disrespect, and I would have informed you of his presence had you arrived traditionally," Navarro said mildly. He spoke idiomatic English with only a slight accent. Navarro didn't appear to be a tall man from where he sat, although his belly indicated a man who enjoyed good food. Gage guessed him to be at least seventy, give or take five years. His hair was stark white and styled nicely. Although his face was deeply tanned, it was blemished by a fair number of acne scars, mainly on his cheeks. The face was round and his nose, while tan and a tad sharp for a man with otherwise rounded features, showed several groupings of burst capillaries, possibly denoting him as an alcoholic, giving him a bright, rubicund appearance. But most pronounced were Navarro's eyes, light amber in color. They were small but vivid and, to Gage, seemed to be the eyes of a person who was highly intelligent.

When Gage didn't respond, Navarro lit his cigarette with a simple disposable lighter. He gestured to the street with his cigarette. "My men are embarrassed."

"Which one is senior?"

"Valentin, the man stationed out at the street, is my *asesor de seguridad*. He's by my side at all times. The other one, Ocho, comes and goes."

"Would you mind calling Valentin over and introducing us—so he doesn't do anything rash—then keep him posted out there for protection? I'm presenting my back to the street—something I do not feel comfortable in doing—and I'm only doing so as a courtesy to you."

Navarro snapped his fingers. Valentin stepped over, flashing a harsh glance at Gage.

"Valentin, this is Señor Harris. He meant no harm in arriving the way he did."

"He was showing off," Valentin said in Spanish. "Showing off at the airport. Showing off here."

"Stop," Navarro commanded, raising his left hand. Resetting his countenance, he motioned back to the mouth of the street. "Now that you know he's here and means no harm, Valentin, please continue to monitor the street for unwanted guests."

"But he's armed, patron, and he took Ocho's pistol."

"I'm not giving up my weapons," Gage said flatly. He shook the silverware from a linen napkin and placed the other man's pistol inside of it, placing it at the end of the table. "For Ocho."

Valentin accepted the wrapped pistol, nodding curtly to Gage.

"That is all," Navarro said.

Once Valentin had walked away, the waiter approached, hands behind his back as he performed a small bow. He spoke rapid Spanish to Gage before Navarro intervened, looking at Gage and saying, "In the interest of time, might I order for us?"

"Please."

Gage wasn't able to understand the request but it appeared by his reaction that the waiter approved. The waiter soon came back with another glass and poured Gage a glass of water.

"Unless you would like something stronger," Navarro said, holding the waiter with an upheld hand.

"Water is fine."

The waiter went back inside.

"This is my real voice, not that regrettable voice you heard on the phone," Navarro said. "I was speaking to you through a ridiculous device." He ruefully shook his head. "My enemies are so desperate to kill me that they have compromised the phone companies."

"They sound advanced."

"They're savages."

Navarro lifted his cigarette from the notched ashtray, dragging on it as he looked past Gage. Studying the man, Gage was almost certain he saw genuine sadness in the man's eyes. A long silence ensued.

"Señor Navarro," Gage eventually said, "typically when a man like you summons someone like me, and pays a travel retainer in the amount you paid, they get right down to the request."

The Spaniard pulled in a long breath, flaring his nostrils. "When I began to make inquiries for a man with your skills, I initially learned about you from the Glaives."

Now it was Gage's turn to take in a sharp breath. He'd been promised that all animosity between him and the Glaives had been quashed. And, while Navarro seemed genuine, it unnerved Gage somewhat that the Glaives still had him on their minds.

"Please don't concern yourself," Navarro said, reading Gage's expression. "The man I spoke to is a friend. He said he knew you…said you made peace."

Gage nodded, realizing Navarro was speaking of Marcel Cherbourg.

"How is he?" Gage asked.

"He's drastically reduced the Glaives' size and, with it, their exposure."

"Despite his choice of vocation, he seemed level-headed."

Navarro took the slight insult with no reaction. "I could have offered this job to any number of qualified men," the older man said distantly, speaking downward as if there were a person under the table. "I chose you because, in all my inquiries, you were rumored to possess a degree of compassion."

"The others didn't?"

"Mercenaries, the whole lot of them. Only in your game for themselves."

"What is the job, Señor Navarro?"

"It involves my son—he's in grave danger." Navarro crushed out the cigarette and straightened in his chair. He smoothed the brim of the fedora before lowering it to the empty chair to his left. "He's in a situation that may soon cost him his life."

"What situation?"

"I've done everything in my power to protect him. But, here in Spain, even someone like me is limited in the resources I can provide. Especially now." Navarro's lips twisted in a sour expression. "Through the years, I've amassed far more enemies than I've accumulated friends or money. And, unfortunately, I can no longer shield him from what he is enduring."

"I don't fully understand."

"I need you to protect my son."

Ten grand to listen. Well, I listened.

Gage leaned forward, placing his elbows on the table. "Señor, I'm afraid there has been a bit of confusion."

"Confusion?"

"I am not in the protection business. I'm not a bodyguard or anything of the sort. My specialty is surveillance and, on occasion, tactical insertion.

There are thousands, maybe millions, of men and women better suited for straight security than—"

"If you'll allow me to finish," Navarro said patiently, cutting Gage off. "What I'm referring to is not a traditional protection job. In fact, you mentioned tactical insertion. Well, in essence, that's what we're talking about tonight. You see, Mister *Harris*, my son is currently—"

The disjointed conversation was again interrupted, this time by the waiter carrying a massive black bowl loaded with mussels in marinara sauce. Navarro slid his chair forward, shaking out his napkin and tucking it into his shirt. He made another request of the waiter who hustled away.

Gage grabbed the silverware from the setting next to him. He shook out the napkin and placed it in his lap, not really hungry but placing a few of the mussels on his plate. After eating one—it was superior—he sipped water and continued the conversation, surprised that his curiosity over this job was mildly piqued.

"You were about to tell me about your son, Señor Navarro."

Navarro shoveled two dripping mussels into his mouth, shaking his head. Once he swallowed the mollusks he dabbed his mouth. "We will dine first; then we will discuss business."

The two men ate two entire bowls of mussels along with a plate of buttered bread. Their only conversation involved the food, with Navarro exalting Gage's choice of restaurants and, as he swallowed his last bite, proclaiming Il Dipinto's mussels marinara as the best on the entire Costa Brava. Gage, who hadn't been hungry prior to eating the first mussel, counted thirty-three empty shells on his plate. He pushed the plate away while Navarro lit another cigarette. As the waiter cleared away the dishes, Navarro ordered two café cortados, then seemed content to smoke in silence. After a few more minutes, Gage learned that café cortados were espressos with a splash of milk.

Happy to have more caffeine, Gage drank his in a few gulps and pushed his chair back while he waited for Navarro. The older man sipped his drink before taking a long drag on his dwindling cigarette, staring over Gage's shoulder with the placid expression of a man listening to a beautiful composition of classical music. After several minutes, he crushed the cigarette in the ashtray and cleared away the smoke of the still air with his hand.

Finally, seemingly sated, he leaned backward and said, "My son, Mister Harris, is in prison. He has been there for about a year and it has been all I've been able to do to keep him alive."

Gage blinked. He fought against repositioning himself in his chair, managing to remain still. *Is he thinking of proposing a prison break?* Gage thought.

Even if it were successful, which is highly unlikely, I'd make mortal enemies of the Spanish government. Realizing he needed to hear the man out, Gage cleared his throat and said, "Please go on," even though he wanted to immediately object.

"The prison, Mister Harris, is probably not the type of reformatory you're thinking of. In the United States, at least from what I know, prisons are dangerous places, yet, at the same time, orderly and predictable."

Though he didn't necessarily agree with Navarro, Gage nodded for him to proceed.

"Here, however, the prisons are small and regionalized. And, upon sentencing, prisoners are supposed to be routed to the penal facility that is commensurate with their crime."

"And your son was convicted of what?"

"Narcotics trafficking. It was an utter sham-job, orchestrated by my political, and economic, enemies." Before Gage could respond Navarro said, "To be fair, and despite my many objections over his choice of vocation, he *was* guilty of narcotics trafficking, Mister Harris, only not in this instance. They framed him by breaking many laws."

"I see."

"Had he been sent to the correct facility, he would be serving his time proudly, and I would be able to protect him in the event of attack."

"I'm guessing he was sent somewhere fierce?"

Navarro leaned forward and clasped his thick hands on the table. "Fierce doesn't begin to describe Berga Prison. Every Catalonian gangster and murderer is there, trying to survive and make a name at the same time. An entirely different order has grown in those walls, one that has no respect for the power that exists outside the prison." A tremor passed through Navarro's tanned face. "The last time I spoke with him, he told me of the violence…and the deviancy." He paused. "I've heard all the stories, Mister Harris, and even served a sentence in my earlier years…but what my son told me I could never imagine, even in the darkest corner of my mind."

This meeting had been far more protracted than Gage had envisioned, and now it was getting personal. Knowing there was zero chance he would ever entertain the notion of intervening with a federal prisoner in a developed country, Gage made his tone polite. "Señor Navarro, I thank you for bringing me all this way. I also sympathize with what you're going through and, if you'd like, I would be happy to connect you with someone I know who might be able to help you intervene by infiltrating the *leadership* of the prison, which is the route I would recommend. But I cannot assist you in helping your son escape, sir. And by continuing our meeting, I'm doing you a disservice."

Navarro listened to Gage without expression. Then, as casually as if he were ordering another café cortado, he said, "I want you to go into that prison disguised as a *prisoner*." He eyed Gage. "I want you to give it one month, and then make your decision about staying further. I want you to protect my son, Mister Harris, and create an overall assessment as to what it will take to keep him alive and well for the balance of the twenty additional months he will remain there. Or, if he cannot be protected for that amount of time, I need to know exactly, from a tactician's eye, what it would take to free him."

"Señor Navarro—"

"Everything has already been arranged. We have layers of redundancy from the government, in the justice department and elsewhere. Your insertion will be highly controlled and safeguarded."

"But, Señor Navarro—"

"And I will compensate you with one hundred thousand dollars, cash, for your initial thirty days."

Gage Hartline fell silent.

"I've looked into your affairs." Navarro's expression was mildly apologetic. "You have few assets and you report no income. My sources tell me that a man like you would do well to earn a hundred thousand dollars in a good year—two-fifty a year if you were willing to live in a hot-spot like Afghanistan or Syria. They also tell me you're the type of man who lives simply, within your means."

Navarro inclined his head, as if he admired Gage for this. "But knowing something about your past troubles, and speaking with you on a personal level, I get the feeling that you would not mind finding your ultimate peace somewhere, be it on a farm, on the side of a mountain, or in a seaside hut. Perhaps you would like to move here to Catalonia and own a small villa in the hills." Navarro's expression hardened, a distinguished salesman nearing the end of his pitch. "My money, Mister Harris, will go a long way to helping you accomplish that and, if you choose to stay on in the prison, I can guarantee you that you will never have to work another day in your life…unless you choose to."

Gage cleared his throat. "Just so I might know what you're referring to, what is the ultimate reward?"

"Fifty thousand dollars, U.S., for every additional month you stay. And when my son exits the prison alive and in good enough condition to resume a normal life—I say that so there's no confusion—I will pay you a cash bonus of three million dollars, Mister Harris. That's more than four million dollars for not even two years of your life. It won't be pleasant," he snorted, "not by a long shot, hence the significant reward."

Gage had to remind himself to breathe. "Please go on," he managed to say.

"An associate of mine has the remainder of the details. Those are, as you say, the broad strokes." Navarro flattened his palms, his eyes alight. "Your thoughts?"

"May we meet again tomorrow?" Gage asked.

"You would like to sleep on this proposal?" Navarro asked with a hopefully cocked eyebrow.

"I'd be foolish not to," Gage said, the very words surprising himself.

"Which means you're considering it."

Gage finished his water. "I don't want to give you that impression."

"If you weren't, you would tell me no right now." When Gage produced his money, Navarro motioned it away. "Please, Mister Harris, the food was my pleasure."

"I will call you tomorrow, señor."

"I'd prefer we schedule a meeting now. Do you feel comfortable enough to visit my casita without disarming my men on your way in?" Navarro asked, smiling as he finished his query.

Gage nodded. "Yes, sir."

"Valentin will give you a new number and pick you up after you call." Navarro snapped his fingers and Valentin appeared.

After Gage had the information and bade farewell to Navarro, Gage stepped to the mouth of the alley with Valentin, addressing him and Ocho. "I apologize to you both if I caused you any problems with Señor Navarro." Gage extended his right hand. "No hard feelings."

Valentin stared at Gage's hand for a moment before shaking it. Ocho followed suit.

Gage walked into the night.

THE IDEA that had struck Gage before his meeting bloomed like a flower. Focusing on the idea and its elements, Gage didn't allow himself to mull Navarro's offer. Not yet. He'd taken the last bus back to Lloret de Mar and gone to his hotel room. After making the bed and brushing his teeth, he stashed one of the Russian's pistols in his suitcase. He grabbed several zip-ties from his suitcase and left the room. Since that time, still working on the fabric of his plan, he'd walked the frenzied streets.

It was now after two in the morning and Lloret de Mar was still going strong. He'd witnessed a fight spill out of a disco onto the cobblestone pedestrian street—two skinny men in trendy clothes took a royal beating from a duo of overly muscled, heavily-tattooed men Gage pegged as Irish. Just when it appeared the two skinny men were beaten, one of them reached into his pants. The appearance of the glinting switchblade ended the entire affair without anything more serious than a bloody nose as the two skinny men yelled after the running Irishmen, insulting them for cowardice.

Cowardice or intelligence? Gage wondered.

It felt good to be back in Europe, back to the unique clash of cultures. Back to the sights and smells. The doner kebabs and the proliferation of smokers. The ancient buildings and the zany fashions.

Gage was home.

He kept going, walking the streets in a grid pattern, never making eye contact with the multitude of barkers doing their best to entice him into their club. He was promised women, men, hashish, and even vodka-laced Italian ice. Like a lion pacing his cage for exercise, Gage put his head down and kept on walking.

Pausing at a church, Gage stared up at the bell tower, lit by twin spotlights. The church was Catholic, situated between the throbbing humanity of the clubs and discos. He found a marker, denoting the building as nearly eight hundred years old. It boggled his mind to think of the changes that had occurred around that old cathedral.

He placed all the money from his pocket in the steel box under the statue of a saint, allowing his hand to linger there for a moment. Then, moving at a faster pace than he had earlier, he walked about a kilometer back to a place he'd visited earlier.

It was the Russian club, Eastern Bloc.

And it was now 2:30 A.M.

From across the main street, as he queued with a group of people smoking outside another nightclub, Gage eyed the door of the Russian establishment. People flooded out, mostly in groups. The last few were either staggering drunk or hanging on a member of the opposite sex's arm. No one went inside. At 2:40, the lights in the front stairwell went out, followed by the red neon sign. Gage hurried a block to the west before navigating to the alleyway behind the club, then he made his way back east.

Behind Eastern Bloc were several cars. There was a large Mercedes, an Audi S4 with numerous aftermarket modifications, and an old Volkswagen van with French plates. Above the rear door of the club was a solitary light with a rain shield over the bulb. Gage found a sandwich wrapper and, standing on a paint can, used the wrapper to unscrew the bulb. The alleyway was now dark. He waited behind the van.

At 3:17 A.M. the rear door opened. A heavily-muscled man exited, glancing up at the darkened light before jingling his keys. The Mercedes chirped, marked by its parking lights casting flashes of amber light over the alleyway. Humming a tune, the car's owner flicked a cigarette that almost hit Gage. He entered the Mercedes, disappearing at idle before the car's tires screeched as it roared away.

Ten minutes later another man exited. Though the alley was dark, Gage's eyes had adjusted and he noticed the burgundy suit of his Russian friend, Dmitry. The Russian staggered to his car, leaning on it for support before vomiting explosively. Gage was only ten feet away from the splattering. By the time Dmitry had essentially fallen inside the Audi, the stench wafted to Gage—vodka, onions and stomach acid.

Doing his best to ignore the stink, Gage watched as Dmitry drove away. As the Audi went by the van Gage was able to see the driver, illuminated by the reddish cockpit lights. Still looking quite nauseous and in no shape to drive, the Russian was rubbing his Adam's apple.

That'll hurt for at least three days, Dmitry. Hopefully you're bright enough to ice it.

A few minutes after the Audi was out of sight, the rear door opened again. A short man held the door as a number of females exited. It only took them a moment to notice the rancid smell, evidenced by them waving their hands in front of their faces as one of them made a joke about it. Gage eyed the group through the window of the van. Standing in the middle, as they waited for the man to unlock the Volkswagen, was Justina. Her arms were crossed in front of her as if she were cold. She did not join the laughter of the other girls.

The van was parked so that the sliding door of the passenger side was nearest the rear door of Eastern Bloc. The old Volkswagen must not have had keyless entry because the girls just stood there while the man entered a sequence of numbers on the building's keypad, grumbling about something— probably the lack of light from above.

There was another joke. Again the girls laughed. Justina's arms remained crossed, her head down. It was the posture of someone who wished she weren't there.

And Gage aimed to do something about that.

While the man cursed the keypad, Gage moved. Star pistol leading the way, he came around the van, using a high shooting position. Despite the darkness, the girls saw him coming, marked by one of them uttering a piercing scream just as Gage reached the diminutive man. The man had just started to turn when Gage pressed the pistol into his neck, causing him to stiffen.

"Do not move," Gage growled in Spanish. He used his left hand to remove one of the thick zip-ties. He wrenched the man's left hand down, moving it up behind his back, the effect creating significant tension on the man's shoulder joint and causing him to grunt. Gage stuffed the Star into his belt and moved his right hand to the man's right hand.

And that's when the man resisted.

The man, a Russian judging by the curses he growled, made an attempt to spin to his left. If someone had advised him on an escape, his choice would have definitely been the best option because turning left, in theory, would relieve the pressure of the hold Gage had applied.

But Gage's grip on the man's left wrist was hydraulic. Sensing the movement, Gage swung his right elbow in a vicious arc, catching the man above his ear and splitting the fresh scab on Gage's elbow wide open.

It was almost the exact same move Gage had used in Waco, Texas only a few days before.

The elbow silenced the torrent of Russian curses. Gage caught the man as he fell, setting him down to the filthy alley floor and securely zip-tying his hands behind his back. Then the American lifted the keys from the ground and walked to the stunned women, all but one of whom skittered backward.

Gage held out his hand to Justina.

Speaking Polish, one of the women yelled what must have been admonishments at Gage. She was visibly confused about what was going on. They all were. All, that is, but Justina.

She stared at Gage's face, then at his hand. When she placed her hand in his, Gage used his other hand to toss the keys to the nearest of the women, telling them in Spanish to do as they pleased.

Leading Justina by the hand, and moving with a purpose, Gage Hartline led her up the alleyway, across the street and into the old city. As they walked, Gage was electrified by the confrontation, by the setting, and by the feeling of the warm, feminine hand in his. When, after a few blocks, they reached his hotel, he turned to her, having not said a word since liberating her.

"Are you okay?" he asked.

"I am now."

Chapter Five

THE BALCONY of Gage's hotel room faced to the northwest. Nearby foothills loomed behind the beachside resort, their ridges marked by blackness. Behind the hills was the panorama of purple night and, somewhere in the distance and unseen, the rugged peaks of the Pyrenees. Between the occasional wafts from Justina's cigarette, Gage enjoyed the sea smell as the wind blew in from the Mediterranean. There were occasional voices below them, in the streets, as the party town wound down from another night of reveling, regurgitating drunks from its many clubs to stagger blindly back to their hotels. Someone in another room had left their balcony door open, the sounds of their intimate union coming and going and, for whatever reason, making Gage slightly embarrassed.

Since arriving at the hotel, Gage and Justina's conversation had consisted only of a few sentences. He'd learned that her last name was Kaminski. He'd also gotten her a glass of water. Justina leaned against the railing, smoking her third cigarette, facing inward. She seemed shaken. Gage stood next to her, facing outward, his eyes moving over the Spanish countryside.

"Thank you," she said for the third time.

"No need to thank me."

She shut her eyes, tilting her head back. "I'm going to be in so much trouble."

"You won't be in any trouble as long as you don't go back."

"I'll have to work somewhere and they'll find me. It's not like I know a trade. I can't be a nurse or a teacher or even a cook." She flicked her cigarette over the railing. "I'm just poor Polish trash who happened to be born with a decent body. Working in a bar, for tips, is all I know."

Just as he was about to speak, one of the copulators from down below reached a noisy crescendo. Gage had been facing Justina but turned his head back to the hills as he spoke. "You haven't been *working*, in the traditional sense. You've been an indentured servant. I'd wager that those Russian club owners have burned that notion into your head for so long that you actually believe it."

"It's true," she said sullenly. "I am nothing."

"So you just work here for the season?"

She nodded.

"What do you do in the winter?"

"Work with my mama's employer."

"Doing what?"

"Cleaning dirty businesses. Emptying trash. Scrubbing shit from toilets."

Gage turned to her, viewing the smooth shape of her face, the protruding high cheekbones, and the swept back blonde hair. "Justina, how many years have you come here?"

"This is my fourth time."

"Do they fly you down?"

"Are you joking?" she scoffed. "They stuff eight girls in that van you were hiding behind. It's made for six passengers, and with luggage even that would be tight."

"All from Poland?"

She nodded.

He wondered how many other local workers suffered under these conditions. "Do they force you to come?"

"No," she admitted. "At the end of last year, when they drove us back to Polska, they told us the date and time they would pick us up—seven months later. As long as a girl has not had a baby, which, according to the Russians, would spoil her body, or as long as she isn't too old or unattractive, she has a chance to be one of the eight that get chosen. It's this way each year. Each year I say I will not come back, but I do, for the money." Justina put another cigarette in her mouth, speaking with it clamped there.

"Two girls were turned away this year. It always happens. They make us strip to our underwear on the side of the busy street. It was freezing cold that day and raining. As we stood there shivering, that little troll you beat up tonight rubbed his hand over every girl's body—if it jiggled, he rejected her." She lit her cigarette, showing the harshness of her expression. "One girl, who I thought was beautiful, had a tiny bit of stomach sticking out below her belly button. It was nothing. The little troll called her '*zhir*,' which is Russian for fat, and told her to piss off. She went away crying that she had no money and no place to stay. It was awful but, I have to admit, I was so happy that day they chose me to come again."

"I understand."

"But now, as I told you earlier, I've decided that I can't take it anymore."

"You weren't feeling that way before you came this year?"

"No, because like that girl that was rejected for her tummy, I have no money…I spend every *groszy* I make helping my family and buying food. Back in Polska, I live in a tiny house with the rest of my family. Coming here, while it's no fun, is a half-year break from scrubbing shit and I am able to come home to my family with a small amount of money at season's end."

Gage had no response to her discourse—her feelings were obviously genuine and justified. While he had no idea of the things she'd endured, he was empathetic.

"I'm sorry for my emotions," she said. "In the past I could get through a season. But this year…"

"Did something happen to you?"

"No," she replied, shaking her head. "I'm just…I don't know…getting older, I guess."

"You'll feel better after you sleep." Gage walked through the room and into the bathroom, brushing his teeth. When he walked back into the bedroom, she was standing there.

"Tired?" he asked.

"You're going to sleep?"

"I am." After turning the bedside lamp off, he removed his shirt, his boots, and his socks. He left his t-shirt and pants on. Then he flopped down on the bed, motioning to the still-lit bathroom. "If you don't find it gross, you're more than welcome to use my toothbrush and toothpaste."

Justina eyed him curiously for a moment. He made his face pleasant, lacing his hands behind his head as he closed his eyes, regulating his breathing. Moments later he could hear her as she brushed her teeth. He heard the water stop and could hear the flick of the light switch. She stepped back into the dark bedroom, standing there, appearing unsure of what to do.

"I won't bite you," Gage said, for lack of anything else to say. She removed her top and the short skirt, sliding into the bed in the bikini he had seen earlier. He recalled how she'd smelled earlier in the day. He smelled her again, the feminine scent making his head spin. She was closest to the balcony door; he was next to the wall. Gage rolled to his right side, telling her to sleep well.

Again he closed his eyes.

When ten minutes had passed, as he neared the welcome cliff of sleep, he felt her hand. She was pulling him to her. Gage rolled over, allowing her hand to situate him behind her, lying there as one. Justina found his right hand and pulled it to her stomach, flattening it there and resting her hand on top.

The American man and the Polish woman slept soundly. Together.

GAGE WAS up after four hours of good sleep. Though he didn't think there was much of a decision to be made, it was time to face the choice that lay in front of him.

He stood from the bed, drawing no movement at all from Justina. As he slid on a pair of old and friendly blue jeans from his pack, he couldn't help but look at her. The sheet covered her lower half. Her youthful, taut body absorbed the sleep like the good medicine it was. Her full lips were parted slightly, altering the pitch between her inhalations and exhalations. Last night, when she'd pulled him to her, she'd held her hand over his for a solid hour, nestling her body back into his as if his human touch was curative. Finally, sometime around daybreak, he'd awoken to find her splayed halfway on top of him. And after that, in his final slice of sleep, Gage's subconscious conjured an ethereal dream about Monika, his former lover whose life had been cut tragically short.

The dream wasn't significant, just the two of them hiking a perilous seaside trail, having an innocuous conversation. As Gage tugged on a long-sleeve t-shirt he paused his reflection, wondering if the perilous trail represented the path he was now on.

And why Monika? He hadn't dreamed of her in months.

He slid on his ancient Asics running shoes and again rotated his eyes to Justina, sleeping peacefully.

She's the first woman I've had emotional interaction with since Monika. He nodded to himself. *That's why.*

He skipped the cramped two-person elevator, taking the stairs instead. Downstairs he found three dozen early-rising tourists wolfing down a buffet breakfast of fried-hard eggs, fruit, and a strange-looking type of processed meat that had been seared on a large skillet. Gage stepped to the attendant, showing him his room key and asking if he could take a mug of coffee on a walk as long as he brought the mug back.

"Certainly, señor," the man beamed. "Our beach is always pretty, but it's especially beautiful at this time of day."

Nodding his thanks, steaming mug in hand, Gage exited and turned right, headed for the shore.

There were rows and rows of touristy curio shops between his hotel and the beach, all shuttered at this early hour. Few people roamed the wet streets, a trace of steam rising from an early morning shower that had already passed by. He descended a narrow street, passing a Scottish bar that looked slightly worse for the wear after what must have been a lively evening. On his left, as he neared the main road, was the requisite McDonalds that is now found in seemingly every European city of decent size. Sipping the stark hotel coffee, Gage walked to the seawall, descending the steps and slipping off his shoes for a stroll by the water.

The distant water was glassy but, at its shore, the Mediterranean offered atypically large waves. Breakers of three to four feet built slowly, crashing in a thundering yet lonely arrival. He turned landward and viewed the horizon over the resort, finishing the strong coffee as he deliberately considered the insanity of voluntarily sending himself to prison. Before he could even consider the offer, there were a number of questions that needed answering, and those needed to be ranked by importance. Floating to the top of the list was Navarro himself: could he be trusted?

And what were the terms of his son's sentence?

What if Gage decided, at any point, that the job wasn't working? How could he get out and how quickly could that be done?

What if something happened to the son that was beyond Gage's limits of control?

Did Navarro have any other people on the inside?

How exactly would Navarro's contacts "send" Gage to prison? Would Gage assume an identity? Who else was in on the job—who were the contacts on the inside?

There were a hundred more questions. More so than any other job he'd ever been offered—in fact, nothing had come close.

All the more reason not to take it.

But, Gage thought, *I've never been offered such money.*

He turned and walked to the southwest. Lloret's castle, flaming tangerine in the morning sunrise, loomed before him, guarding the crescent beach just like Tossa's, both built on the elevated stone headland. The sun was battling the cottony gray clouds for air superiority, enjoying an eastern breakthrough as rich morning light filtered from the castle to where Gage walked. Being here, back in Europe, with thousands of dollars to his name and an attractive, mysterious girl in his bed assaulted Gage with a sudden balminess of tranquility.

Water surrounded Gage's ankles as he walked, continuing to categorize his questions but doing so without much fervor. Because, despite the feelings of goodwill, he knew there was no way in cold hell he was accepting the inane proposition from Navarro. Perhaps he could help in some other way, something he would be pleased to provide. And hopefully Navarro would compensate him handsomely for it.

But Gage Hartline was not voluntarily sending himself to prison.

Chapter Six

THE HOTEL room was empty. Gage stood in the doorway, eyeing the unmade bed. Down the hallway, the maid's cart could be heard creaking along. In the other direction, a door opened and shut, followed by the sounds of a man and a woman. They passed by, a young tourist couple, laughing as they spoke Dutch about their beach day and all it would hold.

But Justina, Gage's Polish fancy, was gone.

Damn.

He stepped into the unlocked room, pushing the door shut behind him. She had slid the balcony door closed, the still of the room trapping her sweet scent. Gage breathed it in deeply, laying back on the bed and resting his hands behind his head as he stared at the dingy ceiling that had once been white. Whatever thought process he'd had going was shattered now, his mind awash in the memory of the Polish woman he had shared his sleep with. Like so many who've lived under loose captivity, probably knowing nothing else, institutionalized in essence, she'd almost certainly fled back to her captors. Gage could only imagine the retribution she would receive—or maybe was receiving at this very moment—for the humiliation he had caused the night before.

Closing his eyes, he shook his head back and forth—he would not go back to the Eastern Bloc again. She'd made her decision and his going back would invite real trouble for all involved.

Damn. Damn. Damn.

As he was biting his inner cheek to the point of drawing blood, he heard a metallic click. The door opened.

Justina.

"Going back to sleep?" she asked, crossing her arms and giving him an impish smile.

"Where were you?"

"Breakfast. I was hungry and they were getting ready to stop serving." She tapped the sign on the back of the door, smiling as she said, "See…it says right here in Spanish and English, breakfast is served from…"

Gage propped up on his elbows, captivated by her vision. He'd only seen her at night and in the dark of the Eastern Bloc. There was something about her, an imperfection that set her apart from the porcelain doll women who made millions by modeling. And whatever that imperfection was, though he couldn't put a finger on it, made her more beautiful, more real in his eyes. He was completely taken with her and he sounded like a schoolboy as he stammered, "I th-th-thought you had to show a key to be allowed entry to breakfast."

"I told the man I was with you in this room," she replied, sitting next to Gage on the bed. "He let me eat and it was probably the best meal I've had since I've been in Lloret." Justina lowered herself beside him and, like the night before, she and Gage lay very close. After a fifteen minute stretch of quiet, Gage spoke.

"I've got something very important to do today, and a big decision to make."

"What is it?"

"I can't really say."

"In Lloret?"

"No."

"Can I come with you?"

He shook his head. "I have to go alone."

He felt her tense. "Where will you go?"

"I'm not sure yet."

"When?"

"Later this afternoon."

"Leave for good?"

"No," he answered, patting her hand. "Just for a while—probably just a few hours."

"After that?"

Gage glanced at her. "I'll come back to you. Maybe we can have dinner, tonight."

She ran her hand through his hair, in the same way she'd done the day before, when instructed by her Russian "boss". But this time she looked upon Gage with warmth, the way a man enjoys being viewed, making his chest swell to the point of separating cartilage.

After another gulf in the conversation, Justina said, "I cannot thank you enough. Yes, I'm still scared about what I will do, and how I will get home, but I am like a bird freed from a cage. It feels good, despite all the questions I have inside."

"Well, relax," Gage said in a reassuring tone. "I've got a little money to get by for a while. Let's just enjoy our day."

"I don't want your money. That's not why I asked you to help me."

"I know that," Gage replied. "Again, just for today, let's not think about things."

"But you said you have a big decision to make today."

"I can set it aside until I have to leave. There are things about the decision that I don't know yet." He rolled over to face her. "A fun day. Deal?"

She smiled at him. "Let's go to the beach."

"The beach?"

"Yes." Her face ignited with whimsy as she bounced from the bed, clasping her hands in front of her. "Let's do like all these rich people do and go to the beach and eat lunch at a seaside café and sun ourselves and play in the water and look at other people and admire the pretty ones and make faces at the ones that should be wearing more clothes. I've come here for four years and have never had a single day at the beach." She leaned forward, grasping him and shaking him as she sang, "Please! Please! Please! A day at the beach! A day at the beach!"

Gage couldn't help but laugh.

"It's a date, yes?" she asked.

Who could say no?

They went downstairs together. Gage gave Justina money to find swimsuits and towels. After paying for an extra night, just to have the benefit of the room for the afternoon, he used the phone in an adjacent hotel to call Valentin on the number Navarro had provided.

His meeting at Navarro's casita was set for six-thirty in the evening. Gage would meet Valentin at six.

And, as it now seemed, he would arrive with a fresh suntan.

FOR THREE hours on the sun-drenched beach, Gage Hartline was twenty years old again. Crossing his mind, however, were Justina's former employers. He had no appetite to run across a group of pissed-off, armed Russians, especially when he was only equipped with swim trunks and sunblock. When he asked her if they would look for her, Justina told him that the crowded beach was the best place for them to be. She was adamant that, despite her absence, everyone involved with Eastern Bloc was either sleeping or preparing for their day. And the last place they would ever look for their runaway Pole would be the main stretch of Lloret de Mar beach—if they even looked at all.

Gage and Justina chose a spot in the center of the action. The temperatures in late May were typically mild and sometimes cool. But on this day, like an unexpected gift, the temperature had soared to nearly 30 degrees Celsius, mid-80s in Fahrenheit, bringing out oodles of tourists and a great many locals.

The beach was splashed with color from bathing suits, towels, coolers, toys, beach balls, and rental equipment. A parasail carried two shrieking tourists out every fifteen minutes, always drawing oohs and ahs from the crowd upon launch, and the occasional sharp cries when the tourists landed a tad hard in the sand.

Summer had arrived.

Once they'd had lunch, Justina took Gage by the hand and led him into the chilly water. They splashed and romped in the waves, with Gage quickly determining his new friend was a competent swimmer.

"How did you learn to swim so well?" he asked.

"We grew up near a lake. The water was cold but since we grew up poor, the lake was free entertainment." Justina winced as she touched the gash on his elbow.

"What happened here?"

"I cut myself at a gas station in Texas."

"Does it hurt?"

"Not as much as what I cut it on."

Shrugging, she moved in front of him. "Throw me."

"Throw you?"

"Can you do it?"

Gage took a great breath, squatting under the water after a wave passed. Digging his feet into the sand, he motioned her over. Justina backed her rear end into his hands and, with a hydraulic burst, Gage launched from the Mediterranean floor, sending her into a three-quarter forward somersault. She came up coughing and laughing and, after many more tries, they perfected the technique, managing to give her a full flip out of the water time and time again. With Gage eventually exhausted they moved beyond the waves, finding a sandbar that allowed them to stand shoulder-deep in the water, well out beyond most of the swimmers.

"I'm beat," Gage said, taking a great breath.

"Are you saying I'm fat?"

"No, I'm just getting old."

"You're far from old," she said, rubbing his shoulder as the water lapped against it. "What's the meaning of your tattoo?" she asked. It was his sole tattoo, the image of Themis, Greek goddess of justice, depicted with an arming sword in one hand and scales in another.

"Just something my friends and I decorated ourselves with back when I was in the military."

"Scales and a sword?" she asked, continuing to trace her finger on his skin.

"Justice can occur in many forms," Gage answered, trying to sound mild about it. "What about you?"

"What about me?" she asked.

"Any tattoos?"

"Not yet," she laughed. Then she asked, "Why did you change the subject?"

"That tattoo represents a part of me that I would never change, but the memories are not all good. Make sense?"

"More than you know."

Suddenly, she playfully clawed at his torso, lowering her head partially into the sea, viewing him through slit eyes. She prowled side to side like a crocodile and he could tell by the lines of her face that she was smiling below the turquoise seawater. Suddenly she lurched forward, grasping his shoulders and locking her legs around him.

Their kiss was instinctual.

Gage placed his arms around her back, holding her tightly, opening his mouth and enjoying the moment for what it was. As they kissed, moving their heads side to side, he parried a sharp attack of Monika-related sadness by reminding himself that he was completely justified in an innocent kiss.

When their coupling resolved itself he continued to hold her close and asked her a question that had been bugging him since he'd first met her:

"Do they abuse you?"

"*Przepraszam?*" she asked, cocking her head in a manner that told him that "przepraszam" meant "excuse me?"

"The Russians...do they abuse you?"

"No," she replied. "We come here voluntarily."

"Not just physically..." He chewed on his lower lip. "Do they require that you..."

"Have sex with them?" she asked eyes wide.

"Yes, that."

She shook her head emphatically. "I wouldn't come here if they did. Thankfully, they think we are trash. The Russians have so much money that they only date the tourist girls and never, *ever* a Pole."

"I don't mean 'date'. I mean, do they ever just use you to, you know...complete their temporary urges?"

"No. I tell you the truth. I have to take off my top at Eastern Bloc and let fat ugly men grab me and rub me, but that is the worst." She unlocked her legs and stood on her own. "It's bad, but not *so* bad, and I did come here voluntarily. I didn't have to come back."

"I just keep coming back to you saying that this year something changed."

"I promise, nothing happened to me. I'm just tired of living a miserable life."

Gage pulled his hands from the water, wetting his face. He eyed her for a bit, imagining the image of their mutual electricity rebounding in sharp bolts between them.

"Happier now?" she asked.

"Only if you've told me the truth."

"Starting seven or eight years ago, I could have made my life much easier by selling myself." Her face was stony, showing the type of tension he'd not yet seen from her. "But I have never done that. I don't judge those who do but, for me, that's never going to be option. And that is the truth."

Gage found her hand under water, clasping it. "If I can support you, would you be willing to stay with me for a while?"

"I don't mind earning my way."

"I didn't say you couldn't work. But, for now, until you find something, will you let me help you?"

"You mean this?"

"It would make me happy."

Justina leapt to him, again locking her legs around him and kissing him. It was an emphatic, and pleasant, answer.

SWIMMING IN the ocean just a short distance away was Xavier Zambrano. He'd actually taken notice of the nearby couple, recognizing the tall, wholesome blonde from somewhere, but unable to make the connection. Her friend, a rugged looking hombre with a few curious scars, was well-built and probably about Xavier's age. There was something cold and knowing about the man and Xavier noticed him looking over more than once, measuring him. Xavier instantly hated him, half tempted to walk up to his own towel and retrieve his pistol. He could conceal the pistol with the towel, walk back and gun the muscled asshole down right here in the surf.

But even Xavier had good sense. He was soon distracted by a clutch of topless post-teens frolicking in the waves. Eavesdropping on their conversation, Xavier learned that they were from the Netherlands. After his first swim, he boldly approached the young ladies and invited them to his villa for drinks after sunset. Surpassing his boldness, one of the young women asked him if he might have any cocaine at his villa.

"And if I do?"

"I'll be your slave," the woman answered, giggling but gnawing on her lower lip as she eyed him hungrily.

Xavier explained where they should rendezvous at the prescribed time. "My associate will meet you there and bring you to my villa."

"We can just walk," another of the young women said.

"I won't hear of it," he replied, winking before walking back to the water, feeling their eyes undressing him as he descended the mild slope of sand.

This was his second day at the sea. Terminally bored with his past two months in Barcelona, and being a man who liked to roam, Xavier had come north to Lloret, a seedy resort in the eyes of many Europeans, but a place where someone like Xavier could find innumerable distractions of the female variety—especially of the type who enjoyed some of his more peculiar proclivities.

He used a powerful free-style stroke to swim to the orange buoy that existed a kilometer out to sea. The chop was significant, making his progress difficult at times. Xavier welcomed it. A strong swimmer, he preferred to be in the water year-round, always swimming outside despite the cold. It was but another mark of his manhood.

After rounding the buoy, he found that the return stroke was a bit easier, making the swim back to the beach pass more quickly. He paused at the sandbar on his way back, and that's when he noticed the couple again. After appraising the tall blonde, he focused on her rugged date, cursing him by muttering the derogatory insult, "*Gilipollas.*"

Xavier completed his swim and exited the water, his muscles expanded by the spread of blood through their fibers. The group of Netherlanders were still sunning, all but one lying flat on their towels. The only one sitting up was the one who'd asked about cocaine. She'd been watching him and gave him a little wave, as if she wanted to make sure he'd made it back safely.

"I bet she's got a nose like a vacuum cleaner," Xavier said to Fausto, his longtime helper who awaited him at the edge of the surf with a thick towel.

"Pardon, señor?"

"The one in the middle," Xavier replied, pointing. The young Dutch woman fluffed her towel as she joined her friends, supine in their collective sun worship. "She wants coke, and a lot of it. How much do we have?"

"I stashed it when we arrived, señor. There is plenty."

"Good, good." Xavier looked at his Breitling, then up at the sun as it was halfway down the western sky. In another hour it would fall behind the high-rises along the beachfront.

"I'm hungry," Xavier abruptly stated. "I will eat this evening as I listen to the monthly reports."

"What would you prefer, señor?"

Scowling at the thought, Xavier ran his hands back through his wet hair, as if such a decision was of momentous importance. Finally, resolutely, he said, "Hearty salad, lobster, drawn butter, broccoli, and some more of that bread I had last night."

"Excellent, señor. I will see to it." Fausto snapped a phone open and walked to Xavier's bag, slipping it over his shoulder.

Xavier walked back to the group of young women, five of them, noting their omnipresent bikini line tattoos and belly button rings. "So, I will see all of you at eleven?"

The young women propped themselves up on their elbows and the one on the end, the only one with dark hair, hesitantly asked, "Should we bring anyone else?"

"You mean *other* men?"

"Yes."

"That won't be necessary," Xavier said, noting that, while cute, she was the least attractive of the bunch. She was probably fearful of being left out. "And just know, ladies, that I can assure *each* one of you an evening of wonderful drink, atmosphere and intense pleasure."

A few of them smiled. All of them seemed intrigued by this handsome, lean and muscular man with his designer trunks, his bejeweled watch, and his air of superiority.

"What's with the neck tattoo?" another one asked.

Xavier showed his best smile, kneeling in front of the girl and tracing his finger up and down her oiled lower leg. "It's my trademark...one of them anyway."

"What are the others?" she asked.

"I'll see to it that you find out first," he replied with a wink.

Another round of giggles passed through the fivesome.

"Until then," Xavier pronounced. He stood and walked to Fausto who was awaiting him at the stairway to the boardwalk.

Knowing the women were watching, Xavier accepted the keys from Fausto. He clicked the fob, chirping the alarm of the gleaming black Mercedes. At the car, Xavier said, "In my bathroom, in the medicine cabinet, I want two small shots of ephedrine and my bottle of pills."

"Indeed, señor," Fausto said, opening the door for his master.

Xavier drove—he always drove—and whipped the Mercedes E63 AMG into a 180-turn as both rear Pirelli tires, 22 inches in diameter, boiled under white smoke. The crowds on both sides of the boardwalk, most of them young, raised their hands and yelled their approval.

As the tires finally gripped the hot asphalt, Xavier roared past, hanging the right turn away from the beach as if the Mercedes was mounted on rails. Standing from the commotion, the five young ladies, having just finished their first year at the lowest level of higher education in the Netherlands, known as MBO, watched his Formula One-style exit, speaking excitedly afterward about their wealthy new friend.

It promised to be a lively evening.

For some of them.

FOLLOWING THEIR fun on the beach, as Justina lounged in the lobby with an English magazine, Gage steamed a black cotton shirt and his pants as he showered. When he came downstairs, he sent Justina up to do the same, asking her to put her things in his bag when she was finished. Then he walked to the nearest Sixt auto rental center, renting an Audi A3 coupe and driving it back to the hotel. He found Justina looking tan and fresh but wearing her clothes from the night before.

"Don't worry," he said, sliding the suitcase into an alcove and moving both pistols to the front pocket of the bag. "We're going to get you some new duds in Tossa."

"Duds?"

"Clothes."

They exited the hotel and drove to Tossa de Mar with the windows down. The warm afternoon was quite dry and felt wonderful compared to the heat and humidity Gage had endured in Mexico. Justina turned the radio up as Gage carved the curvy road between Lloret and Tossa. He felt her hand behind his head, toying with his hair as he drove. It was her habit and he liked it very much. The drive took only fifteen minutes and Gage found a hotel on the outskirts of the inner city, near the main road and up on a hill, paying cash for a room with a sea view, even though the view was from a distance.

Gage gave Justina 200 euro for shopping.

"I feel bad."

"You agreed down on the beach to let me help you," he said. "We're not going to keep having this argument."

"When will you be back?" she asked after kissing him.

He glanced at his Timex, knowing the drive to the rendezvous point would take at least an hour each way. "I'll try to be back by eleven," he replied. "Don't be worried if I'm late."

She waved the four bills in the air. "Thanks to you, I will be waiting for you in new *duds* that don't stink."

Chapter Seven

Ten kilometers away, in the exclusive hillside community known as Serrabrava, Xavier Zambrano held court over the heads of Los Leones' four divisions. The monthly summit meeting was not unlike a corporate board meeting, until things sometimes turned ugly. Los Leones, as usual, was cash-starved, and Xavier wasn't above violent fiscal corrections.

Earlier, after arriving from the beach and washing in the outdoor shower, Xavier sported only a terry robe as he enjoyed a tart glass of Verdejo with his salad. Feeling ravenous, he finished two portions of the fresh garden salad while watching a recap of the week's top soccer matches from around the world. Then, silencing the television, he'd yelled to Fausto for his main course to be brought in, along with his retinue of lieutenants.

As two large red lobsters were placed before Xavier, the men filed in, quite used to giving their monthly briefings as their superior dined. Sitting around the table in the same order as always, the four lieutenants each stared at their notes. Though they probably wanted to, none of them made eye contact with one another prior to Xavier opening the meeting.

Off to the side, eyeing the four lieutenants from behind his dark-rimmed glasses, was a persnickety little man named Theo Garcia. Garcia, an accountant who'd wound up on the Leones' payroll due to two ex-wives and a horrible gambling problem, was one of the few people on earth that didn't seem to be the least bit intimidated by Xavier. His favored phrase, the phrase that Xavier hated, was "The numbers don't lie."

To Garcia, it was always about the numbers.

Once he had wrenched a claw from one of the lobsters, Xavier situated the lobster cracker in the correct spot, crunching down and liberating a large piece of meat from the shell. He dipped the meat into the drawn butter, holding it in front of his mouth and saying, "Proceed."

Each of the lieutenants started with a simple briefing, lasting no more than a minute unless something significant had taken place. There were four divisional business concerns represented at the table, and they were always addressed in the exact same order. First was the smallest concern, known in Los Leones as *Legítimo*. Run by a former attorney, the oldest of the lieutenants and a refined gentleman who preferred tailored suits, Legítimo consisted primarily of legal business transactions running the gambit from property sales to interest on standard investments. Other illegal activity, mostly white-collar crime, fell under Legítimo's watch, including crimes such as union and political vote rigging and some aspects of high interest loans. Xavier expected Legítimo's division to create no less than a five percent monthly return, which, by civilian standards, was preposterously high—but Legítimo almost always managed. When the attorney, a trustworthy man who Xavier had greater plans for, announced an April return of nearly seven percent, Xavier had not reacted but simply flicked his eyes to the next man.

The second lieutenant represented a number of enterprises consisting of human interests. Included were street-level loan sharking, prostitution, human trade, protection, and for-hire contracts. The division, and its lieutenant, was simply known as *Contratos*, meaning contracts. A wily man of sixty, with twin cavernous facial scars courtesy of a rival's clasp knife, Contratos recited his briefing from memory, announcing monthly revenues that were higher than expected. His thin lips crept upward after he finished his oratory. Xavier was emotionless, turning his eyes to Number Three.

The third lieutenant represented gambling and guns, known colloquially within Los Leones as *Balas y Dados*. Having spent over half of his life in various Spanish prisons, this lieutenant was probably the rawest of the bunch, and still enjoyed going out on routine collection runs as a way to stay in touch with his street roots. A muscular man who made no effort to hide his anabolic steroid abuse, his appearance was made all the more comical by his small head. The larger he grew, the smaller his head appeared, making him the private butt of many jokes within Los Leones. His division was typically thought of as Los Leones' most tightly-run division, despite the multitude of hours its top lieutenant spent pumping iron. And steroids.

According to its lieutenant, Balas y Dados had a lackluster month. Since his numbers were typically good, Xavier gave him a pass and moved on.

The fourth lieutenant was charged with *Narcóticos*, as it was unofficially named within Los Leones. From warehouses teeming with snow-pure heroin to sniveling street dealers addicted to their own stepped-on product, Los Leones' narcotics division created more money than all the other divisions combined. Its leader, though the newest of the lieutenants, matched his aggressive business nature with advanced degrees from two Spanish universities. Having been pinched in a drug-dealing arrest twelve years before, he'd created a prison smuggling system so ingenious and so hard to trace that, upon his parole for "good" behavior, he'd rocketed through Los Leones' fourth division in less than two years' time, earning Xavier's trust through sheer revenue.

The fourth lieutenant was a handsome man, if a tad rat-like due to his large and pointy nose. With a lean body and a tight mat of sleek black hair, he was blessed with green eyes, a striking contrast with his dark hair and deep olive skin. Wearing his trademark tailored clothes from Hardy Amies in London, the fourth lieutenant clicked his manicured nails on the table as he recited his numbers. He finished and, although the numbers were low, turned his unapologetic jade eyes at his superior, eyeing him levelly.

"You're short," Xavier said monotone.

The fourth lieutenant, his birth name Camilo, shrugged. "With the restrictions you've placed on me, and considering the lack of help you're getting me from the government, you should be throwing a damned party at those numbers." He surveyed the table, not catching anyone else's eye, before coming back to Xavier. "And unless something changes, *tout de suite*, those numbers will continue to trend downward." The tone dripped condescension and could be described as nothing other than accusatory.

Only Theo Garcia, sitting behind the fourth lieutenant, reacted. His expression was one of horror.

Xavier took the insults without emotion. He finished the second lobster claw, sucking the butter audibly before eating the last chunk of flesh and going to work on the tail. An uncomfortable amount of time passed as he feasted. No one spoke. Halfway through his devouring of the lobster's tail, a clock chimed in the sitting room. Xavier glanced at it, making a mental note to have Legítimo inquire as to the villa's owner's taste for selling the property. In just two days' time, Xavier had grown to love it.

When he finished with the tail, he ate three large broccoli florets, taking a sip of wine and chasing it back with a large swig of water. Xavier pushed back from the table, crossing his leg over his knee and toying with the hairs of his lower leg as he sucked on his teeth. Finally, almost fifteen minutes after the last spoken word, he continued as if there had been no gulf in the conversation.

"I've noted your objections, Camilo."

"Very well."

"I've *also* noted your distractions, and our perpetually short till."

The other lieutenants could be heard shifting in their seats. For the first time since sitting, all eyes were on Camilo, the fourth lieutenant.

"Distractions and short till?" Camilo asked, pushing his own chair slightly back and turning it to Xavier.

"Indeed."

"I don't follow."

"Your receipts don't add up to what came in from the street," Theo Garcia interjected. "I audited them."

"Maybe you need a new calculator," Camilo snapped.

"Shut up, Camilo," Xavier commanded.

Camilo's olive complexion grew splotchy.

"And the distractions I mentioned have been of a *female* variety," Xavier added.

Camilo smiled, forcing a chuckle as he shook his head. "All due respect, señor, but the totals from the street are notoriously inaccurate. Half of those men are addicts. And regarding women...I think we all enjoy such distractions."

Xavier matched the smile, nodding as if he agreed. "Indeed we do, Camilo. Indeed we do." Xavier's mirth evaporated dangerously. "But these other men aren't stealing from me—" Xavier abruptly paused, "—*and* screwing my niece."

The clock that had chimed was the only sound in the villa, steadily ticking sixty times per minute. Fausto, hidden behind the wall of the kitchen with a salad bowl in hand, was frozen, his head turned so his right ear could hear the exchange. He was hanging on every word.

Camilo swallowed, struggling to do so. "I have never stolen money from—"

"Never mind that," Xavier snapped. "I have proof. What about my niece?"

No one breathed.

"Am I restricted as to who I can interact with?" Camilo croaked.

Xavier shook his head and spoke reasonably. "Not at all, Camilo. My relatives, other than my sisters, are all within the sphere of people you might become involved with. I'm not an unreasonable man."

Camilo visibly relaxed, smiling weakly.

"But, Camilo, my niece *is* engaged to be married. And her fiancé is the son of an influential People's Party senator."

Camilo's breathing had become audible, sounding similar to someone who'd just run wind sprints. "She...she seduced me."

"You're completely innocent, aren't you?" Xavier asked coldly.

"No, señor, but I'm vulnerable to women, as I'm sure you are."

Xavier leaned forward, aiming his finger at Camilo. "Do—not—*ever*—compare—yourself—to—me."

If a person were to take a snapshot of the three other lieutenants at that moment, they would see three distinct expressions. The first lieutenant, the cultured attorney, had his eyebrow cocked as he stared curiously at Camilo, as if the trial lawyer inside him were trying to determine how exactly this pseudo-deposition might play out.

The second lieutenant, the wizened old mobster with the twin scars, pressed his lips together, suppressing his grin, anxious for the violent finale to be on its way.

The third lieutenant, his trapezius muscles straining his silk shirt to the point of bursting, adjusted himself in his chair, turning it to allow himself easy access to Camilo. In the event things turned physical, he wanted to get his shots in before it was too late.

And behind them all, Theo Garcia, the persnickety financial man, shook his head, a disgusted expression on his face. He'd been the only one with the balls to object to Camilo's promotion. *Narcóticos* was the goose that laid the golden eggs. There were far too many risks in placing a dirty whiz kid in charge of it.

Xavier, *el capitán*, gnawed on his lower lip while his eyes burned Camilo to the ground. Slight tremors passed through Xavier as he awaited a response, refusing to say a thing as his narcotics lieutenant sat fidgeting in front of him.

"Señor," Camilo finally intoned, sounding more exasperated than sorry, "I didn't realize that my becoming involved with Juana would be a problem, but I will end it."

"I have a question," Xavier stated.

"Fine."

"I know it's fine, Camilo," Xavier said. "Don't tell me that a question is fine."

"I'm sorry."

Xavier stared through gun-slit eyes.

"Please, señor, ask your question."

"Have you gone so far as to have sexual intercourse with my niece?"

Camilo's lips parted. "Señor…"

"Answer me."

Eyes down, Camilo nodded.

"How many times?"

"A few."

"How many?"

Camilo's narrow chest expanded as he took a great breath. "Perhaps ten."

"And she was a virgin?"

"Another nod."

"You've spoiled her. *Eres una rata.*"

Wisely, Camilo kept his head and eyes down.

Xavier stood, walking around the table, never taking his eyes off of Camilo. "Fortunately for you, Camilo, I'm receiving guests shortly." Camilo's relaxation was visible as his entire body slumped.

Xavier spoke to the group. "Money is short. Our friend Theo here says we're operationally inefficient. So, heading into prime earning season due to the tourists, do not dare come here next month without at least a ten percent gain over today's numbers. Understood?"

Everyone nodded.

Camilo quickly pushed his chair back.

"I'm not done with you, Camilo."

Somewhere in the distance, thunder rumbled.

Xavier casually walked back to his seat, taking the greasy lobster cracker in his hand and stepping into the kitchen. Winking at Fausto, Xavier washed the lobster cracker, taking his time to soap it and scrub it with the dish brush. After rinsing it, he patted it dry with the dish towel and walked back into the dining area, noting the keen looks from everyone but Camilo.

Camilo's facial expression resided somewhere in the category of sheer horror.

"Choose two fingers," Xavier whispered. "One on each hand."

"S-S-Señor Zambrano, please," Camilo said, voice quavering.

"We're going to do this," Xavier said. "Now, don't be a little *coño*. Take it like a man, stop screwing my niece, and I will try to rectify the situation with the fiancé. Okay?" Xavier straightened. "Now, choose two fingers."

"I promise I will never touch her again."

"You took my money, too."

"Never again," Camilo shuddered, tears running down his face.

"Choose!" Xavier barked.

Shaking, Camilo extended his two pinkie fingers. Xavier briefly closed his eyes, massaging the bridge of his nose as he shook his head. When he opened his eyes, he considered each lieutenant. The first, the attorney, viewed Camilo with a curled lip. The second, the wizened one, chuckled knowingly. The third, Mr. Steroids, gritted his teeth, eyeing Camilo the way he might a fine cut of meat.

And Theo Garcia, the accountant, grinned triumphantly.

After eyeing Garcia for a moment, angry that the accountant had been right all along, Xavier turned to his narcotics lieutenant. "Well, Camilo, since you attempted to take the easy way out, I'm now forced to choose for you."

Xavier turned to Garcia again. "How many combinations are available?"

"Twenty-five if he's forced to pick a finger from each hand," Garcia said without hesitation.

"You had twenty-five choices, Camilo, and you chose the path of a *coño*." His voice suddenly rising, Xavier yelled, "Extend your thumbs!"

"No!" Camilo cried.

"Do it, or I'll crack every finger." The third lieutenant moved for Camilo but Xavier froze him with a shake of his head. "Do it, Camilo. Be a man and not a *coño*. This is your only chance at atonement."

Somehow, someway, Camilo balled his fists, placing them on the polished wood of the table. Then, like shy snakes emerging from twin holes, both thumbs crept skyward as if Camilo were giving his approval of the situation—though he certainly wasn't.

"Very good, Camilo," Xavier soothed, stepping to his side. He gently situated the lobster cracker on the middle knuckle of Camilo's left thumb. "Are you ready?"

All that came from Camilo's mouth was a croak. Xavier looked at the first lieutenant, the two of them exchanging a grin as Xavier clamped down, using both hands to pop Camilo's thumb with a crack equal to a small caliber gunshot. He had to use both hands to pull the lobster cracker away, as it had bitten into Camilo's skin and stuck there.

"One more, Camilo," Xavier said, moving around the chair.

Camilo was sobbing, his body wracked by pain as he spasmed out of the chair and into the floor, gripping his left hand. Xavier slumped. "I don't have time for this." He looked at his third lieutenant. "Get him up!"

Wasting no time, Xavier repeated the process on the right thumb, this time allowing his lieutenant to assist him in holding the squalling Camilo's arm. He wrenched Camilo's thumb after it had popped, doing more damage than the first as punishment for his womanly crying. Finished, Xavier personally retrieved two plastic bags filled with ice, tossed them on Camilo's lap, and said, "Get that little girl out of here."

When the lieutenants had gone, Xavier turned the music up, retrieving an icy Rosita lager and easing himself, nude, into the hot tub on the porch.

Camilo's sacrifice had left Xavier temporarily sated.

GAGE'S ARRIVAL at the meeting with Navarro was traditional this time. As requested, Valentin picked him up in a small town near the coast. They drove several kilometers before ascending a steep driveway with numerous switchbacks. Cresting the hill, Gage took in the residence that Navarro termed a "casita."

Gage had expected a lavish, modern residence with infinity pools and massive windows. Instead, what he found was a rustic Spanish home, surrounded by lush vegetation in a manner that looked natural but well-ordered. The home was squat and weathered, built with numerous arches and accented in black iron and natural wood. The upper driveway as well as the walkway were covered in crushed shells. To the right of the home, Gage spied the Mediterranean between the numerous cade junipers. While certainly the price of such a seaside retreat would be staggering, its appearance managed to avoid pretention.

The inside of the home could have been photographed and used as an example of a Spanish mansion from the 1930's. The tiled kitchen, while handsome, claimed no modern appliances that Gage noticed. It was illuminated by skylights and, though inactive at the moment, held the pleasant smell of a well-used culinary kitchen. The second room they passed through, a dark sitting room with a sunken floor, contained only books, newspapers and leather furniture. There were no televisions, no digital clocks, no mobile phone docking stations. Two large dogs, gray and resembling wolves, slumbered in the sunken area of the room, just in front of the dormant fireplace. One dog opened his eyes, viewed Gage with mild interest, and resumed his sleep.

Valentin stepped through the rear door. Gage followed him, ending on an elevated porch with ocean views. He turned, able to get a better view of the home from this angle since the front had been greatly obscured by vegetation. As Valentin had mentioned, there was at least a hundred feet of jagged cliff above them. The house was nestled on a broad ledge, with another fifty-foot drop to the sea below it. Hands behind his back, Gage slowly walked the perimeter of the large porch.

There were four bulky chairs in Danish modern style situated between massive planters of flowers and, on the matching table in the center, a pitcher of a red, fruity drink with empty glasses nearby. Peering over the railing, Gage found Navarro, one level down. He'd just stood and was donning a terry robe over his deeply tanned body.

"Good day, Mister Harris. I'm coming up."

An attractive woman was busy packing up a massage table. She glanced up and smiled.

Hearing another voice, Gage turned and looked inside through the open door from which he had come, seeing Valentin leading another man outside. He was small and well-dressed in casual attire, coolly eyeing Gage while Navarro noisily clanged his way up a set of spiral black iron stairs.

"I apologize for my appearance," Navarro said. "I should have taken my massage earlier."

Navarro shook Gage's hand. "Might we use your actual name since we're in a private setting?"

"That's fine."

"Excellent." Navarro gestured to the diminutive man. "Mister Hartline, please meet Señor Cortez Redon. Señor Redon is the senior *acusador* for this area, similar to a state attorney in the U.S."

Gage viewed Redon more closely. His head was ringed by a salt-and-pepper Caesar crown and he had a thin, aristocratic face with a sharp nose. Redon's eyes were dark blue and he seemed to be measuring Gage's soul with his deep gaze. Without a trace of warmth, Redon offered his hand and Gage reluctantly took it.

"Redon's presence here is private, of course."

Gage said nothing.

"A wizard with the law, he has deftly crafted a method to legally place you in Berga that should give you an excellent sense of security."

Gage held up a protesting hand. "Señor Navarro, as you know, I have not yet—"

"Don't say it," Navarro said severely but without venom. He softened his face. "Don't decline me just yet, Mister Hartline. Hear us out. Once you know the specifics, you might change your mind." Navarro gestured to a grouping of chairs. A pitcher of Sangria sweated on the center table. When offered a drink, no one accepted.

"Mister Hartline, what we're going to speak of today is of the highest confidentiality," Redon said, his English perfect though heavily accented.

Gage leaned forward and made his voice stern. "There is no need for a preamble about confidentiality. I'm here because I'm trusted by Señor Navarro. Anything that's said here is between us. Period. Now, at the risk of being rude but in the interest of wasting no one's time, please get on with it."

Redon, like most hardened career attorneys, seemed unoffended by the mild rebuke. He turned to Navarro, who nodded.

"Very well," Redon said. "Some time ago, when Señor Navarro approached me about inserting a man into the infamous Berga Prisión as a prisoner, with the directive of protecting his son, I initially felt there was no good way possible to do such a thing. After doing research, I learned that there were few guards or employees of the *privately*-run prison that I could trust enough to confide in." He inclined his head to Navarro. "Despite this, and after considerable resolve and persistence on the part of Señor Navarro…"

Money in your pockets, Gage thought.

"…I developed a plan that is not only tenable, it's also perfectly legal."

Gage waited and, when Redon didn't speak, he said, "And that is?"

Redon smiled triumphantly. "Inserting you as a paid undercover agent of this government under the guise of a narcotics investigation."

There was a bout of verbal silence. Down below, waves could be heard lolling westward, building, building, then finally crashing into the rocks. Birds skittered about in the trees above, going on about this or that. Gage could feel Navarro's eyes lasering his face from the right. He turned to the man, watching as he removed his Dunhills from the thick robe, taking one out and tapping the filter end on his lighter. After a half a minute he lit the cigarette, blowing white smoke into the air.

"Mister Hartline?" Redon asked.

Gage moistened his lips, surprised at the words that emerged from his own mouth as he said, "That changes things, but only slightly."

Optimism descended upon the Spanish duo. "Why only slightly?" Redon asked, showing a toothy smile that Gage could easily envision being wielded against unsuspecting juries. "This is a good plan and gives us great latitude."

"Be that as it may," Gage said, "since you trust no one in that prison, can you imagine what will happen if I'm somehow exposed as an undercover narc? I might as well have a bulls-eye tattooed on my forehead."

Gage quickly moved on. "And, as I've already told Señor Navarro, my skills don't seamlessly transition to a prison. I'm trained in open tactics. I specialize in weapons, military technology, reconnaissance and surprise to gain the advantage over opponents. Most of all, I prefer nonviolent resolutions." Poking a finger into his own chest, Gage finished by saying, "I'm over forty years of age. While I'm confident in taking care of myself in most situations, I don't have any illusions about fending off a dozen prisoners who are dead-set on killing me…or worse."

"Two people know about this, Mister Hartline," Navarro said solemnly. "Myself and Redon. Even Valentin doesn't know what we're meeting about."

"It's an excellent plan and worth the associated risk," Redon added. "The sort of money you've been offered is unheard of."

Gage leaned forward. "Since we're all being open, I feel compelled to bring something else up. It's sensitive."

"As you said, this is a time to be direct," Navarro said, smoke escaping his mouth as he talked.

Gage aimed a finger at Redon. "You are an agent of the government and Señor Navarro is a known head of an organized crime syndicate. The very fact that you're in bed with him prevents me from trusting you whatsoever."

Redon's tanned face and neck reddened. He pressed his lips tightly together as his eyes blazed. A shiver went through his petite body. Finally, when the boiler could hold the pressure no longer, he stood and began shouting at Gage in Spanish, gesticulating as he spoke, pounding his narrow chest with one hand while the other pointed to Gage, to Navarro, to the heavens and, oddly enough, to the sea. Gage made his own face placid as he leaned back in his chair, crossing his arms as he watched the little man's tirade without affectation.

Navarro glared at Redon.

Valentin appeared briefly, a cigarette dangling from his mouth as he peeked out the window.

Even the two dogs walked to the door, cocking their heads at the outburst.

No one intervened and, when Redon had yelled himself out, he looked spent and without a clue of what to do next. He turned to Navarro who motioned him to sit.

Switching to English, Redon said, "This American prick insulted my name."

"Well, if you can't get over it, then let's me and you take a walk down to the beach and settle things like men," Gage said with a warm smile.

Redon turned his eyes downward.

Thought so.

"Mister Hartline is correct in his reservations," Navarro said. "What he said is the truth. And, Cortez, do not have such an outburst in my home *ever* again."

Redon looked at Navarro as if he'd been slapped. "I'm sorry, señor, but for this...this *jodido* American to have the gall to—"

"Get on with it," Navarro said, cutting Redon off.

The small lawyer wiped his hands on his slacks and regained his composure. "These are the facts. Knowledge of this operation is confined to this group. I have gone to great lengths to create your identity in our justice system. I have manufactured an undercover package that will insert you into the prison under the guise of the crime of murder in the second degree."

"Murder is a respected crime in Berga," Navarro interjected, crushing out his cigarette.

Redon continued. "To provide redundancy, in the unlikely event something was to happen to me, I've created a package of affidavits certifying you as an undercover agent. You'll get a copy and will want to place it somewhere safe. In the event of an emergency, this information can be shown to our government, or yours through your state department, and will provide you with a safe and expedient exit from Berga Prisión."

Navarro leaned forward. "We can stay here and talk all night, Mister Hartline. The job, admittedly, is perilous and will certainly be difficult every day you're there." He rested his hand on Gage's knee. "I know you said your skills aren't a seamless transition to this situation...but whose are? Prisons, this one especially, are gladiator arenas devoid of sanity and absent of reason." Navarro's sun-spotted hand tightened on Gage's leg. "My son is all I have. He is not perfect, nor am I. I've offered you significant compensation for attempting this and now I ask you...I *beg* you, señor...please go to Berga for thirty days and, while you're there, consider staying for the balance of time."

Gage listened to Navarro, pondering everything he'd said, nodding thoughtfully afterward. "Might we discuss the entire process in more detail, item by item, including what you know of the day-to-day activity in the prison?"

"Of course."

The three men talked for another hour before moving inside as the Mediterranean chill swept over the coast. They covered everything from Gage's background story to the "crime" he committed, and to the amnesty he would receive if he were to be accused of a crime while in prison. They spoke about Navarro's son, Cesar, and the people he claimed were his enemies in the prison. Navarro told Gage, according to Cesar, the primary threat was from a rival Spanish crime syndicate known as *Los Leones*.

"Cesar will gladly fill you in on exactly who the aggressors are, Señor Hartline," Navarro said. "Los Leones have been nothing more than an irritating insect for decades. But, perhaps due to my age and my softening demeanor, they've made huge strides in the last years." He leaned back, growing misty. "I've made significant efforts at legitimizing my empire, Mister Hartline. No, I haven't completely stopped my criminal activity, but I've ceased all violent operations."

"You sell drugs, don't you?" Gage asked unapologetically.

Navarro shrugged. "People will get drugs, Mister Hartline, whether or not I sell them. I realize such justification doesn't sit well with some people. But it's my belief."

They spoke further about life inside Berga Prison. Nearly three hours after arriving, when Gage had been briefed on everything he could imagine,

Señor Navarro showed Gage a leather briefcase containing the euro equivalent of one hundred thousand dollars. The bills were in small denominations and were all well used. Navarro promised that they were clean and unmarked.

"This money is all yours as soon as you agree to the first thirty days." Navarro closed the briefcase and set it aside.

Redon, his tone and mood chilly, walked Gage through the insertion package along with the signed affidavits, bearing the stamps and seals of the country of Spain and the autonomous region of Catalonia. "You can have a copy once you agree to go."

"When would you like an answer?" Gage asked Señor Navarro.

"Tomorrow."

"Then my answer is already no."

Navarro frowned. "How long do you need?"

"I want a week," Gage said. "And, even with a week, I'm almost certain I will *not* take this job. If you need to find another man, I will understand."

Gage noticed Redon shake his head at Navarro. The old mobster ignored the acusador's advice as he said, "I wouldn't normally give such time, Mister Hartline, but I like you. A week you want, and a week you shall have. Please answer me *before* the deadline has passed."

"You have my word that I will," Gage said, shaking hands with him.

"Valentin will take you back to your car."

Gage ignored Cortez Redon and walked away, finding Valentin at the front door. They chatted idly on the short drive to Gage's rental car. Once there, Valentin warned about the nighttime hazard of red deer on the rural roads of Catalonia.

Finally alone and motoring southward, Gage felt the thump of his own pulse as he thought about Ernesto Navarro's audacious proposition.

Could I handle myself in a Spanish prison?

Gage's mild intrigue mortified him.

It must be the onset of middle age, he thought, smiling to himself as he drove.

As rapidly as the excitement from the unknown struck him, it was washed away as he realized who awaited him in Tossa.

Justina…

ONCE THE car had disappeared over the ridge of the driveway, Navarro and Redon retired to the sunken drawing room, taking crystal snifters of Gran Duque d'Alba brandy by the crackling fire. Navarro smoked pensively, staring into the flames, holding the snifter off the arm of the chair.

Redon spoke up. "Again, Señor Navarro, please accept my apologies for the outburst earlier. But I do not like that man."

Navarro smoked.

There was a lengthy period of silence. Finally, Redon broke it. "Señor?"

Navarro turned eyes to him.

"Señor, why did you insist that we not tell Hartline about the others?"

The mobster's mouth straightened. He didn't reply.

"I guess you knew there was nothing to be gained," Redon reasoned. "If this Hartline knew that the previous three men all died gruesome deaths in that prison, he'd have run the other way screaming."

"I'm not so sure," Navarro said. He sipped his brandy, his voice velvety. "Regardless, he will learn in good enough time."

"Won't he ask for his release when he learns?"

"I don't think so," Navarro answered.

"And the Berga guard you had hired?"

Navarro shook his head.

"I see," Redon said.

The guard had taken nearly twenty thousand euro through an intermediary. He'd agreed to protect Cesar, and to smuggle occasional items in. But it wasn't long before Navarro learned that the guard was actually working behind his back for Los Leones.

The guard was no longer alive, killed during a violent "robbery" on one of his nights off.

Redon crossed his leg and nervously ran his hand up and down his calf. "Señor Navarro, not to be coarse, but I have a question that's quite personal in nature."

There was a slight dip of Navarro's head.

"Los Leones keeps killing the men you send in, and doing so in ghastly fashion." Redon swallowed visibly. "Forgive me for asking this…"

"Speak, man."

"Why, señor, don't they just kill Cesar?"

The mobster flicked the cigarette into the fire and sipped his brandy. Then, in an uncharacteristic display of emotion, he hurled the snifter into the stone fireplace, the crystal shattering as the brandy flamed in a ball of heat.

He cut blood-laced eyes to Redon, his lips crinkling in anger. "They're doing it to torture me. They're going to suffer Cesar until the final day, and then they're going to gut him."

Shaken by the outburst, Redon smiled weakly and said, "If Cesar can lead Hartline to his aggressors, perhaps Hartline can kill them before they kill him."

Navarro closed his eyes, his voice a whisper. "I pray...*le pio a Dios*...he will take this job and protect my only son."

"Cesar's a fine young man," Redon said obsequiously.

Navarro's eyes opened.

Redon stared at him.

Navarro slowly turned. "Cesar is a piece of shit."

The two men fell silent.

Chapter Eight

OUTSIDE THE bedroom the music blared, making the mirror vibrate on the wall. Having dimmed all the lights, Xavier stared at himself, his hands straining on the edge of the marble countertop. His anger was visible, marked by tremors and bulging veins. Xavier couldn't comprehend that, despite the growth of Los Leones, they were still in financial peril.

Earlier, after the lieutenants had left, Xavier sat naked in the hot tub, trying his best to unwind. Then he was surprised by that little over-educated shit, Theo Garcia. Garcia had not left with the others. Instead, he pulled up a chair and harangued Xavier for the better part of an hour.

As always, Theo had started with hard expenses. These dealt with drug-processing facilities, boats, transportation and people on Los Leones' payroll. "Things have been trimmed as far as possible," Garcia said with a grave expression. He moved on.

His next line item, as usual, was what he called soft costs. These were items Garcia deemed unnecessary, although he was blind to the specifics of many of the actual transactions—something that was by Xavier's design. But the little accountant, degenerate little prick he was, was no idiot. He deftly pointed the dirty end of the stick at Xavier, telling him that "the highest level of leadership is spending well in excess of two million euro per month on security, transportation, meals, housing and *personal* entertainment."

Upon hearing this, Xavier had eyed the little man—stared him down.

"Unless I'm mistaken, señor," Garcia had said, averting his own eyes.

The end of the summary had dealt with mundane items. The net result was essentially this: the top line was up, but only modestly. The bottom line, however, had shrunk. And though he never came out and said it, Garcia most definitely hinted that the bottom line was being vacuumed away by Xavier's extravagant lifestyle.

"We have no cash reserves," Garcia had warned. "One bad month could wreck our entire organization. If you do not have the cash for our government payoffs, or if your legions do not receive the money they're owed, you could be dealing with a mutiny that would result in your certain—"

"Cállate!"

"My apologies," Garcia said, as insincerely as humanly possible.

As he had actually considered grabbing the little accountant and holding him under the overheated water, Xavier, quite overheated himself, sat on the side without covering himself. He took a few deep breaths, finally asking, "Assuming our expenses remain the same, what can we do to increase the bottom line?"

"If all of our expenses remain the same? Including executive expenditures?"

"Yes," Xavier growled through clenched teeth.

"Then you must increase the top line without adding more expense. And the easiest way to do that, rather than encroaching into new geographies, is by eliminating Ernesto Navarro, or his son, and taking over Los Soldados' operations, including their drug and gun inventories."

"Did you say 'the son'?"

"Yes."

Xavier had begun to laugh. He ran his hands back through his wet hair, shaking his head before his laughter had abruptly halted. "You may know numbers, Theo, but you're one of the stupidest, most irritating people I've ever had to deal with. For the hundredth time, Cesar Navarro is a pigeon. We're trying to use him to get to his cowardly old man. But if we kill Cesar, then the old man is a vapor. Do you follow?"

"All I know is you must eliminate the Navarros. If you don't, Los Leones is at high risk. If I were you, I'd be concerned about Los Soldados converting *your* men with the promise of more money. They can afford it."

Xavier wanted to strike back but what Garcia had just said made him stop and think.

My own men turning on me. It could happen.

"There is another option," Garcia said.

"What?"

Garcia looked at Xavier, then averted his eyes. "Never mind, señor."

"Get out of my face."

Garcia began to walk away before Xavier called out to him.

"Yes, señor?" Garcia asked at the threshold.

"Theo…if we have any level of financial failure, I will blame you."

Garcia departed.

The little bean-counter had all but ruined Xavier's evening. Trying to forget the earlier exchange, Xavier now straightened, eyeing himself in the mirror. The many hours spent with his trainers, with his massage therapists, under acupuncture and the injections of various anabolic steroids, had left him with the hard body of a twenty-five-year-old. The day's sun had set his skin aglow, making it warm to the touch. He was further warmed by the drugs and the anticipation of this evening's plans.

Xavier walked to the bedroom door, hearing the young Dutch women laughing and talking out in the main sitting rom. *Lucky* perras...*they don't know what they're in for.*

"But tomorrow," Xavier whispered to himself, affected by Garcia's warnings. "Tomorrow we will increase our efforts to kill Ernesto Navarro."

Xavier opened the door. *Tomorrow.*

GAGE KEYED the door and stepped inside. The small hotel room smelled glorious, of Justina's toothpaste and shampoo and her scent in general. He found her on the balcony, sitting there in a lime-colored cotton dress with her hair down. Beside her was a glass ashtray with three lipstick-marked cigarette butts. One slightly curled division of Justina's blonde hair fell down over her cheek as she lifted her eyes to him. Her freshly tanned skin made her teeth seem all the more white as she smiled at him.

"May I take you to dinner?" he asked, forcing a smile, not yet ready to reveal what occupied his mind.

They found an open seafood restaurant on the crescent beach of Tossa de Mar. There was quite a chill blowing in from the sea so they took a table inside, near the rear of the restaurant. Three different times, as they waited for their food, Justina asked Gage what was wrong. Each time he reassured her, telling her they would discuss it later, insisting they enjoy their dinner first.

Finally, after eating half of his food and struggling to make suitable small talk due to his jumbled mind, Gage flattened his palms on the table. "What would you say to getting out of here tomorrow?"

"What do you mean?"

"I mean you and me get on an airplane, or a train, and leave Spain."

"For good?" she asked, her eyes widening.

"Not exactly. I'm thinking we just go away for a few days. The Costa Brava is beautiful and charming, but I think it would be nice to simply have a change of scenery."

She sipped her water, turning away as she rolled a piece of ice around in her mouth. After a moment, she crunched the ice, her face alight. "I'm in."

"Where would you like to go?"

"Anywhere but Poland," Justina said. "I love my home and family, but not if we're going somewhere to relax."

"Okay," Gage said, listing a number of possibilities.

Justina couldn't decide, finally telling Gage to surprise her. Gage paid the bill and they left the restaurant.

After a brief walk on the beach, cut short due to the chill, they headed back to their hotel. Just before walking up the hillside from the beachfront road, a man in a wheelchair emerged from a darkened alley.

"Good evening, friends," the man said in accented English.

Gage and Justina stopped. The man who stared back at them was muscular with a mop of curly hair and a bushy moustache. He had no legs. His wheelchair was blocking the sidewalk but his expression seemed pleasant as his head rotated between Gage and Justina.

"How did you know to speak English to us?" Gage asked.

"I could tell by the way you walk that you're American," the man said, pointing a finger at Gage. "You've got that American swagger."

"You must have heard us talking."

"I did not," the stranger said. "Not only could I tell you're American, I can also tell that you're a soldier."

Gage glanced at Justina. "I was."

"You *are* a soldier."

Gage took Justina's right hand in his left. "Can we help you with something, sir?"

The man held his hand out to Gage. "I just wanted to say hello to a fellow soldier."

"Is that how you lost your legs?" Gage asked, shaking the man's hand and choosing to be direct about his injury out of soldierly respect.

"Yes, sir. Iraq, February of ninety-one. I was one of the few from the Spanish coalition. I was commanding a Pegaso that got flipped courtesy of a Russian-made anti-tank mine. Been sitting ever since."

Gage nodded his understanding. "Are you from Tossa?"

"Am now," the man said, his English nearly good enough to pass for a native speaker. "Got a shack up on the hill but most days I like to patrol down here at the water."

"Patrol?"

"Yes," the man said. "It's my duty to all our tourists." He motioned up and down the beach. "Watch yourselves around here. With our poor economy, lots of sharks in Catalonia these days."

"We'll remember that," Gage said, shaking the man's hand again.

The man in the wheelchair looked at Justina and said, "*Dobranoc.*" It meant "Good evening" in Polish. He tipped an imaginary cap and wheeled back into the darkness.

As Gage and Justina walked up the hill, Justina was incredulous as she asked, "How did he know I was Polish?"

"And how did he know I was American?"

Justina broke the tension by laughing.

Typically, Gage would have been very suspicious of such an encounter. But, for some reason Gage couldn't discern, he believed the man in the wheelchair to be genuine. He'd instinctively liked the man—and his instinct was seldom wrong. Rather than dwell on it, he decided to focus his attention on Justina.

When they arrived back in their hotel room, the tension was thick. Unsure of what to do, Gage brushed his teeth and asked Justina what time she would wake up tomorrow.

"Well, since I don't have to scrub toilets at Eastern Bloc, I'd like to train my body to sleep a little later."

"I'll be up early," Gage said. "And by the time you wake up, I'll have a trip all planned out, okay?"

As he removed his shoes, Justina leaned down and kissed him. He couldn't be sure, but he thought he felt her gently pushing him backward. Not wanting to seem presumptive, Gage stayed upright.

Though the kiss was glorious, Justina appeared frustrated when she straightened. She walked into the bathroom and told Gage to sleep well.

Later, as Gage stared at the dark wall, Justina pulled him behind her, just as she'd done the night before. Despite the tension, their mutual touch was just the sleep-aid they both needed.

They were asleep in minutes.

NOT FAR away, Xavier Zambrano was having a much more frenetic evening. Before him, five beautiful and naïve young women danced with one another, sufficiently drunk and, for at least two of them, flying high on cocaine. Finger paintings of color followed each woman's movement, highlighted by the hue of her clothing. The house-style music thudded, pulsating from the villa's hidden speakers. Xavier was lounging in a leather chair, sipping his tonic water, enjoying the scene playing out before him as he decided which one, or ones, he would take first.

He'd already forgotten about the thumb-crushing incident with Camilo, his narcotics lieutenant. And he'd managed to set aside the grave proclamations from Theo Garcia. His mind now was solely focused on his own pleasure as he merrily prophesied the dreamy tales of the virile Spanish millionaire these young Amsterdammers would recount when they reentered their pathetic lives in a week.

Earlier, upon their arrival, Xavier had invited all of the young women into the large hot tub. Then still sober, most of the girls politely declined, probably needing to fall prey to alcohol's loosening characteristics before acquiescing to something that would otherwise make them feel slutty—at least in front of a crowd of friends. But one girl, cute but the least attractive of the bunch—the one who, on the beach, had asked if they should bring dates—lingered as her friends went inside in search of alcohol and drugs. Once the friends had moved away from the window, the girl, her name was Erica, bawdily slid her dress and underwear off, dropping down into the water as her hand immediately took a position on Xavier's most private parts.

She was only a few kilos overweight. With brown hair and coffee eyes, she had a cheerfulness about her that she'd probably cultivated to counteract the greater beauty of her friends. Xavier knew enough about women to pronounce her as intelligent: she knew she would be quite plump at some point in the next decade, and she was wise enough to go ahead and have her fun now. And this evening, to Erica, was almost certainly a microcosm of her life. She probably, even if it was subconsciously, realized that this might be her only chance to have sex with him.

He appreciated her efforts.

After a few minutes of stroking him to rigidity, Erica had tried to straddle him. Though it wasn't easy, Xavier had politely resisted, promising the girl much more intensity, but only later in the evening. He didn't want to blow himself out too early, especially with the least attractive one of the bunch.

"Don't forget about me later," she'd said, kissing him. His affirming promise added a radiant glow to her face.

Since then, he'd donned a fashionable outfit of linen pants and an open Versace shirt, getting to know each girl one on one, estimating that, when drunk, they would all be willing to partake in the Roman-style orgy he had in mind. And now, just before he'd come to the sofa, Xavier had popped an erectile tablet in the privacy of the bathroom. Then, adding to his drug cocktail, he'd spiked the ephedrine syringe into his right buttock.

While holding his thumb over the erupted pinhead of stark red blood, Xavier had devoured his own image in the large mirror in a narcissistic bout of self-adulation.

The ephedrine effect, especially when mingled with two lines of cocaine and erectile dysfunction medicine, was intense to say the least. Though no one had touched the stereo, the volume had increased twofold. One of the Dutch women, Julia, with white blonde hair, straight teeth and freshly suntanned skin, was wearing a short blue dress. Earlier, Xavier remembered it being a plain blue, the type of dress purchased off the rack in any cut-rate department store. Now, however, the dress shone in electric cobalt, giving off its own light as Julia turned her attentions to him. The finger paintings of earlier had grown to neon-intensity, dragging brilliance with her every movement. Feeling the hotness of his face and upper chest, probably the erectile pill, Xavier soon felt the benefit of his sudden, and painful, erection. He stood, moving Julia's hand to his firmness, sliding her dress over her head.

Franca, the one who, on the beach, had been so concerned that he might have cocaine, danced to where Xavier swayed with half-naked Julia. Leaving her heels on, Franca dropped her shorts, working them over her elevated shoes and showing everyone that she preferred no panties. In two deft motions her shirt and bra were gone and, cutting in front of her friend, she pushed herself onto Xavier, the two of them falling back on the sofa as she went about disrobing him with her hands and mouth.

Even though he'd had at least a hundred other nights like this one, as several of the girls took turns pleasuring him, Xavier laid there and pondered what a superlative feeling female worship was for a man. It felt as if he were making a cosmic connection back through time with other rulers that had enjoyed power comparable to his. And it was times like this that provided complete understanding of why men in power fought so damned hard to hold onto that power. Through the ages, Xavier knew that other men like him had lain back, accepting the pleasure as payment for all their hard work, thinking similar self-congratulatory thoughts while horny young women battled for their affections.

He lifted his head, surveying the lurid scene and finding that all but one had disrobed. She was holding his mirror, snorting more cocaine. The four naked ones, two on the sofa and two kneeling next to him, stared at him as if he were the only man on earth. He allowed his hands to wander, telling the girls to pleasure one another as he guided Julia, the prettiest one, to his own body. Her lips were locked on Franca's as she began to move with him and, as he'd hoped, the other two girls, Erica from the hot tub and Ami, the shy one, went to work on each other on the floor next to the sofa.

The fifth girl, however, lined the mirror again. She was probably the second most attractive but had been rather distant all night. And despite the intense sensations he was enjoying, Xavier couldn't help but watch the girl as she snorted two more lines. Still standing, she then staggered across the room, allowing the mirror to fall, its shattering made silent by the thudding music.

Staring back at him, she ran her hand under her skirt, feigning ecstasy as her body undulated. Xavier had been seconds from disentangling himself so he could go and take her where she stood.

But it was not to be.

The woman stopped undulating. Her face suddenly contorted into an expression of great pain, followed immediately by two stark red trails of blood from her nose. Then, as if she were controlled by a switch, she collapsed forward, her head striking the tile floor full force.

A chorus of screams went up, briefly defeating the music.

Ten minutes later, the house was deathly quiet. Despite his and Fausto's frantic efforts, the Dutch woman had perished in his rented villa. Xavier massaged his temples, thinking how best to deal with this situation. And he was equally troubled that it had occurred prior to his plan for multiple orgasms.

As the four remaining Dutch women huddled in the bedroom, Xavier, once again in his terry robe, sat on the ottoman next to the fallen girl and dialed a mobile number he rarely called. He slid back onto the overstuffed chair, crossing his legs and taking relaxing breaths as the phone began to ring. Expecting the object of his call to be asleep, Xavier was surprised when the man answered it in a clear voice.

The voice belonged to Cortez Redon, the Catalonian acusador who'd just finished with Ernesto Navarro. And Gage Hartline.

"Where are you?" Xavier asked numbly, his glorious high having faded like dirty dishwater down an open drain.

"In my car, why?"

"I need you. Right now."

"Have you been following me?"

Xavier narrowed his eyes at the out of place query. "No. Why?"

"Never mind." Road noise could be heard during a pause before Redon asked, "What do you need?"

"You'd like me to say this over the phone? Perhaps I should spell out both our names, too?"

"Where do you want me?"

Xavier gave him instructions on where to meet Fausto, then he hung up. He tilted his head to the ceiling and spoke Fausto's name. When Fausto appeared, Xavier told him who he was meeting and where.

"Shall I go now, señor?"

Xavier tapped the barely used mobile phone on his head, thinking. Suddenly, a good idea came to him. "Yes, go ahead, Fausto. He said he'd be there in a half-hour. And when you arrive here with him, remain in the garage and call me."

"Sí, señor."

Footsteps. Door. Engine. Garage door. Tires squeaking on the shiny floor. Garage door. Then, only the murmurs of the Dutch women.

Continuing to tap the phone on his head, Xavier felt the tingling. The pill he'd taken was good for hours and, despite all the tragedy, something had to be done about it.

Licking his lips, he walked to the stereo, turning the volume down. Then he dimmed the lights quite low before softly knocking on the bedroom door, opening it and standing in the slight wedge.

"Everyone okay?"

The women, dressed again, their hair and general appearance unkempt, each of them holding a trembling cigarette, collectively wiped their eyes, their faces beset by running mascara and the sudden puffiness of tearful lamentation. When they murmured their unnatural affirmations, Xavier curled his finger at Erica, the slightly chubby one from the hot tub, saying, "Erica…just Erica…I need your help."

"Me?"

"Yes, just for a few moments." He nodded, smiling reassuringly.

When she passed the threshold, he took her by the hand and pulled the door to. Then he led her back into the living room, watching as she pressed her eyes shut at the sight of her deceased friend. Leading her behind the sofa, turning her so her back would be to the corpse, Xavier kissed her, pushing his tongue into her mouth.

She allowed it for a moment before pulling back and shaking her head. "No…I can't."

"We must and, don't forget, you made me promise." His hands roamed her body, one moving under her dress and sliding her underwear to the side. Her instant protestations suddenly caught in her throat as Xavier, satisfied, felt a tremor pass through her body. Erica's mouth hung open as he manipulated her, pleased with the mouse-squeaks escaping her throat.

"You see," he cajoled, "you can."

They copulated over the back of the couch, the girl occasionally muttering the word "nee" but showing no inclination to truly want to stop things. Somehow, the sight of the dead girl invigorated Xavier, adding a fragrance of animalism to the night that had seemed to come to such a screeching halt.

Finished, their bodies covered in sheens of sweat, Xavier turned Erica to him, noting that her eyes were again clenched shut. He brushed her lips with a kiss, telling her to keep their actions to herself. He also whispered that he'd chosen her, and *only* her, because of her great beauty.

Even an untruthful compliment can melt ice.

Erica managed a smile, reseating her dress as she made a quick trip to the restroom before going back into the bedroom, deceiving her friends by saying she'd helped him with their dead friend's name and names of relatives.

Now Xavier could relax, again reclining in the chair, drinking a cold beer as the warm afterglow of fresh sex swirled around him.

As he waited, he glanced down at the beautiful dead girl next to him, regretting that he'd not been able to enjoy her before she died.

Pity.

AN HOUR later, after a heated exchange over his exorbitant fee, Cortez Redon ingested a double shot of scotch, following it with a strong peppermint. He crunched the mint, taking a sip of water, repeating the script he'd created in his mind in a whisper. When he'd run through it twice, he frowned importantly and nodded at Fausto. "Bring them out."

Fausto opened the door and said a few words to the girls. The quartet sheepishly exited the bedroom. Several of them gasped when they saw their friend, despite her now being covered with a sheet. Redon looked upon the girls admiringly, remembering what Xavier had said about the orgy that had just begun at the moment of the young lady's untimely, drug-induced passing. Their presence, and intoxicating smell, caused Redon to make a mental note, reminding himself of the wicked treasures that could be had in Lloret this time of year, especially at the misdemeanor detention center.

When Redon was just a young prosecutor, he'd habitually pop in and spring a cute coed or two with a quick bribe or a few threats. Afterward, free and clear of charges, they were as pliable as plumber's putty, willing to do all sorts of things to express thanks for their liberation.

The good old days.

He snapped his fingers, speaking English. "Just line up right there. Face me."

He waited until all eight cried-out eyes joined his.

"The gentleman you came here to…*visit* tonight has been arrested for felony possession of cocaine. He called someone in the local coroner's office he thought was a friend when your friend here passed away. I suppose he thought he could hide her death." Redon shook his head and clucked his tongue. "But that so-called friend at the coroner's office thankfully took such lawlessness seriously. And that's why the man you were here doing drugs with is now looking at seven years in prison."

"Who are you?" asked the tallest girl. Though her makeup was gone, Redon found her quite delicious, warring with himself not to be flirtatious.

Removing his credentials, Redon stepped forward, holding them close to every girl's eye as he swept down their small line. "My name is Cortez Redon, and I'm the top acusador in the state of Catalonia. I'm an officer of the court, and of the law. We've had Señor Espinosa on our radar for some time," Redon said, lying about Xavier's last name. "And tonight begins his retribution to the society he has harmed for so long with his illegal drugs." Redon tapped his foot. "But now I am puzzled as to what I shall do with you four."

"But we didn't do anything wrong," the tall blonde protested.

Redon smiled thinly. "My dear, you were taking illegal drugs. There are enough narcotics here that I can charge each of you with intent to distribute. You were also in possession of drug paraphernalia. And, most damning, an attempt was made to illegally dispose of a corpse, along with a potential for those charges to elevate to some sort of wrongful death. If I so desire, I can easily push for time in one of our roughest prisons." He narrowed his eyes. "Just imagine what the prisoners, and the guards, would do for a chance at a lovingly innocent Dutch girl."

"We didn't do any of that," the blonde pleaded. "We just came here to visit."

"You came here to have an *orgía*," Redon snapped, turning his nose up as if even mentioning the word somehow dirtied him. "This, of course, will be a portion of your official arrest reports and, because of Señor Espinosa's high profile and the many leaks with the local police, the media will certainly run with it." He spread his hands above him. "Just think of the headlines and news stories—*bevy of Dutch girls in five-on-one sex romp with Spain's largest drug dealer*." Redon jolted, as if something occurred to him, whispering to himself but purposefully loud enough for the girls to hear. "So *that's* why his attorney insisted that he be immediately examined by a doctor. They're going to collect DNA from his genitals and try to implicate those he copulated with."

Redon glanced up sharply, seeing looks of abject horror on the faces of two girls: the striking blonde and the slightly pudgy one with brown hair. It was all he could do not to laugh.

A few of the girls began to cry. The tall blonde shook her head, eyeing Redon as she pleaded with her eyes. One girl covered her face in her hands.

Let it burn…

Let it burn…

When they eventually began commiserating with one another in Dutch, Redon spoke loudly as he pinched his chin in a pontificating manner. "I suppose there is *one* possibility for you young ladies not to be implicated."

They each looked at him as if he were ruler of the world.

Redon gestured to Fausto, standing off to the side. "This gentleman worked for Espinosa, but has been most helpful on this evening. I'd very much like to spare him the indignity of an arrest—as long as he continues to be compliant." Cocked his eyebrow. "And if you agree to what I'm considering, then I suppose I could afford each of you the same courtesy."

The girls pleaded in three distinct languages. One girl even fell to her knees.

Perfecto!

Redon explained that he had more than enough evidence to convict Señor Espinosa for numerous crimes dating back over a number of years. Then, as if he were working it all out aloud, he again spoke of his desire to prevent a media circus by choosing to ignore what had happened here tonight. "Because, in actuality, it would take away from Espinosa's arrest. I don't want it cheapened by it transforming into a sex story. I want him exposed for the drug-pushing monster he is." His eyes wandered to the sheet, then to Fausto.

"If you were to drive the girls and," he gestured to the corpse, "*her*…back into Lloret, the dead girl could be positioned somewhere on a quiet street, the beach, wherever. Her friends could '*find*' her and she would simply be pronounced as one of the resort's many unfortunate tourist overdoses. And I, in my great benevolence, could make a call to Lloret's *jefe de la policía* and tell him to resist his urge to scrutinize."

Redon turned eyes to the women. "I could also tell him to forget the drug tests they typically administer to the friends of the deceased, provided each of you agree to leave quietly and never breathe a word of this to anyone."

The young ladies eagerly agreed to cooperate. Redon felt they would have done anything he asked.

Fifteen minutes later, after Fausto and the girls deposited the corpse in the trunk of the Mercedes and headed off to find a remote area of Lloret, Xavier exited the bedroom from where he'd listened to Redon's performance, clapping slowly. "Bravo, Señor Redon! That was a stage-worthy performance."

Xavier walked into the kitchen, coming back with a brown paper sack weighted down with several stacks of bills. He pulled it back before handing it over, saying, "And you're certain this won't be traced back to me?"

"Did you have sex with her?"

"Which one?"

"*La chica muerta.*"

"I never touched her."

"Then it won't come back," Redon said, taking the bag and setting it aside. He pressed his lips together, smirking at Xavier.

"Why the face?" Xavier asked, lifting the remnants of a beer and drinking it.

"Because the money in that bag is peanuts compared to what you will soon be paying me."

"What are you talking about?"

"What else was it that you wanted from me?"

Xavier shrugged. "It's been a long night, Cortez. I don't feel like solving riddles."

"Do you recall what you requested of me at the wedding?"

"About tracking a satellite phone."

Redon nodded.

"What about it?" Xavier snapped.

"After a number of painstaking inquiries, I've found a dirty American military general at a joint air base down south in Andalusia." The acusador took a majestic breath, his face triumphant as he said, "If given a region, he can relay all satellite conversations coming to or from that region. When your man is picked out through computer voice recognition, the general can pinpoint him down to the meter."

Xavier, seemingly unimpressed, shrugged. "Very good, Cortez…now all we need is the old bastard to make a call."

Pressing his tongue into the pit of his cheek, Redon trembled with excitement.

"What?" Xavier yelled.

"Well, señor…guess who I had a meeting with on this very evening? Guess who has found a new patsy to insert into Berga? And guess who will be communicating with him…by—satellite—phone?"

"Why didn't you call me?" Xavier roared. "We could have killed him tonight!"

Redon dismissed this with an effeminate wave of his hand. "The precautions that man takes. I was picked up very far away. They searched me, then drove me to another car, checking for tails the entire way. I had no idea where we would meet."

"You could have worn a bug."

Redon shook his head. "They swept me. No phones either. I'd have been brutally killed for trying."

Xavier cursed.

"You've missed the point. As I said, Navarro is back in business. All we do now is pay this American general for his services, and we wait for the call."

"You're certain another man is going into Berga?"

"Almost certain. He tried to act disinterested but Navarro has thrown so much money at him, how could he possibly say no?"

"How much money?"

"Millions for the full tenure."

"Did he pay the others that much?"

"No. It's an indicator of his fear."

A flush spread over Xavier Zambrano. His eyes moved all about the villa as he processed everything he had heard. "This is it," he whispered.

"Pardon?"

"I know it, Cortez. I feel it in my bones. This will be the old prick's death knell—his fatal mistake." Xavier's white teeth gleamed. He opened his arms, leaning back and letting out a victory shriek.

Chapter Nine

AS PROMISED, Gage had awoken early and planned their trip after speaking with the hotel's concierge. That done, he'd found a pay phone and called Colonel Hunter, bringing him up to speed and asking for any information the retired officer might be able to glean from his contacts. Hunter told Gage to call back tomorrow.

Traveling by rail, Gage and Justina's first leg was from Girona, Spain to Marseille, in France. The only available train was a slow-moving regional, making the leg take seven long hours. After a thirty-minute stop and a few tasty donor kebabs outside the train station, Gage and Justina now rocketed to the north on a TGV Duplex train. Though the Marseille to Paris segment of the trip was nearly twice that of the Girona to Marseille segment, it would take only half as long due to the blistering speed of the famed French bullet train. Gage glanced up at the digital display, watching as the train flirted with 300 kilometers per hour, about 185 miles per hour. They were due in Paris just before nine tonight.

He turned his eyes down to Justina, sleeping steadily with her head in his lap. As he swept her hair back from her face, he wondered exactly what this trip might bring. Earlier, before they'd departed, he told her that they would need to pinch their pennies in Paris, drawing laughter from Justina after he'd explained the colloquialism.

"We can just go camping if you'd like," she'd said. "I just want to spend time with you, with no pressures and no worries."

But Gage had insisted on Paris. Partly for his own catharsis.

He stared out the window, past the Rhone River, to the hills surrounding the Rhone valley. The last time he'd traveled to France with a woman, he'd gotten her killed. The sudden burst of horrid memories sent a tremor through Gage. He wiped his palms on his shirt, regulating his breathing.

Never again.

Justina stirred, looking up at him. "Where are we?"

"Near Valence, France," Gage whispered. "Go back to sleep."

"How long?"

"Just a few more hours."

"You're sweating. Are you okay?"

"Sure, I am," he said, forcing a laugh.

"Good." She stared up at him, touching his face with her hand. "This is nice, Gage."

Pushing the unpleasant thoughts aside, he said, "I agree. Very nice."

"I've never been so happy." With that, she nestled her curled body into her seat, again cradling her head into Gage's lap.

Resuming his observation of the French countryside, Gage resumed his vows—screaming the words in his mind.

Never again!

Paris, France

LA VILLE des Lumières was alive with energy. The evening was quite cool and it had rained earlier, but now, despite the bright lights of the city, the brightest stars could be seen twinkling above as Gage and Justina walked hand in hand through the Tuileries Garden. Even though it was almost midnight, they'd just finished their evening meal, having feasted magnificently at an affordable 7th Arrondissement restaurant recommended by their hotelier.

The restaurant itself had been a bit of a shock to Gage. Cavernous and consisting of two levels, the eatery was outfitted with large central screens showing ribald black and white silent films. The films weren't exactly pornographic but did display quite a bit of naked skin of both females and males from what appeared to be early 20th Century footage. Justina had found the movies incredibly amusing, giggling every time the screens showed something bawdy.

Both of them quite full, having crossed back over the Seine, they strolled to the garden park, heading west on the crushed gravel trail, toward the brightly lit Arc de Triomphe up the hill in the distance. Justina suddenly stopped.

"I thought you wanted to see the Arc?" Gage said.

"So, I see it," Justina said, gesturing with her hand.

Though it was dark in the gardens, there was enough ambient light for Gage to tell she was smiling. "Do you want to go somewhere else instead?" he asked.

"*Bardzo,*" she replied in her native tongue.

"What does that mean?"

"It means, 'very much so.'" She grasped his hand, pulling him to the north.

"Where are we going?"

She led him on.

After they crossed the Rue de Rivoli, he asked her again.

"Back to the hotel," she said. "Am I going the right way?"

"Make a left here," he said. "You tired?"

"Not at all," she replied, smiling again.

Their hotel was small and inexpensive—inexpensive for Paris—just a block off the Place Vendôme in the 1st Arrondissement. Despite being basic, the outside of their art nouveau hotel was charming. The building was tall and narrow, faced in glazed masonry with accents of decorative black iron. Justina stopped at a small street-side cart, purchasing a bottle of red wine, a large bottle of water and a pack of cigarettes.

"Now we're really ready," she said, a bottle in each hand.

Upstairs, as Gage's heart hammered in his chest, Justina searched the room for a corkscrew. "*Skurwysyn!* We're in a Paris hotel room and they don't have a corkscrew?"

Gage produced his utility knife and had the cork out in seconds.

"Why, thank you," she said. When she couldn't find a glass, she gave Gage the water bottle, clinking it with the wine. Then she turned the wine up, chugging mightily.

"Careful now," Gage laughed.

"Screw it. I'm on vacation." Walking into the small bathroom, Justina turned the shower on and told Gage to get cleaned up.

His nervousness quelled somewhat by her amusing actions, Gage nodded and complied. When he came out from the bathroom, wearing shorts and a t-shirt, Justina was nowhere to be seen. Moments later she came in from the hallway, putting her cigarettes and lighter on the small shelf by the door.

"My turn." She took another slug of the wine before closing herself in the bathroom. Gage dropped to the bed, taking large, hyperventilation-style breaths.

"Be calm, buddy," he said to himself fourteen times in a row.

After what seemed to be several hours, the bathroom opened, spilling steam into the cool room. Justina, wearing one of his long t-shirts, turned off the light, revealing only her silhouette. He stood. Justina came to him. They kissed, gently at first, growing to heated passion. Justina turned him as they kissed, both of them falling to the bed. They kissed again as her hands slid downward, sliding his shorts and underwear down.

Gage's heart pumped abnormal quantities of blood as she reached under the long t-shirt, sliding her panties down her legs. Then she pulled the long t-shirt over her head, standing still for a moment, her eyes joined with his as he viewed her form.

Justina was tall and lean, and the body Gage had first seen in the bikini in the club Eastern Bloc, and later on the beach, did not disappoint. Her skin had the envious tautness of a person in her early twenties. Her shoulders were square and her breasts full and upturned at their dark points. Two silky curves occurred as his eyes slid downward, inward at her trim waist and back out at the swell of her hips, framing the delicateness of her femininity that he somehow willed himself not to look at.

She climbed onto the bed on all fours, moving to one side of the bed as she slid under the covers, holding them up until he did the same. Then, just as she'd done the two nights before, she rolled to her side and draped his arm over her stomach.

Gage could hardly breathe.

His bodily response was completely involuntary but, judging by the subtle movements of hid bedmate, welcome. She pressed backward into him, turning her head so her mouth was brushing against his.

"Love me, Gage."

Her words set him in motion. Cupping her face in his hands, he allowed her to roll to her back as he moved astride her lean body, kissing her. After a moment he pulled his head back. Justina was smiling.

She was quite beautiful and he told her so.

Justina slid her nails down his back, pulling him into a blissful union that occurred three unforgettable times over the course of the Parisian night.

It was Gage's finest evening in quite some time.

THE NEXT day, after a hearty breakfast and three hours touring the Louvre, Justina napped while Gage made his way down the Rue de Rivoli. After quite a search, he eventually located a phone booth—an anachronism these days, but still useful to a person wanting to make an anonymous call. While the operator asked Colonel Hunter if he would accept charges from a Gregory Harris, Gage checked his watch. It was eight in the morning across the Atlantic in North Carolina.

"Hunter, here."

"Good morning, sir."

"It is a good morning. Gettin' some rain. We need it." Gage could hear the whooshing as his former commander dropped down into his La-Z-Boy. "How's Paris?"

"Not bad, actually."

"Yeah, I spent two months there right after 'Nam, with a task force from the French's Dragon Thirteenth. The French are easy targets for ridicule but, from my point of view, they get a bad rap at times."

"Agreed. So, sir, did you learn anything about the job I've been offered?"

"A little on the folks involved. Sketchy, mainly. Those fellows aren't the terrorist variety, so most of my contacts don't have 'em on their radars."

"That's what I figured."

"Of what I did learn, the son, Cesar, is a certified scumbag. That came from three sources. In the event you did take the job, you couldn't trust him. Ever. He and his pop have had a lot of differences, too."

"Did you learn anything new about Ernesto?"

"Didn't learn anything new. From all I hear, he is what he is, but isn't a bullshitter."

"Okay," Gage breathed.

"But," Hunter said, using a brighter tone, "I did learn a few things about this Cortez Redon fellow."

"We know he's dirty, if he's taking Navarro's money."

"That's a fact, for sure. A contact of mine spoke to a friend in Spain, somewhere in their justice system, and the fellow said Cortez Redon's not only dirty, but he's one of the most spiteful, mean sonofabitches on the Iberian peninsula."

"Is this source good?"

"I trust my guy, and my guy said his source is impeccable. Lie down with Cortez Redon, son, and you might as well lie down in a bed of rattlers."

"Well, that clenches it. I'm out."

"Don't blame you a bit." Hunter cleared his throat. "So, how're things going with you and your new friend?"

"Pretty good, sir."

"I can hear that smile of yours through the phone."

"As usual, you nailed it."

"When will you head back?"

"Not sure. Soon, I hope. Paris is expensive."

"You coming alone, or accompanied?"

"Not sure about that, either."

"Bring her along," Hunter said. "You've got the shed out back and three squares. She's not one of them frou-frou's, is she? Can she handle the shed?"

"She's not frou-frou," Gage laughed. "And your shed'll look like the Ritz after what she's been through."

"Just give me a heads up before you fly."

"Roger, sir."

Once they hung up, Gage stepped from the phone booth, crossing the busy street, back to the Tuileries Garden. The sun shone brightly overhead, warming Paris as many people sunbathed and lounged in the expansive park.

Though Gage knew he needed to put up a façade of confidence for Justina, he at least wanted to settle on a plan of action. Gage hated being without a plan. He found a spot on the edge of a marble fountain and calculated his remaining money, determining that they could easily stay in Paris another five days and leave Gage sufficient cushion to travel back to the States with.

And Gage definitely wanted Justina to come back with him.

As discussed on the call, they could stay in Hunter's "shed", which was a converted shipping container on the backside of his land. It didn't sound appealing, but it was actually quite nice, even equipped with an enclosed toilet and running water. Gage and the colonel had converted it a year earlier, cutting in dual windows and adding a proper door to the front of the container. In essence, it was now not too dissimilar to a mobile home. And mobile homes were quite common around Fort Bragg.

Once stateside, Justina would have a few months to find work and, as part of that process, Gage was certain Hunter could help her with a Visa. In the meantime, Gage could partake in some training as he waited for a job. If things broke right, he and Justina could have their own apartment inside of a few months.

But one thing was certain, after this week, Gage's vacation was over. Being this close to summer, Gage knew Justina's transatlantic airfare would be upwards of $1,200. Gage's round-trip ticket was open, and in business class. He hoped, with some luck, that the airline would allow him two coach seats in exchange for his one expensive ticket. That would be a huge boon to his rapidly decreasing nest egg.

Wanting to let Justina sleep as long as she desired, Gage wandered to the north, turning west at the majestic Paris Opera House. He walked all the way to the Parc Monceau, sitting on a bench as the pigeons swarmed him only long enough to find he had no food. When he'd decided to wait a few more days before proposing his plan to Justina, he ambled back to their hotel, taking the striking, tree-lined Boulevard Malesherbes to Rue Royale.

By the time he keyed the door, he'd been gone nearly two hours. But he hadn't expected to find Justina sitting on the edge of the bed, wiping tears from her face.

"Are you okay?" he asked.

Managing a smile, she nodded, pulling him to her.

"What's wrong, Justina?"

They laid on the bed together before she answered him. "Nothing is wrong. In fact, I'm so happy to be with you."

"Why were you crying?"

"It was nothing."

Gage didn't push for an answer.

After a while, he asked if she slept.

"Not a wink."

"Why not?"

"Because I couldn't sleep for thinking of you," she said, turning and locking her arms around him.

Though Gage would have loved to have known why she was crying, Justina deftly moved his mind in a completely different direction.

Thank goodness.

Chapter Ten

THE FOLLOWING three days were glorious. Gage and Justina spent nearly every waking minute together, discovering exactly how compatible they really were. While there were many things to like about Justina, Gage found himself being most affected by her sense of humor. She had a way of imagining things about other people, total strangers, that would sometimes have Gage bent double in laughter. One afternoon, when they'd wandered into an expensive store just for the fun of looking, Justina had grasped Gage's arm and deftly gestured to a man who was being fitted for a suit. It was obvious the overly-tan gentleman had endured a facelift.

"I think that man's doctor stapled his face a little tightly, yes?"

Gage had pretended to view a tie while taking a good look. She was correct. The man's face was so severely tightened it looked comical, pulled into a permanent smile like the Joker from Batman.

"My goodness, do you think he can even talk?" Justina breathed. "And how does he open his mouth to eat?"

"Stop," Gage whispered, trying not to laugh.

"I bet dogs bark at him when he walks past. Children drop their lollipops."

"Quit it."

"But some women would be attracted to him. They know he has the money for a facelift and, no matter what they do, he always smiles about it."

"Justina…"

"He looks like a doll I had as a child—a plastic doll." She mimed popping a pill. "It looks like someone gave his face a Viagra."

Gage had pulled her from the store before bellowing laughter on the street. There was something about Justina's accent which made such observations even funnier. Her remarks didn't come off as cruel in the least. She was just an observant young lady with a sense of humor, and being with her warmed Gage's heart.

On their fourth day in Paris, after a long walk to the Eiffel Tower, Gage and Justina had a simple meal outside a small café in the 7th Arrondissement. The temperature was much warmer this evening, the air thick with summerlike humidity. The setting sun lingered, beaming through the adjacent buildings and splashing the couple with flattering honey light. Justina ordered a small carafe of wine and, after she'd had two glasses, Gage felt it was a good time to finally suggest her coming with him to the United States. Though he'd have to spend a half-hour on the phone, Gage wanted to make the arrangements tonight so they could depart on one of tomorrow's morning flights.

Just as he'd opened his mouth to speak, he noticed Justina's eyes overflowing with tears. She'd turned, staring up at the Eiffel Tower through the buildings across the avenue.

This was the third time he'd seen her crying since initially finding her crying in their hotel room. Though he hadn't allowed himself to dwell on it, there had been a pit of dread in Gage's stomach, worrying that something might have happened to her at the hands of her Russian "employers."

"What's wrong?" he asked, touching her hand.

She sniffed, shaking her head as her lips trembled.

"Justina, what is it?"

"I'm okay."

Gage steeled himself. "Does this have something to do with the Russians?"

"No, Gage, not at all."

"You can tell me."

"I promise. It's not that."

"Did someone abuse you?"

She wiped her tears with her napkin, smiling reassuringly. "I have never been abused, Gage. Ever."

He wiped his sweaty palms on his pants leg.

"But when I told you about my family back in Poland, I didn't tell you everything."

"Okay," he said with caution.

"As I said, my father died many years back." She took a few steadying breaths. "My mother struggles to make money just for herself. And my older brother can barely pay to keep his wife and kids in food and shoes, so he can't help her." She dabbed her eyes. "All that's true."

"I remember you telling me all that."

"But what I didn't tell you is about my younger brother, Teodor."

"You mentioned him."

"Well, what I didn't say is that he's sick. Very sick."

Gage leaned forward. "Sick, how?"

104

"He has a condition called *Mukowiscydoza*. I don't know how you say it in English, but it affects his lungs. He cannot breathe well much of the time." She snapped her fingers as if trying to recall something. "The international letters for this disease are C.F."

"Cystic Fibrosis," Gage said. "I'm somewhat familiar with it."

"He does okay sometimes, but when he has bad times it puts a strain on my mother. The government pays for his basic care, but she has to *be* there with him. So when his condition is bad, she cannot work her job and then cannot buy what she needs." She twirled her hand. "You get the picture, yes?"

"Yes," Gage said. "I do."

She pointed to the Eiffel Tower, managing a weak smile. "Teodor has an Eiffel Tower poster in his room. It's tacky…showing the tower and two women with painted faces. But, he is a teenage boy." Her smile was weak and distant. "Teodor always says he wants to come here someday and meet a beautiful French girl. Sitting here, seeing the tower in this pretty light, it made me think of him." Her smile faded as her cheek began to twitch. "And the other night, when you came back to the hotel room, I'd just called my mama. They were at the hospital. He's not doing well at all."

"Is being in the hospital normal for him?"

She made a so-so motion with her hand. "He's been in the hospital more than usual."

"And that's what made you cry?"

Fresh tears sprung from her eyes as she pinched her lips together and nodded. Gage felt like he was missing something.

"Justina, is that all?"

She wiped her eyes.

"Justina."

"My mama lost her job. She's been gone too many days."

"Isn't it against the law for her employer to do that?"

"She didn't fill out some form or another. I don't know. She's just a janitor. No one will help her and she's having to spend every moment with Teodor." Justina cried into her napkin.

Gage leaned back in his chair, taking an expansive breath, eyeing this beautiful creature across from him. This was not some manipulation—she had no clue about the possibility of the money he might make. He watched as she pulled her hair back with both hands, wiping both eyes with her hands as she again forced a smile. Then, with trembling hands, she lit a cigarette and said, "Enough about me. We change the subject, okay?"

"Okay," Gage answered. And they might as well change the subject because, in the span of only five minutes, he'd just about changed his mind about Navarro's offer. Although he'd termed the job as a Bolivian Army Ending to Hunter—a phrase the Special Forces had adopted from Butch Cassidy and the Sundance Kid, meaning an unwinnable suicide mission—Gage was confident enough in himself that he could get through the initial month and be flush with cash.

Thirty days, he told himself. *Thirty days for a hundred grand.*

Gage froze, an idea coming to him.

Does it have to be just thirty days?

"Are you okay?" she asked. "Gage?"

What's two years?

"Your face is white," Justina said.

"I'm fine," he murmured, realizing that the idea he was considering was a good one. One that he would deal with in the morning. He reached his hand across the table, holding Justina's. "Don't worry, okay? You'll be able to help your mother and brother."

"How?"

"We change the subject, okay?" he said with a wink, mimicking her accent.

UNABLE TO manage much sleep, Gage finally stood from the bed just before six the next morning. He dressed himself and went downstairs, having a cup of black coffee before taking a walk in the cool Parisian morning. This time, wandering aimlessly, he crossed the Seine, finding himself in the Place des Invalides as the sun rose in the east. Viewing the striking monuments, Gage ran everything through his mind one final time.

Are you sure you want to do this?

Thinking about Justina with tears in her eyes, wanting to care for her mother and brother, was truly all the motivation Gage needed. Though he'd not rationalized it in his mind, Gage Hartline had fallen in love.

But, just to be sure about his decision, he stripped the proposition down to what he felt lay ahead.

Two years of your life…two years naked as the day you were born, with no armament, no spec-ops buddies to call on, no night vision scopes, no exotic high-explosives. It'll just be you and Cesar, the "scumbag" drug trafficker, against nine-hundred-seventy-nine hard-boiled prisoners, many of them well acquainted with the ancient skill of killing.

A shiny plate-glass window on Rue Fabert displayed Gage's reflection: six-foot-one and two-hundred pounds, still well-built but with a few facial lines of age. Gage wasn't surprised when he heard a corner of his mind screaming for the challenge, telling the rest of his psyche that opportunities like this only come along once in a lifetime.

Then, that dueling other corner of his brain started in, the corner every man hates, bringing up all sorts of incarceration unpleasantness—things like shankings, gang rape, riots and, his worst fear, the chance that something could go critically wrong and Gage could wind up in Berga prison for good.

He allowed the two barristers in his brain to make their final arguments as Paris awoke. Once his decision had been finalized, Gage headed back to the north, to the anachronistic phone booth he'd come to know.

As a few clouds arrived from the southwest, Gage stepped into the phone booth and flirted with the notion of calling Colonel Hunter. It was after midnight at Bragg, but he'd woken the colonel up before. And the colonel was so damned good at stripping away the excess of a mission and getting right down to its core.

But Gage was fearful that Hunter would talk him out of it. He'd remind Gage of what a scumbag Cesar was, and would rail on Gage about Cortez Redon's reputation. He would insist that Gage bring Justina back to the States, and together they could make enough scraps to send back to Poland to help her mother and brother.

Scraps…

"Screw it," Gage breathed. He dialed the operator, then gave her the new number Navarro had given him, making a collect call in the name of Gregory Harris. There were a few murmurs before the operator clicked off, followed by a clipped greeting from whomever was speaking into the voice modulator.

Gage shifted the phone to his other ear and asked for the boss. There was a delay before Navarro came on the phone, also using the modulator.

"I will accept the job if you're willing to change several key parameters involving my fee," Gage said.

"And those changes are?"

"The money you offered is not sufficient," Gage said. "And, in exchange for you upping my fee, I will go ahead and commit to the full-term, up to two years."

Navarro took it in stride. "How much?"

"I want twice the monthly amounts you offered me: two-hundred grand for the first month, and a hundred grand for each additional month."

"That's a great deal of money."

"Yes, it is. And if you decline, you will need to find another man."

"You've already asked for this extra week to make your decision, leaving me in a weakened position. One day could be the difference in the life we speak of, and now I don't have time to find another person."

"That was never my intention," Gage said.

"If I double these amounts, and my son departs there in good condition, then I must insist the bonus at the end remains the same," Navarro said.

"Agreed. But there's one other condition."

"And that is?"

"I want more advance money. I want the fee for the first year up front." Gage let that sink in a moment. "And when I go in, I go in. I will not request to be pulled out while your son is alive. I will stay until the job is done and I will do my very best, but that is the *only* guarantee I can offer."

"You're speaking of a great deal of upfront money."

"Yes, I am. It's one-point-three million bucks, meaning one million euro at today's exchange rate, and it's not negotiable."

"You're quite brazen, Mister Harris," Navarro remarked.

"You want me to go into a prison of murderers, señor, and you say I'm brazen?"

"If I agree to your conditions, when can you leave?"

"I'm away at the moment but can be back in Catalonia tomorrow. Have your man bring the money to the main train station in Barcelona. Euros, in small bills, please. Tell him to be at Barcelona Sants metro track L-three tomorrow at eight in the morning."

"*When* can you leave?"

"I can leave three days from today."

"I have your word?"

"You do," Gage said.

"Must I speak of what would transpire if you disappear with my money?"

"I have no illusions about that, señor. And my reputation should give you comfort that I'm a man of my word."

"Very well. I will speak to my associate," Navarro said. "I'm pleased."

"There's one other thing."

"Yes?"

"Your associate, the lawyer…I do not trust him."

"While he's obviously willing to bend the occasional rule, he and I have worked together for many years."

"Tell him, from me, if he double-crosses me in any way, I *will* come for him."

Navarro was silent for a moment. "Is there something about him I should know?"

"Nothing concrete, no. Call it a hunch."

"I will tell him."

"Tomorrow, señor, Barcelona Sants, L-three, eight in the morning."

"My associate that drove you will be there."

"Does he know about this?"

"Not fully, no. But he's my closest ally and can be trusted."

"Fine, señor. Good day to you."

Gage's next call was to Colonel Hunter's regular mobile phone. As Gage predicted, since it was the middle of the night there, Hunter didn't answer and Gage left a two-minute message detailing the high-points of the job. "I'm going to send you a copy of the affidavits in their original form." Gage forced a chuckle and said, "And I don't want to hear any don't-bend-over-for-the-soap jokes either, sir. Hartline, out."

Checking his watch again, Gage exited the phone booth, walking back to the Tuileries Garden. Despite his casual clothes, he promptly did eighty-two military push-ups, breaking the horizontal plane on each one with his upper arms. He jogged through the park, wedging his feet under the legs of a mounted bench as he did more than one hundred sit-ups in the damp grass, touching his elbow to the alternate knee on each one. Then he ran, pushing himself, doing more than the standard quick-time jog. When he was far to the south, he spotted a ticket window awning on a stadium called Charléty. The awning was stout and, after testing his weight, Gage did ten wide-arm pull-ups, touching the back of his neck to the bar and pausing during each repetition. He did four sets of ten.

His muscles sufficiently warmed up, Gage ran for forty more minutes, slowing his pace to a fast jog, timing his run to end near their hotel around ten in the morning. When he went to the hotel room, he didn't tell Justina the news, only that they needed to head back to Spain. Two hours later they departed Gare d'Austerlitz with matching train tickets to Barcelona.

And Gage had no idea how, or when, he would break the news to Justina. But it had to be done. Soon.

That evening, with no immediate worries over money, Gage sprung for a night at the modern Abba Hotel only a few blocks away from the Barcelona Sants railway station.

He wanted to enjoy his brief time with Justina, and his time as a free man.

While he waited for the best time to tell her.

Barcelona, Spain

THE FOLLOWING morning Gage stood outside the gleaming terminal of the Barcelona Sants railway station. He kept his eyes on the short-term lot and, at precisely 7:48 A.M., was pleased to see Navarro's top man, Valentin, enter the lot, taking a ticket from the automated attendant. Gage waited while Valentin parked the gleaming white Jaguar XJL Ultimate. The Spaniard exited the vehicle, carrying a satchel and wearing a sport coat, looking like any businessman at the station to catch a train.

After scanning the area for anyone who might be following Valentin, Gage took up a position behind him and walked into the train station. The station was expansive and busier this morning than it had been yesterday evening. Gage continued to scan for surveillance as he followed Valentin to the sprawling underground area containing the short-distance metro tracks. The Spaniard purchased a ticket, went through the turnstile and walked to metro track L-3, just as he was instructed. He looked up at the clock. It was 7:58 A.M. and he was on the Canyelles side of the line.

Gage walked to the automated ticket machine and purchased two T-10 tickets, running a twenty-euro bill into the machine and pocketing his change. He passed through the turnstile and waited fifty feet from Valentin, keeping him in sight the entire time. When 8:00 A.M. came and went, Valentin began to look around. Gage remained behind a crowd of people on the platform. When the train finally arrived, he pushed forward and, just before the train departed, grasped Valentin by the arm and led him onto the packed subway car.

When the doors had squeezed shut, Valentin eyed Gage.

Gage leaned over and spoke Spanish, saying, "Give me your phone."

"Perdón?"

"You heard me."

Valentin reached into his jacket and handed Gage a rather cheap phone, which came as no surprise. It was likely disposable and, if Gage were to guess, he and Navarro had a drawer full of them. In fact, they probably used a new one every day or two. Gage unclipped the back cover and removed the battery.

"Any other phones or anything else emitting a signal?"

"No," Valentin said, frowning.

"Good. Just stare straight ahead and get off when I tell you to."

They rode the train through several stops. By the time they reached the Vallcarca station, the outbound train was nearly empty. As the doors opened, Gage hitched his head and followed Valentin off. The only other people exiting must have been students because they were all very young, laughing and running with their book bags and matching uniforms. Gage gestured up the long escalator, following Valentin and keeping a watchful eye behind them. Outside, he led Valentin into a grocery, finding a small bathroom in the back. Inside the bathroom, Gage held out his hand for the satchel.

"Shouldn't we talk first?" Valentin asked.

"I'm not going anywhere," Gage said, taking the satchel and popping it open. On top of the money was a canister of shaving cream. Gage lifted the canister, frowning.

"Please take that," Valentin said.

Gage popped the top and squirted some of the shaving cream. He set the canister aside and perused the satchel. Inside were banded stacks of 50 and 100 euro bills. They weren't brand new, thankfully, with each bill showing telltale wrinkles. Gage reached behind his body and pulled a folded vinyl bag from his waist. He opened the bag, dumping the contents of the satchel in and zipping it. Then he tossed the leather satchel into the trash next to the toilet.

"Follow me."

Valentin slid the shaving cream into his jacket.

They departed the grocery, crossing the street to an area with trees and a playground. There, Gage instructed Valentin to sit at a checkerboard built from tile on top of a concrete table. Sitting across from him, Gage unzipped the bag and counted the stacks of money while checking each stack for markers.

"I do not understand your constant caution, Mister Hartline," Valentin said. "We do not aim to cheat you, nor do we want to track you."

"This caution has kept me alive," Gage muttered, finishing with his count. The money was all there. He looked up.

Valentin handed Gage an envelope. "This contains your instructions. Señor Navarro told me to tell you that he is counting on you following through with your commitment every day of your incarceration."

"I understand," Gage said, folding the envelope and stuffing it into his pocket.

Valentin reached into his coat pocket and retrieved a slim, heat-sealed black plastic bag. "This is the satellite phone and an earpiece—the smallest and lightest available." Seeing Gage's look, Valentin said, "The battery is disconnected." He removed the shaving cream canister and wagged it. "On your second day, this shaving cream canister will be replaced with an identical canister with the phone hidden in its bottom. The bottom can be unscrewed."

"Who will put it there?"

"Redon has arranged it," Valentin said, shrugging.

"Who else knows that I've been hired by your boss?"

"Only me and Acusador Redon, along with Señor Navarro, of course."

"When did he tell you?"

"I'm Señor Navarro's eyes, his ears, his hands...I know everything, whether he knows it or not."

"Any thoughts for me?"

Valentin moved his eyes side to side before saying, "Cesar, the son, has *always* been problematic for Señor Navarro."

"In what way?"

"Cesar left when he was sixteen. Went to the south. Lived on hookers and cocaine until his father stopped feeding him cash, and then he used the Navarro name to begin importing drugs from Africa."

"What else?"

"I know nothing else."

"What is Cesar like?"

"It's been many years, Mister Hartline."

"What *was* he like?"

Valentin shook his head.

"Just between us," Gage said.

"Cesar was a little shit and a snake...spoiled, entitled, and very shrewd. Took after his mother."

"Can I trust him?"

Valentin pointed at the bag on the bench beside Gage. "You'll have to. I guess that's what the money is for."

Gage processed that nugget before saying, "Tell me what you know about Berga."

Producing a tan Gitane from its blue package, Valentin lit it with a match, puffing thoughtfully. "Berga is not talked about much in Spain, even in the underworld circles. The reason is its small size. They simply haven't had as many people go through." He drew on the Gitane, trumpeting his cheeks as the smoke exhausted from a corner of his mouth. "The other reason one doesn't hear much is due to Berga's sentences. Most men who go there are sentenced to life—and 'life' here in Spain means just that. Very few men exit to tell their tale." He flicked the ash into a nearby puddle, the ash hissing briefly. "My cousin was there a decade ago. We were very close growing up."

"What was he in for?"

"He was sent there because he killed his brother-in-law in an argument over money." Valentin said no more.

"Did he make it out?" Gage asked.

Valentin shook his head.

"Did he die naturally?"

"No."

"Mind telling me what happened?"

"You've heard of Los Leones?"

Gage nodded. "I read up on the prison. They're a large gang that started there, correct, and have since spread outward?"

"They will be your chief concern. Animals. Vicious. Unpredictable." Valentin took a steadying breath. "My cousin was discovered on only his fourth morning, alone in his cell."

"So he was killed?" Gage probed.

A delayed nod.

"Valentin...how was he killed?"

"There were so many injuries to his body, they don't know which one was fatal," he answered, staring into an unpleasant place. "His hands were chopped off. He'd been scalped. His entrails were out. Many of his bones were broken."

Gage narrowed his eyes. "Was all that some sort of retribution for something?"

"While we don't know for certain, we later learned that he owed an incarcerated member of Los Leones money. The debt was a decade old."

"A great deal of money?"

Valentin eyed Gage. "Less than a hundred euro." He dragged on his cigarette before crushing it out. "In Berga, any insult is colossal despite its size. You remember that."

ASCENDING IN the Abba Hotel's elevator, Gage readied himself for his next challenge. He was more nervous about this one than any he'd encountered thus far in Spain.

It was time to tell Justina.

Gage exited the elevator, viewing himself in the mirror at the landing. He was ashen. When he reached his hotel room door, he placed his hand on the knob, taking a deep breath. Then he keyed the door and stepped inside.

Justina was still in bed, sitting up, the covers to her waist. She looked up from her magazine, studying him for a moment before lowering her eyes to the bag. Her smile faded—she was reading his face.

"What have you done?"

"I've taken a job."

"What job?"

"A job that's going to take me away for a while."

She crossed her arms. "How long is 'a while'?"

"Please, just listen," Gage said, moving to the bed and sitting at her feet. "I have to work, Justina, and my job isn't always pleasant. Far from it, actually." He touched her leg. "My last three jobs have been miserable and dangerous—and none of them made me much money. I risked my life on each one and, had anything gone wrong, I'd probably be dead right now."

Justina didn't respond.

"The reason I woke up and accepted the job this morning, Justina, is completely about us. This isn't about only me." He chewed on his lip, finding the correct words. "I'm fearful of the job I've accepted. I don't have a problem admitting that, but I'm also fearful that, had I told you about it beforehand, you'd have talked me *out* of it."

Her nostrils flared.

He lifted the bag, placing it between them. "This is a million euro."

She stared at the bag. There was a jolt that ran through her but she recovered nicely. "I don't want you because of money," she said flatly. "You could go off on this job, meet some other pretty girl, and never come back to me. It's you I want. Not money."

Gage pulled the curtains back, flooding the room with morning light. "First off, Justina, I don't want to meet some other girl. It's been quite some time since I've been involved with anyone and being with you has brightened my outlook like the sun just brightened this room."

"And where are you going for this job?"

"Before I tell you, I want to know something, and I want the truth even if it takes you a day to think it over."

"What?"

"If I'm gone for a long time, years even…will you wait for me?"

Justina blinked several times. She stared up at him, obviously trying to comprehend what would make him ask such a question. "Why would you be gone *years*?"

"The job could very well take that long." Gage licked his lips. "So, will you, Justina? Will you wait for me? I think we'll be able to communicate sometimes but, even if we can't, will you wait?" She opened her mouth to speak but he cut her off. "Before you answer, I'm going to give you that money. Just know that. That money is for your mother and brother."

There was a lengthy period of silence in the hotel room. Outside, church bells chimed the ten o'clock hour. Then, Justina began to cry, covering her hands with her mouth.

Gage wanted to hug her, to console her, but he kept his distance. Right now, he wanted Justina to be alone in her decision. Eventually, her face contorted through her tears, she shook her head, barely able to get any words out. Several times she said, "I can't…"

"I understand," Gage whispered.

Justina used the sheet to dry her eyes, shaking her head back and forth. Turning her bleary eyes up to Gage, she said, "That's not what I mean. I just can't believe that a man I've known for only a week has been so good to me. Even in my dreams, I didn't believe a man like you lived on this earth." She held out her hand, pulling him beside her. "I will wait for a lifetime for you, Gage. I will dream of you all night, every night. There's *no* other man for me." Justina buried her head into his chest, crying, gripping him, continuing to tell him that he was the only man for her.

He held her, waiting for her to calm down. "I'm going to tell you everything, okay? It must remain between only us. You cannot tell anyone about it, understand?"

"I understand," she whispered, staring into his eyes.

Taking his time, Gage explained what exactly he did for a living. He'd shaded over it before, but now told her about his background and his present life.

Justina took it all in stride.

Then he told her everything he knew about the mission. He told her about Navarro, about his son Cesar, and about Berga. She asked a few questions, most of which he didn't know the answer to. When they'd talked about it long enough, an hour later, Justina opened a bottle of water, drinking it while staring out over the center of the city. Camp Nou, the massive home to Fútbol Club Barcelona, shimmered in the distance.

She turned. "The hardest part of all of this is imagining myself alone. When I was working for the Russians, although I was surrounded, I felt alone then."

"I understand. If you'd like, you can go back to Poland and wait."

"No," she answered, firmly shaking her head. "I want to be near you."

He slid his shoes off, dropping into the chair beside her. "Then you can just send your mother the money. We can't deposit it in a bank, nor can we send it all at once. The best way will be to send it by FedEx or something similar. You'll send it in cash installments, probably once a month. She can't deposit the money either, and will need to be smart about how she goes about using it."

"My mother is wise. I will tell her how to do it, and she will follow instructions, yes?"

"Good." He pointed to the west, saying, "So, now, our first priority is finding you a place to live."

"Near the prison?"

"Within reason," Gage answered.

"Can I visit?"

"We'll have to wait and see. If I think it's safe, we're going to have to take some precautions to ensure that you're never followed. I don't want a soul knowing where you live. Okay?"

Justina nodded. Then, from the table beside him, she lifted a magazine and began to roll it, twisting it nervously in her hands. Gage could hear her breathing, probably trying to come to grips with the seismic upheaval her life had taken in the last week. "Why me, Gage?"

"Why would someone follow you? Well, hopefully that won't ever—"

"No, Gage. Why do you do this for me?"

"What do you mean?"

"I'm just poor Polish trash who you met in a sleazy Russian club. We had a nice week together...okay, great. But, because of that, you want to share your money and your life with me?"

Gage knew this was some sort of defense mechanism, especially from someone who'd never had two nickels to rub together. He allowed silence to settle over the room before he asked, "How do you feel about me?"

"You already know."

"Tell me anyway."

"I love you, Gage. I've loved you since our time in Tossa." Her mouth twitched. "And the hardest part of all of this is thinking of being without you, no matter how much money you make."

He moved beside her. "You can trust me, Justina. I've got no agenda here other than us."

She took his hand, kissing it. "I hope you love me." As he was about to answer, she stopped him. "Tell me on my first visit to Berga, yes?"

Gage and Justina lay back on the bed and held each other.

Chapter Eleven

THEY TALKED about the job during the three-hour drive to Berga. Had they driven straight through, the trip would have taken less than ninety minutes, but they had stopped twice. The first time they pulled over was after Justina calmly asked Gage to stop the car following a gulf of silence. Once he was off to the side of the road, in a mountainous area, she exited and, at her behest, Gage followed. She led him to an overlook at the high hairpin curve, the Catalonian valley falling a thousand feet below the ascending roadway. There was a red picnic table above the rocky escarpment and she motioned him to sit. As soon as he did, Justina began to scream and yell at him. She spoke in her native tongue at first, giving him a tongue lashing any drill sergeant would be proud of. When she switched to English, she called him a maniac, saying she was unable to process how—even for such a large amount of money—a person would willfully allow himself to be imprisoned. Gage let her finish before he again explained his reasons, this time going so far as to cover the high points about his past, his post-traumatic-stress, and even the tragedy with Monika.

When he was finished, Justina, spent, apologized for her outburst.

"You don't need to say you're sorry," he said, pushing her hair back and kissing her on the cheek. "Because you're right, I am a little nuts."

They stopped again, a half-hour later, again at Justina's request. Trying to stifle his irritation, Gage pulled to the side of the road in a heavily wooded stretch south of the town of Ruig-reig. Justina exited, again commanding him to get out. When he did, she led him by his hand down into the damp conifer forest, the gray skies obscured by the canopy of towering trees. In a glade below the roadway's level, a hundred meters from the rental car, at Justina's direction, Gage made slow, passionate love to her on a soft bed of pine needles. When finished, they'd gotten dressed and Justina had lain in the crook of his arm, the two of them peering upward, through the gaps of the Spanish Pinsapo fir trees. Justina smoked a cigarette, toying with Gage's short hair as the two of them enjoyed the moment for what it was.

"Why did you come back for me?" she asked.

"This morning?"

"At Eastern Bloc."

"I guess it had something to do with what you first told me, about being essentially held against your will."

She kissed him. Ten minutes passed as birds zipped overhead, ignoring the two humans on the forest floor.

Justina broke the silence. "We must make love many times in these two days."

Gage turned to her. "Yeah?"

"Two years is a long time, yes? I think we will both miss it."

Their laughter got them moving again.

They travelled to the town of Berga, stopping north of town to view the eponymous prison from the road. It was unremarkable, surrounded by several high fences and guarded by squat towers on each corner. The prison itself, set back a kilometer from the road, appeared to be made of cinderblock. Three stories high, it didn't appear much different than a gargantuan warehouse. Gage didn't care to linger too long, but did make a quick sketch of the exterior features and the surrounding relief.

From Berga, they continued north, the growing gray of the day seeming a bit of a harbinger of things to come for Gage. Despite their lovemaking a short time earlier, he fought to keep his spirits buoyed. He thumbed the window switch for a dose of fresh air, breathing it deeply. Having no idea of where the road would take them, they continued on until they stumbled upon a picturesque lake marked as La Baells. The water, most likely snow and glacier fed, was distinctly turquoise, which Gage knew usually signified an abundance of resident lime. In the middle of the long lake was a towering concrete dam and, just above it, a bridge. They followed the road that circled the lake upward, above the dam, coming to a small town called Cercs around mid-afternoon.

Cercs was situated in the valley of high Catalonian foothills, with the vivid water of the lake behind it. The rustic town seemed more likely to be situated in Scotland or western Canada than in Spain. The marker just outside of Cercs announced its founding in 1379, with a current population of just over a thousand people. In the center of Cercs, like most Spanish towns, was a handsome old church. Gage parked the rental, another Audi, and exited, immediately getting a good feeling about Cercs but vigilant due to its small size. If someone unsavory were to ever take interest in Justina, finding her here wouldn't be difficult. After another glance around the quiet town square, he led her to the church.

Gage guessed the church was at least five hundred years old. The distinct reddish stone building probably seated no more than a hundred people. The stone was badly in need of pressure washing, having been overrun in spots by dark moss. The architecture was quite simple; the most complicated feature was the columned façade that made the church appear larger than it actually was.

Inside, there were several worshipers, praying and meditating, and a number of illuminated candles providing light along with the stained glass windows. Gage and Justina walked forward through the arched nave, passing through two more doors to an administrative area before seeing a light at the end of the hallway. Gage held Justina's hand, leading her to the light where they found a priest sitting in a cluttered office, reading a newspaper while having what appeared to be a glass of hot tea. His face was old and leathery and he arched a bushy gray eyebrow at the couple as he grumbled what must have been a local greeting that neither Gage nor Justina could understand. The way his voice rose at the end made his greeting more of a question, probably because he wasn't used to having people walk into his office unannounced.

Gage didn't speak Catalan, one of the languages of Catalonia, but his Spanish was passable—improving with each day in Spain—and, after greeting the priest, he asked who in Cercs might have a home they could rent.

"You're married?" the priest asked, switching to English without prompting, his eyebrow still cocked.

When Gage hesitated, Justina stepped forward. "Not yet, señor," she replied in smooth Spanish. "But we will be soon. My fiancé here is going away for a bit. He wants me to have a quiet place to prepare for our nuptials."

The priest rolled his chair to the opposite end of the desk, moving his spectacles down to the tip of his Gallic nose, going through an ancient rolodex card by card, eventually grunting and transcribing something on a piece of church stationary. He folded the paper and handed it to Justina.

"Go to that address…Señora Moreno's home. When you exit the church, look to the north, to the south, to the east, and to the west. She owns nearly everything you will see."

Gage cleared his throat. "Will she help us this late in the afternoon?"

The priest continued to look at Justina, adding a dash of humor to his voice though his face remained stony. "If you have money, Señora Moreno will help you *any* time of any day of the year."

Gage thanked the priest who called out as they were leaving. "Young lady, I do hope you will join us for Mass. The times are posted outside."

Justina smiled back at him.

Cercs, Spain

SEÑORA MORENO, real estate magnate, was nothing like Gage envisioned she might be. Short and squat, with a corkscrew beehive of black hair marked by twin streaks of gray, she looked and acted more like someone's doting grandmother. No sooner had they knocked on her door than she had begun fawning over Justina. At Señora Moreno's directive, Gage drove her and Justina down a private road to the lakeshore and followed a gravel road around the lake. Justina was in the backseat with the landlord, the two going on about all manner of topics. Per Señora Moreno, Gage parked at the final house, a picturesque cabin. Gage stood outside the car and waited for the landlady to finish a story about her herb garden. Finally, the two women emerged from the Audi and, using a key from her large ring, Señora Moreno opened the door to the lakeside cabin and gestured them inside.

Other than the dust raised by the forced air from the door, the cabin was still and quiet. The furniture appeared at least half a century old, but otherwise looked completely functional. A few old paintings hung on the knotty pine walls and, at the cabin's rear, a large paned window was covered by brittle drapes.

As Señora Moreno showed Justina the tiny kitchen, Gage pulled the drapes open, viewing the lake above the dam and, on the leaf and pine needle-covered hill below the cabin, what appeared to be an old fire pit. There was no dock at the lake and no worn trail leading down to the water. He guessed the cabin had been empty for some time, confirming it when he turned on the kitchen water, waiting as pipes rattled and frightening gurgling sounds could be heard below the cabin. It sounded as if a giant suction hole had opened in the earth and was close to swallowing the cabin and everything around it. After no less than ten seconds Gage was rewarded by an explosion of muddy water, punctuated by explosive air bubbles until, after running a bit, a smooth stream of clear water eventually emerged. He splashed the water in the sink to move the sediment down the drain and walked into the far room in search of the two women.

"…was to be hers," Señora Moreno said to Justina, standing before a medium-sized bed, clasping Justina's hands as she looked her up and down.

Gage felt, judging by Señora Moreno's tone and expression, that he'd just interrupted a weighty story. He stood silently. Justina turned to him, her face awash in sympathy.

"Señora Moreno built this cabin for her daughter."

Unsure of the context, Gage nodded and dipped his head.

Señora Moreno shooed the sympathy away. "It's been many years now, and she would want someone staying here." She turned to Justina. "You remind me of her."

"I don't know what to say." Justina took her hand. "Thank you."

Señora Moreno beamed.

"We've been learning how much we have in common," Justina said to Gage.

Señora Moreno gave Justina's hand a final squeeze. "Perhaps we'll have time to get to know one another better."

"I'd like that."

Justina walked to Gage, leaning close. "Well, what do you think?"

"It's not what I think…it's up to you." Justina's radiant smile, and a deft squeeze of his butt, provided his answer. He looked at Señora Moreno. "How much is the rent?"

The businessperson emerged from sweet little Señora Moreno in a flash. Her mirthful face turned serious as she clasped her hands in front of her. "Being on the lake, in this popular region, it's *not* inexpensive." Eyeing Gage levelly, she said, "Twelve-hundred euro per month."

"Is that negotiable if we choose to extend the term?"

"No," she responded with a firm shake of her head. "This is a prime vacation cabin in a desirable area. Long leases do me no good. Come July and August, I can rent this cabin for three times the monthly number I gave you."

"True," Gage responded, admiring the little lady's spunk, "but in December, January, February and probably March, you'll be lucky to even get a showing. Furthermore, judging by the plumbing and the dust, this house could use a renter to get it back into shape."

"Be that as it may," Señora Moreno said, obviously unaffected by Gage's negotiation tactics, "if I were to want to rent it, I *could* rent it." She turned to Justina and smiled. "And until today, I had no desire."

Expertly stonewalled, Gage smiled humorlessly back at the older lady. He turned to Justina. "Well?"

"Can we afford it?" she whispered.

"Yes."

She pecked him on the cheek.

Gage walked to the Audi to retrieve a month's rent. As he stood outside, a light rain falling on him, he felt as if he were wearing a leaden suit, the realization thudding down on him that this time two days from now he would be inside the four walls of Berga Prison. And here, all alone, would be the beautiful Polish lady he'd so quickly grown to love.

He tilted his head skyward, blinking the mist away, trying to imagine exactly what he would be doing on his first day of incarceration. He tried and tried, but he had no idea.

It's a good thing he didn't.

Chapter Twelve

THE VAN was without any rear windows, equipped instead with a steel cage inside its cargo area. And in the midst of that steel cage sat Gage Hartline. There was no seat or bench. He sat on the hard steel floor, his backside already aching a mere twenty minutes into the ride.

It was mid-morning and he knew, from Barcelona, the drive to Berga would take about an hour-and-a-half. He knew this because he'd left the cabin at four in the morning to drive to Barcelona, idly wondering how many men had ever voluntarily driven themselves to the place where they would be arrested. Next to him was a brown paper sack containing a bruised apple and a hard piece of bread. There was a bottle of water loose on the floor, rolling between two bars each time the vehicle turned. Gage had eyed it earlier—the seal had been broken by someone else, leaving him without much thirst.

He'd purposefully hydrated himself over the last two days and, though he knew he should eat, he had no appetite.

Gage closed his eyes and thought about last night. Justina had surprised him with a small cake and wonderful meal, which they ate early, before sitting by the fire pit down by the lake. After ten minutes of discussion over how they should communicate while Gage was in Berga, Justina stood from her Adirondack-style chair and sat in Gage's lap. He ran his hands up and down her long, smooth legs, the feel of her skin making his hands tingle. They kissed for what seemed an hour, a small fire crackling before them.

When the blissful moment had passed, Gage had eyed Justina in the dusk. "You forgot your cigarettes," he said. Justina always had a smoke after a meal.

"No," she replied with a shake of her head.

"Are you out? You could have gotten some when we went to the store."

"I am out. But I didn't want to buy any."

Gage had stared at her.

"I quit, Gage. I quit for you."

"You didn't have to do that."

"You've never complained, but I can tell you don't like them. It's okay," she smiled, playing with his hair. "I only smoked as a way to pass the time. Now, I have something better to think about."

"You're gonna want a cigarette when I'm gone. It'll be boring out here."

"Every time I crave a cigarette, I will write to you."

"Remember what I said."

"I know," she replied. "I will use the fake address. I will never write people's actual names or use real places. I will only mail the letters from far away."

"That's my girl." The firelight had danced on Justina's face, somehow making her more beautiful than she already was. "Thank you, Justina."

She kissed him.

Gage had carried her back to the cabin where they made love well into the night. The last time, Justina insisted it be slow and simple, holding Gage to her the entire time, his face next to hers. When they had finished, as Gage brushed his lips over hers, he tasted the saltiness of her tears. She had silently cried the entire time.

Remembering the beauty of last night, Gage tapped his head against the bars of the van's cage, trying to stifle his anxiety over where he was headed. While he was anxious about Berga, the thought of being without Justina for two years made his stomach churn.

Gage shut his eyes, banging his head again.

"Knock it off!" one of the guards yelled. They had talked sporadically throughout the trip. Their Catalan was beyond Gage's grasp other than a snippet here or there. The one in the passenger seat turned and glanced at Gage on occasion, usually curling his lip as if he were observing a mangy dog.

Stretching out as far as he could, Gage rested on his back, using the bottle of water as a makeshift pillow. He lifted his cuffed hands in front of his face, viewing the tempered steel's numerous dings and gouges that dug into his wrists with every subtle movement.

"Be glad we didn't hogtie you, *pajillero*," the morose-looking passenger guard sneered, switching to Spanish. "We were told to treat you nicely, and that's why you've got food and water. Be thankful."

Yeah, Gage thought, *everything's just peachy back here*.

The two men spoke more Catalan, both of them suddenly braying laughter. Again the passenger turned, rattling his coffee thermos on the cage just as Gage had shut his eyes.

"Hey, *Pajillero*, do you know about Berga?"

"What about it?" Gage asked, keeping his eyes shut.

"Do you know about it? I shouldn't have to say more." More laughter.

"I know it's a prison for murderers."

"You brave man, eh?" When Gage didn't open his eyes the guard clanged the thermos again. "Look at me when I talk to you, *puta!*"

Gage opened his eyes, taking a calming breath. *Two years of patience, buddy boy. Live it, breathe it, accept it, hour by hour.*

"The men in Berga are going to rip your ass apart. Literally." The guard laughed so hard that his wheezing overpowered his words. When he recovered, he said, "They're going to make you into a beautiful woman if they don't kill you first."

Gage held the man's eye.

"Look at you, acting tough now, but just wait. I hope you packed plenty of petroleum jelly." The guard translated this to the driver and they both roared with laughter.

Closing his eyes again, spurred by the man's mocking, Gage reviewed everything that had been in the notes provided with the money and satellite phone. There had been a layout of the prison and the yard. Gage used Google Earth's satellite view to augment this information, spending two hours on a library computer memorizing every feature of the prison property. Also included was an estimate of how many gang members existed in Berga—the estimate was nearly eighty percent of the prison population—and what each gang stood for. Such intel could be very useful to Gage in the coming days.

As the van drove on, Gage thought through all he'd ever learned about hand to hand combat.

Most earlobes will detach with a strong yank from pinched fingers.

Eyeballs can be pressed in with thirteen pounds of thumb pressure.

Pinkie fingers are the easiest digit to snap, with adult male pinkies typically cracking at their base with no more twenty-three pounds of pressure.

The best bodily weak points for attack are at the temples, base of skull, larynx, kidneys, genitals, and the tibial nerve at the back of the foot.

Feeling his pulse coming up, Gage reminded himself that he was going into a prison for violent murderers. *There's no reasoning. No talking. No fist fights. No ignoring. When you're confronted, you attack. When you attack, you attack to kill. It's them or you.*

Deep, steadying breaths.

Them or you.

GAGE'S FIRST experience in Berga Prison was nothing like he imagined. Expecting to see an arena of unpainted concrete and rows and rows of iron bars, instead, the inside walls of Berga were painted a soft yellow. The floors were linoleum, their color an extremely faint blue and buffed to a high shine that reminded him of his Army days. He'd not been treated to an outside view, though he'd seen it the day before during a reconnaissance drive.

Today, when they'd approached the prison, the guard in the passenger seat, Gage's heckler, dropped a black shroud down over the front of the cage, shutting off all of Gage's vision. Several times the van stopped and voices outside the van could be heard, speaking Spanish. Eventually the tires thumped over a ridge and the sound of a garage door shutting could be heard. Once stopped, the rear doors were opened and Gage was led from the van by two new guards, both with a hand on his upper arm. Once situated, his cuffed wrists were unlocked and re-cuffed behind his back.

Glancing around, happy to stand up, Gage surveyed the details. He was facing the garage door the van had just driven through. It was electric. Sliding his eyes upward, Gage looked at the door's motor. He then followed the heavy-duty stainless steel conduit's path to the switch housing. It was inside a raised guard shack with mirrored windows on the outer wall. His eyes moved down to the garage door itself. He noticed, on both sides, clamp-style electromagnetic locks that probably disengaged when the door switch was flipped. Though he had no plans of trying to escape, perhaps such a reconnaissance was in Gage's blood, and he felt somewhat silly over his crestfallenness that Berga's security measures seemed, at least initially, quite good.

The rest of the warehouse-like room was unremarkable. With a high ceiling of horizontal steel supports under a corrugated, slightly canted roof, there was little else to see. Painted the faint yellow, the walls were standard cinderblock, probably one layer thick and likely bolstered by internal rebar. To the left of the garage door were a number of cardboard boxes of various supplies. Beyond that, where the wall made its ninety-degree turn, Gage could only see empty shelving. When he dared look beyond his left shoulder, he was viciously pinched in his left upper arm, followed by a growl from the guard telling him to stare straight ahead.

Then they waited. And waited. No one talked and Gage assumed the two guards in the van were still sitting there. After what must have been fifteen minutes of numbing silence, Gage heard a door click followed by one person's footsteps approaching from the rear. They were exactly what he expected, coming quickly and marked by their distinct tapping. The room must have been quite lengthy because there were a total of 62 clicking steps and they didn't change pace, meaning *she* was almost certainly walking in a straight line. He did the math...*Calculating those clicks at an average 27-inch female pace count, added to the thirty or so feet in front of me to the garage door, I'm going to make the room as about 160 to 170 feet long.*

Gage's primary assumption was confirmed as a woman emerged. She moved well around him, circling and standing a good ten feet in front of him. This would be the warden—*la capitana*, actually. He'd learned a little about her but he hadn't envisioned her looking this way.

She was of average height for a woman, her long brown hair held up in a tight bun behind her head. Wearing a powder blue lab coat like that of a doctor or a scientist, she held a clipboard in her right hand, rounding out her erudite appearance. Gage guessed her age as somewhere in her mid-forties and, while she was still certainly quite attractive, he assumed she had once been striking. Her face, due to the heavy makeup she wore, now seemed somewhat severe. But her full, smiling lips and large brown eyes softened her appearance. She was trim with a proud bust-line and, from below her knee-length skirt, what appeared to be well-toned runner's legs. As he surveyed her, she surveyed him, finally asking him, "Habla Espanol?"

"Sí, un poco."

Despite his answer, she spoke excellent English as she viewed her clipboard. "Gregory Harris, United States citizen, convicted of second-degree murder in Melilla, our crime-riddled province next to Morocco." She looked up, viewing him behind her large glasses. "And whom did you kill, Gregory?"

"A fisherman," Gage replied, having memorized the cover story.

"You admit this?"

"I do."

She beamed, showing very large white teeth with a distinctive gap in their center. "Well, Gregory, kudos to your honesty."

Gage said nothing.

"And why did you kill this fisherman?"

"We had a business disagreement. Things got out of hand."

"Hmmm," she purred. "Weren't you and the so-called *fisherman* exporting narcotics to Europe, and the disagreement revolved around that?"

"I wasn't convicted for that, ma'am. The reason was simply a business disagreement."

"Where in the U.S. are you from?"

"All over, really. I grew up in the north."

"Not that it's pertinent here, but I adore the United States. I go every year. My preference is Manhattan, but I also love San Diego and even the heartland of Nebraska, where I've a good friend whose husband is an airline pilot."

Unsure of what to say, Gage said, "That's good to know."

"Did you attempt to have the United States intervene in your case?"

"Yes."

"And?"

"They did nothing to help me."

"No shock there," she said. Then she reset her countenance. "I'm the administrator here, Gregory. My name is Capitana de la Mancha. I've been charged with Berga for thirteen years now..." again the dazzling smile, "...thirteen *successful* years, and I take my responsibilities very seriously."

She narrowed her eyes as the mirth slid away from her expression. "Gregory, you have an intelligence about you, I can tell, so I will not patronize you by mincing words. Forget what you know about prisons. Berga is nothing like any penitentiary you might find in the United States, or Spain for that matter. We're truly unique here." Capitana de la Mancha began taking slow steps toward him as she spoke. "My job isn't about rehabilitation or nurturing—not at all. Rather, it's about shielding the Spanish citizenry, and our *tourism* which, as I'm sure you know, is a large portion of our economy and is responsible for putting food in the mouths of our beloved people."

She stepped directly in front of him and lowered her voice. "I'm assuming, since it was Africa, that you were exporting either opium or, with the burgeoning industry that I hear has popped up, poorly-produced *africano* cocaine. These drugs are quite important to our tourism here and I truly could care less if people choose to use them."

Had Gage been given a hundred chances to hypothesize what the warden's welcome to Berga would be like, he'd have never come close to guessing anything such as this. Capitana de la Mancha was close enough that he could smell her perfume, which was quite strong.

"But enough about me, Gregory. In short order, you will be inserted into the population and, according to our detailed statistics, there is a twenty-seven percent chance you will be in the prison hospital within one hour. That number rises to nearly fifty percent after twenty-four hours. Those who can survive the first twenty-four hours without a hospital trip typically fare quite well here." She lifted her free hand, tipped with long red nails, starting with his left shoulder, running her hand downward over his chest and stomach, lingering at his belt as the corner of her mouth ticked upward.

"You've a nice, hard body, Gregory. Most Spaniards aren't as big as you and, while that could portend well for your future, my fellow Spaniards are also a proud people. Expect them to come at you with ferocity. They won't like the fact that you're a *gabacho*, and they won't like the fact that you're large, well-muscled and, I must say, quite handsome." Her hand brushed downward, below his belt, before falling back to her side. Then, with surprising force, she knifed the plastic clipboard upward, striking Gage's testicles and sending him lurching forward in agonizing pain.

"I'd suggest you pick up your game because you'll need faster reflexes than that, Gregory." As he tried to catch his breath, her heels could be heard again as she said in Spanish, "Have him examined and then get him in-processed."

The two guards hoisted Gage to his feet and took him to the infirmary.

AFTER INVENTORYING his scant personal items, the supply worker told Gage that everything other than his toiletries would be kept in a locker until his release. That done, Gage was herded to another station where he was issued four pair of thin green pants and four lightweight shirts. The clothes were cousins to hospital scrubs, probably made flimsy for a multitude of reasons. His boots were taken and he was issued flat thong sandals, like a person might wear in a public shower. Gage's sandals were a few sizes too small and, when he mentioned this, the attendant, a small prisoner with only one eye, mumbled something to Gage about stopping his bitching.

"If I'm going to wear sandals, I'd like the correct size."

The diminutive attendant slung another pair at Gage, hitting him in the face. Gage didn't budge, didn't even twitch. He continued to eye the little man until the guard behind him nudged him with his baton. Once Gage scooped up his new sandals and slid them on, he continued on to the end of the stark hallway, to a door marked *Enfermería*. The guard opened the door and, with a painful whack to Gage's right kidney, propelled him inside. He'd been there ever since.

Standing alone in a white room with no chairs, it occurred to Gage that he didn't know what time he'd arrived. He estimated that he'd been in the infirmary for about ninety minutes, an hour of which constituted waiting. He'd first been given a cursory physical by a gruff man he assumed to be a doctor. The man had been quite old, and he stunk of far too many cigarettes. His skin was sallow and, due to his foghorn voice and bizarre accent, Gage had hardly been able to understand his Spanish.

Next was an x-ray and a cavity search in the presence of two guards. Their jokes tested Gage's patience. He closed his eyes and counted the seconds.

Mercifully finished with the physical, the guards shoved Gage out and instructed him to follow the painted yellow line. They walked quite a distance in a bright, hospital-like corridor. At the end of the corridor, built into the wall, was a gray clock mated to an intercom system. The clock was the same type a person might find in a school or hospital, almost certainly wired to the other prison clocks for precision. To the right of the clock, Gage noticed a series of wire glass windows.

"Stop at the door," the escorting guard barked. From a hallway on the left, two more guards, these outfitted with riot masks and shields, appeared. They both carried leather-handled batons. The guards took up a position just behind the door and waited.

The first guard moved beside Gage. "You will be escorted to your cell, after which time everything will come clear as you experience a few days. Evening meal is at eighteen-hundred-hours and will be announced by three blasts of the alarm. Lights out, in your cell, will occur at twenty-three-hundred. Got it?"

Gage nodded.

"Toe the door."

Gage walked to the door and did a military right-face. He sucked in a great breath of air, wondering if he'd be alive in twenty-four hours. The attendant punched a metal knob on the wall with his hand, making the door swing out.

From behind him, Gage heard one of the two guards yell "Entra!" Putting one foot in front of the other, Gage stepped into the gladiator's arena, immediately smelling the piss and sweat of the prison's male inhabitants. The din slowly faded away as the mostly tattooed, largely bald prisoners stopped what they were doing to turn and stare at the new arrival.

In all his years, Gage could honestly say he'd never felt quite so singled out.

Behind Gage, standing at the door, Capitana de la Mancha had appeared. She discreetly crossed herself as she whispered, "Que Dios esté con usted." Even with no idea who Gage really was, de la Mancha found him interesting.

She also wondered if his first trip back through the door would be to the infirmary or, perhaps, to the walk-in kitchen refrigerator that doubled as a makeshift mortuary.

Chapter Thirteen

THE WALK to Gage's cell passed without incident. The main bay, as it was called, was hexagonal and three floors high. Wide concourses ringed the top two floors of cells, protected by floor to ceiling chain link fencing—presumably so no one would take an accidental, or deliberate, tumble to the floor of the main bay. The center of the main bay, on the first level, was the common area. There were built-in steel tables and chairs, along with Plexiglas encased televisions mounted on several large columns.

As the guards instructed Gage to climb to the second floor, he viewed the prisoners staring back at him. Some had been playing cards, others watching TV. On the concourses, men who had been shooting dice, stacks of strange-looking money in piles by their feet, eyed Gage with dripping contempt. There were clumps of men standing on the concourses and, as Gage could see when he passed by each cell, occasional prisoners reading or chatting on their bunk.

Every prisoner stopped what they were doing to stare down the new arrival.

Ignoring the gawkers, Gage turned to take in a sweeping view of the main bay as he ascended. Despite its modern appearance, it was the devil's gut, churning with acidity, eating away at every man forced to call it home. The smell intensified with each step upward, redolent of sweaty men in need of soap and deodorant. Gage halted, memorizing the image, forcing himself to accept it as his new home. A baton poked his already sore lower back as his escort growled at him to keep moving.

There were a total of six staircases leading to the higher floors, one on each line of the hexagon. At the top of the tall flight of stairs, Gage was told to move straight ahead before being ordered to halt. Next to him was an open door of a cell. One man was inside, on the lower bunk, reading. Upon hearing the guards he sat up, sneering at Gage.

"Meet Salvador. He's your new best friend," one of the guards chuckled. "Go in and make your bunk according to the diagram on the wall." At the end of the top bunk, military-like linens and a blanket lay "stockaded" much in the same way Gage recalled from Army basic training. There was a small diagram affixed to the wall at the end of each bunk, showing a properly-made bed. Both guards laughed before their heavy boots could be heard clanging back down the steel stairs.

Inside his cell, Salvador, Gage's new best friend, stood and tossed his book on the bed. Unlike many of the other prisoners Gage had seen, Salvador had a full head of hair with a pronounced widow's peak. His face was lean and menacing as he rolled a toothpick steadily back and forth between his narrow lips. Salvador's most prominent feature, obviously a mark of his gang, was the massive tattoo of a horse emerging from under his prison uniform. Done in black ink, the horse's head exploded from his narrow chest and terminated on the highest area of Salvador's neck. The tattoo was dominated by the steed's piercing red eyes. Therefore, Gage pegged Salvador as a Semental gang member. Based on what he'd read, the Sementals had a small presence in Berga.

Despite the menacing tattoo, the remainder of Salvador was unremarkable. He appeared to be about 5'9" and weighed at least sixty pounds less than Gage. Maybe seventy.

Upon entering the cell, Gage got a full whiff of Salvador's scent as he perused the square confines of his new home. The bunks were naval style with rounded corners protruding from the wall and supported by hinges so they could be folded to the wall. The mattress was very thin, like two magazines stacked on top of one another. Next to the bunks, also built of stainless steel and rounded, was a sink. Beside it, a pubic hair-encrusted toilet with no lid and no seat. The far wall held three recessed shelves, all holding paperback books, and the rest of the wall, and nearly the entire cell, was covered by pictures of a woman and two boys in various stages of youth. All in all, the cell was bigger than what Gage might have envisioned, approximately fifteen feet square. He nodded to his cellmate, seeing a clear plastic container on his bunk containing his toiletries. Gage noticed the bottle of shaving cream.

Prisoners began gathering outside the cell.

Ignoring them and Salvador, Gage reached for the container on his bunk. Salvador grasped Gage's arm and threw it backward, shouting an unintelligible threat and leveling a finger at Gage's face.

Shit.

Hating the fact that he was already being challenged but steeling himself to stick with his plan, Gage took two steps backward.

Salvador came forward and swiped at Gage with an open hand but missed.

Gage raised his fists and bounced on his toes. Outside the cell, the prisoners stood ten deep. Money began to change hands as bets were levied.

Salvador took up a fighting stance and began to circle.

Here we go.

Salvador's smile was broad and menacing, glinting at the corners due to his gold-capped canines. He must not have thought much of Gage, or he was a good actor, because Salvador looked like a sneaky fox who'd just been granted access to the fattened hens' coop. His first action took Gage by surprise as he suddenly dropped and attempted a front sweep by spinning himself with his right leg extended.

It was a piss-poor fighting movement for this setting.

Gage was far enough back, and in an athletic enough position, that he countered the sweep by taking one step back before he unleashed a hard straight right, catching the exposed Salvador above his right ear and knocking him unconscious. Because of his vulnerable position, Salvador fell unnaturally on his already bent left leg. It twisted abnormally before springing out, leaving the prisoner spread eagle on the concrete floor.

It was not a dramatic fight at all. Outside the cell, "oohs" and "aahs" were followed by derisive laughter. Gage heard a number of prisoners mocking Salvador.

Despite knowing he was being watched, and judged, Gage simply couldn't bring himself to continue to beat on an unconscious opponent. Suddenly, the sound of sandals slapping the concrete floor took priority over everything. Whirling right, making sure to leave few feet between himself and the back wall, Gage surveyed the situation. Two men, tattooed like Salvador, stormed into the cell, yelling a similar battle cry. Gage had no illusions that this next encounter would be as easy as the last. The lead man was as large as he was, muscles rippling as he thrust forward with his arm pulled back for a punch.

Though he didn't feel natural by remaining still, Gage held his ground until the man swung, ducking the telegraphed punch as he caught the man in the midsection and thrust his own body upward, cartwheeling the man over his head and sending him crashing down onto the toilet in a hail of grunts and curses. By the time he turned to the man's partner it was too late to see the punch coming. It caught Gage in the nose and cheek, instantly making his eyes water and giving him the taste of salty blood in his mouth.

Rather than give the man a clean shot at another punch, Gage leapt over Salvador, putting his back to the bars at the front of the cell as he glanced down. Salvador was now awake but didn't seem inclined to get up. The man who had hit the toilet was coming to his feet, gripping his shoulder and cursing as he grimaced in pain. The third gangster, the one dancing in front of Gage, was tall and wiry and seemed to move with fluidity.

Having a distinct feeling that the man in front of him had a boxing background, Gage did the only thing he knew to do. Ignoring the looping punch that grazed above his ear, he plowed forward, catching the man as he tried to whirl away. The two fell hard against Salvador's bunk and, after scrabbling, tumbled to the floor next to the wide-eyed, still motionless Salvador. As Gage struggled to mount his skilled aggressor, he noticed the man with the wounded shoulder staggering out of the cell, saying something to someone. No one else seemed to be wading into the fray, leaving Gage free to ignore the pestering blows from his downed quarry as he rained down his own elbows and punches.

Hand-to-hand combat had never been Gage's favorite skill to practice, but he'd always been good at it. An uncontested left elbow caught the downed man's temple and, as soon as it connected, Gage knew he had him. The man's eyes rolled back in his head, causing Gage to slow the thundering right he was bringing down. Gage glanced to his left, seeing Salvador still lying motionless, like a saucer-eyed possum. Just as Gage was about to dismount his opponent, a ripping, stinging pain sent him tumbling forward.

As he fell, the nerves in his upper back relayed enough of their frantic message to Gage's brain for him to realize that he'd just been stabbed. By the time the second thrust caught him, this time in the shoulder, Gage had spun, grabbing the stabber's knees and twisting him to the floor. Gage quickly cinched his legs around the stabber's left leg, also grasping it with his arms. Once the man was under control, Gage confirmed that he was the muscular man that had been flipped to the toilet. The man struggled against Gage's hold, known in grappling as a knee-bar.

His own anger redlining, Gage repositioned his arms on the man. With his forearm as the lever on the muscular man's heel, Gage torqued his own body as hard as he could, leaving no chance.

The tendons popping in the man's knee might have been .22 rounds going off in the enclosed space. He shrieked like an adolescent girl.

Gage's back and shoulder were on fire. He ignored the pain. With Salvador still catatonic and the boxer sleeping nicely, Gage looked outside the cell at the rapt audience of prisoners.

It was time to leave an impression.

As Gage had done with the boxer, he slid up the muscular man's body, mounting him securely with his knees holding steady pressure on the man's torso. When the man ceased his yelling long enough to open his eyes, Gage said one thing to him.

"*Poner su lengua.*" It meant "Stick out your tongue."

Gritting his teeth in pain, the man shook his head. Gage placed his left index finger below the man's right ear, digging his fingernail into the auricular nerve, changing the man's yell to a squeal like that of a pig.

"*Poner su lengua,*" Gage growled, easing the pressure slightly.

The gangster stuck his tongue out, but barely. Gage dug his fingernail in again and told him to stick his tongue out farther. His eyes wide with fear, but his fear overridden by the powerful nerve pain, the man obeyed. When he did, Gage unleashed a ferocious uppercut, making the man's teeth snap shut with tremendous force.

On his tongue.

Blood spurted, then ran down both sides of the man's face. He writhed a moment more before falling into a semi-conscious state, moaning in his delirium. Salvador was up on his elbows now, staring with awe at Gage as he stood. Gage motioned to the tall, skinny boxer that had been unconscious.

"What's his name?"

"Enrique," Salvador breathed reverently.

Gage stood over Enrique, who was already blinking as if he was in a dust storm. He smacked Enrique's face several times and, when he seemed lucid enough, told him to drag his partner out and never come back.

A full minute later, while the crowd dissipated, buzzing with delight at what they'd seen and, as Enrique pulled the muscled body of his felled, and now crying, fellow gang member into the concourse, Gage ripped open his plastic container and removed the lone dingy washcloth. He found Salvador's shaving kit, rummaging through until he saw a small pair of nostril scissors, clipping the end of the washcloth, then ripping it apart with his hands.

Gage dropped onto the lower bunk, not breathing for a full twenty seconds due to the growing pain in his back and shoulder. He raised his eyes to Salvador, who had shrunk to the rear corner of the cell.

Remembering what he'd been told about Salvador's gang, and what he'd read on the Internet, Gage asked, "Should I expect any more of your fellow Sementals today?"

Wetting his mouth several times, Salvador shook his head as he mouthed the word "no".

Gage pressed one half of the washcloth to the wound on his shoulder, probing at it and estimating that he'd been stabbed with something about the size of a large nail. He tried to reach over his shoulder, but the wound on his back was too far down. Salvador shuffled over.

"I look?" he asked in English.

Gage raised his eyes.

"Trust," Salvador whispered.

"Me trust *you*?"

"When you arrived, señor, I had to do this."

"What about your buddies, did they have to try to kill me?"

"Sí, señor, they did. Every man here must be tested. Had I not, had we not, would label us to everyone here as *coños tímidos*. It would be an invitation to our own death."

"Coños tímidos?" Gage grunted.

"Scared pussies," Salvador clarified.

Gage pondered Salvador for a moment before he leaned forward. Salvador bent over Gage, lifting his shirt and switching to Spanish. "*Sí*, the wound here beside your spine is deeper than the shoulder wound. Juan must have hit bone on the shoulder, but the wound on your back went all the way in."

"How wide is it?"

Salvador straightened, showing his pinkie finger. "He got you with what we call a *'perforador.'* I didn't see the one that was used, but probably a nail or a sharpened piece of plastic." He patted Gage's other shoulder. "Wait." Unsteadily, Salvador exited the cell and turned left.

Not knowing whether or not to trust Salvador, Gage stood, moving into the corner of the room protected by the beds on one side and the front wall on the other. Salvador returned momentarily, carrying with him a plastic vial and a weathered box of what looked like detergent.

"Please, sit."

Gage stared at him.

"Please," Salvador said. "Now, remove your shirt." Gage complied. Salvador went into his personal items and came back with a handful of cotton balls. He opened the vial, turning it over to soak it on a cotton ball then pressed it to Gage's back wound.

Searing, burning pain.

Salvador did this three times, then repeated the process on Gage's shoulder. Finally he retrieved the detergent. "You know Celox?" he asked, holding it up.

"Clotting agent, yes. I've used it before. You guys keep that lying around here?"

Salvador grinned. Gage could feel the granules being poured over his back, then his shoulder. Salvador took the washcloth pieces, pressing them against the wounds filled with the styptic granules. "Now lie back."

"Want me to climb up on my own bunk?"

"It's okay," Salvador said.

Head spinning slightly, which was disconcerting, Gage rested, feeling the pressure of the makeshift bandage pushing against his back. Salvador wet another washcloth, handing it to Gage. "Your nose, señor, it may be broken."

Having forgotten all about the punch he'd taken, Gage wiped the already dried blood from his face, pinching his nose and deciding it actually wasn't broken, just sore from a solid strike. Footsteps could be heard on the stairs—boots, not sandals—followed by an approach on the concourse. Gage's eyes were closed but he saw the darkness created by the figure just outside the cell.

"You need to come to the infirmary," an authoritarian voice said in Spanish.

Gage opened his eyes, seeing one of the two guards from earlier, his mouth twisted into a smirk.

"I'm fine," Gage replied.

"You're not fine," the guard said, motioning with his baton. "I know what happened. Let's go."

"I'm fine," Gage said. "Please, let me be."

"Yeah, piss off, Guevo," Salvador barked.

The guard snorted before turning and walking away.

Gage moved his right arm under his head, rotating his eyes to Salvador. "So, did I receive the standard welcome?"

Rummaging around on his bookshelf, Salvador retrieved a box of toothpicks and placed a fresh one in his mouth, massaging his jaw as he did so. "That was your first test. The Sementals are very small in number here. But the others will now know that you're a force to be reckoned with."

"What's that mean?"

"It means that everyone is now talking about you. And it will be a source of great status to be the one who kills you."

Well, that's just great. Damned if I do, damned if I don't.

"But I think you will be left alone today," Salvador ruminated. "Although that's by no means certain."

Gage reminded himself of the phrase he planned to adopt as his mantra here: *One hour at a time.*

THE FIRST twenty-four hours of Gage's incarceration were marked by increasing pain and little rest. Somehow Gage managed to shuffle to the evening meal, noting the curious, often malevolent, stares as he took his tray of food and sat alone, unable to eat a bite due to his lack of appetite—and not aided by the food's vomit-like odor. There was still no sign of Cesar and, especially due to his current condition, Gage knew it would be far too obvious if he began overtly looking for him. No incidents followed and Gage rested on his bunk for the balance of the night, having to endure numerous stories from Salvador, most having to do with his children and his passion for kung fu.

Eventually, mercifully, Salvador fell asleep.

During the previous decade, Gage had experienced more seismic shifts than most people experience in a full lifetime. The accident on Crete. The abrupt scuttling of Colonel Hunter's team. A permanent move overseas. Losing Monika, followed by the business with the Glaives. As a guard walked by, whistling annoyingly while people were trying to sleep, Gage closed his eyes and remembered the cool air of the Catalonian forest, as Justina lay below him, her cheeks flushed as they completed their spur-of-the-moment show of affection for one another. She'd rubbed her soft hands up and down his triceps, whispering that she would wait for him if he promised that he would come back to her. When he made his vow, she pulled him to her, locking her legs tightly around him, and held on for what felt like dear life. Her grasp wasn't sexual—it was emotional. Purely emotional.

That was three days ago. Three days. *And now I'm in prison, on day frigging one, with stab wounds in my body and seven-hundred days to go.*

Justina…

Not a man prone to regret, Gage felt the despondent, rusty stab of the disgusting emotion. He imagined what it would have been like if he and Justina had blown off this ridiculous job and taken the train to Germany, back to the land he knew so well. There was no longer any heat from the incident with the Glaives. The only thing that had kept him away from his beloved Germany had been the pain of Monika's death. But, had he been able to stomach going back, he could have called Colonel Hunter, along with others he knew, and put out the word that he was in business again. Justina spoke a little German, and her English was good. Had they settled in the right place, Gage had no doubt he could have talked to some of the local American military and helped her get a job at a PX or BX. Their existence would have been simple, lean when Gage wasn't working.

But they'd have been together, and he certainly wouldn't be nursing these damned stab wounds.

Torturing himself even more, he imagined their evenings in a dingy little rental flat, eating inexpensive food followed by hours of lovemaking while good music played in the background. Maybe, during the summer months when the light lingered to nearly midnight, they would have walked to one of the thousands of hilltop castles that dot the German landscape, exploring its ruins and scaring each other at every opportunity, laughing so hard no noise would even escape their—

Stop it, dammit.

You're wounded and showing loathsome weakness. He took two deep, back-splitting breaths. *You're not in Germany, Gage, because you took Navarro's money. Your intentions were, and are, good. You made the decision, it was all you, now deal with it. Sleep and, tomorrow when you wake up, stop acting like a pussy and do what you've been paid to do.*

Work hard.

Don't let up.

And be ruthless.

His real self was a welcome presence in Gage's mind. He managed a few fitful bouts of slumber, but mainly lay there sweating in his pain. His mind, however, remained hard throughout the night. And it pleased him.

Chapter Fourteen

Cercs, Spain

AT EASTERN Bloc, especially when the season was in full swing, Justina often lost track of what day it was. With everyone in Lloret for vacation, and her receiving no days off, the days of the week were meaningless. To Justina every day seemed a weekday while, to the teeming revelers, every night was Saturday night. And now, in the tedium of the lonely lakeside cabin, for a completely different set of reasons, she'd again lost track of the days. As she planted summer flowers in two weathered window boxes, she tried to recall exactly which day it was, thinking to herself that, for some reason, today felt like a Thursday.

Gage had left yesterday. She was now one day closer to having him back.

The air was thick with humidity and, despite the cloudless azure sky, Justina predicted afternoon showers in the next few hours based on what had happened on the previous days. As she gently pressed the rich potting soil around the hibiscus, hoping the flowers would waterfall from the boxes as the summer lolled on, a squeaking sound startled her. She turned, using her forearm to push wisps of hair from her sweaty face, seeing Señora Moreno on an ancient, three-wheeled bike.

"Those will be pretty if you see that they get enough sun," Señora Moreno said, climbing off the wheeled machine and reaching into its wire basket, retrieving a covered picnic basket. Her plump little hand pulled back the red cloth to display a trove of delicious-looking food. "Might I entice you into taking a break?"

"Sure," Justina answered, dropping her soiled gloves and wiping her face and hands with a wad of paper towels.

After a wonderful lunch of salad, a shrimp dish, and a lemony flan desert, they sat in the rocking chairs on the back porch, drinking something called *tinto de verano*, essentially red wine mixed with lemonade.

"This is often enjoyed by the poor here in Spain, much simpler than the sangria we're so famous for," the older woman said. "But it reminds me of my past, and summers, and the early days with Mateo."

"He was your husband?"

"Oh my, yes," she said gaily, her mind clearly hearkening back. "A fine man...the finest. He worked in a tire factory until his thirty-second birthday and that's when he threw down his gloves in disgust and, on a whim, we picked up and moved here. They'd just dammed the river and we used our savings to purchase a parcel of land on what would eventually be the new reservoir." Señora Moreno glowed, rocking steadily as she allowed a brief silence to settle in, as if they were eating a fine meal and she wanted to make certain Justina enjoyed each bite.

"The lake there, I remember when it was just a small river down in the valley. We watched it rise about one meter every two or three weeks."

Justina stared at the broad expanse of water, unsuccessfully trying to picture a craggy valley in its place.

Still staring back into her past, Señora Moreno said, "People told Mateo that no one wanted to live on a manmade lake, and that the south of Spain was the place to invest our pittance. But Mateo, in his patient, Catholic way, would just nod politely and continue making his plans. Two years later, he had finally built our cabin...built it by hand. Up until then, we'd been living in a shack in town."

She looked at Justina. "I remember the exact moment that I walked in our cabin. Mateo had been fanatical about never letting me in before. I remember the smells of creosote and fresh paint—and I remember his smell, his glorious smell, permeating the place." She turned her head back to the distance, back to the memory. "Oh, how we loved that cabin. Then, as the reservoir filled to its higher levels, when it really looked like a lake, people began to arrive. Mateo divided our land and sold three lots. He used that money to buy more land...and so on."

"Did you tear down your cabin?"

"Oh, no, darling. We just added on to it. When you come in my home, the first rooms are still a part of the old cabin. Same wood, same floor, same ceiling, all laid down by my Mateo."

A bird zipped past the porch. Señora Moreno stopped rocking and made a slight shushing sound. The bird landed in a nearby scrubby tree, its head quizzically darting left and right. It was green, distinguished because of its long curved beak, with notes of white and orange around the head. Suddenly it lurched into the air, tumbling then fluttering, an insect trapped at the tip of its beak. Then it was gone, off to lunch in private.

"A bee-eater," Señora Moreno said. "One of my favorites and the first I've spotted this year. They winter in Africa, you know." She let out a contented breath. "Summer's here, my dear."

Justina sipped her drink, finding it a tad harsh, guessing that it was probably an acquired taste or a bit heavy on the Tempranillo. "And your Mateo, his business here grew?"

"Yes, dear. I became involved after the cabin was built." She stopped rocking, leaning over and conspiratorially whispering, "I'd never had one whit of business experience. Back then, Circs was controlled by the local parish priest. He was a good man but had grown too used to the locals fawning over him. Power can do that, even to good people."

"I can imagine."

"Once I straightened him out, made him see things my way, made him understand that things could be better here if he'd fall in behind me, things were just grand." The Spanish lady rested her hands on one another. "Soon after, I opened a mercantile in Cercs—very, very busy in-season and steady through the winter due to the workers from the dam and the power plant. I quickly learned what to stock in the different seasons. That led to another shop, then a petrol station while Mateo built cabins. When those sold, we hired others to help us run things while we speculated on real estate. Mateo always gave me equal voice…such a fine man."

"Señora Moreno, your husband…"

"Seventeen years ago, darling. Automobile accident, but the coroner felt he actually died of a heart attack beforehand. He'd had heart troubles for years." She spoke of his death in the flat, practiced manner of someone who'd found peace and maintained it by not dwelling on the details of the tragedy.

"I'm sorry."

"I'm fine, dear. I was blessed to have him for the time I did."

"Has there been anyone else since then?"

"No," Señora Moreno answered with a firm shake of her head. "He was the one man for me."

There was a bout of silence, marked only by the occasional thumping of the rocking chairs.

"As I told you, this cabin was to be my daughter's."

"I remember," Justina said, afraid to pry.

"Her name was Isabel—she died in Madrid, while at university. Spinal meningitis."

Justina reached across the small table and touched Señora Moreno's arm. "I'm so sorry."

"Years ago, after Mateo died, I lamented not having more children. But I found peace, and decided to live my life on my terms."

"Good for you."

"Mateo and Isabel are together now," the older woman beamed. "Receiving their reward in heaven." Before Justina could say anything, Señora Moreno turned to her. "As I said, you remind me of her. You have a quiet spirit about you, just like she did."

"That's so nice of you to say. I'm honored."

The placid face returned as Señora Moreno resumed her rocking. "Now I get my pleasure by going to church, running the business, and moments like this."

Justina tasted the drink again, feeling a tad awkward but not knowing what else to say.

"And what of you and your squire, my dear…is he *the* man for you?"

Feeling sudden heat in her cheeks, Justina nodded and said, "I truly hope so."

Señora Moreno placed her drink on the wicker table between them. She tucked one of her legs up underneath her and turned her body to Justina. "Well, if that's the case, dear, then why don't you tell me the truth about him?"

Feeling her eyes blinking spasmodically, Justina stammered, "Señora Moreno…I…I…"

"I know a false story when I hear one and, until today, I decided to let it be. But beautiful young Polish women don't usually show up here at the foot of the Pyrenees with quiet American men nearly twice their age to stay anonymously, *hidden away*, for a long period." She reached across the small table and touched Justina's arm, briefly closing her eyes as she said, "He's married, isn't he? He was here for work, paid you some flattering attention, you two got involved, and he told you he'd go home and cut all the strings." Señora Moreno pulled in an audible breath. "They're snakes, dear. Cunning and alluring, but snakes the whole lot of them. It's just how they were created. And, I can tell you from my own experience as an attractive young lady, all he'll do is come back a few more times and take what he wants before—"

"He's *not* married," Justina said, bursting out with good-natured laughter.

Señora Moreno tapped her lip with her index finger. "You're sure? Older gentlemen, in their prime, can make you believe all sorts of things."

"Positive."

She showed the palm of her left hand. "Wait. Don't tell me. I'm old and lonely and such a mystery as your handsome American is spice to my daily monotony." Narrowing her eyes, she stared off into the woods, taking a moment before she said, "He's gone away on a job of some sort. Something different..."

Unsure of what to tell Señora Moreno but feeling very close to her after the stories of her husband and daughter, Justina said, "Yes, he has."

"And he has money, but he works with his hands...I could tell by how rough they were." She spoke the words in the affirmative, but added a slight lilt at the ends of her sentences to indicate the possible presence of a query.

"He does work with his hands."

"And has money?"

"Well, not exactly."

"He had money when I met him, dear."

"Yes, but he doesn't typically have money."

Señora Moreno's face lit up. "Ah, a windfall. He's into something quite illegal, isn't he? Something afoul—sinful." She spoke without censure, actually sounding quite gleeful at the revelation. "Don't worry yourself, dear. The secret is quite safe with me. All humans have their peccadilloes. I just knew there was something illicit about him..." She looked away, her round face alight. "And he's such a handsome devil. I can see how you would readily invite him into your—"

Justina cut her off. "He's not a criminal, Señora."

The elder lady opened her hands. "Then, pray tell, please just tell me what in the world the nature of your relationship is. Start at the beginning, speak slowly, and leave nothing out. I want all the juicy details."

Tugging at her earring, Justina smiled nervously. "I can't do that, Señora. We agreed that I'd keep everything to myself."

"Look at me, dear," Señora Moreno cajoled. "This is my seventy-second year on this earth. I have two men who work for me and both avoid me at all costs...it's not that they hate me, but I think they find me old, irascible, unpleasant on the eyes and difficult to please. My tenants are now all set for the summer—and all very boring—and my television shows are wrapping up their seasons. So now all I'm left with are reruns, my books, the arriving summer birds and my two old cats, one of whom seems to be on his last legs." She tilted her head. "So humor an old woman. If this is a secret, it's safe with me. I want to treasure the friendship of a beautiful young lady. And her telling me her story will do nothing harmful to her, or her beau, but it *will* add a firm foundation of trusting in another."

After letting out a long breath, Justina took a large quaff of the tinto de verano, finding it more palatable as the ice had melted and diluted its strength. "His name is Gage, Señora, and we only met a few weeks ago. I was in Lloret, working for the season at a horrible job, when he arrived at the bar one afternoon. I didn't know him at the time."

"Go on," Señora Moreno said reverently.

"Initially, our meeting was quite odd. More odd was what he did to my abusive boss."

"Abusive?"

"Not physically. I worked with other Polish girls—they treated all of us like slaves."

"And what did your Gage do to this boss?"

"He came into the bar during the day. A few minutes after he came in, he knocked my boss to the floor and..." Justina told Señora Moreno the entire story of their first day, up to Gage's liberating her in the back alley.

When Justina came to the portion of the story about their first night alone together, in Gage's Lloret hotel, Señora Moreno again stopped her with a raised hand. "This is just grand, dear and, please, do go on. But when you get to the romantic parts..." she crossed herself, "...you know, the sex, do *definitely* be detailed, my dear. All I'm left with are memories so, perhaps, I can enjoy the interludes vicariously through you. Mateo and I used to do the most wonderful things on afternoons such as this, but now..." she said wistfully, her voice trailing off.

Justina listened to this, struggling not to appear amused. She cleared her throat and resumed her storytelling. After relaying their rather innocuous first night, she gleefully told the story of their day at the beach, and Gage's taking a most unusual job for a large sum of money. She told her about Berga Prison, pausing when it looked like Señora Moreno was going to say something, but continuing when Señora Moreno, rapt, twirled her hand impatiently. And, of course, she detailed the few romantic encounters she'd enjoyed with Gage, watching as Señora Moreno appeared breathless, hanging on every detail.

Finished with her story, Justina watched her landlady cross herself again, kissing her rosary and whispering a litany of thanks. Then she said, "My dear, that was beautiful. Absolutely breathtaking and, despite your wonderful imageries, I gather there are more details."

"Well," Justina said, drawing it out and shrugging.

"Have you plans tonight?"

"No, señora."

"Splendid. Please finish planting your flowers—don't press the soil down too hard...leave it loose—then go and get cleaned up. Be at my house at eight, where you and I will do something I rarely get to do any more."

"And that is?"

"We'll drink fine wine and cook a feast just for the both of us. While we cook and drink, I want to treat you to the music of my favorite classical pianists, Valentina Lisitsa and Yuja Wang, both of them as spectacular as that story you just told me. Afterward, we will retell your story of Gage, with additional backstory on you and more detail about this prison…as well as the, well, the steamy areas of the story."

"It's a date."

Señora Moreno clasped her hands, placing them under her chin as if she were a child, eagerly awaiting Christmas morning.

After finishing her flowers, Justina craved a cigarette. So she wrote Gage a letter.

THE FOLLOWING day, after morning chow, a very sore Gage trudged back to his cell while Salvador "attended to some business." Feeling feverish and in a state of torpor, Gage lay on his bunk with a wet towel over his head. In his sickly state, he worried that he might be a tantalizingly easy target for someone. *Well, there's nothing I can do about it right now,* he reasoned, closing his eyes, hoping that there was some manly prison code that frowned upon inmates taking out a wounded duck.

Around mid-morning, he heard the casual shuffle of sandals scraping into the cell. Blinking sleep from his eyes, Gage realized he had dozed off. When his eyes cleared, he saw Cesar Navarro standing in his cell.

Gage sat up, wincing from the stab of pain. He'd been shown dozens of pictures of Cesar Navarro at the meeting with his father and Cortez Redon. But he was taken aback at the way prison had affected Cesar's appearance.

Roughly five-and-a-half feet tall, Cesar probably weighed 150 pounds. He and Salvador, in regard to size, were close matches. In the pictures Gage had seen, Cesar had once had wavy sandy hair, worn down to his shoulders like that of a soccer player. Now, his hair was buzzed to his scalp, showing only perhaps a week's worth of growth. Cesar's thin arms were covered in sleeves of tattoos. Large bags drooped under his eyes, far too heavy and dark for a man of only thirty-four years of age. His prominent nose that seemed to fit his face so well in the pictures now looked oversized and cartoonish and, when he spoke, Gage noticed a broken tooth.

"My father sent you," Cesar said in a soft voice.

Gage carefully lowered himself from the top bunk, holding the bedframe as the blood rushed away from his head. "Did your father tell you that?"

Cesar shook his head, a sneer on his face. "I can always tell."

"Perdón?"

"I said, I can always tell."

"Always?"

"Yeah, you deaf?"

Alarms. Loud, cacophonous klaxons clanged in Gage's mind.

"What do you mean you can *always* tell?"

"Not one of you has fit in here," Cesar growled, the tendons in his neck showing with his strain. "It's obvious as shit and if I wasn't smart it would get me killed. I don't need you looking after me, *pelotudo*."

Gage's chest tightened from the sudden onset of stress brought about by Cesar's words. "Cesar, please tell me exactly what you're talking about. Are there others, here to protect you, besides me? Because, if so, I need to know that."

Navarro's only son cocked his head. "He didn't tell you?"

"Tell me what?"

"That devious old bastard. He thinks if he tells someone like you the real truth they'll cut and run."

"And what is the real truth?"

"Here I am, papa, doing your dirty work again," Cesar spoke to the concrete ceiling before his eyes came back down. "There've been three men before you, all sent here with the mission of protecting papa's little boy." Cesar studied Gage enigmatically, then showed his broken tooth in a wicked smile. "Each man, *mi amigo*, now lives with the maggots."

Wanting to respond, wanting to grab the diminutive Cesar by his sneering head and judo flip him out of the cell, Gage instead shut his eyes and regulated his breathing.

"I can see you're upset," Cesar remarked, crossing the cell. He leaned against the wall, removing one of Salvador's books, thumbing through it before dropping it to the floor, holding his fingers open as if he'd been handling a soiled diaper. "Understand this, *gabacho*, I do not want, or need, your help."

Gage didn't respond.

"So you do me a favor, faggot…you stay the hell away from me."

"Cesar…"

"Don't say my name again, *puta*."

Backing away, Cesar made double hand pistols before firing them at Gage. Then, when he grinned, Gage realized his tooth wasn't broken—it was capped in gold, along with several others. Outside the cell, when Cesar turned and walked away, several prisoners greeted him, slapping hands before they descended the stairs together. The other prisoners wore the distinctive neck tattoo of a gang: a long barreled revolver, canted upward with smoke trailing from its barrel. There was an "L" emblazoned on the grip of the pistol.

He'd seen many others with the same tattoo.

The gang, as Gage had read before coming here, was called Los Leones. It was the largest gang in Berga and the fastest growing crime syndicate in all of Spain.

Wide awake now, Gage shuffled from his cell, noticing a few nearby inmates back away. He crossed the concourse to the mesh fencing, staring downward as Cesar waded into a large group of prisoners. A dangerous-looking bunch, they seemed to welcome him, laughing and making gestures common to gangs the world over.

A half-hour later, when Salvador returned, Gage played dumb and asked him about the pistol tattoo with an "L" on the grip.

Salvador snorted, picking up his fallen book, staring at it a moment, then placing it back on the shelf.

"What about the tattoo?"

Head whipping around, Salvador said, "Come on, man. Don't act like you don't know."

"I don't. Tell me."

Glancing outside the cell, Salvador walked to Gage and stood very close, lowering his voice to a whisper. "That's the mark of Los Leones. My *banda*, Los Sementales, are less than fifteen men," he said, holding his hands close together before opening his arms wide. "Los Leones number in the hundreds. If you see anyone with that tattoo, turn and walk the other way."

"They're the biggest gang here?"

Again Salvador checked the entry to the cell. He turned back, saying, "The biggest here and in every Catalonian prison. But now they're in and *out*, growing everywhere." He cocked his head. "And if you were pinched for murder, I would think you would have known that."

"I was convicted in Melilla."

"Where?"

"Melilla, it's a Spanish territory in Morocco."

"Morocco? In Africa?"

"Yes."

"How is Spain in Africa?"

Gage shook his head. "It's just a territory of Spain. Doesn't matter."

"Why you asking?"

"A few men came by while you were gone. They had the Leones tattoo."

Salvador straightened. "What did they say? Did they mention my name?"

"No, Salvador. They were here to see me."

"What did they say to you?"

"Not much."

"But they were here to see you?"

"Yes."

Salvador closed his eyes for a moment, his hand going to his forehead. "What did they want?"

Gage sat down on Salvador's bed. "They gave me a warning."

"A warning about what?"

"They just told me to watch my step."

His chin tilting upward, Salvador closed his eyes, crossing himself praying aloud. He prayed for Gage's salvation.

Chapter Fifteen

IN BERGA, down a locked hallway from the main bay, next to the laundry, was a storage room. Teeming with linens, blankets, and towels at the front, the rear of the room was constructed of unpainted cinderblock. The back of the storage room doubled as an office. On a table was a small television, numerous packs of playing cards and several bottles of liquor. Situated in the middle of the rear space was a card table with four folding chairs. And sitting at the table was the most powerful prisoner in all of Berga, a man named Sancho Molina. Though his name was Sancho, no one dared call him that. He went by his nickname of *El Toro*, a moniker given to him for his powerful build as well as his bullish nature. To match his name, El Toro wore a gold ring, pierced between his nostrils. It was one of his many trademarks in Berga.

In front of El Toro was a bottle of Portuguese ginja and a shot glass. Standing before him was Cesar Navarro and one of the Berga guards. Cesar stood there looking every bit the part of a man on trial, waiting while El Toro took shots. The guard, despite being on the payroll of Los Leones, was a proud man and, though he didn't come out and say it, refused to stand before El Toro. He'd moved off to the side and was twirling his baton, smoking a cigarette.

El Toro poured a third shot of the reddish-gold berry liqueur, gunning it and baring his teeth afterward. He'd listened to what Cesar had said and ingested his shots while he considered it.

"How many days ago was this?"

"About a week."

"You're sure this is the man your father hired?" El Toro asked. He'd been personally told by Xavier Zambrano that there was an American coming to aid Cesar, but had no way of being absolutely sure Gregory Harris was the man. There had been Americans in Berga before, and a mix-up was certainly possible.

"Yes, El Toro," Cesar breathed with reverence. "This is him. He essentially came out and admitted it."

Turning his eyes to the guard, El Toro said, "And you?"

"His cell is clean. I checked his shit when he arrived."

151

"Did he plug one on the way in?" El Toro asked, tugging on his nose ring.

"He was X-rayed and the doc did a cavity search," the guard said with a trace of irritation, dropping the cigarette to the floor and grinding it under his boot. "I told you, he *doesn't* have a phone."

"Have you tossed his cell since?"

"No," the guard snapped.

"You giving me an attitude?"

"No."

El Toro eyed the guard from the corners of his eyes. "Your name is Pendulo…you got hired about a year ago."

"Yeah," the guard answered, maintaining his superior air.

"You live in Avià, don't you?"

The question visibly shook Pendulo. "Why do you ask…and how did you know where I live?"

El Toro straightened. "Do not *ever* question me."

"Yes, *jefe*. I am sorry."

"Now, answer the question."

The guard licked his lips. "Yes, I live in Avià."

"And you have a wife and a young child, if my memory serves me? A boy?"

"Yes, he's two."

"I've seen a picture of your wife." El Toro divined her by staring at the ceiling. "A tiny lady, if I remember correctly. A peasant *paleta* for sure, but young and firm and attractive."

The only sound for fifteen seconds was the washers and dryers tumbling in the adjacent room.

El Toro poured another shot, guzzling it in a flash. "Either you get on board with me, Pendulo, or I will have your little wife brought to me, kicking and screaming, while some of my friends look after your son." He cocked his eyebrow. "Get it?"

There was an obvious battle of emotions on the guard's face.

El Toro hitched his head in a dismissive gesture. "Now, get the hell out of here."

When the guard was gone, El Toro turned to Cesar. "So you told the American about the others? Was he surprised?"

"Shellshocked."

"He needs that phone," El Toro whispered to himself.

"Yes, he does. He didn't know about the others before me, and he didn't know my position with Los Leones."

"We will need to watch him closely, but we don't want to intervene. He *must* get that phone." El Toro nodded. "You've done well."

"Thank you, jefe," Cesar breathed with reverence. "What do I do now?"

"If you see the American, tell him you won't protect him much longer. Tell him you are a Lion, and protected by Lions. Tell him that by being here, he is inviting death. That will get him moving."

"I will do as you say."

El Toro politely dismissed Cesar. As soon as Cesar walked down the hall to the main bay, El Toro removed his mobile phone from his pants and called his local lieutenant. The lieutenant, also in Los Leones, was situated in the town of Berga to handle items outside the prison walls, mainly the importation of drugs. But occasionally he handled other items.

Such as this.

"Do you know anything about a satellite phone coming in to an American?" El Toro asked.

"Yeah. That's in this week's shipment, from Xavier himself," the lieutenant said. "I would have rushed it but Xavier said it was important that it come in as normal, so that no one would be suspicious."

"When?"

"Tomorrow."

"Perfecto."

"You need anything else?"

El Toro was about to hang up, but was struck by an inspiration. "Yeah. There's a young guard here named Pendulo. He's a hick and not very smart, but he's too proud. Go to his wife and quietly offer her money to come and visit me in the wood shop. Tell her I'm the top Lion here and we will see that her husband is occupied during the visit." El Toro smiled. "Tell her I'm in love with her and I want to start a sultry, passionate affair with her and give her all my seed."

"Okay, *jefe*," the lieutenant chuckled. "When would you like her?"

"As soon as possible." El Toro thumbed the phone off, pouring another shot and leaning back with it. His first thoughts were with the American, and his association with Ernesto Navarro. Xavier had been most pointed, dangerous even, when he'd told El Toro that the American had to call Navarro by the satellite phone.

Then, setting those thoughts aside, El Toro thought of the guard's young wife. Though he always reviewed the backgrounds of everyone who was on the take, he'd quickly dismissed the wife until today, when Pendulo tried to be a man. Well, now he would pay for that.

El Toro grasped himself, warm with the thought of a new affair, despite the fact that the wife was nothing more than a rural peasant. "She'll come," he whispered before taking a sip of the liqueur.

"She'll come again and again."

Life was good.

OVER THE balance of the previous week, Gage had grown accustomed to the Berga routine. As with nearly every major injury he'd ever sustained, the stab wounds had reached their worst point on the third day after the incident. Now, though they still burned and appeared semi-wet when he viewed them in the mirror, some healing seemed to have taken place as the redness around the wounds had turned a healthier pink. Relieving Gage the most was the fact that there had been no more fever.

All in all, he felt much better.

An elderly prisoner shuffled by, dropping two letters on the ground at the entrance to the cell. Salvador retrieved them, handing one to Gage. Gage eyed the return address, a made-up post office box in Barcelona. The letter was postmarked Sabadell, which Gage knew to be just north of Barcelona.

Good girl.

He tore into the envelope.

Dear Gregory,

Every tick of the clock brings me a second closer to you. I will never forget our last night, our glistening bodies joined together as one, hearing your breath in my ears. It was heaven, and we will experience it again.

We will.

Be strong. Worry about your situation there and don't trouble your mind worrying about me. I am fine and have made a wonderful new friend in our landlady. I remind her of her daughter and find her amazing to be around. Maybe I can learn from her and, when you return, I can become a real estate queen like she is. Ha!

This may sound improper, Gregory, but it's the truth. Every night when I lie down in bed, I will think of you in the most intimate way. It's my connection with you and, I want you to know, I would wait for you until the end of my life if need be.

You saved me. And that was the first building block of my love for you.

I do love you.
In sweet love,
Justina

P.S. My English has improved but I did use the online thesaurus for this note. Ha again!

While Salvador lounged on his bunk with his letter, occasionally laughing to himself, Gage reread the letter before tucking it away in his personal things. Feeling a large measure of stubble on his face, Gage decided to shave. He removed his shaving tackle from his container, immediately noticing how heavy the shaving cream felt. Deftly, Gage unscrewed the bottom just a fraction, pleased that his satellite phone had arrived. He could now make plans to call Navarro.

Gage briefly thought about the acusador, Cortez Redon. Valentin said he was the one who would arrange for the phone to be delivered. Gage had no use for Redon, and Colonel Hunter's intel had said he was not to be trusted.

So who did Redon use to deliver the phone? Whoever it was, in Gage's mind, now knew more than they should. Gage hated leaks. Leaks get people killed.

Pushing the concern aside, Gage soaked his face and prepared to shave without shaving cream. Before he did, he noticed two men in the paper-thin aluminum mirror—both were adorned with the distinctively large Semental neck tattoo.

Gage turned. It was the two aggressors from his first day. The tall, thin boxer and the muscled Semental with the nasty tongue bite. They were waiting outside the cell's threshold, saying nothing. As Gage eyed them, feeling the thud of his own pulse, the muscled one, supporting himself on crutches, nodded to Gage. The tall one nodded as well. Gage didn't respond in kind but bumped his leg against Salvador's bunk. Salvador glanced at him and Gage lifted his chin. Seeing his hombres, Salvador thanked Gage as he stood and slid his sandals on.

"You want to meet with them in here?" Gage asked. Salvador stared back in amazement. "Go ahead," Gage said, wiping his face one more time before hanging up his blood-marked washcloth and making his way out of the cell. The two Sementals moved out of his way, both dipping their heads until he passed.

Gage noticed that the large man's mouth wasn't closed completely. He could see the man's swollen tongue.

Ouch.

Gage walked to the fence, not seeing much going on in the main bay. Having never made a full revolution of the concourse, Gage decided to do so, stretching his legs as he tried to walk at a regular gait despite the throbbing ache radiating from his back and shoulder.

Estimating that a full revolution of the second-floor terraza was nearly a quarter-of-a-mile, Gage wondered if anyone ever jogged it for exercise. *Bet that'd go over big*, he thought. His eyes were drawn to a cell not far from his. As Gage passed, he looked inside, seeing a man holding another to the wall, his forearm under his neck as he harassed him with slaps to the face. A third man was standing outside of the cell keeping watch, the revolver visible on his neck. He eyeballed Gage.

Gage ignored the scene and continued to walk.

Halfway around the terraza, Gage noticed that every time he passed a Leones gang member, the Leones would see him coming, as if they were looking for him, and each time the gang member would nod as if to say, "I know who you are, and I have respect."

It didn't feel right.

Two-thirds of the way around, when he glanced down through the wire mesh to the main floor below, he noticed Cesar, standing in the center of the floor, motioning to him. Gage stopped and stared.

Cesar opened his arms as if he were some long lost friend then, again, he beckoned Gage.

There was not a more public place to meet in the entire prison. And Cesar had told Gage to stay away. Something, indeed, was very wrong here.

Not exactly knowing how to react, Gage decided to comply with Cesar's request. He descended the two flights of stairs, crossing the main floor to where Cesar stood, hands on his hips as if he owned the place. As Gage approached, the other prisoners that had been nearby, all marked with Los Leones neck tattoo, dissipated.

"You talk to my papa yet?" Cesar barked as Gage approached.

Gage moved close enough to ensure their conversation would be private. "No, Cesar. Today is actually my phone day, but I don't have a number to call your father."

"Yeah, right. Well, when you do talk to papa, and I know you will, you make sure you tell him I'm fine and I don't *need* his help."

"I heard you the first time, Cesar."

Cesar thumped his own chest then pointed at Gage. "But you should know, *cabrón*, that it's me protecting you, and not you protecting me."

"What do you mean by that?"

"Los Leones are staying away from you because of me." Again he hit himself, slapping his chest as he snarled, "And only because of me."

"Really?" Gage said, making sure his tone was one of boredom.

"By now they would have turned your asshole into the Vielha Tunnel. And then, when you could pleasure them no more, they would kill you in the worst way you could imagine."

"But instead, in all your benevolence, you've saved me?"

"You don't seem very grateful."

Turning his eyes, Gage noticed the stares. All around him, even on the terraces, he noticed every man with a Leones tattoo staring at his verbal exchange with Cesar.

Again, something didn't feel quite right. Gage began to feel the way he always had in the military when he'd been given bad intelligence, at the moment when all was quiet but, somehow, someway, he knew a shot was about to ring out from an area that had been pronounced all clear. It felt exactly like that.

Struggling to wet his mouth, Gage said, "Well, thank you, Cesar. I appreciate your intervention." He turned and began walking away.

"Que mierda!" Cesar bellowed. Gage turned, watching as the wiry man stalked to where he stood. "You never walk away from me, or any León, unless told to, *comprende?"*

The feeling had been crawling in Gage's direction since he'd first met Cesar. And now, as he stood toe-to-toe with Navarro's only son, Gage knew he'd somehow been had. The elder Navarro wasn't in on it, at least Gage couldn't see how or why he would have any motivation to incarcerate Gage and risk his money in the process. No, the father's worry for Cesar was genuine but, for whatever reason, he didn't know about Cesar's "membership" in Los Leones. Earlier, Gage had recalled the elder Navarro's words, telling him that Los Leones were going to torture his son until the end of his sentence, at which time they would kill him.

Now, standing inches away from Cesar, Gage read the situation in a completely different way. Cesar acted as if he were in charge. Los Leones did seem to be taking orders from him, hence the leeway Gage was now given. But there had to be more to the situation than that.

And, for whatever reason, Cesar was not marked with their tattoo.

Regardless, such a situation was treacherous and, until he figured out what was going on, Gage knew he'd be wise to comply. He dipped his head a fraction. "I apologize and I won't turn my back on you again."

Somewhat mollified, Cesar's voice was pure arrogance. "See that you don't."

Gage nodded then waited.

"My protection ends very soon, *maricón*. If you were smart enough to come here with an escape route, I'd suggest you use it." Cesar twirled his hand all around the prison. "Because, whenever I'm tired of you, I will snap my fingers and laugh as these men eat you alive."

Cesar shooed Gage away like he would a pesky gnat.

As Gage trudged away, it was all he could do not to vomit.

WHEN THE encounter was over and the American had moved out into the yard, Cesar walked to the area where El Toro stood, doing business with several others. When the others were gone, Cesar was beckoned over.

"Did you see the American approach me, *jefe?*"

El Toro nodded.

"He will call my father now," Cesar said. "I left him nowhere else to go."

"You've done very well," El Toro said, patting Cesar's face with affection.

Based on his reaction, a person might have thought Cesar had just won the lottery.

When Cesar was dismissed, El Toro turned to his top man. "Watch that American every second of the day. He's hiding that satellite phone somewhere."

Chapter Sixteen

Lunch chow consisted of a watery soup that was imbued with some sort of gamey, stringy meat, reminding Gage of a possum he'd once eaten during a survival training block at the Army's JRTC. Following lunch, with the aftertaste still coating his mouth, Gage stretched his body in a corner of the main bay before climbing the stairs and walking to his cell.

And that's where he found trouble.

Standing in the cell, above Salvador, was a large man with the distinctive tattoo of Los Leones. He was probably at least fifty years old, but in incredible shape for his age. He had a rounded face with beady brown eyes. His pants were around his knees and his hands were gripping Gage's bunk. The man was steadily growling curses at Salvador, who was leaning back on his own bunk, shaking his head. The man was thrusting his erect manhood at Salvador.

It was a disgusting scene as the man was clearly trying to take something that Salvador had no interest in providing.

Gage took two deep breaths and stepped to the threshold.

"What the hell is this?"

Without pulling up his pants, the man turned to Gage, his voice a growl. *"Vete a la mierda, maricón."*

Gage lurched forward, shoving the vulnerable man against the sink, making him fall to his knees. Without taking his eyes off the intruder, Gage said, "What's up, Salvador?"

Salvador kept his eyes down. "Because you beat me up, he now considers me one of *los más débiles.*"

"The weak?"

"Yes. But here, that means men who act as women."

The muscular León was on his feet now, having pulled up his pants. Gage watched as he balled his fists.

"Leave now, before you get hurt," Gage said, hitching his thumb to the door.

The León charged Gage.

Knowing he was in no physical condition for a brawl, Gage sidestepped the onrushing man, attempting a kick that was largely futile. Salvador began to come off his bunk but Gage motioned him back.

Uninjured and huffing loudly, his face and neck splotchy with rage, the León turned and faced Gage. Judging by his initial bull rush, Gage believed he could use the gang member's aggressiveness against him. Gage stood his ground, telling him to come and get some.

Gage's challenge, and the insulting word Gage added to the end, were too much for the León to bear. He rushed forward, cocking his arm for a strike. Gage waited for it, ducking when it came, and catching the man in the gut with his own shoulder. They struggled there in the middle of the cell, both men at a disadvantage on the concrete floor with the thin prison sandals.

A long grappling match would not favor Gage. He was weakened due to the stab wounds and knew he wouldn't be able to hold out long against the muscular gang member. Still in a clinch, Gage had the advantage of underhooks, ignoring the pestering slaps coming from the León who was steadily cursing Gage.

The two men struggled and turned, and that's when Gage noticed a group of Los Leones gathering outside the cell. They seemed inclined to watch, but Gage didn't know what they might do if Gage were to defeat their fellow León.

Just then, the man in Gage's grasp pulled backward, sending a left hook into Gage's face as they broke from one another. Briefly dazed, Gage was simply too weakened to provide a game fight for the gang member—unless he could come up with a fight-ending sequence in short order.

Your legs are just fine, Gage. Use them.

Circling each other, the muscular, but older and wiser, León must have been aware of what Gage did to Salvador and his Sementals. He was being very wary, cursing Gage with every insult in the book as they prepared for the next sequence in their fight.

When the León had his back to his fellow gang members at the cell's entrance, he called for a *puñal*, holding his hand backward as if expecting to have it handed to him. Gage had heard the word *puñal*, but didn't know exactly what it meant. He thought it had something to do with a person's hands.

He found out soon enough.

One of the gang members reached through the doorway, putting a homemade knife, a shiv, into Gage's opponent's outstretched hand. He grinned maniacally at its feel, his eyes never leaving Gage.

"Attack now," Salvador hissed at Gage. "Don't wait."

It was good advice.

Using what strength he had remaining, and remembering his own advice about his available leg strength, Gage rushed forward into the clench again, using both of his arms to control the man's right arm. The two men grunted and growled. But Gage knew that such a close quarter battle would eventually be futile so, still holding the right arm, he spun to that side and unleashed a powerful knee into the side of the man's right thigh.

Such a strike is known as a lateral femoral assault and, if used correctly, can completely disable a person's leg. The key is the branching lateral femoral cutaneous nerve that runs down the leg. It's more than a pressure point—it's a motor point. If stunned with great enough force, it will drop a man, as it dropped this León. He went down on his side, his leg cinched up as he yelled curses and insults.

Gage unloaded with a right hand, catching the man in his jaw and watching as he went briefly limp, his hand releasing the homemade knife.

And that's when numerous feet could be seen surrounding the downed León. Gage kicked the knife away and stepped back to the sink, his chest heaving as he viewed the assembled members of the Leones gang.

For whatever reason, they weren't on the attack. Instead, though they eyed Gage with contempt, they lifted their fellow León and dragged him from the cell. When the group had cleared, Gage saw two men standing at the fence of the terraza, staring at him. One was the man with the nose ring, known as El Toro. He was a member of Los Leones, and Gage had heard Salvador say he was the most powerful man in the prison. Next to El Toro stood Cesar. Both men glared at Gage.

"You see, *puta*," Cesar said, pointing his bony finger, "I have saved you again. Soon, I will let them rape you both, for days, before they gut you."

Bent double, hands on his knees, Gage had no response.

Laughing, the two men shuffled away.

Salvador stood momentarily before dropping back on his bunk, covering his face with his hands. "You saved me," he muttered, his voice shaky. "You saved my life."

Gage leaned against the cool bars, catching his breath, trying to make sense of what was going on.

"I will never be able to thank you enough," Salvador said, unsteadily standing and holding the bars.

Gage shook his head.

"Do you hear me?" Salvador asked.

Gage turned to his cellmate. "I did what anyone would do."

"Not here, *mi amigo*. Not here."

"Maybe you and your friends can watch my back, too."

Salvador nodded, clapping his cellmate on the good side of his back.

Unbeknownst to either man, the León who had fought with Gage, and the man who provided him the homemade knife, were mercilessly gang-raped after nightfall. A week earlier, all Berga members of Los Leones had been given implicit instructions not to harm the American named Harris. The gang rape was their initial punishment and, according to Los Leones tradition, the two would be on probation for a period of ninety days.

If they didn't please their superiors in every way possible during that period, they would be marked for death.

Most members of Berga's Leones gang felt they were let off too easily.

HIS SITUATION here untenable, Gage decided to make the call on the following day. It baffled Gage that a man with Ernesto Navarro's power wouldn't know about his son's traitorous behavior. Wouldn't there be someone here who would report such matters to Navarro?

Maybe there had been, Gage thought. Maybe everyone with Navarro's interests in mind had all been eliminated. And after spending a few days in Berga, Gage wouldn't be the least bit surprised.

Once the yard was open, Gage found Salvador on his bunk, reading. "Ten minutes of privacy?" Gage asked.

"Sure," Salvador replied. "Need more?"

"No. That's all." Taking his book with him, Salvador quickly departed.

Gage unscrewed the bottom of his shaving can, removing the phone and the skin-colored hands-free device. Acting as if he were using the sink, he powered up the AAA battery-powered phone, making certain it was set to silent. He quickly learned that the device had already been programmed for silent-mode only, and that the light behind the LCD keyboard and display had been disabled.

Dropping the phone into his right pocket, Gage tried to view himself in the inadequate mirror. Deciding that the phone, while slim, might be noticeable through the thin fabric of his pants, he used a flattened wad of toilet paper to break up its outline.

Glancing down and now satisfied that no one could see the phone, Gage exited his cell, walking downstairs and outside to find a suitable location to call Señor Navarro. This entire job had been a fool's errand and Gage intended to tell Navarro just that. Cesar seemed quite safe in Berga, unwilling to accept Gage's assistance—and was now openly threatening to sic hundreds of men after Gage's ass. Literally.

Navarro was a businessman and Gage expected to find him relieved, and perhaps bewildered, at the news of his son's clout. Gage would tell the mobster the unvarnished truth and propose that Navarro's flunky district attorney, Redon, extract him immediately. Once Gage was safely out, he would refund Navarro a prorated portion of the initial payment he had received and everyone could go about their business.

As Gage stepped into the warm sunshine of the Spanish afternoon, his warmth was far outweighed by a temporary visualization of Justina. The payday for this mission would still be substantial. And, if Gage applied himself, he knew he could probably double what he'd been making before beginning this job. That would provide enough money for him and Justina to live, and would hopefully leave enough left over to send to Justina's mother and brother.

Surveying the prison yard, Gage shook his head over the turn of events. He was no quitter, but staying here would be a suicide mission.

"Let's set these wheels in motion and go home," Gage whispered to himself.

He had no idea of the wheels he would actually set in motion.

EATING SUNFLOWER seeds one at a time, El Toro sauntered through the main bay. Working the split hull of a seed to the tip of his tongue, he spit it out, watching as it separated into two damp pieces, fluttering to the shiny floor in random patterns. Standing in the main yard doorway and keeping the American in sight, he eyed his relay man at the far fence. As a type of commo-check El Toro scratched his forehead, watching as the man across the yard repeated the action.

"*Aquí vamos*," he whispered, shuffling into the sunlight.

SINCE ARRIVING, Gage had only been out in the yard a few times. He could see no reason to make a habit of it. Gage was not one to tempt fate. He knew that the breadth of the outdoor area would be far more likely a place to invite attack or retribution. But, especially after Cesar's decree and the treatment he'd gotten after the fight in the cell, Gage felt safe walking to the far side, viewing the road through the fences.

Outside the outer fence, the occasional car sped by, its occupants surely blissfully unaware that only a few hundred meters away existed an entirely different universe. A universe of rape and extortion. A universe where certain tattoos were the equivalent of senatorial power. A universe that cared only about itself and its occupants, ignoring the realities and reason of the outside world.

He moved to one end of the fence before turning halfway around. This would keep his right side to the fence and would only be visible to the lone guard in the center tower. And unless that guard was viewing Gage through a high-powered scope, Gage saw no way he could see the flesh-colored earpiece device he'd just slid into his right ear.

As he ambled slowly, making sure to turn his head and eyes naturally (a person with a still head looks quite unnatural) Gage reached into his pocket, blindly dialing the number he'd been told to memorize.

A European ring tone was then heard, tinny and distant. One ring. Three rings. Five rings. Eventually, just as he'd been told, a person answered but said nothing. Then Gage spoke the code he'd been instructed on, using Spanish. "Buenos días, es esta la farmacia?"

As promised, the caller on the other end of the line didn't even respond. They simply hung up. Gage counted as he walked the fence back to where he'd started. By the time he reached sixty-five, the phone in his pocket vibrated. Gage tapped the earpiece and whispered, "Bueno?"

"Señor Harris." It was Navarro.

"Sí."

"Are you secure?"

"I'm in the yard. I may sound strange because I don't want to fully move my lips. Can you understand what I'm saying?"

"Yes, it's quite clear."

Ahead of Gage, a small man in dark sunglasses sat alone at a picnic table reading a J.T. Ellison paperback. While he read, he scratched his chin, his hand moving slowly up his face before scratching his shaved head.

"Señor," Gage whispered, keeping his eye on the reader but not yet thinking anything of him. "Things here are not as all as you thought."

"In what way?"

"For starters, your son is aligned with Los Leones." Gage took ten more steps before hearing a response.

"That's...that's impossible."

"He told me so. And I've hardly seen him when he wasn't surrounded by members of Los Leones. He's also confronted me several times, telling me he doesn't want my help and that *he* is protecting *me*. In fact, I was in a fight and Cesar intervened. He's told me that my protection won't last much longer."

Spanish curses, spoken in anguish, could be heard. Footsteps were also audible before he heard Navarro snap his fingers and dismiss Valentin. The background sound changed to slightly fuzzy, denoting a breeze. "Has someone there turned you?" Navarro asked.

Gage stopped momentarily, glancing up to the sky as he felt a throbbing begin in his temples. "No one has turned me. I speak only the truth."

"If what you say is true—"

"It *is* true."

"Then something more sinister than I feared is going on," Navarro said, sounding out of breath. "Cesar doesn't have the shrewdness to be a true León. If they've brought him into their fold, it's being done as a ruse, as a trap. You *must* tell him this."

"He won't listen to me. He doesn't even know me." Gage let that settle for a moment. "Why don't you tell him? You could come here and see him face to face."

Out on the road, two loud trucks rumbled by, forcing Gage to tell Navarro to wait. When they had passed, Navarro responded. "As I explained before you went there, I am doing all I can to sanitize my operations, to be legitimate as the saying goes. But it's Los Leones who have made things the most difficult for me. They've beaten and killed my men in all corners of Catalonia. They've robbed my concerns. They've spread disinformation about my empire, all to their own end.

"While I have not operated by the letter of the law, my organization has always been honorable. Those who strayed from my ethical code were dealt with, and harshly. But Los Leones kills the way you and I breathe. They do it from instinct."

Movement caught the corner of Gage's eye. The man at the picnic table had spun so he straddled the bench with both legs, trying to appear natural as a man simply shifting his position. Now, as Gage changed direction, the man flipped back around, still holding his paperback. Gage could hear Navarro saying something, but he was too zoned in on the reading man. *Now he's putting his hand on top of his head and rubbing his scalp.* Gage slyly followed his gaze, seeing a man on the far wall casually mimic the gesture. Then, at the main door, Gage could see El Toro, his musculature obvious even at such a distance.

All three men were members of Los Leones.

Gage rapidly blinked his eyes as if there was dust blowing. But there was no dust. Permutations of possibilities took place in his mind. He'd just seen a simple code relayed, that was for certain. The reader from the picnic table ambled away, doing a quick rendition of a flamenco dance with stuttered, strutting steps while keeping his hands at his waist. When he reached his relay man they shared a laugh, performing some sort of ritualistic handshake.

"Señor Harris?" Navarro persisted. Gage was too deep in thought to acknowledge him.

Studying the angle of the relay—edge of yard, center yard with an eye to doorway, inside of doorway—Gage pondered the reasons for the message. It had to be his own actions, talking on this phone. Did they aim to steal it? Certainly a possibility—a phone in prison would be one of the most treasured items a prisoner could own. But if that were the case with Los Leones, why didn't they just come take it?

"Señor Harris!" Navarro yelled.

Startled by the shout, Gage said, "Señor, where are you?"

"That's not pertinent."

Gage's voice became a razor. "The phone you're talking on, the satellite phone…"

"What about it?"

"You devised the farmacia-wrong-number code solely for the purpose of knowing when to turn on the satellite phone, correct?"

"Yes, of course."

"Is the man with the phone I called, the first number, is he there?"

"No. He's hundreds of kilometers away. As I've told you, I take great precautions."

They're after the satellite phone's signal. Shit!

"Why do you ask?"

"The house we met in, the one on the coast under the cliffs, does anyone know where it is?"

"That wasn't my regular home, Señor Harris, it was a rental I use on occasion. I've insulated myself to the point that I bring no one to my permanent homes other than Valentin."

Gage rubbed the stubble of his face. "What about your son, does he know where you are now?"

"Only Valentin knows where I regularly stay," Navarro said with emphasis. "As I told you about Cesar—we've been estranged for many years, since I began to legitimize my operation."

"Have you ever visited him here?"

"Yes, once."

"Was the visit announced?"

"Of course not. And I took great precautions upon leaving there not to be followed."

Swallowing, his tongue feeling as thick as a tire tread, Gage said, "Los Leones, would they profit from knowing where you are?"

"You know they would."

"But to be clear, are they looking for you?"

"Everyone is. It's why I live the way I do."

"You compromised me, señor, by telling me none of this. You didn't tell me about the others you had inserted before me, and you certainly didn't tell me about the fact that Los Leones are looking for you."

"What are you saying?"

"Have your acusador get me out of here today."

"What?"

"Today. But before you do that—right damned now—hang up that satellite phone, remove the battery, and run like hell. Change your position."

"But it's untraceable."

"Nothing is untraceable," Gage snapped. "Do as I said and change your position immediately!"

"You're actually serious," Navarro said.

"Of course I am. They *know* I'm on the phone. They waited for us to speak and someone is now tracking your signal. Disconnect the battery and go!"

"This is nonsense. This phone cannot be traced."

"Go now!"

"Keep that phone on," Navarro said. Then the line went dead.

Gage surveyed the yard. There were at least a hundred men outside and no one seemed to be paying him any notice. Inside the three outer guard towers, Gage saw one guard casually smoking a cigarette. The other two, leaning over their respective railings, radios in front of them, seemed to be having a conversation, a funny one judging by their laughter.

Am I just being paranoid?

Crossing the yard, Gage stepped inside the main bay to see Cesar, standing in the center of the cavernous room. A shit-eating grin dominated his ratlike face and his arms were straight out to his side—he could have easily been taking an ovation after an opening night on Broadway. Around him, Los Leones slapped him on the back, grabbing his shoulders and shaking him with their congratulations.

It was a scene of jubilation.

A cold shiver passed through Gage.

Morón Air Base, near Seville, Spain

MINUTES EARLIER, in the southern province of Andalusia, an old-fashioned pager vibrated in General Brian Yelding's pocket. The pager had been modified to vibrate twice as hard as a normal pager would—so there was no mistaking its presence when it performed as designed. Yelding had just taken a bite of a late lunch when he felt the buzzing. The vibration scared him at first but the fear quickly turned to thrill. The general was about to get paid.

He excused himself from the table of officers, stepping outside into the hot afternoon and dialing a number.

"Got it?" Yelding asked, breathless. He listened for a moment. "No...no coordinates. The person I'm dealing with wouldn't know a frigging coordinate from the length of his dick. Just give me the exact address."

Yelding waited. After a moment he scribbled the address on a scrap of paper, tucking it into his shirt pocket. He listened to the defense satellite engineer before saying, "You'll get paid when I do. And just remember who we're dealing with here. Don't tell your wife, your buddies, anyone. And don't deposit the money, either." He hung up.

Yelding then went through the folders of his phone, finding the number on a note he'd created. He slid the cursor over the number, dialing it. The phone was answered immediately.

"I found your friend. Respectfully, I'd like the Gibraltan bank account number before giving the address." After a moment of listening he removed the address from his pocket and scribbled the bank account number. "Just a moment, please." The general removed another sheet he'd prepared, showing the sequence of numbers in Gibraltar banks. The number he'd been given appeared to be genuine.

"Thank you. The address you're seeking is in the enclave of Cadaques. The address is number one, S'Aranella."

After confirming the address, the man on the other end of the line hung up the phone.

Yelding, unable to restrain the mirth from spreading over him, placed his phone on the ground, smashing it under his heel. He ground his foot back and forth, pulverizing the mobile device. Once he'd discarded the pieces, he stepped back into the dining facility, resuming his late lunch. He didn't feel one bit of remorse—criminals killing criminals makes the world a better place.

The bland meal tasted exquisite, especially now that he was a quarter-of-a-million dollars richer.

Chapter Seventeen

Cadaques, Spain

ERNESTO NAVARRO had removed the battery from his satellite phone, eyeing the two parts with a cocked eyebrow. He was at his villa on the northern shore of Cadaques, the seaside enclave famous for inspiring artists like Salvador Dali and Pablo Picasso. Tapping out his last Dunhill, Navarro crumpled the pack, leaning back on the white leather sofa and pondering what he'd heard on the phone. Was it possible, Cesar in bed with Los Leones?

Don't be his papa right now, be the cold and calculating man who once ruled the north of Spain with an iron fist. The man with fifty million euro spread throughout the world's banking havens. The man who once took down the world's most powerful mobster with only three men, two shotguns and a pair of osmium balls.

Closing his eyes, Navarro reasoned it out. Cesar had always been his own man, unwilling to stand in his father's shadow, returning any act of paternal kindness with a bite of Navarro's hand. Even as a small boy, back when Navarro's wife had been alive, Cesar would become angry at something trivial and smash his favorite toy as revenge.

But...

Cesar as a León? Yes, it's theoretically possible. Opening his eyes, Navarro whispered, "Quite possible," feeling as if he'd just ingested a cup of vinegar.

But this American...What was his name?...*Gage Hartline.* What was he up to? Though vouched for as a man who lived life simply and well within his own means, he'd certainly turned at the prospect of Navarro's significant offer. And why wouldn't he do it again, especially when Los Leones could easily portray Navarro as just another mobster? They could tie hundreds of murders back to him so that a soldier-like mercenary such as Hartline would have no compunction over flipping from one thug to another.

Unsure of exactly who to trust, Navarro was still somewhat unfazed over the warnings from the American. The phone call had startled him at first, but he relaxed as he thought back through his scrupulous preparations. He'd been assured by a top scientist with Spain's *Instituto Nacional de Técnica Aeroespacial*, a man who regularly helped Los Soldados with surveillance, that a satellite phone was untraceable except at the very highest levels of government and military. While Navarro had grudging respect for Xavier Zambrano's skills, Navarro still felt that he and his top Leones were nothing more than a collection of thick-skulled thugs. It would be one thing to track a cellular signal—any iniquitous idiot at a wireless provider could provide such a service. But it would be an entirely different process to crack into a satellite's feed. It would take the government's help and, for more than three decades, Navarro had owned all corners of the executive government. If Zambrano had made inroads, Navarro would have already learned about it.

Now, on to another question.

Should he pull Hartline from Berga? It might help determine if he'd flipped. And, if he had, he'd have to be eliminated. That would leave Navarro in a precarious position with his American allies.

"*Merda*," Navarro mumbled. He thumbed the handheld radio. "Valentin."

"Yes, señor?"

"I spoke with Hartline at Berga. He was concerned about my satellite phone being tracked. Does that concern you?"

"No, señor. We were given assurances that such a task is impossible. Also, if you'll recall, this American is overly cautious. Too cautious, in my opinion."

"You have no concerns?"

"*Cero.*"

"Do you see anything unusual outside?"

"Nothing, señor. I'm viewing all the monitors now. What did Hartline tell you about Cesar?"

"I'll tell you later. I want some time to think."

Navarro put the radio down and dropped the crumpled cigarette pack on the coffee table. He then lit his cigarette. The Mediterranean waves could be heard outside, the warm sea breeze pushing the filmy fabric in through the open French doors. Hoping the fresh air might clear his head, he walked outside, sliding off his Gucci loafers and standing barefoot on the white wood of his porch. Navarro's two wolf shepherds padded out with him. Having been run earlier, they quickly settled in on the deck and resumed their slumber.

This was his primary residence in the summer, not the safe-house twenty kilometers to the south where he'd met with Gage Hartline. No one knew he was here, although the very thought of being found sent a spike of fear through the elder Navarro.

Deep breaths.

He thought about Valentin's counsel, and the advice of his own primary attorney. They both urged him to pick up and go. To announce himself as fully retired, to give up his interests and move to Monaco or Montenegro or Cyprus where he could finish out his final ten or twenty years in the sun and casinos. There he could eat good food, enjoy the ministrations of skinny women, and utilize the world's best medicine to remain above ground for as long as possible.

"How much money do you need?" Valentin had urged on the chilly night after the Hartline meeting, once Hartline and the smarmy acusador, Redon, had taken their leave. "If you leave now, even that maniac who runs Los Leones will gladly trade Cesar's life for the control of your interests. He'll leave him unharmed and send you on with his blessings."

The fire had danced before Navarro, the seasoned alder cracking and popping.

"Why won't you do it, señor?" Valentin had pleaded.

Navarro had finally turned to him and said, "I will *never* run away." Then he'd stared until Valentin dropped his eyes.

Since then, there'd been no more talk about retirement.

Ever since Francesca's death almost a decade before, when Navarro had begun pulling back in the Spanish underworld, the rival organizations began pecking away at the void like pigeons pushing into a seed pile. At first it had seemed that Lima's group from the south might emerge, before the fateful explosion on that yacht at the Port of Santa Maria. Then it had been the originators of the Santa Marian fireball, the Italians, but their reign had only lasted a cup of coffee before they were sent away in a Neapolitan cargo ship loaded with body bags. When Los Leones had followed the flood of Italian blood, bringing with them the brutality they'd dominated the prisons with since the mid-century, Navarro had known his time was coming to an end. And he'd stepped aside gracefully.

In *most* areas.

For five full years he'd negotiated with Los Leones' leader at the time, Severo Santana, "Sevi the Knife," his moniker depicted by the twin daggers on the backs of his hands. Navarro had only angled to keep a few of Los Soldados' best moneymakers. For a hardened criminal, Sevi had been a decent man. While he was a ruthless negotiator, he was at least practical, until that day five years ago when he'd been disemboweled by his top lieutenant. The lieutenant, Xavier Zambrano, a lean, chisel-faced ball of contempt, had arrogated the mantle and never looked back. He'd ceased all discussions with Navarro, sending word of a one-week truce before he declared war on Navarro's entire operation.

That had been five years ago.

As the salty breeze pressed in, Navarro pulled one last drag from his Dunhill, pressing it into the planter at the corner of the patio. The sun was now behind his enclave, descending, adding comfortable, eastward shadows to the patio. Pressing his thumb and forefinger to his closed eyes, he recalled his initial indignation at the threats from the largely unknown León, Xavier, who'd spent the majority of his adult life in prison. For three days Navarro had sat awake, smoking and thinking, watching the sun and the moon travel across the sky, waiting as rival factions warred in his own mind. At the end of his patient cogitation, Navarro had summoned Valentin telling him what to yield and what to protect.

Now, rather than live under the shroud of a large guard force, Navarro had chosen to live independently, in anonymity. He prepared his own meals, or sent Valentin to retrieve them. When he desired entertainment, like the young woman who currently lay nude in his bed, Valentin delivered it in the blind rear of the Mercedes.

No one outside of his tight inner-circle knew exactly where Navarro's three retreats were. Sure, there were rumors. People had seen him in places like Cadaques. But he only went there, or to a place like Tossa de Mar where he'd met Gage Hartline, under the watchful eyes of multiple guards.

He lived a very private, secure life.

Before Navarro told his dogs to stay and stepped back inside, he glanced southward down the beach, staring at the ribbon of sand and red rock that disappeared into the belly of Spain. The thought of the initial meeting with Hartline made him go back to what Hartline had said on the phone, about someone tracing his call. If that were true, Navarro thought with a measure of satisfaction, he could just imagine Xavier's anger when he was told that, for whatever reason, the phone on the other end of the line wasn't a regular cellular phone, it was a satellite phone and untraceable to a specific location.

But Navarro's good humor slid away from him, bringing back the vinegary taste as he remembered what Hartline had said about Cesar. Why would Hartline lie? Unless the Leones had somehow turned him, he wouldn't. And Cesar…he was just stupid enough to be taken in by Los Leones, who probably promised him all manner of shiny objects in return for his papa's head. Cesar was certainly gullible enough to believe them.

As he crossed the bright white sitting room, an encouraging thought struck Navarro. This situation, as bizarre as it was, might work to everyone's favor. Cesar knew nothing. Since he and Navarro had become estranged, which was before Xavier took over Los Leones, everything had changed. Navarro's three retreats had all been purchased through an untraceable shell company. Cesar had no knowledge of anything other than Navarro's previously jettisoned narcotics operation so, as long as Los Leones felt he was worth keeping around, even if Hartline decided to pull out, Cesar might be kept alive for the balance of his sentence.

That meant Navarro had twenty months to try to figure out some way to bring his son out alive. And twenty months was a long time. In that time, rather than try and protect Cesar with commandos like the American, perhaps Navarro would usher in a capable rival gang, teaching them of the macho Leones' many weak points.

Yes, Navarro thought, his hand on the door of the bedroom, a flush spreading over his florid face. It will be much better to have a predictable enemy than a band of dishonorable convicts like Los Leones.

It's a very good plan.

And now he would celebrate by letting the leggy young visitor bring him off before he ordered his evening meal. Reaching into his pocket, Navarro removed an erectile pill, biting down on it and letting it dissolve on his tongue so that it would work quickly.

The miracle of modern medicine.

He stepped into his bedroom.

"YOU'VE GOT a visitor," the guard said to Gage. Gage had just come back inside from the yard, and still had the phone in his pocket.

"A visitor?" Gage's right hand hung naturally, concealing the slight bulge from the phone.

The guard pointed to the cage-covered clock above the doors. "Yeah, and your twenty minutes started six minutes ago."

His mind still occupied by what had happened with the satellite phone, Gage followed the guard's instructions, walking ahead of him through a series of bright yellow doors. He was made to enter a holding cage and told to back to the bars on the left side with his hands clasped behind him. There his ankles and hands were shackled, quite tightly, before the far door slid open. A voice from the shadows told Gage to walk forward and to sit in the third cubby. When he did, the guard walked behind him and slid a musty curtain over the space. There was a screened hole in the thick glass in the front of the cubby and, on the other side, a gray stool inside of an identical space. Particles of dust settled slowly through the air, lit by the harsh light above the cubby.

One of Navarro's people? Surely not Justina. Not yet.

After a minute of waiting, listening to snippets of muffled conversation from the adjacent prisoners, a light flashed on the other side of the thick glass and in she came. It was, indeed, his Justina, a lone peony in a field of scraggly weeds. For an almost uncontrollable instant, Gage wanted to scream a protestation over his inability to touch her. Instead, he bit his tongue and drank her in, feeling a tremor pass through his body. She was bronzed, wearing the same clothes she'd bought in Tossa de Mar, her hair pulled back in a ponytail. When his moment of agony had passed, Gage forced a smile, watching as Justina's smile faded to concern, then something akin to horror.

"My God, your face," she said, pointing. "And your shoulder, is that dried blood on your shirt?"

"Shhh," Gage whispered, shaking his head. "Not here. Not here."

"But what happened to you?"

"Remember my name?" he asked, arching his eyebrows.

"Gregory Harris."

Winking, he lifted his chin. "I'm going to be fine, okay?"

Justina looked unconvinced, continuing to look at his shoulder.

"And..." he said, drawing it out, "I've told *them* to pull me out."

Justina's green eyes widened. Her lips parted and, though she looked very much the part of someone who wanted to be dissatisfied, glee overcame her as she clasped her hands. "Are you serious?"

"Quite."

"When will that be?"

"I'm not sure, exactly. But I can't do anything about the situation here. My being here is pointless." He decided it best not to inform her of the threats against his life.

"Will you make it until then?" she asked, looking at the blood.

"I went through a little trouble at first, but that's been taken care of. Don't you worry about it, okay?" Wanting desperately to touch the glass, Gage wrestled with his cuffs. "Would you want to go back home, back to where you're from?"

"I'm not leaving here."

He shook his head. "Not now...when I get out."

"I just want to be with you."

"Think about it, okay? Anywhere you want to go."

"Anywhere?"

"Anywhere but here."

They chatted about a number of things, mostly about what she'd been doing with herself, Justina growing more relaxed as the conversation flowed.

She told him all about "Señora", and how they'd spent nearly every evening together.

"Her daughter died and she goes on and on about how I act like her."

"I'm glad you made a friend."

The guard stepped behind Gage, sliding the curtain open. "Two minutes."

"Have you gotten my letters?"

"One. I loved it."

"There should be more on the way. I've written one, two, sometimes three a day."

"I will treasure every word. Now, listen," Gage said, leaning forward and becoming serious. "When you leave here, you make sure you aren't followed, okay? Find a long road that gives you a view for at least a kilometer behind you, and make sure there are no other cars. If there are, you drive as fast as you can, never once stopping, to the police down in Manresa, okay?"

"I remember all that you told me," she said reassuringly. "So what happened to your shoulder?"

Gage dipped his head. "When I arrived, two men tested me."

"And since then?"

"No one has bothered me and I'm certain no one will."

They studied one another for ten more of their precious seconds. Before the guard arrived, Justina said, "Be careful, *Gregory*. I feel like you're not telling me everything."

"I will make it out of here."

Just then, Gage was lifted by his arms, watching as she touched the glass and mouthed her love. The guard jerked Gage's cuffs and led him away.

JUSTINA SAT in the cubby until she was retrieved. She was numb on the walk back to the car. She didn't even check the road when she crossed it, earning a blaring horn from a passing car. As Justina drove away, recovering her senses, she thought about her brief meeting with the man she loved.

Though his reassurances had comforted her a little, she was very much unnerved by his appearance. He'd said he'd gotten into a fight when he arrived, but some of the cuts and bruises on his face were fresh.

And the quantity of blood on his shirt was far too large to have come from a regular fight.

Justina was also unnerved by something else, though she couldn't quite put her finger on it. It was just something she sensed.

She was right to be unnerved.

NAVARRO PUSHED the bedroom door open. On the ocean side of the room, just as they had in the sitting room, the filmy curtains fluttered in with the sea breeze. The bed's inhabitant, a young Barcelonan beauty whose name Navarro had unfortunately forgotten, lay prone and swirled in his Egyptian cotton sheets, her tanned rear end propped up by a pillow underneath her midsection.

"Mmm," she said after hearing the door click. "Who says modeling is the easiest money for a *mujer hermosa?*"

Navarro undid the belt on his robe, allowing it to fall away as he drank in the young lady's splendor, feeling a doleful quiver in the pit of his belly. There was a time, back when ETA was assassinating enemies in the streets—back when Navarro could win a woman like this with nothing more than his looks and charm. But now here he was, old and paunchy and drug-aided, forced to pay ten thousand euro for a few days with a young woman who surely was disgusted by his appearance.

At least her willingness *seemed* genuine, he noted with some measure of satisfaction. She went to all fours, moving to him as he stood at the bed's end while she swept her hair back and went to work on him. He touched her shoulder, rubbing it, feeling the fine, taut skin of her back, briefly wondering if she'd ever even heard of him.

Probably not, he decided, satisfied as the crushed pill went to work, pushing blood into his dear old friend.

The dogs barked outside.

"Calla!" he yelled, irritated at his wolf shepherds' constant barking at any small breeze. It was this house, for whatever reason—they always seemed on edge here.

Suddenly, the hair on Navarro's neck stood on end. Hartline's warning…

No, he reassured himself. *Valentin said it was impossible, as did the aerospace scientist. You're on edge. Relax.*

Navarro took several steadying breaths, coming back to the moment.

The girl…*Pilar! Sí, Pilar*…she pulled back, sweeping her hair to the other side of her neck in a practiced motion.

Modeling, my ass.

Pilar smiled up at him, her lips glistening as she said, "That feel good?"

"Yes, darling," he murmured, pulling her back into position, thinking back to his heady days as an up-and-comer in Barcelona's El Raval, when he was in his early twenties, clipping rival hoods and banging nightly beauties.

Oh, to have it all back.

Underneath his right hand Pilar's back suddenly tensed, showing the striations of muscle as her skin tightened over her ribs. She pulled away. Simultaneously, a piercing scream echoed through the room, making Navarro lose his balance. The erectile dysfunction tab he'd just taken elevated his blood pressure and the sudden shock was a violent spike to his system.

He managed to catch the bed as he tumbled down, striking his rear end on the hard tile floor. The sharp pain from his tailbone breaking was eclipsed by the scene from the doorway he'd entered only moments before. Standing there, propped up by two gloved men, was his trusted friend and *asesor*, Valentin. The entire front of Valentin's clothed body was covered in thick red blood. Though he was dead, his eyes were wide open and his partially severed tongue hung obscenely from his mouth. Behind the threesome, on the white deck, Navarro could see the remains of his wolf shepherds.

The two men shoved Valentin's corpse into the room with a thump as Navarro scrambled to get away. Pilar lurched from the bed, sprinting to the open balcony door as one of the men raised a pistol, his arm elevating mechanically. An arrow of flame burst from the pistol's barrel as Pilar fell forward, striking the doorframe and lying motionless.

"What do you want?" Navarro demanded, his back against the sturdy bedside table, while his right hand climbed the side of the bed as if it were independent of the rest of his body. The men were Leones; he could see their hideous neck tattoos.

One man was brandishing a short shotgun, casually holding it on Navarro, watching as the other shooter moved to Pilar's body. He clucked his tongue, telling the other one that he'd have loved to have screwed her before he killed her.

Their collective laughter could only be described as evil.

Enraged and stunned by their impudence, Navarro could find no suitable words. Instead, he chewed his lower lip to blood, craning his head to the side, viewing Valentin, his old friend. Navarro hated himself for the tears and shudders that had suddenly erupted from his body.

"Señor Navarro, we are here to kill you," the one with the shotgun said. "Eventually."

"How did you find me?" Navarro muttered, his mind currently too jumbled to remember Gage's warnings from an hour before.

The man with the short shotgun said, "We've been waiting here in Cadaques for almost a year."

"You knew where I was for a whole year?"

As the one with the pistol stepped back to Navarro, his thick black utility boots leaving marks with each step on the white floor, the one with the shotgun knelt down. Navarro got a good look at his face. First and foremost was the cruelty of the youthful eyes, like a person who might kill tame dogs for fun. The man was quite ugly, his face round and dominated by heavy jowls, out of place for a man of his lean stature. Below his pronounced widow's peak, which both men claimed, was a scar only a few degrees from vertical, starting at mid-forehead, creating a valley through his nose, over his lips and terminating at his chin.

He lightly rapped the single barrel of the shotgun, a tactical Benelli that Navarro would have once enjoyed shooting, on Navarro's knee and said, "No, Señor Navarro, we only knew you had a home in this *area*. Other duos like us are stationed in other areas in Spain where you are rumored to have homes...homes that you hide in like a scared little *niña*." He motioned to Valentin. "And, before I sliced that piece of shit's tongue, he gave me just about all of the information I needed. Tonight, because of your death, Julio and I will be heroes."

Navarro squeezed his eyes shut and arched his head back to the heavens. This was the end. Seventy-four revolutions around the sun. A poverty-stricken child taken advantage of by a perverted uncle. An anonymous escape into the military, followed by an awakening that revealed the world as a treasure box just waiting to be opened. After he came home and killed his uncle, the pesetas turned to hundreds—turned to thousands—turned to millions. Navarro had spread innumerable pairs of beautiful legs, all while raising a mostly-charming family. Three daughters went their own way before Cesar defied logic as he went his. Then Francesca, his doting wife, had died in a twitching, agonal breathing mess that Navarro had prayed daily he might someday forget. But he'd had an eventual, glorious rebound, followed by many enjoyable years. And now it had to end like this. Why did the ending have to be so awful?

A strange thing occurred, as the sadness and great melancholy was swept out with one blast of wind from the sea that had meant so much to Navarro in his seventy four years. It was a burst of joy, and resolution, over one final challenge. A chance to write a fitting ending to his story. Resigned to his death, recalling a spurt of his impassioned youth, his constitution crackled as he pondered the exclamation point he might place on his denouement.

Because, though he'd grown far too comfortable in his life these past years, he recalled the tour Valentin had given him when the villa was brand new. There was something about two guns, deftly placed underneath the bed, able to be reached with one arm from a sleeping position on either side.

"I placed them myself," Valentin had proudly said on that rainy morning, lifting the heavy bed skirt to show the drop brackets.

The kneeling man had been talking all the while. He smacked Navarro across the face, bringing him back to the present, the challenge now cemented in Navarro's mind. Though it wasn't hard to do, Navarro made himself cry more, truly weeping.

"Ayeee," the standing León said, aiming his Glock 19 at Navarro's torso. "He has no self-respect. Crying like a little bitch."

"Wait," Navarro blubbered, putting his left hand out. "Please wait. I know you must kill me; I'm at peace with it. But, in return for your making it fast and painless, I will tell you where I have a store of cash nearby. You two can keep it for yourselves. It's millions...*millions* in untraceable American dollars."

The one with the shotgun narrowed his eyes and stared coldly at Navarro. "You will tell us whether your death is slow or not. I can see to that, *pinche*."

Navarro lifted his chin. "You can't be sure of that. I've a bad heart and I may die as soon as you begin torturing me. And then, *mi amigo*, all your efforts will have been in vain. Because, I can assure you, you will not find that money on your own."

Again the two Leones exchanged glances. The one with the pistol said something unintelligible, continuing to hold his Glock on Navarro as the one with the shotgun stood to confer.

And that's when Navarro gripped the weapon.

Seasoned by years of shooting, Navarro recognized the shotgun by touch alone. He and Valentin had practiced with this model years earlier, entranced by its compact size and close-range firepower. The shotgun was made by Serbu, its moniker the Super Shorty. Not much larger than a long revolver, it packed a deathly, close-range wallop with its 12-gauge shotgun shell. Navarro said a three-word prayer that Valentin had left the 2+1 shotgun cocked. He jerked it from its banded mooring, hoping the blast would take both men in the process.

But the man with the pistol had never fully let his guard down. He twitched at the sight of movement, falling away from his shotgun-toting partner. As Navarro unleashed a round whose spread would have definitely taken both men down, the man with the pistol fired, catching the elder mobster in the neck.

The very last thing Navarro saw, providing him with a brief moment of satisfaction, was the León with the shotgun flying backward, spun by the ripping lead shot, his silk shirt dotted by flowers of fatal blood.

Ernesto Navarro, longtime don of Los Soldados, slumped down onto the floor of his villa, dying in a matter of seconds.

Chapter Eighteen

Port Hercule, Monaco

THE EARLY evening lights of the tiny principality beckoned Xavier Zambrano as the captain piloted their yacht to its mooring. Xavier enjoyed a cold beer at the bow of the rented yacht, the water below him audible as its gentle swell kissed the bladed centerline. Xavier nodded his thanks at the galley attendant who told him his meal would be ready in fifteen minutes, after which time he would launch into the quartier of Monte Carlo for a night of gambling and debauchery. Glancing to the southwest, seeing the remnants of tangerine light disappearing in the sun's westward race, Xavier was pleased with his decision to get away. The leisurely cruise from Barcelona had taken a full day, around 240 nautical miles according to the yacht's Greek captain. Xavier had slept for more than half of it and now felt as refreshed as he had in weeks.

While not the finest yacht he'd ever rented, the 95-foot Farocean Marine provided him adequate comfort, especially since he was traveling alone. But it was the crew that set this cruise apart. The specialty charter company Xavier used exclusively catered their crew to the renter's tastes; in this instance, they'd sent only the harmless old Greek captain and five beautiful, capable shipmates.

As he stood from the bow's chaise lounge, the attendant returned, carrying Xavier's mobile phone. "This was ringing, señor," she said, allowing her hand to brush his as she handed the phone to him.

Realizing he was now in Monte Carlo's cellular range, he appraised the number, cocking his eyebrow because his lieutenants knew not to disturb him during his one-week vacation. He'd even given Fausto the week off, sending him back to his hometown of Rubi to attend to his dying mother.

The girl, a galley helper and the lowest ranking of the crew, lingered, eyeing him hungrily as she gnawed on her lower lip. "Señor, would you prefer your meal in the dining saloon or the afterdeck?"

Xavier was still staring at his phone before blinking his thoughts away. The girl, probably no more than twenty, was short and voluptuous. Her face wasn't incredibly pretty but her body was built like a tempered five-kilo hammer. Pulling in a sharp breath through his nose, Xavier convinced himself to wait for the evening in Monte Carlo to play out. He still had four days of fun ahead and could bed this one all the way back to Barcelona if the mood struck him.

He moved close, touching her chin as he said, "I'll dine on the afterdeck, my dear. And please see that my dove gray *Dolce y Gabbana* suit is steamed and ready, and along with it my white McQueen shirt and black Gucci points."

"Of course."

"Until later." He sent her on her way.

Xavier watched her go, waiting for her to look back. When she did, he puckered his lips in a kissing motion, satisfied as she covered her smiling mouth with her hands, racing into the galley to brag to the other girls that he'd paid her significant heed.

He hurriedly swigged the rest of his beer, a damn good German pilsner called Licher, and touched the number that had just called him. When lieutenant number two, Vasco, the scarred sixty-year-old in charge of Contratos, answered, Xavier could tell he was out of breath.

"This better be good, Vasco," Xavier warned, eyeing his nails and wondering if he should have them done before taking the launch over to Monte Carlo. Perhaps he could have the voluptuous one do it. *No, because you'll end up taking something from her, and that will ruin some of your motivation tonight in the casinos.*

"Señor, you know I wouldn't bother you if it weren't important," Vasco said, his voice juddering with barely restrained emotion.

"What the hell is wrong with you?" Xavier snapped. "You sound like you just ran wind sprints."

"Nothing is wrong, señor. Nothing! In fact, all is perfect!"

There was something different about this call. Vasco never yelled.

"Perfect, you say?"

"Claro!"

Xavier blinked, unwilling to believe, after all this time, that it might have finally happened. *No…it can't be.*

He gripped the brass rail to steady himself. "Tell me, Vasco…tell me without any preamble."

"El Voltor, señor…he is *gone.*" El Voltor is Catalan for "the buzzard", the code name that had come to represent Navarro.

"Are you certain?"

"Oh…quite, señor. A small amount of collateral damage on our end, but El Voltor, as well as his adjutant, have been brutally dispatched."

Xavier allowed the news to sink in. When he felt steady again, he padded across the teak deck, surprising the feverishly working women as he entered the galley and retrieved another beer, biting off the cap. He stepped back out into the chill early evening, viewing spangled Monte Carlo as his chest swelled from the shatteringly good news.

"Señor?" Vasco asked for the third time.

"I'm here…just basking in it."

"It was the help from *above* that did it, señor."

"Finally…"

"Should I dispatch payment to the yankee jingoist and the acusador?"

"Absolutely. In fact," Xavier said, feeling magnanimous, "pay them an extra ten percent as a bonus."

"Garcia won't like that."

"Piss on Garcia."

"Very good," Vasco chuckled. "A few more items, señor. The one we'd lured in, the baby vulture in Berga, what about—"

"End that with prejudice," Xavier said with a snort, the thought of Cesar Navarro's agonizing death warming him. "And make sure he suffers."

"I know our friend El Toro will enjoy hearing that," Vasco said. "And, I realize I'm getting in the weeds here, but what of the other man, the *gabacho* who El Voltor sent in?"

Xavier laughed openly, arching his neck to the indigo sky. "Tell El Toro to do as he pleases with that one. Our Berga-Bull deserves a chance to have some fun after all this cat and mouse."

"There is one thing…"

"Yeah?"

"He was paid in advance. Word is, it was a very large sum of money."

"Who was?"

"El Voltor paid the American."

"Then just get the money before you kill him."

"You want El Toro to do that?"

"He's not bright enough. Use Angelines, instead."

"The warden?"

"Yes. I've got to go." Xavier thumbed the phone off.

Surveying the sea, Xavier suddenly realized he'd finally, after all the years of trying, reached the summit. Then, relinquishing his self-control as a point of celebration, he strode back into the galley, taking the voluptuous galley helper by the hand and hurriedly escorting her to his stateroom, ejecting the stewardess who was busy steaming his suit. While she, too, was quite comely, he had his mind set on the tight little package who stared at him as if he were the last man on earth.

When they were alone, he destroyed her clothes, ripping them from her body before he took her without preamble.

His boiler had redlined and the excess pressure had to be relieved somehow.

Fifteen minutes later, ignoring the miffed expressions of the rest of the female crew, Xavier, smelling of fresh, wanton sex, dined famously on prawns and seasoned Argentinian steak. He skipped the wine and downed four more of the German beers between his ravenous ingestions of the heavily seasoned food.

That evening, while getting stinking drunk on complimentary Jean-Marc XO over ice, he lost nearly fifty thousand euro at Monte Carlo Casino, eventually passing out alone in the Winston Churchill Diamond Suite at the exclusive Hotel de Paris.

The next morning, despite his gambling losses, saddled with a splitting headache and a room bill of more than 15,000 euro, Xavier couldn't stop smiling. He imbibed a loaded Bloody Mary on the penthouse's sprawling terrace, afterward enjoying a hot oil massage from two lovely Swedes.

And, though he knew he'd be best suited to rush back to Spain and claim all that was his, Xavier decided to remain in Monte Carlo for the weekend—he felt he'd earned it.

WHEN THE following morning and early afternoon came and went with no word from anyone about his release, Gage decided to go ahead and make satellite phone calls to Colonel Hunter, then to the Catalonian acusador, Redon. Pushing the fear from his mind, Gage wouldn't allow himself to consider the possibility that Navarro had been located after their satellite phone call. Because if Navarro had followed Gage's instructions, it was highly unlikely that they could have closed in on him that quickly.

But this useless charade had to end, and end soon.

As Gage walked through the main bay, headed back to his cell to get the satellite phone from its hiding place, he heard a commotion coming from the top terrace. Glancing up, he witnessed a clustered mob in one of the straight areas of the uppermost hexagon. They were shouting and chanting, facing inward to one of the cells. Everyone on the floor of the bay stared up at the scene except for the three guards. They were each at their posts, studiously ignoring the commotion.

Gage stopped before a prisoner he'd spoken to a few times—he was Gage's "neighbor" from two cells down. A Frenchman of approximately Gage's age, he was tall and lean, with tan skin and a tight mat of black hair. With a spare, dour face and dark eye sockets, the Frenchman looked like a tough customer who was terminally bored. Today he stared upward, but without emotion.

"What's going on up there?" Gage asked in Spanish.

The Frenchman placed an unlit cigarette between his lips as he said, "A betrayal."

The mob was almost directly above Gage's cell. As Gage considered the location, he realized the horde was gathered close to Cesar's cell. "What kind of betrayal?"

"Do you know who Cesar Navarro is?"

Gage's head snapped around. "Yes. What's going on?"

The Frenchman glanced around before whispering, "It's Los Leones...they've turned on him."

Oh, no...

At that very moment Gage knew that Ernesto Navarro was dead.

He thought back to the men who'd been here before him, with the mission of protecting Cesar—the men who were all dead. Los Leones had probably tried to locate Navarro through each of them, but somehow they weren't able to close the deal. But yesterday in the yard, as soon as Gage saw those signals being passed, he was certain they were trying to track down the source of the communication.

And after all Navarro's precautions, they'd done it. Somehow, someway, they'd tracked the signal. Gage knew that tracing a satellite phone was no small task. It would take serious coordination, government help—and a great deal of money.

These are no rank amateurs, Gage. You're dealing with an advanced organization.

"Why've they turned on him?" Gage muttered, looking up at the pulsating mob.

"Who knows?" the Frenchman said with palpable disgust. "Los Leones are hyenas."

"Have they killed him?"

"Oh, no," he said, poking out his lip. "He's not dead yet. In my seven months here I've come to know that this is a common practice of theirs."

Hitched his head to where the nearest guard stood. "The pigeons have been paid off. This Leones' *extracción* could go for days."

"Extraction?"

"That's what they call it."

"Why?"

"They're extracting not only his life, but his dignity."

Gage squeezed his eyes shut for a moment as he said, "Are they beating him, or raping him?"

"You know the answer," the Frenchman whispered, shaking his head in disgust as he ambled toward the yard.

Gage stood there and watched the scene for several minutes, allowing his blood to come up. There was no inner war, no deliberation. He already knew how to respond. He focused on the men behind that top terrace's wire mesh. To a man they all wore the mark of Los Leones. They all laughed. They all chanted. Some high-fived, some rubbed their crotches. And while a man, a human being, suffered in that cell, those sons of bitches out on the terrace acted as if they were watching *El Clásico*. So, rather than deliberate, Gage made up his mind but let it burn. After three minutes and forty-two seconds, despite his still-healing back wounds, he balled his fists and stalked across the floor. Not at all nervous, Gage took the first level of steel stairs at a steady jog, as if he was headed to his own cell, ascending with his head down.

As he reached the landing from the first flight of stairs, Gage saw Salvador, standing against the fencing with his fellow Semental, the one on the crutches. Both men stood with an upturned ear, listening to the commotion above them. As Gage turned to the second stairwell, he heard Salvador's urgent protests and running feet. Five steps up, a thin León wearing an eye-patch had been looking upward. Seeing Gage coming, he dropped down one step and put his forearm on Gage's throat to stop him. Gage clamped the man's arm with his left hand, twisting harshly, making the smaller man turn to relieve the pressure. But Gage didn't stop, he wrenched the man's arm upward until he felt the deep and satisfying pop as the punk's shoulder dislocated, yanking the humerus away from the scapula. Still holding the man's left wrist, Gage thrust the man's neck forward with his right arm, hammering him onto the stairs so hard he wondered if he might have killed him. Satisfied the stair guard was out of commission, Gage climbed the stairs.

At the top, on the second terrace, the mob of Leones, which must have consisted of two hundred men, all faced inward, chanting and yelling. The smell of the electrified, inflamed humanity was sickening, angering Gage further by the second. As he spun from the stairs onto the terrace, a young

León turned, eyes going wide as Gage's forehead rushed to his nose. The head-butt was perfect, crushing the gang member's proboscis in a spray of stark blood. The man went down in a heap, holding his nose and squirming about as if he'd just been doused in acid.

Due to the noise and the remainder of the gang staring inward, Gage was able to push his way forward. In ten more seconds he was at Cesar's cell, shoving his way inside, repulsed to see one man violating Cesar while another pleasured himself on the far side of the cell. Aware that he wasn't a León, someone grabbed Gage around the neck, taking a vicious elbow to the face for his efforts. Gage turned, fielding punches from another León while the one he'd elbowed crumbled below him. Grasping the puncher by the sides of his head, Gage pressed inward with his thumbs on the man's eyes, satisfied with the agonized scream in response. That man, too, went down in a pile on top of the unconscious gang member.

As the two downed men temporarily clogged the doorway, Gage thrust a front heel kick to the masturbating prisoner, who was eyeing Gage with temporary shock. When Gage's heel mashed into the man's swollen member and testicles, the man's shriek was so loud in the enclosed space that Gage felt it might have damaged his eardrums.

The rapist, in his own sick world, was still rutting on Cesar. Due to the noise, he had no idea what was happening behind him.

Knowing his own death was near, and resolved to go out in blinding flames, Gage grasped the rapist by the neck, digging his fingernails in as he yanked the surprised man off Cesar's back. As the rapist rolled to the floor, Gage began to kick the man, aiming for his head.

Following a half-minute of kicking, Gage, his body burning from the exertion, ceased his action. The rapist's breathing was ragged, his face bloody and unrecognizable. Gage staggered to the back wall, hearing only Cesar's muffled sobs.

It suddenly occurred to Gage that he hadn't been attacked, and all had gone quiet. Despite the two men who'd clogged the doorway earlier, Gage should have been torn apart by now.

When he turned, Gage saw a León blocking the doorway, the rest of the men standing behind him. The León was about Gage's size, bald, with a thick golden ring between his two nostrils, like that of a bull.

It was the notorious prisoner El Toro.

In his right hand was a curved linoleum knife, glinting from the solitary light of the cell.

Despite the presence of El Toro and his menacing blade, Gage welcomed the brief respite, sucking in air as he surveyed the cell. The masturbator was still on the floor, huddled in the corner of the cell and whimpering, both of his hands cradling the smashed treasures at his midsection. Below Gage, the man whose face he'd pulverized was now laboring to breathe, the maw on his face making wet, sucking sounds like a person sucking the remains of a soda through a straw.

And next to Gage, managing to cover himself with his wool blanket, was Cesar, curled in a small ball on his bunk.

Gage watched as the man with the nose ring and linoleum knife spoke quick Catalan to the mob, using the word "*extraccio*" several times. The mob listened intently and, when he finished speaking, they sullenly evaporated.

El Toro then put on a little show with his hooked knife, moving it back and forth between both hands, twirling it, eyeing Gage the entire time. When he stopped, he aimed the blade at Gage. "You, *meu amic*, are to be commended for your balls of brass."

Gage, still catching his breath, didn't respond.

"I've instructed my men to cease the *extraction* of Cesar." El Toro lifted the knife, pointing it at Gage. "You paid that price for him, which is honorable. But, *gabacho*, you've paid his price with your own life."

Before Gage formulated a response, boots thundered up the stairwell. El Toro, his actions casual, concealed the knife in his uniform, stepping aside and lowering his head but continuing to view Gage from the corner of his eye.

Arriving from three directions, Berga guards in full riot gear converged on the cell. Upon surveying the bloody scene, the center guard rushed in and struck Gage, who made no effort to stop it, on the top of his head.

Gage fell. His last sensation was that of his legs failing him, as the guard and the bars and the lights rushed upward.

Blackness.

WHEN GAGE awoke, he felt the rough cut of the heavy-duty zip ties that hogtied his hands and arms, each movement sawing into his flesh. The ripping pain of his back wounds was outweighed by the pressure on his shoulder joints, making both feel as if they might dislocate at any moment.

Enraging Gage, he heard the casual banter between the guards lugging him around the terrace, carrying him like a fattened pig to a routine slaughter. Though his vision was blurry, he oriented himself, realizing he was still on the top terrace. They were nearing the stairwell all the way across from Cesar's cell, with the open air of the main bay between the stairs and the cell. One of the guards, his voice gravelly, halted the procession.

"*Muéstrale*," he rasped. Gage was able to make out some of the man's Catalan, something about a good place to view it from.

Gage was lifted so that his chest rested on the rail below the chain link fence. His eyes were still blurry from being struck in the head—he blinked, clearing his vision enough to see two men standing across the void in Cesar's cell.

It was the gang leader, El Toro, and he was holding Cesar up. Cesar was still nude and his arms were behind him, as if he were handcuffed. Gage realized the entire bay, for the first time ever during the daytime, was completely silent. El Toro, murmuring something in Cesar's ear, led him outside the cell, showcasing him in the middle of the terrace.

A cheer went up, hushed immediately when El Toro lifted the blade above his head. Then…

The overhead lights glinted off the curved blade of the linoleum knife as it plunged downward.

"No!" Gage shouted, lurching and tugging, trying futilely to free himself from his bonds.

El Toro struck Cesar under his ear, ripping the knife across his upper neck, ear to ear, going back and forth several times, the scraping and cutting and gurgling audible across the expanse. He lowered Cesar's limp body to his knees, holding the dead man up under one armpit.

The main bay was a cacophony of frenzied cheers and catcalls.

In a move that surpassed the sickest of fertile imaginations, El Toro reached into Cesar's ghastly incision, rooting with his hand for a moment. Then, lifting Cesar and using some sort of fashioned hook, he propped Cesar's body outside of his cell, hanging him there as if he were standing. Taking a wet towel from inside the cell, El Toro diligently cleaned the blood from the face and neck area until his ghastly masterpiece was visible for the screaming masses of Berga Prison.

El Toro had pulled Cesar's tongue out through the neck wound. Gravity pulled the complex muscle downward, giving it the unsettling appearance of a necktie.

El Toro stood next to Cesar, admiring his work with a sickening grin on his face. After a moment, he moved to the fence and raised his arms in victory.

The main bay exploded in noise.

Chapter Nineteen

GAGE ESTIMATED that he'd been on the concrete floor for about a day. There wasn't one bit of light seeping through the doorway, which was probably sealed by gaskets on the outside of the heavy metal door. Using his hands, he'd done a methodical probe of every square inch of the square room, finding only a fist sized air vent and a small drain in the center of the floor.

They didn't even provide him with a bucket.

As time had worn on, Gage's head hurt to the point of making him lie down and close his eyes. While he wouldn't describe the state he'd experienced "sleep," whatever it was, and for whatever period of time, had helped alleviate some of the pain, most of which came from the top of his head where the baton had struck. After awakening and sitting up, Gage flexed his right hand, feeling the pain and swelling, idly wondering if he'd cracked a bone on some León's face.

Around the time his internal clock passed twenty-four hours, the door opened, spilling painfully bright light into the cell. When Gage's eyes had somewhat adjusted, a man in cheap slacks and shirtsleeves politely motioned him out. Gage had never seen the man before, noting his holster and Sig pistol. The man waved his hand in front of his face, muttering something in Spanish about Gage's smell before he cuffed Gage and led him through a series of hallways until they reached a private bathroom.

The man rapped on the steel door and said, "You've got twenty minutes. Use the toilet, shave, shower, and comb your hair. All the toiletries you need are in there, and I will inventory them afterward. You'll be on camera so don't be cute."

"Why am I getting a private shower?"

The man eyeballed Gage's build and pulled several pieces of fresh prison clothing from a rack on the far side of the hall. He opened a box and removed a new pair of thong sandals, still held together by a plastic band, speaking as he worked. "You're going in to see Capitana de la Mancha." He clucked his tongue. "She's a fanatic for cleanliness, so I suggest you scrub yourself very well." The man pressed a button on his watch, motioning to the door.

"Twenty minutes. Enjoy it."

AS IF he were a vice president in a Fortune 500 company, awaiting a meeting with the chief executive, Gage was allowed to wait in a pleasant sitting room as Capitana de la Mancha's assistant pecked away at her Lenovo computer. The only two things marking the waiting area as a prison setting were the thick safety glass protecting the assistant, and the armed guard who sat next to her. This was the eighth unique guard Gage had seen thus far. The burly guard sported an M1911 pistol, probably in .45 caliber—not in his holster, but in his hand. There were gun ports in the glass, presumably there in case Gage became enraged and started tearing the Spanish version of People magazine apart.

Ignoring the reading material, Gage leaned his head back against the wall, closing his eyes as he ordered his thoughts. Cesar's ghastly ritual killing had unnerved Gage badly. But with Cesar and, presumably, Ernesto Navarro dead, it was time to pull the curtain down on his entire incarceration. Gage had seen wanton corruption before. It was obvious that Los Leones were running the guards here and, although it sickened his righteous side somewhat, Gage planned to leave and never look back. Oh, sure, he'd probably talk to some people once he got stateside. One of Colonel Hunter's best connections was a friend to both U.S. senators from North Carolina. Perhaps they'd put a little well-timed pressure on the Spanish government.

Regardless, Gage's top priority was exiting Berga. Afterward, he would collect Justina and they would depart Spain as fast as could be arranged.

What a stupid decision this entire stunt was, Gage thought, admonishing himself. *Old Navarro knew what he was doing, Gage, when he tempted you with that pile of money. But you should have known better.*

There was a beep from behind the glass.

"Señor Harris," the assistant said, beaming as she touched her phone earpiece.

Gage stood.

"La Capitana will see you now."

The guard didn't move, just flicked the Colt to Gage's right. When Gage moved to the door, it buzzed and he opened it.

The smell was the first sensation to affect his senses. Perfume: citrusy and pungent. The second was the visual treatment the captain's office had received. While the last room he'd sat in had pleasant mauve paint, padded chairs, a fake plant, and magazines, this office would certainly seem out of place in any prison. With a burnished wood floor, oriental rugs, bookshelves loaded with leather-bound books and several original oil paintings, the inviting room would be more suitable as a chancellor's office at a fine university.

"Just so you know," Capitana de la Mancha said in her nearly unaccented English, her voice surprising him since he couldn't see her, "you're only the third prisoner ever to enter these walls since I took over. You should feel honored."

Gage stood there, unmoving, just inside the door he'd entered through. He heard a tinkling of glass and a spurt of running water, then the footsteps he recalled from his first moments in Berga. De la Mancha burst in from his left, wearing the lab coat, crossing the office to take up a seat behind the massive mahogany desk. Recalling his woodworking apprentice work during his recovery after Crete, Gage appraised the fluting and columning of the desk's finish, and the gorgeous wood itself—he pronounced the desk as hand-carved and probably worth an average year's salary in Spain.

"I didn't build this office," she said, reading his eyes. "It was done by my predecessor, a man with a huge ego who was owed a number of favors." She surveyed the room. "I guess this was one of the favors."

Gage stood motionless.

"Hmmm," de la Mancha mused, her plucked brows tilting as she settled herself into the low-back leather chair, "I'd heard you were a bit taciturn. Please, do sit."

He obeyed, moving forward and sitting in the lone chair set about six feet in front of her desk. He allowed his eyes to wander the walls and ceiling behind her.

"You're no doubt looking for cameras. There are none. No one watches me."

"Good for you."

She reached into her coat, lifting a compact revolver by the trigger guard. "See this?"

Gage narrowed his eyes at the pistol, marking it as a Smith & Wesson 340 series—a concealed-carry pistol. "That's a decent Smith," he said, "but not what I would recommend for you to carry in a prison loaded with animals."

"What's your suggestion?"

"Have a look at the Springfield 1911 compact. It's larger but packs a wallop."

She moved the pistol to her left hand and scribbled a note on a yellow pad, stabbing the paper afterward. "Thank you," she said, moving the pistol back to her right hand.

Gage committed her actions to memory, finding her loose and too relaxed *if* what she said about cameras was true. *Good.*

De la Mancha settled back into her chair. "It's my contention that, in the event you lose your mind and lurch at me, I can shoot you before you reach me." She drummed her left fingers on the left arm of the chair. "So, you'll excuse me if I go ahead and hold the pistol on you, *Gage Hartline.*"

There was no point in appearing surprised at the mention of his name. He shifted in his seat, nodding. "I'm happy you know my real identity, *capitana*, because that saves me a long explanation. Unfortunately, with the murder that occurred yesterday…well, I think it was yesterday but I've been locked in a blackened tomb for some length of time…regardless, my reason for being here in Berga is no longer practical. You see—"

She stopped him by raising her left hand.

"Mister Hartline, you were hired by career mobster Ernesto Navarro to protect his sniveling son from the Spanish criminal syndicate known as Los Leones." She cocked her head. "That's the truth."

Gage inclined his head. "*Capitana*, despite who, or who wasn't, involved, my *official* mission here is under the oversight of the Catalonian, and Spanish, governments and, as I said, is no longer practical. Therefore, it's pointless for me to stay here."

De la Mancha smiled indulgently at him as he spoke, like an acting coach listening to her freshman pupil delivering stilted, yet slightly improved, lines. When Gage finished, she said, "Ernesto Navarro paid off Acusador Cortez Redon to insert you into Berga as an undercover agent." She began explaining about Redon and Navarro, all while holding the Smith casually aimed at his chest. Her final words clapped like thunder:

"You have been thoroughly deceived, Mister Hartline, by the state attorney Navarro thought was his confidant. Redon was taking Navarro's money while also working with Los Leones. They cooked up this entire deception so Los Leones could find Navarro, and kill him. In the process, you were sold out."

As she spoke, Gage fought to keep his vision steady. A whirling occurred in his mind, the type that was once a precursor to his old post-traumatic-stress migraines, the debilitating cripplers that once haunted his every day. And, although he would certainly approach this situation with reason in the hope that this little lady would lower her guard, the sixth sense deep in Gage's organism, the one that had warned him about potential trouble on the isle of Crete, the one that sent him hurtling on a cosmic collision with Nicky Arnaud, and the one that had kept him alive over a dangerous twenty-three year career, told Gage that he'd been bent over and screwed, for lack of a better comparison.

"If that's true," he rasped, "why wouldn't Acusador Redon just tell Los Leones when and where he would be having a meeting with Navarro? Why use such an elaborate setup, instead?"

"You already know the answer, Hartline. Navarro was unconscionably vigilant. My source tells me he never announced where the meetings were, and would send for any and all visitors with his own security people."

Gage pondered what she said—it made sense—but the onset of stress was preventing him from thinking clearly.

Slow down, Gage. The game just changed. Slow down and think.

He turned his thoughts to Capitana de la Mancha. Given her tone and body language, this woman, this warden, wasn't about to let him escape from here. He had a distinct feeling that this prison, her fiefdom, had lined her pockets with Europe's dirtiest money, creating a cinder-block killing machine for Spain's burgeoning gang, a place where many walked in and no one walked out.

Had he been blessed with the luxuries of ample time and freedom, Gage would have loved to do a forensic accounting of de la Mancha's finances—not to mention the banking records of her gangster guards. He shifted slightly in his seat.

"One question, *capitana*, comes to my mind. Don't you fear for your life when working with Los Leones? If you're complicit with them, and being paid as I suspect, why don't they ask you to allow their prisoners to escape or put ridiculous demands on you?"

"There have never been any escapes from Berga, nor will there be."

"And what of the ridiculous demands?"

"Since you jumped ahead with your assumptions, I will, too. As you know, Navarro and his son are no longer threats to Los Leones. I don't like killing, Mister Hartline, I'm not that cold." She paused, resetting her expression. "But these people, all of them, the Navarros *included*, are savages. They'll kill one another whether I'm here or not. And trying to stop them is, as you Americans so eloquently say, like shoveling shit against the tide. It's useless."

Gritting his teeth, Gage said, "So you figure, screw it, I may as well get rich off their blood."

"That's not it."

"Well, what is it?"

"It's either cooperate or die," she said with indignation.

Though her statement didn't exactly make sense to Gage, he moved on, asking, "And what about me, *capitana?*"

"Yes, well, your deal is a bit more tricky, Mister Hartline. And you destroying that León's face yesterday didn't help things, either. You nearly killed another one on the stairs." Clucked her tongue. "You're quite violent."

"I don't cotton to gang rape, *capitana,* though you obviously have no problem with it."

"I had no idea that was happening. When I learned of it, I ordered it stopped but you had already halted it."

"I was too late. Then the guards you sent to stop the rape *allowed* Cesar to be killed."

"I won't argue that."

"Why do you allow it?"

"Los Leones run things here. They did. They do. They will. And had I, or any of the guards, tried to stop the killing of Cesar, it would invite certain death."

"So you can stop a rape, but not a killing?"

She shook her head. "I don't expect you to understand."

"If fear rules your life, then you don't need to be a prison warden," Gage said, disgust dripping from every word.

"Understand this: given my broad powers here at Berga, if I decide to send you back out in that bay, you're dead inside of ten minutes." She tilted her chin up, waiting for him to respond.

Gage was emotionless.

"Rather than do that, I'd like to propose a deal, Mister Hartline."

Gage sucked on his teeth, viewing her paintings.

"Mister Hartline…did you hear me?"

He ignored her.

"I *said* I have a proposition."

"Listen, lady…my proposition is for you to open the doors and let me walk out. Now. Even if Navarro was double-crossed, there is official paperwork on me, filed in the U.S., stating that I was hired by the Spanish government to be placed into Berga as an undercover agent."

She shook her head. "That won't work, for two reasons."

"What reasons?"

"First, if I allow you to make contact with the U.S., it's *me* who will die."

"How will anyone know?"

"Los Leones now have a bounty on you, Mister Hartline. I'm the only person keeping you alive. It was me who had you thrown into that dark cell, thereby protecting you."

"Why?"

"While Los Leones may be vicious, they're not very bright." She gave Gage a tight smile. "They know you were paid a large sum of money. If you can produce that money, I might be able to bargain your life with it."

Given the tenor of the conversation leading up to this point, this demand wasn't at all surprising to Gage. He believed every word. He also believed her choice of words, using "might," was key. She *might* be able to bargain his life.

Yeah, sure.

Once she had the money, he'd be getting a necktie to match Cesar's.

"If I don't agree?" he asked.

"I think you already know the answer to that question, Mister Hartline." She gestured toward the main bay. "I'll send you out to the floor with word that you won't cut a deal. Then I'll come back in here and have a mineral water as I polish a monthly report that goes to the Bureau of Prisons. I may squeeze in a workout on my elliptical and, by that time, my chief of guards will bring me one of the little pink notes I'm so familiar with. It will detail your tragic, and gruesome, death."

Gage pressed his hands over his face and back through his still-damp hair. "That all sounds real tidy, but there's one thing I don't think you're considering, *capitana*, and that's the official state paperwork I was given. Regardless of what I have been paid, my person in the U.S. is going to get suspicious when I don't call on time. We created a system—they will be expecting to hear from me."

"Please, go on."

"When my paperwork is shown to the U.S. State Department, they'll split this place open like a cheap tin can to get me out. And with the U.S. holding those papers, you know what'll happen if you let these animals kill me before I'm released. Your entire flow of money will come to a halt because you'll have CNN, the BBC, and every other news organization crawling all over this place, not to mention the United States State Department. And then, when they crack the corruption—and, believe me, they will—it'll be you who will be in prison, fending off the inmates who want to meet you for all sorts of reasons."

"All true."

Gage stared.

"If it were to play out as you said."

Gage made no response.

"But it won't."

It was a struggle for Gage to make no response.

"Remember when I said there were two reasons your proposition was flawed?"

He arched his brows.

Capitana de la Mancha walked back around her desk and opened the center drawer. When she did, Gage noted the bluing of another handgun in a larger frame and caliber. Filing the desk gun to memory, he watched as she produced a rigid overnight envelope, marked by thin bills of lading dangling and crinkling as she waved it.

Holy shit.

"Mister Hartline, is this the paperwork you thought was filed in the U.S.?" She tossed the heavy envelope to him, the hanging bills of lading fluttering loudly as it spun.

Gage caught it, immediately ripping open the pull tab. Noting the shake of his hands, he tugged the sheaf of papers from the inside, studying his hand-written note on top, running his hand over the back of the paper as he felt the indentations from his own pen.

"Acusador Redon, wily little snake he is, had all outbound shipments tracked and this was pulled for him by someone at the shipping company." She frowned. "He also knows you didn't email or fax these papers because the dirty American on his payroll, some Air Force general, the same one who tracked your satellite phone conversation, used your own country's imperialistic power to monitor all electronic transmissions outbound from Spain to the U.S. Of the millions of communications that occurred in the few days between the two countries, those documents were not part of them."

"Sonofabitch," Gage breathed.

"You're in check, Mister Hartline, and you have only one move available."

Lifting his eyes, Gage thought about his phone conversation with Colonel Hunter, and Justina's knowledge that he was here. So, at the very least, two people knew he was here. He'd need to somehow get to his cell and call as soon as he could get a signal with the—

Breaking his train of thought was his compact satellite phone being wagged across the desk. She'd pulled it from the other pocket of her lab coat. "You're recalling the people who you told you were coming here, and you're thinking of calling them. But it's going to be hard without this," she teased, shaking the phone back and forth.

Staring down at his lap, Gage took steady breaths, allowing the situation, the wretched situation, to sink in. Justina, a Polish national who probably didn't even have a visa, wouldn't be able to create any pressure. And Colonel Hunter, despite his considerable pull, didn't have a clue that Gage was in any distress. For all he knew, Gage was going into this situation long-term. Gage had promised to reach out when he could—but there was no timeframe.

The situation was perilous.

"It's all quite simple, Mister Hartline. Acusador Redon already told Los Leones that you were advanced a million euro. Now, where is the money?"

Fists balled, head down, Gage ground his hands against the other.

"Hey!" she snapped, finally losing her cool. "Look at me when I'm talking to you." He looked up. This time she asked it slowly, her painted lips readable even without the sound. "Gage—Hartline, where—is—the—money?"

"I'd have to make a phone call."

"We'll call for you."

He rubbed his face. "Capitana, if I can produce that money, who is to say I won't be killed upon its delivery?"

She shrugged. "There's no guarantee."

"So, why do it?"

"You want to live, don't you?"

He narrowed his eyes, thinking the situation through. The call he mentioned was a call to Justina, of course. As soon as that call was made, he'd instantly endanger her along with himself. The vivid picture of Cesar's bloody Colombian necktie burst forth in his mind, stark and chilling. Again he thought of Justina, waiting tables for Russian mobsters and now sitting alone in a cabin, loyally waiting for him to return.

A cold dagger of pain pierced him as he hearkened back to that rainy Frankfurt night when Monika was ripped from this earth.

He thought of Monika's smile.

He remembered watching movies on her sofa, the two of them entwined as one.

And now she's gone. Murdered.

Not again.

Not again.

De la Mancha said he had only one move—and she was correct. Gage licked his lips and swallowed a few times to wet his mouth. He shifted in the seat, joining eyes with Capitana de la Mancha. He shook his head once, resolutely, and made his reply loud and clear.

"No."

She tilted her head. "Pardon?"

He repeated himself.

"What do you mean, 'no'?"

Gage crossed his arms, setting his chin, making sure the corners of his mouth ticked upward. "No means no, in English, Spanish and Catalan. I can do it in German, French, Russian, Italian, Portuguese, and probably a few others, but I'd need some time to think on it."

She straightened, the mirth of her face replaced by anger. "You stupid, macho bastard! Do you have any idea what they'll do to you out in that bay?"

"No. I'm thinking about what they'll do to you."

"Idiot!" she snapped. "You hand over that money and pray they spare you."

"Not happening."

"There is no other answer here, Hartline, other than compliance!"

He smirked. "Look at you."

"What?"

Gage nodded knowingly. "You're scared."

"They will torture you for that amount of money, Hartline. It will be worse than anything you could ever dream."

"Tell them to have at it. I'll die before I give up the money. That's my guarantee." He pointed at her, making his grin menacing. "Try me."

There was a lengthy period of silence that made him feel better—for now—about the decision he'd made. When de la Mancha finally spoke, her tone was reasonable.

"I honestly don't think they'll kill you if you pay. Especially if you insist that you sent another copy of this paperwork by...say...courier. Los Leones may be savages, but they don't want to make an enemy of the U.S."

"You're wrong," Gage said. "They will kill me because they know, if they release me, I'm more dangerous to them than the U.S. is. The U.S. will play by the rules to avenge all of this—I won't."

A torrent of emotions flashed through her expressive face, ending with exasperation. "And what if I can broker some sort of deal?"

"Why do you care so much?" Gage asked, narrowing his eyes. "I know you're getting a cut, but is there something more?"

"I'm scared, *cabrón*! I was vulnerable when I took this job and they took advantage of that. Every day of my life, I wonder if I, or my family, will be murdered due to some misstep I've made." Her eyes welled with tears. "And if you don't get them that money..."

She wept.

"So I was right?"

"You have to give up that money," she mumbled, a tissue over her eyes.

Gage didn't respond.

Monte Carlo, Monaco

THE COMPLIMENTARY drink, a Bombay Sapphire gin with a splash of tonic and extra lime, was placed on the subtly-branded casino coaster next to Xavier's right arm. It was daytime on the French Riviera and, despite his presence at the highest minimum Baccarat table, Xavier's time there had already grown boring. He'd had his fill of fine meals and certainly enjoyed his romps with beautiful, store-bought women. He'd gambled away nearly a quarter-of-a-million euro but, especially without that little shit Garcia around, even such a loss wasn't enough to get his blood moving.

Was this how life was going to be now that he'd toppled Navarro? Was it going to be a struggle to find something to get him off?

He already knew he could have damn near any woman he wanted. And killing didn't do it anymore—oh, sure, the occasional murder was a useful tool, but Xavier wasn't a savage.

Sonofabitch, he realized, *I'm done. There's nothing left to conquer.*

"Monsier?" the croupier asked, gesturing to Xavier's cards. Xavier stared at a king and a 3 in this thousand-euro hand.

He nodded.

The bank was showing a jack and a four, meaning a third card was coming for the bank as well.

As the croupier went to the shoe, Xavier could feel his phone vibrating inside his jacket. He ignored it, glancing around the half-empty casino, pondering what to do next. Earlier in the day he'd briefly flirted with changing his yachting plans, thinking of crossing the Ligurian Sea to La Spezia, in Italy. He possessed a few arm's length La Cosa Nostra contacts there and, on his last visit, had secretly bedded the local don's seventeen-year-old daughter. Unquenchable and deliciously curious about the taboo, she'd clawed his chest upon his leaving, vowing to Xavier that he could take her anytime he pleased, even after her papa had pledged her hand.

"A good way to get killed," Xavier whispered to himself, remembering Camilo and the lobster cracker. He glanced down to see a 3, a loser, as the croupier slid the stack of chips away. The phone buzzed again.

"*Joder*," Xavier muttered, retrieving his phone with one hand as he waved his other hand over the table. Once he was beyond the red velvet rope, he glanced at the number, not immediately recognizing it.

"Yeah?"

"Señor, this is El Toro. I was told to call you directly."

"Right," Xavier said, using his curt "don't waste my time" tone of voice with his underling. "I told him to have you call me. Speak."

"Well, señor, it is an honor to finally talk with you after so long," El Toro said with annoying and highly obsequious gravitas.

"Skip the dramatic salutations and just bring me up to speed. I'm quite busy." Xavier winked at a bikini-clad woman who was passing by with her male companion, headed from the pool to the elevators.

"The son is gone, señor."

"Then it's done," Xavier said with finality, his thumb preparing to end the call.

"Please, wait, señor, there's one other thing."

"Hurry," Xavier snapped, focusing on the derriere of a lady who'd just taken a seat at his baccarat table.

"Señor, it's the American, the most recent one who was brought in, the one who we took the signal from."

"Yeah?"

"Señor, under advisement from my superior, we are to make him believe that we're willing to cut a deal with him."

"I heard about this. I want the warden to get the money."

Xavier motioned to the croupier to play the hand without him and ascended the carpeted stairs, looking at the rear pool and the assemblage of hot-tubs arranged in a pattern. There were a number of oiled women sunning themselves and suddenly he didn't feel quite as jaded with his vacation.

"Señor, should we trust her to handle this?"

"She knows what will happen if she screws up."

"Yes, but I have never truly—"

"I already told Vasco this," Xavier said, cutting him off. "Do it my way."

"Of course, señor. It will be done. And it has been good to—"

Xavier clicked the phone off as El Toro was speaking. He headed back to his table, deciding that he would play another hand or two before donning his swim trunks and bathing in the sun.

The sight of the thong bikinis had gotten his blood moving.

Chapter Twenty

THERE HAD only been a brief gap of time since Gage had told Capitana de la Mancha that he would not make a call to retrieve the money. Since then, she'd done a poor job in remaining calm, crossing the room to a wet bar, running water in a tumbler and guzzling it so fast a stream ran down her neck and into her blouse, temporarily marking it with a dark stain. She must not have feared him rushing her because she showed him her back, muttering curses in Catalan.

While her attention was diverted, Gage flirted with the idea of diving for the other handgun, the one in her drawer. Unfortunately, there were too many holes in such a reckless plan and, even if it were loaded and he could spirit it out without getting shot beforehand, how would he get away from Berga? Sure, he might be able to hold Capitana de la Mancha hostage long enough to get a news crew here to hear the truth, but getting from where he was to that point would be prohibitively difficult.

Added to that, he wasn't in the U.S. anymore. While Spain is an advanced and cultured country, he had no idea how their news organizations worked—to them, he'd likely be just another crazed murderer spouting off on fanatical discourses about corruption in the Spanish justice system. Certainly Acusador Redon would arrive on the scene, calmly pronouncing Gage as a lunatic, showing manufactured evidence of his murdering a man in Africa (almost certainly at a time when Gage had no alibi,) condemning the United States and its elitist attitude, and saying this was one Yank that wasn't going to get away.

C'mon, Gage. You'll probably not get this audience again. This may be your only chance. What is her weakness?

As his mind raced, he eyed the phone on the table next to where he sat. A single unit, wafer-flat, it was probably chosen due to its inconspicuous profile. A wired phone, it was nothing more than a one-piece handset with a single switch hook button, gravity-aided when seated on a flat surface, and the keypad between the transmitter and the receiver. Gage eyed the outlet on the floor, sprouting with several plugs and cable jacks like one seen below a conference room table.

De la Mancha's back was still turned.

After another moment, she stalked back to her desk, the pistol trained on him as she remained standing. "I walked away to see if you might make a move. Kudos to you for at least having some sense."

An idea was coming to him.

De la Mancha tapped her telephone. "I don't want to send you back out to the prison population. So, will you please stop fencing with me and get that damned money here?"

"I already gave you my answer."

"Look, I promise to do all I can to protect you *if* you pick up that phone and get the money, now."

"Just send me out to the main bay so we can all get on with it," Gage replied.

Capitana de la Mancha, for the third time, sat behind her desk, collapsing into her chair. She placed the pistol on her blotter and rested her head in her hands. It was the picture of a person in distress. Gage could tell that she'd never have thought that he might turn the deal down. What sane person would, especially after seeing what those animals did to Cesar? And when he did decline the offer, she had no idea how to react.

While her head was down, he leaned over, unclipping the phone cord from the jack.

Her head was still down.

He spirited the phone away, pushing it behind him, making sure the cord was safely under his rear end. Now he had to divert her so she didn't mention the phone again.

De la Mancha lifted her head.

"Send me back out there," Gage said, adjusting his body to cover the phone. "Send me out into the main bay and let's get it over with."

"Will you stop saying that?"

"No."

She threw her head back.

He used the time to tuck the phone into the rear of his pants. That done, Gage decided to propose the idea that had come to him. It wasn't perfect—it would involve his losing all his money—but, in his current situation, his life took priority over money.

"There is one other avenue we might take," he said.

Showing her age despite her mask of makeup, she muttered, "What's that?"

"I'll get you the money."

"I thought you said you wouldn't."

"Listen to what I am saying. I'll get *you* the money." Gage stressed the word "you".

"You'll get *me* the money?"

"Yes, I will. Minus the small amount that's been spent, you can have it all." He lifted his index finger. "But I won't get it for those savages, not one single euro."

It appeared as if switches had been thrown in Capitana de la Mancha's mind. Dozens of minuscule markers immediately sent out external signals to a scrutinizing eye. The rise and fall of her chest quickened. Her left hand clawed the armrest of the chair. Both of her eyes twitched, bouncing a few degrees to the left and right. Her tongue barely pressed through her painted lips, pushing at her right upper canine. Her swallow was evident from the movement of her Adam's apple. She blinked several times. Her feet shuffled. Gage suspected her body had released a rush of scarcely discernible pheromones.

No matter what she's preparing to say, she's intrigued.

"You're mad," she snapped.

Ignoring her, Gage said, "There's about nine-hundred-fifty grand left, in euro, all for you." He leaned forward. "I'm guessing you bring in…oh, I dunno…maybe the equivalent of a hundred grand U.S. here. Maybe a little more. Then, from your dirty money, you probably double your salary, maybe triple it. And that, of course, is tax free. But," he said, sitting back and making his voice grave, "you're in bed with the devil, and you know that. And sooner or later, despite all that you tell yourself about corruption in Spain and Los Leones' wide net of protection over you, someone who matters is going to turn the microscope to Berga Prison." He studied his fingernails, speaking matter-of-factly. "It could be a politician looking to buck the system or just some rich asshole whose relative was killed in your prison.

"You've put a little money back, probably in cash for fear of banking it and getting investigated over its source. And nine-fifty, also in loose, spendable *cash*, sounds mighty good right now. That's well over a million dollars, U.S., and a quick run up to Zurich would allow you to set up a new life elsewhere." He glanced around.

Gage stacked his hands in his lap and continued. "Despite the situation you tell yourself you were thrust into—one which has made you a shitload of money—and all the comforts you've come to know and love, you hate living this existence. Every single day you awaken and wonder, is today the day?" His voice grew quiet as he finished, saying, "The money is yours if you simply let me walk. You've a decision to make."

Capitana de la Mancha's face had clouded over. She stared through slit eyes, her lips parted, no longer making movements of any type.

Gage remained silent.

After about a minute she held a hand to her mouth and cleared her throat. "Do you realize what they would do to me if I participated in your plan?"

"They have to catch you first, Capitana. And they'll eventually eliminate you, whether or not you do this. At the very least, this will take them by surprise and you can be long gone before they know what's happened."

"I really don't think they'll eventually kill me," she said with no confidence whatsoever.

"Really? Go have a look at Cesar Navarro's body at the morgue. And I'd be curious to know how they killed his father. You yourself said they're prehistoric."

"In the way they deal with their enemies."

"And you know what they do to their enemies. Rape and murder. Rape steals a person's soul and murder does away with it."

She averted her eyes, and Gage noticed.

He leaned back, willing his intensity away, softening his voice. "Capitana de la Mancha, at some point you will serve no more purpose to them and, when that day comes, because of all you know, they will kill you."

She sipped her water, abruptly standing and walking to the barred window, staring out. "I need some time to think."

"You can have all the time in the world, capitana. But if you send me back out into that bay, according to you, I'm a dead man."

She turned, briefly gnawing on one of her painted fingernails. "They won't kill you if they think you're cooperating."

"What does that mean?"

"I'll tell them you called several times but your contact wasn't there."

"And who is my contact?"

She walked to her desk, flipping open a file and tapping the sheet. "The girl who came to visit you. That's who has your money, correct?"

"No."

"Whether she does, or not, that's who I will say you called."

"Don't do that," Gage warned.

"Why not?"

"That girl doesn't exist."

"Olga Nemcova?" de la Mancha asked, reading the paper.

"That's not her real name."

"Well, that's the name listed here. And it had to have been on her identification for her to get in."

"It's not her name," Gage said authoritatively. "And they won't find her, either."

"So, that *is* who has the money."

"Doesn't matter. You won't find her or anyone else."

"They have plenty of money, Mister Hartline. Make things too difficult, and it will be easier for them to just kill you."

"If that happens, you won't see any of the money. And..." he said, drawing it out, "Los Leones will blame you. Or, as I've said a dozen times, you let me walk and the cash is all yours."

"You're sure of the amount?" she asked.

Gage nodded.

Capitana de la Mancha paced the room for a full minute. "If I'm even to consider this, I've got to move fast. I won't be able to hold them off very long before they want to question you."

The money suddenly seemed supremely unimportant. "How soon can we leave?" Gage asked.

"I haven't agreed to anything, yet. Until I decide, I'm going to stick you in the *aposento*."

"Aposento?"

"The apartment I told you about. It's used by a few select prisoners for visitation."

"Conjugal?" Gage asked in Spanish, curling his lip.

Ignoring him, she walked behind her desk and lifted her phone, speaking rapid Spanish that he could barely follow. Carefully replacing the receiver, Capitana de la Mancha motioned him away. "Go back out the way you came and follow the guard's instructions."

As Gage left, he thought he heard a stifled sob.

TEN MINUTES later, when she'd stopped crying, Capitana de la Mancha opened the top right door of her handcrafted desk. In the back of the drawer was a directory of Spanish Judicial System phone numbers. Tucked in the center of the directory was a stack of pictures of a boy in various stages of life.

Her son.

She studied each one, kissing the last one before hiding the pictures away and replacing the directory.

Suppressing her nausea, she lifted the phone, summoning a prisoner.

THE SEX was fast and animalistic. He was on top of her, holding her face down and to the side, mashing it, leaning his weight on her as he thrust, his powerful triceps showing all three distinct heads of the long upper arm muscle. When he was unable to climax, he pulled her hair, earning grunts of pain as he twisted her head, making her turn over. Again, as was his habit, he held her down by her head as he worked from behind, cursing her as she began to moan.

He had no idea she was faking.

Her sounds aroused him, bringing him to his climax. El Toro collapsed into the chair behind him and cleaned himself with her underwear.

Capitana de la Mancha didn't move.

"You didn't seem to like that," he eventually grumped, crossing the room and pouring four fingers of straight whiskey.

"I did," she replied, trying to keep her smile from being tepid as she pulled her skirt down. "It was amazing as always, the highlight of my week." She stepped into the bathroom to use the toilet.

He dropped onto the chair again, taking a slug of his whiskey, tightening his lips over his teeth. After the flush he yelled, "So, when do I get my money?"

Capitana de la Mancha froze, staring at herself in the mirror. She watched as her lips moved but only tiny sounds escaped.

"Damn it! Are you deaf?" thundered El Toro's voice off the tile walls.

Lie, damn you, lie!

"He called several times," she managed, satisfied with her casual tone. "His contact wasn't there and he's going to try again tonight. He almost cried when I offered him the deal…that's how happy he was." Mopping beads of makeup-tinged sweat from her forehead, she turned and walked back into her office, making sure her feigned afterglow was evident.

"He's got one hour," El Toro barked. "One hour before he dies." His sweaty face split into a wicked grin. "Then, once I get my money, he dies anyway."

"Do you really have to kill him, Sancho? I know the situation with Cesar goes back many years, but this is just some American who was hired to—"

A raised hand silenced her. He extended his thumb, jabbing it in a pointing motion behind his head. "Just shut up and rub my neck, bitch."

Capitana de la Mancha moved behind the gangster, massaging his rough skin with her fingers, allowing her long nails to occasionally scratch over the tattooed ectodermal tissue. She closed her eyes as she rubbed, repulsed by the sweat-tinged, sour smell that arose from her tormentor.

"Hell yes, I have to kill him," he said. "Even if he hadn't beaten Gio, even if he brings me a dozen roses along with the money and sucks me off three times, yes, I still have to kill him. Rub harder, bitch," he grunted before loudly slurping his whiskey.

De la Mancha cursed the situation under her breath.

"Who is he anyway?"

"What?"

"This is twice I've had to repeat myself," he warned. "Who the hell is the American? You said you were pulling information from his prints."

"Oh, that," Capitana de la Mancha said, again trying to sound blasé. "His real name is Hartline—just a small-time, bodyguard type."

"That's it?"

"That's it."

"And *you* met with him in here?"

"Yes."

"In your office?"

"Yes."

"Just you two…no one else?"

"No one else," she said in an audible exhalation.

"He's a pretty big hombre."

She kept rubbing.

"Did you ever once even think about fucking him?"

"Sancho, don't—"

"No more calling me Sancho. And answer the question!"

"No, I didn't."

He tilted his head. "Don't lie to me."

"I'm not lying to you."

"Don't do it!" he bellowed, lifting his clenched fist as if in warning.

"Okay, Sancho, if you insist…if you're going to force me to go down that road, then I did fantasize about him. He's attractive, okay? He's attractive and I wondered, for one quick second, what it would be like to be with him. There, I admitted it. Satisfied?"

His body vibrated as he chuckled in a smug manner, muttering chauvinistic insults. "So, speaking of you and your nasty little habits, exactly how many men have you been with, capitana?"

Gritting her teeth, de la Mancha rubbed her face with her free hand. She hated when he took a turn to the perverse. It meant only one thing: degrading her as he again grew aroused, only to be followed by another symbolic rape episode, the next one almost certainly more violent.

"Sixteen."

"Sixteen, my ass!" he snarled, laughing in a malevolent manner. "You're so full of shit. What are you now, forty-four? Your box has got more miles on it than an old city bus. I bet you screwed sixteen guys when you *were* sixteen. Now tell me the damned truth."

"That is the damned truth," she snapped. "Three between the time I was nineteen and twenty-one. Only one, my husband, until I was thirty-three, and the rest since then, the last one being you."

"Right there," he groaned, hitching his thumb again. "Yeah. Dig into that knot. That's it, right there." When she'd rubbed the knot out, he lifted the heavy tumbler to his shoulder. "Go refill my glass, bitch. Fill it up."

As she poured, he asked, "Who did he call?"

"What?"

"That's three times!"

"Sorry."

"*Who*," he emphasized, "did Hartline call on the phone?"

"I was listening, but they didn't answer. He claims he was calling a woman."

El Toro nodded. "Yeah, that'd be the one who visited him. Your guard Consuelos said she sounded Russian, or something. Said she was gorgeous, a premium *pedazo de culo*."

"Great," de la Mancha said without enthusiasm.

"What's her name?"

Why is he asking all these questions? "She signed in as Olga Nemcova," de la Mancha answered mildly.

"How did she get here?"

211

Capitana de la Mancha stood to his side, handing him the brimming tumbler. "We don't know. The lot was full and she came from the overflow across the road. There are no cameras there."

"Did you get the number he called?"

"No. I don't have that capability on my phone."

He glared up at her, curling his lip. "You're a completely useless twat, you know that?"

Unable to hold back, and without any venom, she politely said, "Please don't call me that. I hate words like that."

Whiskey sloshed as he stood. She saw it coming, letting it happen. If she didn't, the resulting beating would be worse.

El Toro slapped her so hard across the face that she fell and slid all the way to the sitting area on her side. He moved above her, shouting Catalan curses before spitting on her. Then, just as she'd known he would, he pushed his pants down, displaying his excitement. El Toro mounted her on the floor, biting her neck as he began their forced union. Bearing the humiliation in silence, Capitana de la Mancha wondered if she'd broken her wrist in the fall.

Fortunately, as she knew from at least three previous episodes, violence inflamed Sancho "El Toro" Molina. This would be the last episode of the day and, if it played out as it had since he'd taken the top spot at Berga, probably the last time for a few weeks.

Her palms flat on the floor, accepting the violation that was occurring to her body, and despite the pain in her face and her wrist, Capitana de la Mancha closed her eyes and thought of where she might go and who she might become.

Who am I? Why am I here? What have I done with the pretty and demure girl who graduated con honores grandes, *full of promise and with a resolution to affect change through dogged determination and a career in criminal justice?*

From there to here, face down on a cold floor, taking it like an alley cat in heat.

Capitana Angelines de la Mancha, for the first time in years, despite what she was currently enduring, felt the energy of renewal.

When he was done, El Toro stood and strutted across the office. He filled another tumbler, shooting at least four shots of whiskey in one gulp.

"You gonna cry now?" he asked with a sneer.

She lay still, not looking at him.

"Where's Hartline?"

She twitched. Then, lying there and still not facing him, she said, "In *el aposento*."

"I want to see him."

She turned her head. "No."

"What did you say?"

"You heard me. After what I put up with, you can at least give me a day to get his money. And Vasco told me it's my responsibility anyway. If you go in there alone, none of us will get a single euro because you'll end up killing him, and Vasco will relay that to Xavier." Doing something she rarely did, she eyed El Toro. "Vasco said that *no one* better foul this up."

By his hesitation, she knew she'd trumped him. El Toro feared no one in Berga, but he knew what Xavier was capable of.

El Toro eventually smiled, his gold teeth glittering as he said, "You just want time to screw him, don't you, bitch?"

"Give me until tomorrow."

El Toro studied de la Mancha with narrowed eyes. "Send for me tomorrow morning at nine, and not a second later. When you do, you'd better be telling me that money is on its way here." He pointed a finger in the direction of *el aposento*. "Or Señor Hartline will get what Cesar got."

El Toro left.

Alone, Angelines de la Mancha lay on the cool hardwoods.

She didn't move for a half-hour.

Chapter Twenty-One

THE "APOSENTO," as Capitana de la Mancha had termed it, was nothing special but certainly a far cry from Gage's prison cell. Painted exclusively in buff, a bland color common to government buildings the world over, it seemed to have once been a single room. Gage estimated the dimensions of the entire unit as twenty-five feet by ten. A wall with a drape-covered pass-thru had been installed in the center, cutting the large room into two. The first room had a small stove, a miniature refrigerator, and a tweed couch with disgusting flaky whitish stains all over its cushions, like sugar crust from a glazed donut. Relics from all the conjugal visits. There was a throw rug and, behind a bolted-on piece of safety glass, an old television.

The pull drape revealed a bedroom with a twin bed, a nightstand and a toilet in a corner. Fortunately the bed had clean sheets and there was an extra sheet on the nightstand, presumably to cover the ejaculate-infused couch.

Gage studied the toilet for a moment. It wasn't the type in the cells, gravity-fed, built into the floor, similar to what one would find in a sports stadium. This was a standard European toilet, like one might find in a home, with a reservoir that was bolted down and held by a clamp. He passed back into the sitting area, using the spare sheet to triple-cover a spot on the sofa. Reasoning to himself that he'd sat, and slept, in far filthier environments, Gage perched on the edge of the sofa and studied the kitchenette. He eyed the stove, briefly remembering the natural gas explosion he'd once created outside of Metz, France.

That's got to be nearly a thousand kilometers from here, he mused. *I did that back when I was a prisoner to grief, but free. Now I'm no longer grieving, but I'm imprisoned.*

He pictured Monika, recalling the blackness of her death, shaking the image away with a wobble of his head. Then his mind created a vision of Justina, in bed next to him, viewing him as if he were the only male on earth, moving her hands through his hair, drinking him in, touching him, loving him.

Though he'd told the captain he wouldn't reveal Justina even if tortured, Gage knew enough about torture to know that every man has a limit.

So, don't let it come to that.

214

Gage refocused his efforts. Unfortunately the stove was electric, small and chintzy. He turned his eyes to the refrigerator. It was about three-and-a-half-feet tall, not unlike the type found in an office or a college dorm room, quietly humming as it impotently cooled a few presumably empty cubic feet of air inside itself. He bounced several times on the couch, listening for the squeak of springs. After a glance through the drape to the bed and nightstand, his eyes drifted up to the overhead light, which was nothing more than a single bulb, the glass fixture having been removed. His gaze rotated through the unit and...

There! Right there in the corner above the door, black and with a plano-convex lens for fisheye viewing, only about the size of a Sharpie pen's tip, was the security camera's aperture. There would certainly be another one in the bedroom.

But did you spring for night viewing, Capitana de la Mancha? Did you pay the big bucks, or did you spend that on one of those paintings in the office you claim you didn't decorate?

Sliding backward on the disgusting sofa, he furtively pulled the phone from behind him, using his right hand to push it, cord and all, down into the cushions.

That done, his eyes drifted left, to the outer wall. He'd knocked on it on his way in. It wasn't brick or mortar—probably laid in sheets of some sort of hardboard. The camera was on that wall, as was electricity, marked by the wall outlet. Next to the electrical outlet was a rectangle, the same size, covered in a steel plate. Gage focused on the plate, seeing dual holes—like eyes—on the screws. The screws were spanner-drilled, meaning whoever installed the plate didn't want tampering.

Fighting to keep from smiling, Gage felt almost certain the plate covered an old phone jack. And, if so, was the jack live?

"We're going to find out," Gage whispered inaudibly, hoping.

Eyes moving back to the kitchenette, and back to the overhead light, he licked his lips, suppressing his excitement over the tiny chance that had bloomed on this dreary prison day.

CAPITANA ANGELINES de la Mancha emerged from the blistering hot shower, turning on the exhaust fan and using her hair dryer to blow the condensation from the full-length mirror. As the chill air of the office swept into the bathroom, she studied herself in the mirror, fighting to view her familiar features objectively. This time she wanted a cold appraisal.

Her face, minus the arguable benefit of her trademark caked-on makeup, still held its shape for the most part. Sunspots dotted her temples and forehead. Tiny random bumps, pigment-free moles according to the dermatologist, had grown in a few areas of her face. The spots and bumps were easily taken care of with makeup, but the crow's feet and the slight wattle of loose skin under her chin couldn't be readily concealed. She bared her teeth, one of her best features along with her full lips, satisfied with their bleach-aided whiteness and straight, square appearance.

De la Mancha took a few steps back, feeling gooseflesh as the powerful exhaust fan ushered in more cold air. Squinting her eyes at her reflection, pretending she was a man viewing her form on a beach from a distance, she knew she could pass for thirty at a quick glance. She'd birthed her son, Jordi—her secret son—thirteen years before and had worked hard to regain her form afterward, especially on the loose skin that gathered below her navel. Being hyper-conscious about her body, she'd chosen not to nurse Jordi and, ever since she'd given him up to her mother, she'd spent at least ten hours per week in exercise to combat and slow the inescapable aging process.

With a trim stomach and a decent set of medium-sized breasts, she admitted to herself that she'd done a nice job with her fitness. But, despite all the hard work, a slight gathering of extra flesh had grown just below her waistline, on her hips, a shadow of the wideness her mother had carried nearly her entire adult life. Despite that small flaw, she possessed a killer set of legs and even her feet and painted toes seemed cute and dainty.

The grin that had grown quickly dissolved as she had one final place to view. Desiring to get it over with quickly, Angelines de la Mancha turned, looking over her right shoulder at the ass she'd grown to despise.

If polled, there would be hardly a man on earth who found her rear end as grotesque as she. In fact, though she'd never admit it to herself, most men would find it quite desirable. It looked perfectly at home on a fit woman of her age. Nevertheless, she loathed her backside, wearing uncomfortable body shapers and tights under her outfits to help improve her shape. Her butt was trim and without cellulite or deformity but, to Angelines, it now had one very fatal flaw. Since she'd turned forty, her ass had begun a faster-than-wanted trip southward. In other words, it sagged. Not a great deal but, despite all her running and time spent sweating on the elliptical, her ass had not gotten the "stay in shape" memo.

She whirled back around and, using her thumbs, gently tugged backward on her temples. The crow's feet disappeared.

Bringing her thumbs downward, she touched her neck, lightly pulling under her ears, watching as the gentle wattle became youthfully taut under her chin.

Taking a steadying breath and turning, Angelines touched her dimples of Venus with her oh-so-helpful thumbs, briefly closing her eyes and pretending she was again 28. Then, with some pressure and a tug, she watched as her butt gloriously levitated to the one she once knew and loved.

After staring at it for a full minute, she donned her robe, lit an ultra-light cigarette and walked into her office, dropping a few rough cubes of ice into a highball glass and pouring mineral water in, hearing the crack of the protesting ice.

"Nearly one million euro," she said aloud, thinking about what Gage Hartline had said about Zurich. Sitting on the leather sofa, she flipped the cover over on her iPad and made sure she was on her cellular connection and not Berga's WiFi. She typed in a quick search about the world's best, and most affordable, plastic surgeons.

Singapore was mentioned often.

After reading a few top-search entries on the high quality of available Singaporean plastic surgery, she reclined on the sofa, a wistful smile on her face as she searched the nearby countries. There were a bevy of affordable homes for rent in Indonesia, and the pictures were captivating.

A year with her mother and son, mending fences and washing the sludge of Berga Prison from her mind.

She dropped the iPad on the sofa beside her, pointing her toes and stretching, groaning from the pain. Angelines' groin area ached from earlier—not because El Toro, sicko, was well-endowed. Not in the least. The pain was from the beginning of their copulation, before her body was able to provide its own natural lubrication, when he'd jabbed her with his fingers and his pint-sized organ. She blew smoke upward in a lacey stream, telling herself that, along with plastic surgery, she'd get some psychiatric help to blow away (or at least hide) her hellish prison memories.

Setting aside the sexual abuse she'd endured, she recalled the scornful expression Gage Hartline had worn when she'd justified the killings that had occurred under her watch. She'd always told herself (especially after enduring one of her frequent nightmares) that the men she'd allowed to be killed were dead anyway. They were in Berga Prison, the definition of hell on earth, for life with hardly any chance at parole. Yes, often their end was fraught with suffering but, wouldn't a person be better off with a few moments of pain followed by death over a lifetime spent in misery, also followed by death?

Sipping the bracing mineral water, she closed her eyes again, resetting her thoughts and making a mental note to line up the psychiatric help first— even before the butt lift.

So, getting the money from Hartline was priority one. Added to her savings and the cash she'd squirreled away, she would have well in excess of a million euro. Then, as quickly as possible, she'd have to collect her mother and son and go to ground. They would need new identifications, disguises, and rail transport out of Spain.

"Assume Los Leones will find out within hours," she whispered to herself, her voice quavering. "Just accept it and understand what you're up against."

Because when El Toro figured out that she'd escaped, he would immediately tell Xavier Zambrano. And, if Xavier caught her, a well-compensated trustee, double-crossing Los Leones, her end, and that of her family, would be beyond her darkest fears.

"Unless El Toro is dead," she whispered, a smile relieving the lines of stress on her face.

A final drag and a swill of her drink. It was time to put herself back together, to forget about the "rape," and to go home for the evening. Assuming she could make all the arrangements this evening, she could awaken early, with the dark, for a long run in the Aviàn forest. It would be the very first physical step in the cleansing after the disgusting liaison with El Toro—and to prepare for what it was she had to do on the morrow.

In the bathroom, Angelines lifted the hair dryer but paused. She slumped forward, dropping the hair dryer onto the counter as she supported herself with her arms. The hair dryer switched on in its tumble, running loudly and twirling back and forth like an untended garden hose on full blast.

Though hurtful pieces of her life would occasionally strike her like cosmic debris hitting a hurtling spacecraft, this time, at this very moment, the thudding realization of what she'd become crashed down on her with the weight of the prison itself.

"I'm their whore," she rasped, her voice well under the sound of the hair dryer.

Unable to hold herself up, she crumbled to the floor, curling up on the shaggy throw rug, shaking in her sobs.

"I've got to get out," she whispered through the tears. "I've got to get out."

SITTING THERE on the coverlet, eyes closed, his hands laced behind his head, Gage prayed the lights would soon go out. With no watch, no clock, and no windows, he could only guess at the time. He had plans, lots of them, but had no idea what direction they might take. Tonight he would be drawing on several arcane blocks of military training, melding them with his own creativity, imagining contingencies, dreaming up scenarios, and numbly hoping for an opportunity or two.

Finally, there was a loud electrical click, like a breaker tripping. Then darkness.

Gage went to work.

He moved into the bedroom, stretching as if he were preparing for bed. After stripping off his shirt, he climbed under the seemingly clean wool blanket and leaned over, switching off the lamp, an item he was surprised to find in the apartment. He was certain, before a person was allowed to leave the apartment, that the guards would probably inventory the apartment's items—the power cords being first on the list. Once in bed with the lamp switched off, chancing the fact that he could no longer be seen, he emerged from the bed, padding to a spot next to the main door where he touched the metal cover over the outlet. The only illumination in the entire room was a strip of light coming under the door from the hallway. There, licking his lips, he waited for his eyes to adjust, wondering if the sliver of hallway light would be enough to work by. While he waited, he made his way to the sofa, removing the phone. Then he flipped the sofa over and went to work on the springs.

At least an hour later, when he'd finally torn three springs from the underside of the sofa, Gage moved back to the front wall, trying to decide if he had enough light to proceed. The light from the gap under the door—it was nearly an inch—was sufficient, allowing him to see the wall plate and the two dark dots on each spanner-screw. Using one of the springs, he slowly and steadily picked at the top screw, trying to be quiet even though he'd found no evidence of a resident microphone. After ten minutes he flirted with the idea of burrowing into the hardboard wall but, following a few more tries, he managed to get the first screw moving. Once he'd turned it one revolution, he was able to remove the screw by hand and followed it by removing the next one in a third of the time.

Screws in his pocket, Gage opened the socket, feeling inside, well aware that, in the event the socket was electric, he could get zapped by the European standard 220 volts. There was a coiled wire inside, too thin to be electrical. He tugged the wire out, finding a great deal of slack in the wall. Holding the wire beside the light of the door gap, Gage was happy to see the familiar old D-station wire like he'd trained on years before. Using the sharp point of the spring, he ripped at the rubber coating at the wire's end, finding the universal colors of black, yellow, red, and green.

Phones typically use 48 volts, twice that when ringing, but not a lot of amperage. Gage knew this as he stripped the wires away from the coating, taking what seemed forever to strip the thin wires with his smallest spring. That eventually done, Gage went back to the sofa, reaching into the filth behind the cushions and spiriting away his stolen phone. He'd found a semi-sharp edge on the back of the refrigerator. He gripped the phone's springy cord on both sides, sawing back and forth until the cord separated. Then, repeating what he'd done with the wall cord, but this time using his teeth on all four, Gage stripped the wires and, in the scant light, set about matching the colors and twisting the wires together.

With no electrical tape, he had to bend the four wires out, so they wouldn't touch one another. After making each of the unions fast, Gage took a breath as he prepared to twist the red wire together. This was the hot wire and, as deflating as the prospect was, Gage was afraid the phone wire might be dead and this entire project completely futile.

He touched the wires together. There was no spark. No light from the phone. Nothing.

"Damn it," he mouthed, twisting the two copper leads together and carefully lifting the phone to his ear. It was dead.

Gage leaned against the outer wall, his head pressing backward as he closed his eyes, a tiny piece of him reasoning that he might as well just get some sleep.

A sound jolted him.

It came from just outside the door. Gage opened his eyes and looked at the strip of light, seeing two dark patches in the long strip. He heard metal jingling.

Keys.

Shit!

He looked at the phone wire, seeing that the green wire had actually come undone when he'd lifted the phone. Unable to worry over that, he jerked the three other splicings apart, coiling the wire and stuffing it in the jack housing.

The key scraped at the door, sliding into the lock.

There was no time to cover the housing. Gage grabbed his three springs, his phone, and the outlet cover.

The lock turned, the sliding bolt sounding like trains uncoupling to Gage's highly attuned ears.

He leapt from his spot, lurching through the space, diving into the bed and scattering his items under the chintzy wool blanket, sprawling the way people do once they're well asleep.

His closed eyes were aware of the antiseptic hallway light spilling into the room. Footsteps, slow and steady, thudded across the floor. They didn't sound like sandals. Gage wondered if the drape between the two rooms was swaying.

And please, don't look at the open wall outlet.

The steps stopped in the bedroom, by the bed.

"Bé, bé, aquí està el senyor important," came the deep, raspy voice, speaking Catalan. Gage felt something prod the bed. Feigning sleep, he turned, shielding his eyes.

Standing there above him was a guard Gage recognized by silhouette—the one Gage called "Weeble Wobble" because of his pear shape. He usually worked nights, dragging his baton along the bars to awaken the inmates as he prowled. Short and quite portly about the midsection, the guard's belly strained his uniform shirt, making Gage briefly wonder if the thread on his buttons had ever been reinforced. Though the guard's wide face was cast in heavy shadows, Gage could feel a malevolent air coming from the man.

"Habla Espanol?" Gage asked. "Yo no hablo càtalan."

"Sí, sí, Espanol," the guard chuckled, switching to Spanish. "You're a very important man, Señor Harris. I was told by my night commander not to bother you by orders of la capitana."

Gage didn't like where this was headed.

"Have you anything to say?" the guard asked.

"Just trying to sleep," Gage said, making his voice slack in a poor acting job.

"Good, good," the guard said. "My friend, El Toro, told me to tell you to sleep well, important man. He said you will have something for him tomorrow morning by nine. And nine will come soon. So, roll over now, *puta*, and go back to sleep."

Gage stared at the man.

"Roll over," the guard said, an edge in his voice.

Reluctantly, Gage rolled over. The guard's feet scraped once, making Gage hope he was taking his leave.

And please, mister, don't look at that wall outlet because I—

His thoughts were cut short by the brief slicing of air. And, in that fraction of a second, Gage's experienced ears knew exactly what was coming. The sound was made by the baton. The ripping air was loud enough, and of enough duration, that Gage knew the guard had taken a mighty swat, not unlike a clean-up hitter swinging for the fences. Still, in that tedious fraction of a second, Gage ruefully wondered where the guard was aiming. If it was a head strike, it might be fatal. A body blow would certainly break ribs. He thought about the wounds on his back and shoulder, knowing such a blow would rip them—

The baton thudded home, making Gage growl in pain.

But he remained mostly still.

Let it burn, Gage. Let it burn. Take it as further tax for this foolhardy job you accepted.

Footsteps shuffling idly away, and whistling, followed by, "Sleep well, princess." The door slammed, the bolt shot, and Gage was left with a searing kidney.

And relief.

Chapter Twenty-Two

A LAKE breeze whispered through the evergreens, bringing with it the smells of the lake's sulfury water mingled with the fragrant scent of the hillside Aleppo pines. Crickets chirped at a near-deafening volume but, at the same time, the sound didn't seem too loud or out of place. It was the chorus of summertime in the country.

Justina was quite full, having enjoyed a sumptuous meal of salad, shrimp, fresh vegetables, and rice, at Señora Moreno's cozy home. Señora Moreno had sautéed nearly everything in heavy enamel cookware. The food had been liberally spiced and, though the extreme amount of spices Justina had seen go into the dishes worried her, the dinner wound up being delicious. In fact, though they'd spent nearly every evening together, it was Señora Moreno's finest culinary creation to date.

And that was saying something.

Justina's cabin was only a kilometer from Señora Moreno's. *Oh, how good would a cigarette taste right now*, she thought, her feet scraping along the gravel road. *No. I told him I would quit. I haven't broken down once. Each day without a cigarette is a victory. To yield now would only invite the habit back.*

She recalled her final night with Gage, and the way he'd squeezed her so tightly. She'd hardly been able to breathe but, at the same time, it had been heaven. The mere thought of Gage's pleasant presence provided a stab of melancholy to Justina's stroll, making her realize how intense her short time with him had been. She touched her stomach through her thin top, remembering his powerful hands, marked by their rough skin, and how he would hold her to him as he slept, their bodies entwined but providing complete comfort for slumber.

Tears arrived like uninvited guests. She wiped her face, glumly kicking at stones, coming around the bend to see the sparse indoor lights of her cabin ahead. She'd forgotten to leave the porch light on. Moments later, when she arrived on the darkened porch, she briefly wished she'd not left the comfy confines of Señora Moreno's home. For the past two hours they'd done nothing but talk. They talked about life. About their families. And after hearing much more about Señora Moreno's late daughter, they talked about Gage. And talking about it, in someone else's presence, had made Justina feel almost as if Gage had been there, living the story with her.

But now, all that awaited her was the cold loneliness of the cabin. The quiet bed. The lifeless kitchen. She thought back to her life in Lloret, living in a filthy bay with a host of other women. But even there, though she'd hated it at the time, at least she'd had companionship, grating as it often was.

"Be inside, Gage," she whispered, pushing the glinting silver key into the lock. "Surprise me and be inside, ready to hug me and shower me with kisses."

A turn of the key.

A click of the knob.

The smells of her new life.

She'd left a few lights on in the bedroom, casting amber light into the sitting room.

The cabin was deathly silent.

Justina was all alone.

Surprising even herself, she screamed out his name.

GAGE DID ultimately vomit, twice, turning on the lamp to inspect the vomitus for blood. Though he didn't want to, he made himself urinate, wincing from the pain. Again, no blood. He knew, however, that a kidney strike like the one he'd taken could take hours, or days even, to show itself in the form of an infection.

Again playing for the cameras, Gage staggered back to his bed, imagining the guard watching him on closed circuit, laughing with his buddies. *Fat little prick.* Gage pulled the blanket up and switched off the lamp. He waited five minutes before painfully creeping back to the outlet, phone in hand, back to the strip of light.

This time, despite the biting of stiff copper wires into his flesh, he twisted each one tightly, checking to make sure all were secure enough to remain fast in a tug. Lifting the telephone, Gage tapped the switch hook three times and held the phone to his ear.

Dial tone!

After murmuring a litany of thanks, Gage squeezed his eyes shut, recalling the numbers to the prepaid wireless phone he and Justina purchased on his last full day. A few numbers into the dialing sequence he heard something that sounded like a fast busy signal. *Slow down, Gage.* He hung up then pressed nine, listening as the dial tone blipped before it went back to normal. He dialed the number again, waiting…waiting, finally hearing a low, steady buzz that represented the Spanish phone line's connection. After two rings he smacked the floor when an automated message answered, telling him in computer-generated español that the number he'd dialed was long distance and could he please try the number again. He did, hoping the prison's phone system would accept the long distance call. It didn't, and this time he received a different message.

Thankful that he'd memorized the toll-free access number, he dialed it followed by his calling card number. Gage listened, punching his leg when the nice woman informed him that he had only two minutes remaining and asked if he would he like to purchase more time.

No! No! No! That's why you never wait to recharge your calling card, Gage. Damn it!

Gage had memorized a host of numbers, but he'd never memorized the damned number to his own low-limit Visa card and now here he was, with two measly minutes to get his point across.

He pressed "1" to put the call through, listening to the ringing, listening…listening…voice mail. "Are you frigging kidding me?" he mouthed. He repeated the process again, getting voice mail after going through the maddening series of numbers. A third time, same result.

His lower back throbbing, his mouth parched, Gage stood in the dark room, wanting to yell. Instead, he stretched. Stretched his neck. Stretched his back—*pain*. Put each hand, one at a time, between his shoulder blades and tugged on his elbows to give his triceps a good stretch. Stretched his quads and, leaning against the wall, his calves. Feeling about one percent better, he squatted to his makeshift phone, almost laughing at the impotency of having a phone in jail but no way to use it.

For the third time he dialed the numbers, fighting the urge to break something when the operator told him he had only one minute remaining. He'd burned up the other minute listening, each time, to the blasted voice mail message.

Shit.

Hoping the AT&T computer kept track of minute fractions he stabbed the number "1," steadying himself as he prepared for the voice mail.

But this time, to his gleeful surprise, a groggy Justina answered.

Gage spoke at machine-gun pace. "Justina, listen to me and don't talk. We have one-minute, and that's it. First, no matter what happens, don't call this number. Don't call it and don't speak to anyone other than who I tell you to, okay?"

"Gage, what in the world are you—"

"Justina!" he barked. "I'm sorry to be short but there's no time. Listen, the man in the government—Acusador Redon, from Barcelona—double-crossed me. I need you to go to the American Consulate General there and tell them *everything*, Justina. Tell them everything you know and tell them I'm being held ransom here, okay? Tell them to call Colonel Hunter, too."

"What? You mean you're not coming home in the next few—"

"Just tell me what I said!"

"Acusador Redon in Barcelona double-crossed you.   Go to the American Consulate and tell them everything. Call Colonel Hunter, too."

"Leave now. Get rid of this phone, too, because I don't want anyone tracking you. Leave now and find someplace safe and hole up until morning, but get away from that cabin and go tomorrow, as quickly as you can."

"Okay, Gage," she answered, voice trembling.

"Also, Justina, make sure you leave the remaining money in the cabin with one of my pistols. Take a little to Barcelona, just what you need, but—"

The line clicked, followed by the friendly AT&T computer operator informing Gage that, if he wanted to continue, he would need to pay the piper.

Flattening himself on the cold concrete floor, Gage lay there, staring up into the darkness. Then, futilely, he tried to make a collect call to Justina. The operator, a nice enough lady, came back and gently told him that doing such a thing wasn't possible to a prepaid cellular and the phone he was trying to call was definitely a prepaid cellular.

It was all Gage could do not to yell.

Justina is smart. She'll do her part.

After calming himself, he repeated the process, informing another operator that he'd like to make a collect call to the United States, to Colonel Hunter. To Gage's surprise, the operator put the call through. Gage listened to the ringing and to the brief conversation as Hunter accepted the charges. When the operator clicked off, Hunter became immediately terse, the way he always did during periods of high stress.

"Where are you?"

"Still in Berga, sir. I've been double-crossed."

"No shit. I never got your paperwork and then I started getting pieces of intel from all the hooks I'd put in the water."

"Listen, sir, I'm on an unsecure line that could be compromised any second. I need you to get me out or I'm going to have to do something drastic that probably won't end well."

"That's the problem, son. I've been trying for a full week to get you out. No one'll do a damned thing to help."

The room suddenly became cold. "Explain that, sir."

"When I didn't get your paperwork, I called my guy there, the one who gave me the intel on that lawyer, Redon. My guy confirmed you got sent up to Berga. He did some digging and couldn't find shit about you being undercover."

"Wouldn't that kind of thing be compartmentalized?" Gage asked, more hopeful than confident.

"It would, but he knows the lady who heads up their *Audiencia Nacional*. She pulled every scrap on you. There was nothing but papers showing you as a normal murderer. Then she pulled all the undercovers in Spanish prisons, even the ones that had just been filed. Nothing there either." Hunter cleared his throat. "We didn't connect you to Redon, with her, however. I was concerned that, if the wrong people got wind of it, doing that might get you killed. Since then, my guy there has called in every marker he's owed and no one has near enough juice to even get your case reviewed."

"So everything Redon said was lip service."

"There's more."

"Navarro," Gage said flatly.

"You know what happened?"

"I do. And yesterday I watched the local gang here give the son a Colombian necktie."

"Have they connected you with him?"

"Oh, yeah. They want the money I was paid or they're going to kill me, too. For the moment, that cash is all that's keeping me alive." Gage let that sink in. "But I know as soon as I hand over the money, they're going to kill me, regardless."

"Sounds bleak. I think I'd better call in a marker with my senator friend."

"There's no time," Gage said. "That'll take days and I don't have days."

"Are you suggesting a bust-out?"

"That's my only prayer."

"Finding operators willing to do that, in hours and not days, is probably impossible and, if not, would take more money than either of us ever dreamed."

"I'm working on a plan," Gage said, massaging his tired eyes. "There's a bent-screw here."

"Guard?"

"The warden."

"You're kidding."

"No, sir. She's been coerced by this gang, Los Leones, for years. Got in bed with them. Took their money. I think I've managed to convince her that she'll wind up dead if she hangs around."

"Will she help?"

"We're going to find out soon."

"How soon?"

Gage told him about El Toro's deadline.

"You're in a damned two-out-pickle, ain't you? What can I do?"

"For now, not much. Just keep the phone on you."

"I'm sorry about all this, son. As soon as I heard who the originator was, I shoulda hung up the damned phone."

"I'm the dumbass who took the job."

"Give me an update ASAP."

"There's one other thing, sir."

"What's that?"

"I had a satellite phone. Someone traced it. And Navarro swore it wasn't anyone in the Spanish government."

"When was this?"

"Two days ago. That's what burned Navarro. Someone had to have major pull to track that signal, sir."

"I'll look into it."

After hanging up, Gage remained on the cold concrete floor, despondent. His kidney felt like a swollen grapefruit, the area around it radiating heat. Finally he stood, stretching as best as he could manage.

Think.

So many questions came to him. Surely Redon couldn't have faked trial paperwork. And what about the man he was accused of murdering in Melilla? An investigation would expose the fallacies in all of this.

You're forgetting something, Gage. All this stuff is true, but unless you can figure it all out before your nine A.M. meeting with El Toro, worrying over it's like pissing in the wind.

He'd have to trust that Justina would come through. Rather than waste time feeling sorry for himself, he decided to get to work. First, he disconnected the phone, reaffixing the wall plate but leaving the screws a tad loose, just in case. He hid the phone in the cushions of the sofa before going to the small refrigerator. After unplugging it, he carried it to the scant light by the door.

The back was covered in a template-cut sheet of soft, bendable aluminum. Behind that aluminum was the coil, loaded with refrigerant.

Useful items.

Monte Carlo, Monaco

IT WAS past two in the morning when Xavier got the call. He was on the launch, nearing his yacht, planning to take an overnight cruise to Italy. Tomorrow he would romance the don's daughter, hoping the illicit liaison would get his blood moving.

The water, roiled by a passing storm, was choppy, making the launch's ride loud and rough. The sky was now clear, the flower moon casting the water in purple light. Xavier pressed his phone against his head with his finger in his other ear, barely able to hear his persnickety financial man, Theo Garcia. Xavier told Theo to wait as they reached the yacht, the pilot taking a line from the captain and sidling to the deck at the stern.

"Good evening," the sleep-frosted Greek captain mumbled to Xavier once he'd climbed aboard. The captain was wearing his bathrobe topped by his crooked hat.

"Keep everything quiet," Xavier commanded, stepping into the saloon.

"Speak, Theo."

"We have no money at *all*," Theo said, his tone accusatory.

"What are you talking about?"

"I've been telling you for weeks. Our spending is outpacing our income. When I paid off the parties involved in the satellite phone, and then you went and blew nearly a half-million dollars in Monaco, money that the casino took straight from the bank, and put a huge yacht rental on your bank line of credit, it stripped away all of our cash and strained what remaining credit we do have. All I'm doing now is fending off bankers."

"What about cash from Los Soldados?" Xavier asked, massaging the bridge of his nose. "That's surely coming in now."

"No, it's not," Theo replied, raising his voice. "That could take weeks…months, even. Your lieutenants are pushing, but they're being pushed back. We've got wars in the streets trying to take over their operations while you're off playing baccarat!"

"My Leones are capable, you little shit. They'll handle it."

"We don't have time. We need cash *now*."

"Well, what about Navarro's cash reserves? Have you found them?"

"I've been through everything," Theo snapped. "And I've got accountants combing the records we've found. We're finding nothing. It was probably all in his brain and your moronic Leones killed him before getting the information."

"Impossible. Surely there are records of where his money is."

"It's not impossible, it's brilliant. And our organization is a huge mouth to feed. For months we've been struggling along, taking in money as fast as we can spend it. Now we're dry and, until we collect from the people who owe us, we have no cash."

Several notions struck Xavier at the same time. "Theo, what if I produce a million euro, in cash? Would that get us by?"

Theo was quiet for a moment. "For a week or two. Provided our regular income remains the same, and there are no more unusual or *excessive* expenditures, it would definitely put us back on our feet."

Xavier ignored the veiled barb about expenditures. "Regarding Navarro's cash hoard…do you think Cortez Redon would have any ideas about it?"

A sharp laugh. "If I had to guess, I would imagine he's spending his every waking moment looking for it."

Xavier smiled, because he agreed. "I'll be in touch," he said, thumbing the phone off. He stepped back into the night air, finding the captain leaning against the rail, his chin bobbing as he tried to stay awake.

Xavier moved toe-to-toe with the man and demanded to know what the yacht's top speed was.

"Well," the captain said, smacking his lips, "that depends on a number of factors that could include—"

Xavier slapped the captain across the face. The older man staggered to the rail while his captain's hat rolled away like a crooked wagon wheel. His lower lip trembling, the Greek straightened, his shock outweighed by his humiliation.

"I asked you what the top speed was," Xavier demanded in a razor voice. "From right here, right now, to the Spanish port at Roses."

Mouth opening and closing like an oxygen-starved fish, the captain finally managed to say, "Thirty-two knots on glass. With the chop, between twenty-five and thirty knots."

"Very well," Xavier said, his tone changing to polite as he flashed his teeth. "See how easy that was? Now, set a speed course and don't waste a single second. And I will be awakened when we are precisely one hour away from Roses."

"Of course, señor," the shaken captain said, dipping his head.

"Go."

Moments later, as the yacht roared to life, Xavier pondered what his actions should be on the morrow.

Do I go to Berga and claim my million? Or do I trust that whore de la Mancha and, instead, travel to Barcelona, and have a tête-à-tête with Acusador Cortez Redon?

His mind awash in a multitude of thoughts, the decision didn't come to Xavier. Trying to clear his head, he walked belowships, finding the low-ceilinged crew cabin containing the bunk-style beds.

With no consideration at all, he flipped on the harsh overhead light, listening to the immediate protests from the women until they realized who it was who had illuminated the room.

The smell of the sleeping women aroused him, spent as he was. And there, starboard side, second bunk, lay the object of his desire, her large tits unbound inside her long t-shirt. He held his hand before her, satisfied over her radiance at once again being chosen. He pulled her lightly and she emerged from the bed, a flash of her pink underwear providing him further rigidity.

As the remaining crew whispered frantically behind them, Xavier led her astern, back to where he'd just dressed down the captain. There, over the same rail the captain had used for balance, Xavier took the young crewmember, their sounds drowned out by the churning twin screws making maximum turns to the southwest.

The copulation didn't take long. When finished, it was well into the night. Xavier kissed the girl gently on her lips, telling her to come and sleep next to him. He instructed her to bring him a toothbrush, toothpaste, and a bottle of water. Once he'd brushed his teeth at bedside, he asked her to use a warm washcloth to wash his penis. That done, he climbed under the covers, telling her to shower quietly and climb in bed with him.

"And sometime tonight, as I sleep, take me into your mouth but do not wake me."

Her face was troubled as she stood before him, nude, holding a towel for her shower. "Don't wake you, señor?" she asked in her cob-rough peasant Spanish.

"Yes, my dear, don't wake me. Because a good blowjob while a man sleeps means a dream of the finest sort. Remember that when you're someday married and, if you really want to get to your husband, surprise him with it, but later *do* tell him where you learned the trick."

Feeling magnanimous, Xavier slid under the silken sheets and was asleep in minutes.

That night, two hours before he was awakened by the petrified Greek captain, Xavier had the sweetest of dreams.

Chapter Twenty-Three

BRIGHT, STINGING light. And an instant headache.

Gage squinted, groaning as he came to his feet despite the bowel-watering pain from his kidney. But, despite his stab wounds and bruises, getting up fast was his trademark—he would continue to do it as long as he was able. To him, it wasn't unlike the theory of jumping into a cold swimming pool. Why deal with the series of shocks one takes when slowly entering the water? Might as well jump right in and get it over with.

After the phone calls, Gage had "worked" in the relative dark for what he guessed was at least two more hours, maybe three. He'd then gotten about four hours of sleep and, although he was fatigued, he was strangely heartened over what might happen on this day. Because, if all went well, he'd be leaving Berga. And if Justina came through for him, with the consulate's help, he might have a chance to clear his name and leave the country unmolested. Possibly with the money.

Wearing only his underwear, he padded around the small apartment, viewing each of the items he'd worked with, seeing nothing that appeared out of the ordinary. Satisfied, he went back into the bedroom area, stripping his skivvies and taking a shower behind the waxy curtain. Once dressed, he sat on the covered cushion, waiting for the prison's excuse for breakfast.

Perhaps tomorrow I can have a cup of strong coffee, he thought in a rare moment of indulgence. He knew that such hope, even over small things, can provide a person extra degrees of motivation.

And I will enjoy my coffee with Justina.

HAVING DRIVEN into Berga through the three gates, breaking what were surely numerous government rules but not giving a damn—the same way she hadn't given a damn since having been given the keys to the place—Capitana de la Mancha eased her Opel Insignia, the nicest auto she dared own, up the ramp to the same garage door Gage's prisoner transport van had entered not even two weeks before. When Guillermo, the normal morning guard, flipped the switch, the door slid up, allowing her to drive in. She drove across the large warehouse to a mini-garage of sorts, created by a structure of stacked boxes in the back corner of the massive room. It was just past 7:00 A.M. She was almost two hours earlier than normal.

De la Mancha's heels were a tad taller than her usual footware. She was nicely dressed in a dove-grey skirt suit with a cream blouse. Carrying her requisite planner and iPad, she smartly walked to her office, managing to appear composed while her mind raced.

It raced because last night she'd made a number of plans. Her first call, of course, was to her mother. *Bitch.* After a brief shouting match, followed by Angelines' familiar, tired threats to reveal a few secrets about good old mama, she finally convinced the former mistress-cum-blackmailer to grab only her essentials, to collect Jordi from the local fútbol field, and to drive the two of them in her car to Girona, Spain.

"Find a large car lot somewhere, back the car in, remove your tags, and leave the car there. Then walk to a hotel that's nowhere near the car, and pay cash for a room. Use your old skills, mama, and sweet talk your way into a hotel room without revealing your identity," Angelines had said, struggling to be patient.

"Why?"

"Because we're leaving."

"Who is?"

"The three of us."

"Leaving to go where?"

"Doesn't matter where. We're going far away, and it's for good. You, of all people, should be thrilled to hear this."

"And what on earth do I tell Jordi?"

"Just tell him I will explain everything. And take his mobile phone away the second you see him. Destroy it."

"Who's financing this?"

"I am."

"Where did you get the money, Angelines?" She only called her daughter by her full name in times of high stress, or distrust.

"I've been saving."

"Not enough to take us away like this." Her mother's tone turned skeptical. "And you sound scared. Something happened."

"Never you mind."

"Well," her mother had said, her voice turning syrupy sly, "how much money are we talking?"

"It's enough, mother. Enough for me to escort you two away from this place. Enough, added to my other savings, for me not to have to work for a while. Enough to get to know my son, really know him, before it's too late."

"I see," she said coldly. "You want to spend time with him but not your own mother."

Typical mama—a rainbow of emotions in just one conversation. "I'm taking you with me, aren't I?"

"Yes, but you've got me removing my plates," her mother said knowingly. "Meaning you *stole* the money."

"You know, mama, whether I did or didn't, you're one to talk. All those years I watched papa drinking himself to death, wailing through nightmares in the middle of the night, defeated. When I was young, I thought you were working a night job and his sorrow was from missing you. I had no idea that, all along, you were out blackmailing local politicians with your pimp boyfriend."

"I paid your way through college," her mother said sharply.

"Yes, mama, you did. And now I will pay your way to a new life."

Angelines had hung up the phone—then completely broken down. She'd had all she could take and she couldn't imagine having to spend more than a day with her mother.

In her weakened state, she'd even pondered leaving Spain all alone. Maybe she could find a way to continue to send the checks to her mother. Maybe once she set up the new life she could come back for Jordi. Maybe she'd even be able to—

Her thoughts had been chopped off by an icy realization: Such a plan would never work. *If I disappear with their money, Los Leones will go directly to mama and Jordi. Go to them and butcher them.*

Gulping her wine, she pushed the conversation from her mind and consulted her iPad, having already identified where she wanted to go. From Zurich, once her banking was done, they would make their way to Athens.

Athens, as her searches revealed, was highly corrupt. She'd found a website devoted to pirating and, for a highly developed global city, Athens was a favorite for criminals in search of sanctuary. Once she left Berga, going anywhere was a risk—but staying in Spain, even in hiding, would be far more dangerous. And, once in Athens, Angelines would somehow have to find new identification for her and her family. The pirating website listed a restaurant in Kolonaki, reputedly owned by the largest mob in the Athens underworld. One person wrote of it: With enough money, a person can dine at the restaurant and, after a discreet inquiry, purchase anything they desire, to include murder, followed by dessert.

Then, with fresh identifications, they would travel to Indonesia. Angelines planned to stay there for at least a year, getting to know her family again as they planned their new lives.

So, last night's work done, on this, an early morning of her most fateful day, Capitana Angelines de la Mancha flipped on the lights to her office. She stood there, in the hidden rear doorway, feeling the heavy rise and fall of her chest.

In that room, still left over from the brutality she'd received yesterday, she smelled the sour scent of El Toro, distinctly mingled with the sweat of her own fear.

With a shaking, aching left hand, she removed her cigarettes and lighter. As she stood in the doorway, the cigarette calmed her nerves. She smoked it all the way to the filter, crossing the room and crushing it out.

"Last day," she breathed to the empty office. "Last day."

GAGE HARTLINE stood as keys jingled in the door. He figured it was the guard coming back to retrieve the food tray. He'd choked down the foul-tasting meal because he knew the nourishment might serve him well later. But his visitor was not a guard. Instead, Capitana de la Mancha, looking quite alluring today, and without her trademark lab coat, stood in the doorway. She jangled a pair of handcuffs, twirling her finger so he might turn around. Gage obeyed, placing his hands behind him as the cuffs were clicked shut, though not overly tightly.

"Please, sit," she said. He did, on the protective coverlet, perched forward to keep pressure off his wrists.

"I want you to listen to me before you speak," she said. "Do you understand?"

"That's fine, but what about the cameras in here?"

"They're off," she said dismissively. "The only guard that has access is the one with my assistant, and he's not here yet."

"Understood."

"I've decided to do as you suggested. And I think you're right—it's the only way you could possibly survive Los Leones." Hands clasped behind her back, she began to pace. "There are two sizeable problems, however. The first is the question of how to physically get you out of the prison."

"The second?"

"My involvement."

236

"What do you mean?"

"I will help you, but it needs to appear that I'm your hostage."

Gage was silent.

"That way, in case you're caught in the escape, I can deny involvement."

"Crafty," Gage said in a low voice, simultaneously trying to keep the cuffs from jangling.

"It's the *only* way I will participate and, therefore, your only hope of getting out of here."

"I suppose you still want the money?" he asked.

She snorted.

"All right, well, how about the million-euro question? How the hell do we get out of here, with you as my *hostage?*"

"We have to get all available guards in the main bay. That will leave us with only the warehouse guard, and the tower guards to deal with." She crossed her arms. "And El Toro."

"What about El Toro?" Gage asked, focusing on the furtive actions taking place behind his back. *Upper notch until it seats, then slow, strong pressure in the direction of travel.*

"It was all I could do to buy you the night in this *aposento*. He wanted to meet with you yesterday, but I was able to hold him off until this morning."

"Yeah, I heard about the meeting at nine."

"How?"

"Your little pear-shaped guard came in last night and brought me a message from Mister Toro. I think he ruptured my kidney with his frigging baton."

She closed her eyes and shook her head, mumbling something to herself.

"Regarding that asshole, El Toro, we need to leave before his deadline."

"No," she said, her voice firm.

"No?"

"Before we leave here, Hartline, you're going to kill El Toro for me."

"What are you talking about?"

"He's the critical link between our actions and Los Leones. With him dead, the resulting confusion in Los Leones will buy us time."

"Why don't we just leave now? We'll have a few hours' head start."

"I can't get you out of here without a reason," she snapped. "We need chaos and confusion and, as part of it, El Toro will wind up dead."

"A riot."

"Yes."

"Do you have thoughts on how to start one?"

"Of course I do. I've been here a long time, remember?"

"Can you do it without El Toro's knowledge?"

"That's going to be the trick."

Gage turned his eyes in the direction of the main bay. "I may be able to help with that. We'll come back to it." He tilted his head. "About El Toro…"

De la Mancha's lips parted.

"Why do you *really* want him dead?" Gage asked, making his tone skeptical.

No response.

"There's more," Gage said, nodding knowingly.

Tears welled in her eyes.

"Why, capitana?"

She squeezed her eyes shut. "I want him gone. I want to sleep at night knowing he's no longer of this earth."

"What's he done to you?"

Her hands over her face, she shuddered, shaking her head.

It was obvious that whatever her reasons happened to be, and Gage had a powerful hunch about those reasons, they were deeply personal. In an effort to settle her, he moved on. "So, back to the plan, we create a riot and I supposedly kill El Toro—then what?"

It took a few moments before she composed herself, finally saying, "You and I escape in my car."

"Your car?"

"Yes. It's parked in the warehouse where you first came in."

"How do you manage to drive your car into a prison?"

"I'm in charge and, besides, I've always done it."

"Do they search your car on the way out?"

"Never."

"Even if there's a riot?"

"If I'm cool and collected, no one would dare question me."

"Is your car parked out in the middle of the warehouse?"

She shook her head. "Parked at one end, obscured by boxes."

"Why is it obscured?"

"Because, whenever we have inspectors, even though they're paid off by Los Leones, we can't have my car parked out in the open warehouse. When we tour them through, my car is parked in such a way that they can't see it."

Gage screwed up his face. "So, even though they're paid off, you still hide your car?"

"It's the way things are done, okay? Rules are broken, but we're discreet about it."

"Fine, whatever. Do you have a trunk?"

"Yes."

"How many eyes will we pass between here and your car?"

"None, if we can generate a riot."

Okay, other side now. Slowly, no big movements…there's no rush.

"Tell me exactly what happens when you get in your car to leave," he said. "Exactly. Leave nothing out."

She did, going over every detail from her backing out, to waiting for the garage door, to passing through the heavily-fortified inner gate and the final pass-through at the narrow rear gate of the facility.

"Even with a riot, the outer guards will stay at their posts?"

"Yes. They cannot leave unless they're relieved, no matter what."

"And they've never searched your car?"

"Never."

"So, to summarize, you meet with El Toro. I pop out somehow and, with luck, I kill him. We create a riot in the main bay, to keep the guards there. Then, you and I drive away with you as my hostage."

"Essentially, yes."

"But, in a riot, they're not going to let you drive out."

"You're going to drive," she said. "You'll bust us out."

"Where will you be?"

"I'll be your hostage."

He nodded his understanding. Then, slowly, so he didn't startle her, he brought his hands around, the cuffs attached to only his right wrist.

Her mouth fell open. "How did you do that?"

"I wasn't completely sure how this meeting was going to go." As he stood he showed her the straightened piece of metal from the refrigerator with the S-bend at its tip. "Just an old trick. But it demonstrates to you that I'm placing my trust in you. If I'd wanted to, especially with the cameras off, I could have taken you hostage now, and blown off this business of killing El Toro." He held out his manacled wrist.

De la Mancha unlocked the other handcuff and walked to the door. "We've got less than two hours."

"There's one other thing." Gage reached into the sofa cushions and removed the phone, holding it in one hand and the frayed wire in the other.

"That's the guest phone from my office," she said quizzically.

"Correct. You never noticed it was gone and I used it last night to call my contact."

She stared at the phone as her lips parted.

"I told my contact everything, *capitana*. Everything about this prison, about your involvement, the works. And today, as we speak, my contact is headed to the U.S. consulate." Gage muddled the details on purpose. "Once there, my contact is going to tell them everything." He motioned toward the main bay. "So, if you get cold feet, you can send me out to the main bay and, yes, they'll probably eat me alive. But your little reign here is about to end." Gage licked his lips, satisfied at her horrified expression. "And Los Leones will lose a million euro, and a prison empire. And they'll blame you."

She swallowed a few times before finally speaking, her voice meek and unsure. "You couldn't have called anyone."

"Really?" He walked to the wall plate and quickly thumbed off the loose spanner screws. He freed the phone line from inside and quickly twisted each of the corresponding wires together. Then, after tapping the button a few times, he held the phone out to Capitana de la Mancha.

With leaden feet, she trudged over, listening as he held the phone up to her ear.

"Dial tone," Gage said.

Capitana de la Mancha had to support herself with the door handle.

"It's called mutually assured destruction," Gage added. "Keeps everyone honest."

"I wasn't going to back out."

"C'mon…we're wasting time." He walked back to the sofa, reaching under and removing what looked like a hobo's bindle minus the stick. The bindle made a metallic tinkle when moved. "Can you get this back to your office?"

"What is it?" she asked.

"Just some items I scrounged. Can you get to the janitorial supplies, too?"

"Yeah," she answered. "Why?"

Working on the fly, and with her knowledge of Berga, he quickly formulated a plan.

Chapter Twenty-Four

SEÑORA MORENO placed a heaping breakfast plate in front of Justina. They were in the sitting area, located in the original portion of Moreno's home, easily denoted by the cabin's saddle notches at the corners. Señora Moreno sat across from Justina, who was cradling a cup of coffee in her hands. The older woman eyed her houseguest.

"Did the valium I gave you help you sleep?"

Justina, her head somewhat swimmy, nodded and sipped the coffee.

"Do you feel like talking now?"

Another nod.

"My dear, you were hysterical last night. I thought we were going to have to take you to the hospital."

"I'm okay, really."

Señora Moreno leaned over the table and squeezed Justina's knee. "You've fresh fruit and eggs there, dear. Eat some, and drink all that coffee—it will help you wake up."

"Thank you."

"I'm not going anywhere, dear. And, as you can see out front, Sven has been out there all night. And Amancio is out back. They've been there to protect you." She looked away. "With all you were saying last night, I didn't really know what else to do."

Justina peered through one of the windows, able to see half of Sven, one of Señora Moreno's "property men." He was sipping from a cup of steaming coffee and in his arm he cradled a long rifle of some sort. She'd seen Sven tinkering around the lake homes, an older gentleman from Sweden with a kind nature. Like Sven, Amancio had to have been in his late sixties. Despite their advanced age, their presence did give Justina a measure of comfort, as did the sunshine coming through the windows. The renewal of a new dawn seemed to always have that effect on her.

Not wanting to dwell on it, but seeing the worry on Señora Moreno's face, Justina knew that last night, after the call, she'd been an absolute basket case.

Don't start all that...

Justina sipped the coffee. It was good and strong and black, but not too hot. She gulped the remainder and looked at Señora Moreno. "What time is it?"

"Around eight, dear."

"I've got to leave!"

"Please wait just a moment."

"I can't. I've got to go."

"Where are you wanting to go?"

Justina shook her head. "I'm not supposed to tell anyone anything."

"Dear, last night, after you took that valium, you told me a number of things. Only none of it made any sense."

"I've got to get to the American Consulate in Barcelona," Justina said, standing and glancing around, feeling the unwelcome mania of the night before rushing back in.

Señora Moreno stood, moving around the small table and hugging the much taller Justina. "First I want you to relax, darling. Shh. Shh," she murmured. Señora Moreno gently reseated Justina and knelt next to her.

"Last night, you were all over the place, talking about consulates and ambassadors and acusadors and double-crosses." She used her thumb to wipe away the tears from Justina's face. "You've told me most of Gage's story, involving Berga Prison. Now, calmly, slowly, and eating a bit of that breakfast, I want you to tell me the rest, and then tell me what Gage said last night." Señora Moreno's voice was soothing as she said, "Ten minutes of talking isn't going to hurt anyone. And, when you're finished, I will personally drive you to Barcelona this morning, okay?"

Justina pulled in a long breath through her nose. "I wasn't supposed to tell anyone."

"I'm not just anyone, I hope."

Justina smiled. "No, you're not."

Señora Moreno handed her a piece of fruit, sliced pomegranate. "More coffee?"

"No, thank you," Justina said, chewing the fruit. "Okay," she said, exhaling. "I've told you nothing but the truth about Gage. But last night, after I'd gotten home, he called me."

"From the prison?"

"Yes. He said he only had one minute and, no matter what, I was not to call him back."

"You're doing fine, dear," Señora Moreno encouraged.

"He said he'd been double-crossed by Acusador Redon, from Barcelona."

"Acusador Redon?"

"Yes."

A quick shake of her head. "Don't know him. Please, go on."

"He said they're not going to let him go. He said he's being held for ransom."

"By this Acusador Redon?"

"He didn't say. But he told me to leave the cabin at that very instant, and to leave most of the money where it could be found, along with one of the pistols. Then he told me to go to the American Consulate General in Barcelona and to tell them everything."

"How much money is left?"

"It was a million euro. We've spent some of it."

"Hmm," she frowned. "What else, dear?"

"That was all. We were cut off by an electronic message…something about a calling card." Justina looked at the clock on the wall. "Señora, we must go. I'm afraid he's already dead. I just have this horrible feeling…"

Señora Moreno hushed her again. She stepped to the front door, conversing in rapid Catalan with Sven. She came back into the room, her voice soothing. "Sven said not a soul has driven up the road to your cabin. So the money is still there, dear, meaning your Gage is not dead."

"You can't possibly know that," Justina cried.

"I know all about money, dear. If it's there, he's alive. And now it's time for us to make a move." Señora Moreno walked away, coming back with her iPhone. Her fashionable red reading glasses perched on the bottom of her small nose, she swiped through several pages before making a satisfied sound. She touched the screen, dropped the glasses around her neck, and pressed the phone to her ear, smiling reassuringly at Justina.

"Hello, I'm calling for Jorge." Listened. "Yes, I'm aware this is his mobile—that's why I'm calling it," she snapped, using a tone unlike any Justina had heard from her before. "Well, I don't care if King Juan Carlos is in the shower with him. You go and tell him Lydia Moreno is on the phone with a dire emergency." She listened for a moment then winked at Justina.

"Sometimes people need a little push, dear."

Justina sipped her orange juice, relaxing slightly.

It wasn't a moment before Señora Moreno had a brief conversation with Jorge, a man Justina would soon learn was one of her Barcelonan attorneys. Justina struggled to follow the Catalan, but most of the focus of the conversation was Acusador Cortez Redon before it ended with a brief discussion about the American Consul General in Barcelona. Finished, Señora Moreno dropped the phone on her chair and stared out the window for a moment. Justina could hear the clicking sound as the lady of the house tapped her teeth with her fingernail. Finally she turned and told Justina to hurry back to the bedroom and to shower quickly.

"There's no time," Justina protested.

"There *is* time. Now go shower, my dear. We'll make our plan in the car."

As Justina showered, Señora Moreno made two trips to her Volvo. On the first trip she placed two bottles of water in the cup-holders. On the back seat she placed a small stack of clothes and a case loaded with her finest makeup. On the second trip she came back with only one item, first stopping to show Sven, who nodded. She placed it under the driver's seat, her Mateo's beautiful Modele 1892 revolver, fully loaded, touching it afterward to make sure it was securely seated in the folds of the automotive carpet.

Afterward she stood outside the car, eyes up. Clasping her rosary, she stared into the trees, fresh with leaves and pine needles, smiling because, for the first time in years, she felt the zing and zest of imminent danger.

It was pretty damned invigorating.

A thought—actually, an inspiration—came to Señora Moreno. She thought of her assets, so many of them—cabins, homes, lots, buildings, a parking garage in Madrid, a fabric plant in Girona, and millions upon millions of euro in all manner of investment vehicles. It was an empire that Mateo had begun and she'd grown but, now, in the twilight of her life, she could never possibly use it all—and she had no one to leave it to.

"What good is all that wealth doing anyone?" she said aloud.

There was no point in answering herself.

As she wended her way down behind the cabin, into its high basement, and through the two hidden doors, Señora Moreno hummed quiet thanks to Mateo for his prescience. She opened the old safe on the very first try, removing the thick sheaf of linen paper as she eyed the other important documents, stacks of cash and the inviolable instructions for her battery of attorneys in the event she was ever kidnapped.

"Sweet Mateo," she sang, carrying the sheaf back around the cabin. "You knew that someday these papers would come in handy."

THE TWO women sped to Barcelona, taking the E-9, an international road with occasional tolls. It runs from Orleans, France to its terminating point at the Via Augusta in Barcelona. From Berga, in the foothills, the road quickly flattens out on its way to the Mediterranean plain and the surrounding area could easily be mistaken for the wine country north of Santa Barbara, California. Once she'd settled the turbo-charged Volvo S80 in at a blistering pace, Señora Moreno kept her eyes on the road as she spoke to Justina.

"My lawyer said the consul general is worthless if you want quick action. They'll have to call the embassy, then the embassy will have to call the United States—everyone's asleep there, you know, and politicians and appointed officials will be more worried about how this affects them than you and your gentleman."

Justina glanced over at the speedometer, seeing it hovering around the 200 kilometers per hour mark. She buckled her seatbelt. "I'm only doing what Gage told me to do."

"Well, Gage isn't from Spain, now, is he?"

"No, but he's experienced in—*Look out!* Look out for that truck!"

Señora Moreno eased the wheel to the left as both left side tires tore through dirt and weeds to pass a tractor trailer lolling along in the faster left lane. The underside of the car sounded like it was being struck by bullets from a machine gun. When they'd made the pass, Señora Moreno smoothly centered the car in the left lane and, beaming, looked back at Justina.

"The salesman said this is the safest car on the road, dear."

Justina scrutinized the dashboard in front of her seat, making sure the Volvo came with dual airbags. "Do you normally drive this fast?"

"No, dear. In fact, I don't think I've ever driven this car over a hundred kilometers per hour. I must admit that I find driving this way exhilarating."

Justina pointed to the turn selector. "Pull on that lever to flash your headlights. Most people will get out of the way and that might prove better than any more passes in the grass."

As they rapidly closed on a car, Señora Moreno flashed her lights, marveling at how the car quickly moved right. Again she smiled, adjusting her fingers on the wheel. "I feel so free."

"Señora, you said your lawyer didn't think the consulate was the best place to go."

"Yes, dear. He suggested we find another angle that might provide us much greater leverage."

"And what's that?"

"I didn't like his suggestions. Too safe and obvious."

"But you have an idea?"

"I do, dear. This Ernesto Navarro…there have been countless news stories about him since he was killed. He was worth many millions, dear, and the news outlets seem to think his fortune is well-hidden."

"How does that help us?"

A blue sign flashed by, displaying Barcelona as only 77 kilometers away. "Before I tell you, in the interest of time, climb into the back. You'll find my makeup in the case. And I put some of my grand-niece's summer clothes back there. She's tall and pretty like you…and dresses like a tramp."

"What's wrong with what I'm wearing?" Justina asked.

Señora Moreno risked a glance. "Your platform sandals will do, but those jeans and that shirt are too baggy. Back there you'll find some items that will accentuate your gifts. And once you're changed, tease your hair out and go heavy on the makeup."

Justina turned and rummaged through the clothes.

"We want you to appear *lujuriosa*."

"I don't think I know that word," Justina said.

After flashing her lights at another car, Señora Moreno briefly turned. "I think the English word is 'slutty.'" She motioned with her head. "Go on now. I'll slow down just a bit, but not too much." She flashed her lights again. "I'm having too much fun to drive normally."

Choosing to follow along, Justina climbed through the seats into the back. The clothes, while tight, did fit.

"No brassiere, dear," Señora Moreno said, looking at Justina in the rear view mirror.

"Are you sure?"

"Quite."

After resignedly removing her bra, Justina opened the case and went to work on her face. "Make myself *lujuriosa*," she mumbled, eyeing herself in the mirror as she applied Vichy foundation to her face.

As Justina worked on her face, Señora Moreno explained her plan.

"You think it will work?"

"I do," Señora Moreno answered with conviction.

Justina grew silent.

"Dear?"

"Yes?"

"I need to tell you something else."

"Okay."

"I left something else for your boyfriend...left it with Sven."

"You did?"

"Yes. Just in case."

"What was it?"

"Before I tell you, I want you to promise that you'll try to understand *why* I did it."

Their eyes converged in the rear-view mirror. "I will try to understand."

"These past few weeks with you have been wonderful." She adjusted her hands on the wheel. "I truly feel like my Isabel is here with me again."

"As I've said before, I cannot imagine a greater honor than to remind you of her."

"And it's because of that..."

The Volvo sped southward as Señora Moreno explained.

Chapter Twenty-Five

AS HE'D done the day before, Gage waited in the outer office while the big guard stared at him from behind the glass. The pain around Gage's kidney had worsened, as if there was a pipe clamp around the organ, cinching tighter by the minute. After Capitana de la Mancha's visit, Gage had relieved himself, doubling over from the pain that seemed to have spread to his bladder. When he'd recovered enough to straighten, he peered into the toilet—his urine was now flecked with blood.

That meant infection—or worse.

But there was no time for him to worry about it now. For the moment he was just a prisoner who was expected to deliver nearly a million euro this morning, and he had to assume that everyone in the prison's employ knew this fact.

The assistant, looking somewhat disheveled this morning—Gage had heard her confiding in the guard that she had drunk way too much last night with a man she'd had no business seeing, and she'd sounded gleeful about it—stepped back into her little office, sloshing milk-laden coffee and reaching for the buzzing phone. She picked it up, listened for a moment, then said something to the guard. The guard looked at Gage.

"You remember the drill?"

"Yes."

"I'm right outside this door and it would make my year to have to come in there and deal with you, got it?"

Not in any condition to tangle with a guard, Gage nodded with closed eyes. The door buzzed. He entered.

De la Mancha had taken off her heels and was rushing all around the office. On the leather sofa was a cardboard box containing a thick plastic bottle, similar to a gallon bottle of bleach, sticking from the top of the box. Without speaking, Gage went straight over to the items.

The large bottle was half-full of industrial drain cleaner. *Perfect.* Next to it was a pair of needle-nose pliers, as well as a hammer. Also in the box were a number of empty soft drink bottles. Gage turned to her.

"Where am I meeting him?"

"In here. I'm summoning him now." She lifted the phone, having to repeat her instructions twice.

When she hung up, Gage asked, "Is he on his way?"

"Yes."

"Good. Now, I need both of your pistols."

She was rummaging through a file drawer, removing folders when she turned. "How did you know I had two?"

"I saw it when you opened your middle drawer. Just like I stole your phone. You're careless, and that needs to end now."

"Go ahead and get it," she said, shrugging. "The drawer isn't locked."

He opened the top drawer. There was no pistol. Wondering if he'd been mistaken about which drawer, he opened all them, making quite a racket.

"What's wrong?" she asked, walking over.

"No pistol."

"You're kidding." De la Mancha pulled each of the drawers out, rifling through their contents.

"What kind of pistol was it?"

"An AutoMag."

"Where's that Smith you had?"

"Purse," she said, going back to the top drawer, removing each item as if she were somehow overlooking a large handgun.

He opened her purse. Inside he found the Smith, in a single movement pulling it out and popping the cylinder from the chassis.

Empty.

"Where are the bullets?" Gage barked, the pit of dread in his stomach outweighing the pain of his bladder and kidneys.

"Oh no," she mouthed, with hardly a sound escaping.

"El Toro?" Gage asked.

Capitana de la Mancha's large eyes darted around the room. She began to cry.

"C'mon, now," Gage encouraged. "No matter what, you have to focus."

She looked at him, wiping tears as she nodded.

"Do you have any spare bullets?"

"Not here."

"What about the guards?"

"If I go raiding their supply room, it'll raise suspicion."

Gage willed himself to remain calm. "Well, I'm sure as hell not going to bring an unloaded gun to a gunfight." He searched the room, his eyes settling on the cardboard box loaded with implements.

"What is it?" she asked.

He lifted several of the contents, eyeing each one before his eyes drifted out the window.

"What are you going to do?"

"I'm still thinking about it. Get a sheet of paper and diagram the layout between here and your car."

As she drew, she pointed to the paper and said, "The hallway has two turns from the back door of my office. We leave and walk straight to the end of the short hall. We turn right from there and—"

"What's to the left?"

"That's the long hallway. Infirmary and then the main bay."

"I remember. So, turn right and walk to the end?"

"Sort of. Before we reach the end, which was where you were brought in, we take the single door to the right and that's where my car will be."

"Type of car," he demanded.

"It's an Opel Insignia."

"Heard of it but not familiar. Describe."

She looked away for a moment, trying to contain her trembling chin. "Will you please ease up? One of my guns is gone, we've got no bullets, and now you're making me more nervous than I already am."

He grabbed her wrist, turning her wristwatch. "We've got twenty minutes before you're due to call El Toro in. And he's armed, which is mind-boggling enough as it is. When I got here, I was stabbed by a shank made from a nail. But I've never heard of a prisoner armed with a frigging handgun."

"Now who's wasting time?"

Toning it down, he said, "The car, please."

"Like I said. It's an Opel Insignia, four-door, not huge but larger than most cars in Spain."

"Manual or automatic?"

"Manual."

"Front-wheel drive?"

"All-wheel drive. It's the nicest version of the car available."

"Horsepower."

"No clue."

"Fast?"

She shrugged. "Fast, I guess."

"Diesel or gas?"

"It takes high-octane gas."

"I was hoping it was diesel," he breathed, looking outside the window.

"Why?"

"Torque."

"What?"

He made a dismissive motion with his hand. "How does the car start?"

She went to her purse, removing the chunky key fob. "As long as this is in the car, you push a button to the left of the radio."

He nodded, rubbing his stubble. "Okay. When we get to the car, I'll drive and I want you beside me. We're going to have to smash through that garage door and, whether we make it or not, we're probably going to get a face full of airbag."

"You don't want me in the backseat?"

"I want to give them a reason to *not* shoot at us." He wiped incipient sweat from his face. "Next item. Tell me about the procedure for an escape alarm."

She motioned for him to follow, walking to the rear door of the office. Mounted on the wall was a heavy-duty keypad with three buttons. "These are encased in the hallways, the guard stands, and other strategic locations around the prison. A person needs a key to open the case. When pressed, this first button signals an internal alarm not fed into the prisoner areas."

"What's the alarm for?"

"All available guards muster when it's pressed. It's usually used for large fights and that type of thing."

"I didn't realize you ever broke those up."

Ignoring him, she said, "The second button rings an alarm throughout the prison and the third—"

"Notifies the external police of a prison emergency," Gage finished for her.

"That's correct, except for one thing. When that alarm is triggered, the 'C' alarm, it's possible to cancel it if one has the proper cancellation code."

"And you have it?"

"Of course. Once we're clear of Berga, I'll call and tell them to ignore all signals for the next hour, that we're having problems with our system and testing it."

"Will they buy that?"

"They will if it's me calling. They know me."

"Will anyone else here call the police?"

"Possibly, but they'll think the alarm did its job. I would think most calls will go to Los Leones."

"It might give us the head start we need."

She gestured to the door. "Can you still handle El Toro?"

Just as Gage was about to answer, the phone buzzed. She spoke for a moment, telling her assistant to wait one minute and send him in.

"Cuff me," Gage said. "And when he comes in, put him next to me and then excuse yourself to go to the bathroom."

"Okay."

"I need some money, too."

"How much?"

"Just twenty, thirty euro."

She gave him forty euro from her purse. Gage held a handful of the aluminum pieces he'd taken from the back of the refrigerator along with the money. She cuffed him and he sat in front of her desk just before the prisoner was shown in.

Wearing manacles, Salvador the Semental was escorted in before she dismissed the guard.

"Please sit," she said to Salvador. He stared at Gage with saucer eyes, certainly having never been summoned to this office before.

Just as de la Mancha opened her mouth to speak, she stared at her mobile phone, excusing herself and walking into her bathroom, feigning a conversation.

Speaking conspiratorially, Gage said, "Do you still have that clotting agent?"

"What?"

"The clotting agent you used on me."

"Yeah. It's in Nico's cell."

"Can you get it, and a few plastic bottles?"

"Why?"

"Sal—can you get the clotting agent and some bottles?"

"Yeah."

"Okay. I want you to make as many bombs as you can, and I want you to set them off up on your terrace."

"Bombs? Th'hell are you talking about?"

Gage handed over the aluminum chips. "Get the plastic bottles. Mix that clotting agent with water in the bottles, then drop these aluminum chips in. Screw the tops down, shake them up and roll them out on the terrace."

"Why?"

"Because I'm going to try to escape, that's why."

"What?" Salvador said loudly.

"Shhh," Gage said, eyeing the main door. "Wait until the guards are mustered in the main bay in riot gear, then mix those items and do as I said. Watch the center clock and drop the aluminum chips in at nine-oh-two on the button." With his cuffed hands, he handed over the money.

Salvador eyed the cash. "How do you know the guards will be in the bay?"

"I just know."

"Am I supposed to throw the bombs at the guards?"

"No. This is just a diversion. Start screaming and yelling after they go off. Burn toilet paper. All that stuff you guys do when you riot."

Salvador was dumbstruck.

"Can you do it?"

"Yes." Salvador glanced at the bathroom. "I'd heard you were in *el aposento* and were due to pay money to El Toro this morning," Salvador whispered.

"Word travels fast."

"He's going to kill you," Salvador said.

"He's going to *try* to kill me."

"Is *la capitana* in on it?"

"Yes, but she's with me." Gage pressed the money into Salvador's hand. "You're my only friend here, Sal. Keep all this quiet. Just hurry out, get those items, and get everything ready in the cell. You'll see the guards mustering and—"

"At two minutes after nine I should make the explosions."

"Exactly."

Salvador extended his cuffed hands, bumping fists with Gage. "You saved me."

"Now you can save me."

"Make El Toro cry like a *perra*, okay?"

Gage smiled at his friend. "Hide those items and go to work. There isn't much time."

As Salvador stood and tucked the aluminum and money into his underpants, de la Mancha wrapped up her call. She hurried back into the room, asking if all was set and ready.

"Yes," Gage answered.

"Oh," she said, reaching into her bag. She produced a bundle of letters, tossing them to him.

They were from Justina.

"Where were these?"

"They were holding these from you, probably on orders of El Toro."

"But I got one of them," Gage said.

"The mail is run by trustees. I'm sure El Toro let you have one to tease you."

"Prick," Gage muttered, eyeing the envelopes. There were twenty-five of them.

"That's typical of the little tortures around here," Salvador said, clapping Gage on the knee, his cuffs jangling.

De la Mancha called her guard back in, telling him to un-cuff Salvador and release him back into general population. As he was led out, Salvador nodded at Gage.

"Nine-oh-two, *mi amigo*."

When the two men had left, she un-cuffed Gage. "Salvador's in," Gage said.

"I just hope his timing will be right."

"He'll mix the items at nine-oh-two. After that, we can't control how long the reaction takes."

"Gage, how will you subdue El Toro? He's got a gun."

"I need a bag or backpack or something that looks like it might have the money in it." She started to move but he stopped her. "Just know, when this goes down, there's no turning back."

"I'd rather die than turn back," she answered with conviction. "So you've now got a plan?"

Gage explained.

THE MAIN bay was unusually quiet for the hour just after breakfast. Typically, other than late afternoons, this was one of the most raucous times of day. It was when prisoners, cooped up all night with their cellmates, enjoyed a brief respite from the man they were forced to spend their remaining lives with. Conversations ranged from debts owed, to loved ones, to who was copulating with whom.

But on this morning, as El Toro and a select few stood near the doorway to the long hallway, staring through the wire glass, the remainder of the prisoners talked in quiet voices. Los Leones, all of them, were the quietest. While they didn't know exactly what was occurring, they'd heard whispers that today was to be a landmark. The other non-Leones prisoners were obviously alert enough to sense the sea change and some, like Salvador, had gotten word of a coming windfall for Los Leones. Rather than risk a beating, or worse, most prisoners kept to themselves, quietly speculating about what might happen.

At 8:48 A.M., when Salvador had been released back into the main bay, he was stopped by a hulking León and questioned by El Toro about why he was summoned. Salvador lied, saying that he took a phone call telling him that his mother was in the hospital and would die soon. El Toro shoved Salvador away, telling him he hoped his cunt of a mother would die in screaming agony.

A short time later, as the steel minute hand on the large main bay clock audibly clicked to 8:57 A.M., one of the guards appeared in the hallway. Baton in hand, he opened the door, pointing it at El Toro, motioning him from the main bay.

El Toro wasn't searched, wasn't even escorted away with any measure of caution. The two men could have been old friends. In fact, as they passed by the windows in the hallway, El Toro could be seen laughing at something he'd just been told by the guard.

And at his back, just above his waistline, bulged the hard outline of the .44 caliber AutoMag.

Chapter Twenty-Six

CAPITANA DE la Mancha stood by the back door of her office. Even though Gage couldn't see her, her breathing was audible from where he stood in the bathroom.

"You can't release emotion like that, de la Mancha," Gage commanded. "Calm down."

"I'm trying, damn it. And I think it's about time you start calling me Angelines."

"Okay, Angelines, keep your head about you when this all goes down. I have no idea if the guards will hear the explosion."

"But Teresa will," she said, walking to her desk. "Can't believe I didn't think of that."

"Who?"

"My assistant." Angelines spoke on the phone for a moment. "She's leaving."

"What reason did you give her?"

"I sent her home because of her hangover. She probably thinks she's getting fired."

Gage surveyed his items. On the counter next to him was an overnight bag. In front of him were two soft drink bottles, both made of green plastic. He'd washed them out before fitting broken, pill-size chips of aluminum, taken from the back of the refrigerator, down inside of each bottle. In his right hand was the liquid drain cleaner. He viewed himself in the mirror. His forehead was greenish-blue, marked by yellow at the edges of the bruising. His right hand, gripping the drain cleaner, was also bruised and topped by abrasions on his knuckles. His elbow showed the gash that he'd first sustained at that Waco gas station—the gash that he'd ripped open several times since. He felt nauseous due to the pain in his kidneys and, after the activity of the last few days, his back and shoulder ached.

As he stared into his own eyes, Gage briefly thought about the fantasy that was Navarro's payoff. Go to prison for a few years and never work again. And while he still believed Navarro to have been mostly genuine—even though he'd left out some crucial pieces of intelligence—Gage was angriest with himself for falling into such a pit of greed.

Gage knew that, with his vocation, his life was likely to be short and marked by numerous valleys. That, despite the cherry highs—his loving parents, making it through Special Forces selection, Monika, Justina—his life's destiny was one of great pain.

"And shit situations like this," he ruefully whispered. Though he'd never admit it aloud, he didn't think he and Angelines would make it out of Berga alive.

Today was probably the day his number would finally get punched, courtesy of a thuggish Spanish criminal syndicate.

Gage Hartline had been fed to the lions.

But that didn't mean he couldn't do the world some good on his way out.

So, when the phone buzzed and Angelines placed her hand on the receiver, Gage vowed to make this first leg of the plan successful—and eliminating that scum El Toro would be a fine start.

It was now exactly 9:00 A.M.

Angelines lifted the phone, telling her guard that, after sending El Toro in, he should assemble all available guards in the main bay in full riot gear. She stared at the ceiling as she listened. "Because I said so!" she yelled back. "I've got good intel that something's about to happen. Don't say anything to El Toro, either. Just wait about thirty seconds and send him in. Then make the call. Got it?" She listened, giving Gage a tight smile. "Good." She hung up.

Gage immediately poured each soda bottle a quarter full with the drain cleaner. Moving as fast as he could manage, he capped them both, doing all he could not to shake the bottles as he placed them inside the overnight bag.

This was the tedious part.

Leaving the bag unzipped, he rushed across the office, placing the bag in one of the desk chairs.

The clock now showed 9:02 A.M.

C'mon, Salvador!

After a moment, the door buzzed and El Toro strutted through. The guard, talking urgently on his radio, closed the door behind him. Then the outer door could be heard closing. Gage was standing to the right, near the window, behind the sofa. His hands were in front of the sofa's back rest, the handcuffs around his wrists, appearing locked. Angelines was beside the back door, at the far end of the room.

El Toro swaggered across the floor, evil-eyeing Gage and stopping fifteen feet from the bag where his money supposedly sat.

He wasn't close enough.

Gage had capped the bottles just a few moments before. The seconds ticked in his mind...*13, 14, 15...*

El Toro reached behind his back, producing Angelines' .44 AutoMag, distinctive due to its long vent-rib barrel. He aimed it at Gage's head, point-blank range.

"I have your money," Gage said.

"I asked Viejes about visitors," El Toro replied, saying the words toward Angelines. "And I was told there *weren't* any, other than that skinny shit Semental."

"*La capitana* got the money from my friend on her way in," Gage said, hitching his head at Angelines.

Lowering the pistol a fraction, El Toro's animal eyes flicked across the room. "You didn't tell me nothin' 'bout no off-site meeting, bitch."

"I-I-I didn't know about it yesterday," she stammered.

Get it together, Angelines!...32, 33, 34...

"Mmm-hmm," El Toro mused. "Bet you went back to the *aposento* last night and let this *marieta* do you, didn't you." He turned to Gage.

"Què diu el meu gust xufa agrada?"

Knowing it was an insult but having no time for Catalan translations, Gage spoke Spanish as he said, "Can you just take your money so I can leave here? I don't want any more trouble from you and your friends."

"I don't want any more trouble," El Toro mocked in a feigned little girl voice. He narrowed his eyes. "Where's the money?"

...50, 51, 52...

Please let Salvador's bombs explode first!

Again Gage hitched his head, this time to the coral-colored bag on the guest chair. "As you'll see inside that bag, the money is in small, unmarked bills."

As if his street-smarts sensed that something was wrong, El Toro stood motionless. Only his eyes moved to the bag. He sucked on his teeth, curling his lip to show a flash of gold. "Get the bag for me."

Taking care to keep the loose handcuffs pressed against his body (so they wouldn't clatter to the floor) Gage started to move.

The pistol came straight up as El Toro said, "Not you, *marieta*." The pistol traversed to Angelines. "You."

...58, 59, 60!

Gage could see Angelines trying to stifle her panic. "Sancho," she protested meekly. "I was standing back here by the door in case you were, well...in case you were going to do something to our prisoner."

"Oh, I'm going to do something to him if my money is not in that bag."
He twisted the pistol, holding his aim on her as he screamed, "Now get the
damned bag, bitch!" Spittle flew from his mouth, a thin line of saliva hanging
from his snarling lower lip as he stood there huffing.

Gage turned to Angelines as he worked the conundrum in his mind.
The aluminum chips were thicker than anything Gage had ever worked with.
In fact, he'd been trained with standard aluminum foil, only a fraction of the
thickness of the refrigerator's soft aluminum. How long?

He nodded at Angelines.

...72, 73, 74...

Though her first step showed hesitation, she got herself moving, coming
up behind her desk, around it, and confidently grasping the overnight bag.
Gage held his breath as she gave the bag a few good shakes, then slung it at
El Toro.

Good girl!

The bag thudded at the prisoner's feet.

IN THE main bay, as the prisoners were trudging back to their cells, the
guards were huddled in the center, grumping that there appeared to be no
sign of a riot whatsoever.

"This has got to be another of that stupid bitch's drills," one of the
guards said.

"Yeah, but did you see who she summoned right before?"

"Who?"

"El Toro.   Maybe she sent us out here so we wouldn't hear
her moaning."

"I dunno. Rumor is he forces himself on her. Something about Los
Leones killing her son if she doesn't cooperate."

"Man, I bet that's some good stuff. Got an ass that won't quit!"

"El Toro better not hear you talking about his ass like that."

Laughter all around, followed by more bitching.

As the group of guards chuckled, three explosions rocked the building
from the second terrace, followed by large clouds of acrid white smoke.

"Holy shit!" the lead guard said, lowering his riot mask.

Chaos reigned as the guards thundered as one unit to the second floor.

Fights broke out.

Burning toilet paper descended like confetti.

To a man, every prisoner yelled and screamed and raised general hell.

Salvador the Semental had come through.

BACK IN the office, just after the bag had landed at El Toro's feet, a thud in the direction of the main bay made everyone turn. It was followed by another. And another.

Then the phone rang.

...80, 81, 82...

"The hell was all that?" El Toro yelled.

"There's construction on the new roof," Angelines said dismissively.

As the phone continued to ring, El Toro turned his eyes back to the bag at his feet. Despite his rage from a moment before, the toss of the bag clearly surprised the man who was used to having his way with the prison's captain. Then, as his mind came back to the impudence she'd shown, he adjusted the pistol on Angelines and said, "Who the hell do you think you—"

BOOM!

Despite the office's cavernous size, the explosion was cataclysmic inside its enclosed walls.

Of course, creating a hydrogen bottle bomb from aluminum mixed with a potassium hydroxide-based drain cleaner was an imperfect science. The drain cleaner was the first variable. Gage had no way of knowing its makeup other than the active ingredient that had been printed on the bottle. He'd assumed, since it was a commercial brand, that it might have had a higher concentration of potassium hydroxide than something a person could buy off the shelf—and perhaps it did.

The second major variable was the aluminum. What was its purity? He'd trained with aluminum foil—would the density of the aluminum change the reaction time? Had he made the chips too large? Too small?

And the third was the bottles. How thick were they? And did he mix in enough of the drain cleaner for the amount of aluminum he'd used? Also, did the amount of oxygen count? Here in Berga, if Gage remembered correctly, the altitude was around 2,400 feet. He'd done his bomb training just above sea level.

All things considered, with the numerous variables in play, it had taken about twenty-five seconds longer than Gage had expected. But, in the end, the desired result was the same.

Thankfully.

One thing Gage did know, however, since the explosions were created from only pressurized plastic, followed by a reaction with the highly-oxygenated air, they would likely not be fatal, even to a person standing at ground zero. And especially a healthy, well-built human being like El Toro. But, as Gage also knew, even a single bottle's explosion had concussive effects—double with two bottles.

Instinctively, Gage had dropped behind the sofa during the explosions, avoiding most of the collateral residue. Ears ringing, he lurched a second later, finding El Toro writhing on the floor ten feet from where he'd stood. The chemically-charged smoke burned Gage's eyes. After a few seconds of searching, and despite the stinging, he found the AutoMag.

In one fluid movement he checked the handgun's operational status, finding it locked and loaded. Gage aimed it at the squirming El Toro, his hands clawing his eyes as he alternated between yelps and moans. Using the three-and-a-half pound pistol like a hammer, Gage brought it down on top of El Toro's head. Twice.

El Toro was knocked unconscious.

"Make the call!" Gage yelled to Angelines, satisfied when he heard her radio Viejes, her personal guard that was usually stationed in her outer office. Though Gage's ears were ringing, he could hear Viejes reporting the riot situation. Angelines told him to disentangle himself and come to her office, ASAP.

Gage touched the "A" alarm on the keypad. He situated Angelines before taking up a blind spot to the side of the main door. Then, pistol ready, he waited.

Concentrate.

"Don't kill him, Hartline," Angelines said. "Viejes is a decent man."

Concentrate.

He's going to see the broken door, and probably some of the smoke. He's going to come in heavy.

But don't kill him.

Gage wiped his palms, one at a time, on his shirt.

Finally, the partially ruptured door was yanked open and, with no effort at being tactical, the big guard from outside clamored through, his pistol straight out in front of him.

Though he didn't think about it as he aimed and squeezed, Gage had aimed at Nicky Arnaud in the same manner a year-and-a-half before. The large bullet from the AutoMag impacted the guard's Sig Sauer just forward of the rear sight. Gage couldn't imagine the pain of the tightly held pistol being yanked from a person's hands with such force. He did get treated to a good visual, however, as the guard was thrown as if he'd been clinging to a ski rope attached to an accelerating boat. He went down in a heap, howling and rolling, clutching his broken hands to his large belly.

Gage lurched and, like before, brought the butt of the pistol smashing down on the side of the guard's head, silencing him. Gage's shocked eardrums had recovered enough so that he heard the klaxon alarm from the pressed "A" button.

Standing and turning, he witnessed Angelines running to him from the rear of the office. Her eyes were rheumy, her face was wet, and she was marked by a small cut on her forehead. She opened her hands, as if wanting instruction.

"Make the next call!"

Angelines lifted the radio and asked for a status report. After listening, she told her guards to make sure all prisoners were secure—every last one—and to get a headcount. She also insisted that the riot not be reported outside of the prison walls.

"This is our problem! We will handle it in-house." Angelines shoved the radio into her waist band and looked at Gage. "We've got about five minutes."

Gage struck the still unconscious El Toro again, seeing him twitch as a result. Then Gage dragged the guard to the bathroom, stripping him and zip-tying his hands and feet, shutting him inside the toilet room. Three minutes had passed before he arrived back in the office to find El Toro awake on the floor, Angelines standing behind him.

She'd zip-tied his hands and feet. El Toro writhed, staring at Gage as he yelled, "You're a dead man!"

Gage produced the needle nose pliers from his cargo pocket and rolled El Toro to his stomach. Sitting on El Toro's bound arms, Gage grasped El Toro's hand, burrowing the needle nose pliers underneath his left middle finger's nail.

El Toro's shrieks rose above the blaring klaxon alarm.

Twisting the pliers, Gage denailed El Toro's finger while struggling to hold him in place.

"What was your plan?" Gage asked, leaning down to his ear. "Tell me now or all nine of your nasty fingernails are coming out."

"No!"

"Tell me!"

"I was just going to get your money," El Toro grunted. "I was going to get it and let you go."

Taking all of ten seconds, Gage removed the left thumbnail next, estimating that it took twice as much twisting force. There was considerably more blood with the thumbnail.

"Ayeeee!"

"The plan?"

"Okay...okay...once I had the money, I woulda killed you," El Toro sobbed. "That was the plan."

"Who was the money for?"

"For Xavier," El Toro said, sounding surprised that Gage didn't already know.

"Xavier's the head of Los Leones," Angelines added. "Hurry, Gage!"

From all Angelines had said, and from his own research, Gage certainly knew about Xavier Zambrano. "And is Xavier nearby, waiting for the money?"

"I don't know!" El Toro shrieked.

Believing there was nothing else to be gained from this thug, Gage slid the pliers into his back pocket. He grabbed Angelines' shoulders, leaning close to her ear. "I know you wanted to kill him, but if we do that, it changes our status in the eyes of the authorities."

Her eyes blazed. "And what about Los Leones?"

"They want us dead anyway."

Angelines took the pliers from Gage's pocket. She yanked El Toro's light prison pants down. And, to Gage's shock, and satisfaction, she wrecked both of El Toro's testicles.

Before they departed, Angelines spit on the sobbing El Toro. And kicked him.

Chapter Twenty-Seven

Barcelona, Spain

CORTEZ REDON'S office was located in a pleasant yet nondescript building on the Carrer de Pau Claris. The one-way street, lined with flowering Jacaranda trees, was dominated by apartments and office space over the street-level retail establishments. Hundreds of scooters and bicycles littered the available areas of the sidewalk, though no automobiles were permitted to be parked on the busy thoroughfare. This would work in Justina and Señora Moreno's favor.

Justina was now driving, circling the block as Señora Moreno settled into a street-facing chair in a modern café one block south of Redon's office. She consulted her notepad, memorizing the key points she'd been told by her own attorney. Finally, when she was confident she knew what she wanted to say, she dialed Redon's office number, touching her rosary and whispering a one-sentence prayer that he would be in today. The woman answering the phone sounded young.

"Hello," Señora Moreno said. "Acusador Redon, please."

"He's in a meeting. May I take a message?"

"No message, dear. Please interrupt his meeting and tell him I'd like to speak with him about Ernesto Navarro."

"I'm sorry," the woman said with unconcealed irritation. "He is *in* a meeting. I can take a message."

"How long will his meeting last?"

"A while. And he has more meetings immediately afterward."

"Then you must go tell him something for me, dear. I promise you, he will be upset if you *don't*."

The young woman's voice was even and deliberate. "Like I said, I can take a message."

"Understand this: my reason for calling is an *emergencia* for the acusador. Interrupt his meeting and watch his eyes when you give him my brief message."

There was a brief pause and an outbreath. "What message do you want me to give him?"

"Please pull him aside so it's private—no one should hear this but him. Tell him I'm in possession of a large amount of Ernesto Navarro's wealth and, now that he's dead, I need to speak to Cortez about what to do with the money."

"Ernesto Navarro, the dead gangster they talked about on the news?"

"He was a businessman, too, dear."

The assistant sounded unimpressed but seemed to jot it down because she read it back to Señora Moreno, word for word.

"That's correct, dear. Please go tell him."

As she waited for Acusador Redon, Justina approached in the Volvo and Señora Moreno nodded and pointed to the sidewalk. She watched as Justina pulled the car all the way up onto the walkway, between two trees, in an area forbidden to vehicles of any type. Just as she'd been instructed, Justina exited and depressed the air valve on the back rear tire. A man on the sidewalk stopped and Señora Moreno watched as Justina shook her head and waved him on. Then, just as they'd planned, Justina dragged the scissor jack and assorted tools from the trunk, scattering them haphazardly around the flat tire. The stage was set and, just in time, Acusador Redon came on the line, sounding quite breathless.

"Who is this?" he demanded.

"Is this Acusador Redon?" Señora Moreno asked in her professional voice.

"Of course it is. Now who are you?"

"I'm not willing to reveal my identity, yet."

He cleared his throat. "Well, what's all this nonsense about supposed money belonging to Ernesto Navarro?"

"He rented a large mountain chalet from me, Cortez...may I call you Cortez?" When he didn't respond she continued. "He rented it through a shell company for years and would come and go at the oddest times, only with his assistant. I knew who he was, of course, from the news, but never reported it since he paid handsomely in cashier's checks, regular as clockwork."

Redon could be heard groaning before he spoke in an admonishing tone, saying, "So, he was your renter? That's why you called me?"

"He left something behind, Cortez. Something of great value that I now have."

"Money?" he asked in a low voice.

"Negotiable financial instruments. When I saw on the news that he'd been killed, I confiscated them."

"And why are you calling me?" he asked, his tone one of suspicion mingled with hopefulness.

"I saw your press conference. I thought you might be interested in," she cleared her throat, "*partnering* with me to make sure these instruments are converted."

"Madam, am I to believe that you are truly holding negotiable securities that were owned by the notorious gangster, Ernesto Navarro?"

"It's the truth, and I'm ready to make a deal that will sufficiently compensate me for my trouble. After that, Cortez, I don't care what you do with the remainder of the money. Understand?"

Redon's response was thunderstruck silence.

Smiling because she knew she had him, Señora Moreno said, "I'm sitting a few blocks away from your office, Cortez. El Café de Limón. You will come alone, right now."

"Why don't we meet here?"

"I may be a widowed landlady, Cortez, but I'm not stupid. Now, let's have a chat here in public, shall we?"

"Very well. In the interest of the good people of Catalonia, I'm on my way."

Señora Moreno touched the screen, ending the call. Justina was adjusting the scissor jack under the car. When she turned, Señora Moreno pointed to her own eyes and motioned up the sidewalk.

Justina tugged her short shirt upward, then pulled her thong up into view over the waistband. Laughing, Señora Moreno gave her a double thumbs-up.

"Now let's just hope your libido overrides your greed, Acusador Redon," Señora Moreno whispered. Mineral water at her right hand, she leaned back to watch the show.

"JUST PLAY it straight, Cortez," Acusador Redon murmured to himself, slipping his mobile phone and business cards into his pocket. He'd struggled for a full minute, trying to decide whether or not to wear his suit jacket. In the end he'd donned it, feeling it might make him look a tad more official, more formal. Breath mint clicking in his mouth, he stepped from his office, telling his assistant he needed to step out.

"What was with that woman?" his assistant asked with a sneer.

Cinching his tie he said, "Just another crazy. It seems we grow them here in Catalonia." He popped his cuffs. "Grabbing a bite. Be back soon."

Cortez was off, skipping the cramped elevator and padding down the stairs from his third floor office. If this woman was serious, and did hold negotiable financial instruments—*negotiable* being the operative word—once owned by Ernesto Navarro, Cortez would be in an enviable, yet precarious, position. Xavier Zambrano, of course, felt he was entitled to anything owned by Navarro and, in the unwritten code of the underworld, he did. But, as Cortez reminded himself as he shoved the stairwell door open, emerging on the cool morning sidewalk, Xavier didn't have to find out about this.

"And that's why we play it straight...at first," he said to himself, setting a quick pace down the street. "Let's allow her to make the indecent proposal and then let's see if these are indeed negotiable instruments." It had been quite some time since he'd brushed up on investment law. He began summarizing a list of negotiable instruments at the only crosswalk between his office and the cafe.

"Promissory notes, cheques, bearer bonds, warrants, debentures..." Acusador Redon muttered to himself while waiting at the crosswalk. Then his discourse was cut short when he noticed a tall, well-built blonde fumbling with a scissor jack beside her flat tire.

He glanced left, seeing the café just past where she was parked, but his eyes were drawn back to the bombshell struggling with the jack—and, of course, her pink thong panties jutting from the small skirt that contained her deliciously-proportioned rear end.

Feeling his neck flush at the ribald sight, he shuffled audibly to a stop, watching as she slumped, the jack lying impotently on its side with two narrow bars extending from its eye-hole.

She turned and looked at him and, in accented Spanish, said, "I hate days like this."

Flashing his jury grin, Cortez motioned to the jack. "May I help you with that, *preciosa?*"

The woman stood. She was nearly half a head taller than Cortez and her frustration was evident. "Will you help? I'm clueless about these things."

She stood in his space, her large breasts straining against her tight shirt, close enough for him to smell her scent, making him forget why he'd even left the office. Cortez looked up at her and said, "I must say you're quite beautiful. And what's your accent?"

"Polish," Justina replied. "I'm visiting Spain and, as you can see, not doing too well."

Cortez shed his jacket, hanging it from the Volvo's mirror. He lifted one of the tire irons. "What brought you to Barcelona?"

"I came down for the summer to visit my sister and her husband. This is their car."

"How long have you been here?"

"Couple of weeks."

"Do you like it?" he asked, seating the jack and looking up at her.

"I guess I like Barcelona but I don't like my brother-in-law. I don't think he wants me staying with them." She glanced away. "I'm just lonely."

Cortez squeezed his eyes shut. In his mind he screamed "gracias!" to the God he didn't believe in, because this was going to be too easy.

"Well," he said, "let's see if we can't get you fixed up."

Not having much experience with changing tires, he consulted the diagram on the black vinyl bag that had held the tire tools. After loosening the lug nuts, he positioned the jack just in front of the tire and elevated the right rear corner of the car from the sidewalk. Reading the diagram he said, "Now, all you do is finish taking off those nuts, then pull the tire off and replace it with the spare. Twist the lug nuts back on, lower the jack, then tighten the lug nuts in a star pattern." Smiling, he handed her the diagram. "Can you handle it or do you want me to stay?"

"I can do it," she replied, again standing in his space. "Being here, in a different country, knowing hardly anyone, is more difficult than I'd thought it would be. But then someone like you, a new friend, comes along."

"Is that what I am, a new friend?"

Her face took on a rueful expression. "With my luck, I'm sure you're married."

Ignoring the comment, and in a practiced motion, all while feeling the throbbing, elevating arousal between his legs, he pressed a business card in her hand. "I'd like you to call me, darling. Perhaps you'd let me show you around a bit."

She read his card. "Acusador...you sound important."

He made a shooing motion. "Don't be intimidated, my beauty." He tapped the card. "Just call. Call soon."

With no nod of agreement, the frustration coming back to her face, the girl placed his card on the ground as she went back to work on the tire.

Cortez watched her for a few seconds, finding himself struggling to swallow. Finally, cursing the deadline imposed by the woman on the phone, he grabbed his jacket, said goodbye again, and walked away.

The girl didn't respond.

Feeling suddenly dejected, he crossed the side street, turning left as the door bells jingled at El Café de Limón. Sitting to the left, the only patron in the café, a diminutive woman with a beehive of black and gray hair climbed off her high stool and headed to him, her right hand extended.

"Acusador Redon, I am Maria Herrero and I am pleased to make your acquaintance."

After glancing through the window, able to see only the taillight of the Volvo, Cortez forced a polite smile as he shook the woman's hand. "Please understand, Señora Herrero, that I'm only here in the *duty* entrusted in me by the people of Catalonia."

This seemed to throw her, as a troubled expression briefly crossed her round face. "I see," she said distantly. "I guess I probably shouldn't ask you what I'd planned, then."

Between two forces of gravity, lust and greed, Redon felt himself transferring from one field's pull to the other. He clasped the older woman's hand, sandwiching it with his left. "Let's don't be hasty. You suggested a chat, and a chat we shall have."

She tugged her hand away. "But I don't want to get myself in trouble."

"What trouble?" he asked in a breezy tone. "We're just two acquaintances having a friendly discussion." Signaling the young man behind the counter, Redon asked for another mineral water. He took Señora *Herrero's* water and led her to the sitting nook in the corner. Once they were both seated, Cortez leaned forward, clutching his hands together.

"Now, please tell me, dear lady, without fear of consequence, what you wanted to tell me."

PERUSING THE feed on Facebook, Mara, Cortez Redon's assistant, heard the ding of the elevator out in the hallway but paid it no mind. They shared the third floor with an engineering firm and the firm's early workers would be heading out to lunch.

As she read a thinly-veiled posting by a friend, clearly an insult to another girl they both knew, Mara's phone buzzed. It was the front receptionist.

"Yeah, Pilar?"

"There's a man here to see the acusador."

"He's out," Mara said, already refocusing on the snide comments below the posting.

The front receptionist, Pilar, a heavy, middle-aged woman who liked to live vicariously through Mara's nocturnal adventures, lowered her voice to a whisper. "Let me send him back anyway. I'm flushed all over…you've got to see him."

Mara hit the red X at the top right of the screen. Pilar might have been a frump, but she had an unerring instinct in men. "Okay, give me thirty seconds and buzz him through."

Grabbing her purse, Mara quickly applied fresh lipstick and powdered the shine from her nose. She glanced down at her cheap department-store blouse, unbuttoning another button and spreading the collar. A moment later, the buzzer buzzed, the handle turned, and in walked a gorgeous specimen of a man, prowling forward with the rippling confidence of a Bengal tiger.

He was tall and lean, but muscular in the right places. Complementing his rich tan, his dark hair was flecked with spots of light brown, burnished by the sun. His clothes were casual but chic and appeared tailored—probably from a fine fashion designer. He oozed superiority, infused with animal sexuality. Despite his chiseled face, his alluring body, and his fashion-magazine wardrobe, the most prominent of all the visitor's features was the large tattoo of a smoking pistol on the side of his neck.

Mara knew, as soon as she saw the tattoo, that he was a member of the notorious Leones gang.

Not that she cared.

Moving around her desk without invitation, he took Mara's hand and kissed it, saying, "*Buenos días,* beautiful lady. My name is Xavier Zambrano and I am here to see the acusador."

Addled, Mara blurted something about the acusador having stepped out.

Xavier stood his ground, glancing at his large, expensive-looking wristwatch. "He doesn't take *el dinar* this early, does he?" he asked, having switched to Catalan.

"No, he just said he was stepping out."

Stepping forward so his body actually made her chair wheel backward—the action nearly caused Mara's heart to burst…she thought he was making an advance—Xavier leaned over her, allowing her to smell the tastefully faint citrus scent of his cologne or lotion. When he straightened, she ruefully realized he'd not been making a pass. As Mara dipped her head, he slowly sounded out the message she'd just taken from the woman on the phone. Mara used a modified shorthand—"medium-hand," she called it—because the acusador liked to be able to decipher her notes.

He stabbed the paper. "When did this call come in?"

"Just fifteen minutes ago," she replied, her voice sullen as she was still fretting that he wasn't coming on to her.

"Did he leave to meet the person who called?"

"I don't know."

"Was it a man or a woman?"

"An older-sounding woman," Mara answered formally, disliking this man's mounting intensity.

"Did he tell you where he was going?"

"He said he was going to pick up a bite to eat."

"Where?" he barked.

She glanced away, finally shrugging. "He didn't say."

Xavier leaned down again, veins visible at his temples and on his neck. "Think! Are you certain?"

"I'm *quite* certain."

"Tell me everything about the phone call from that woman," he loudly demanded, "then tell me *exactly* how long it was before Redon left."

Mara touched three digits on her phone, leaving it on speaker.

"Yeah, Mara," came a man's voice.

"I have a troublemaker up here, Roberto."

"On my way." The line clicked dead.

Feeling a measure of vengeful satisfaction, Mara narrowed her eyes. "The acusador doesn't answer to a León, Señor Zambrano, and neither do I. Roberto is a very large security guard and he'll be here in a few seconds."

Xavier straightened, nodding once as he backed away. "What a pity."

"A pity?"

"I apologize for my intensity, but the acusador and I are actually acquaintances."

"Yeah, right," she replied.

"But that's not the pitiful part. I was going to suggest drinks after work. *Dinner* and drinks." Xavier Zambrano turned as Roberto, the obese security guard, burst in from the hallway door, breathing like he'd just run with the bulls in Pamplona. Xavier, smirking, put his hands up innocently as he showed himself out, pausing at the door as Roberto, huffing his way through the query, asked Mara if she was okay.

"He didn't do anything wrong," Mara murmured sullenly.

Xavier winked at her, then stepped away. The last thing she heard was the stairwell door being yanked open, followed by the shuffle of the gangster's feet as he hurriedly descended.

Chapter Twenty-Eight

HAVING DUCKED under the cold shower for a few seconds, Gage donned the guard uniform and moved Angelines into the running water. She was yelling that there was no time but he ignored her, having witnessed the amount of airborne drain cleaner that had soaked her body. Still wearing her clothes, she ran her hands through her thick hair while he dumped shampoo over her. She made a sudden hissing sound.

"Clamp your eyes shut," he whispered, taking care not to allow the captive guard to hear them. "You're getting mild chemical reactions but it'll all wash away. You might look sunburned for a few days, but that's it."

Shutting off the water, Gage pulled her from the bathroom and handed her a towel. "We've gotta go, but you should make another call. Remember, you're in charge here. Your guards don't yet know what you're up to. Until then, *you* call the shots."

Gage watched as her uncharacteristic timidity seemed to evaporate. She looked away for a moment, nodding. Then, pulling away from him, her clothes still dripping, she stalked across the office and grabbed the handheld radio.

"Where's my headcount? And I want a status update from each unit."

Feeling slightly emboldened, Gage stepped to the rear door of the office, the remaining greenish smoke having settled on the lower half of the room. She told him to wait as she listened to the status reports coming in.

"Salvador's bombs caused all sorts of commotion. There's a host of fires in the main bay. No one mentioned the bomb in here."

"Good. How long?"

"They're getting the last of the stragglers in their cells. We need to be gone in two minutes."

"Will the guard at the garage door be in his station?"

"Yes, but I've got a better idea than you driving."

"What's that?"

"Let me drive. I'll tell them I got burned by an acid bomb and I'm rushing to the doctor. Given what just happened, they'll believe me. It's all they've been hearing on their radios."

"But when they find the guard and El Toro, they'll determine that you're in on things," Gage protested. "And the headcount will show me as missing."

"They're going to figure that out anyway. And it beats being shot on the way out."

She had a point.

Hoping he could pass muster as a guard, Gage opened the rear door of the office, seeing an empty, brightly lit hallway that led to a T-intersection to his left. Holstering the AutoMag, he stepped into the hallway, obscured by the riot shield. Angelines would follow a moment later.

It was time to escape this hell known as Berga.

ACUSADOR CORTEZ Redon placed his mineral water on the table, swishing the water in his mouth before swallowing it. He was deliberately taking time to digest the fantastic story, trying his best to poke holes in it, but overwhelmed by the possibilities in the event the woman's tale was true.

For what it was worth, she seemed quite genuine. There was a grandmotherly quality about her but, in a matter of minutes, he was able to discern the fact that she was certainly moneyed and the twinkle in her eye suggested that she would like to keep a portion of Navarro's money, with his help, of course.

In Redon's experience, wealthy people were among earth's greediest.

"So," Redon said, drawing the word out. "You've got what were allegedly Ernesto Navarro's bearer bonds."

"Yes," she replied, unblinking.

"I'm not a lawyer who specializes in finance or banking, but I thought bearer bonds were an anachronism."

"Whether they are or aren't, these are genuine. They don't expire for a few more years."

"And you found them when you determined that he wasn't coming back."

"When I saw you on television commenting on his death, I went to the home to see if Navarro's...*person*...had come for his things. Nothing had been touched and then, when I read the paper, I saw that Navarro's right-hand man had been killed along with him." She patted the back of Redon's hand. "Cortez, the only other people they ever brought to that house were young women…prostitutes. So, in my thinking, no one knew where to look for the money once he'd been killed."

Redon stopped her. "Weren't you concerned with him as a renter? He was notorious."

"Not really. I didn't even know it at first."

"How did you know to call me?"

"I saw you on a special news report. You were dashing, Cortez. So in control."

He adjusted his tie, smiling. "Please, dear lady, go on."

"When I went to the house, everything was still there, untouched."

"How often did he stay there?"

"It was hard to say. Sometimes for a few days, other times for weeks."

"Alone?"

"Like I said, just with his assistant who always paid the bills. And the women."

Breathe, old boy, breathe. Redon fought the urge to dance around the café. "Tell me about these female visitors."

Señora Herrero pursed her lips. "Harlots," she said with disdain. "Buxom, wearing sinfully skimpy clothing. Drinking and probably drugs…late-night frolicking in the hot tub." She looked off in the distance and shook her head.

So she's against his bringing hookers to her home but she'll gladly steal his money, he thought, sticking his tongue into his cheek to avoid a smile. Redon leaned forward, having waited to ask the most important questions. "Where did you find the bearer bonds?"

"In a briefcase. It was well-hidden."

"Locked?"

She smirked and diverted her eyes.

"Where were the bonds issued?"

"A bank in Luxembourg."

"Are you completely certain they're genuine? Like I said, bearer bonds are outmoded. Although, to be fair, I'm not surprised a man like Navarro held some—they're most certainly a favored instrument of money launderers."

"Acusador Redon," she said sharply, "while I may look like I should be home baking cookies, I'm an accomplished businesswoman. The bonds each have a face value of fifty thousand U.S. dollars and have matured completely. They're no longer drawing interest, but they're absolutely viable."

"I hope you haven't fallen prey to some sort of prop," he said. "Because I've not seen bearer bonds since—"

Redon was cut short by the older woman's action. She reached into her large purse and removed a single sheet of folded linen paper. Taking her time, she unfolded the thick greenish paper, flattening it on the table before them, turning it so he could read the text.

It was, indeed, a bearer bond—or a fake of the highest quality—marked by several official seals. "Fifty thousand United States dollars," he croaked. Redon's mouth was dry, very dry. After a long draught of the faintly sulfuric mineral water he reverently touched the paper as he asked the critical question.

"How many of these bonds did you recover?"

"Just so you know, I do *not* have them with me."

He nodded. "The amount, please?"

"Well, there's an entire sheaf of those bonds."

A sheaf! His throat was so swollen and dry he couldn't even swallow. "How many?" he managed, knowing his squawking voice sounded ridiculous.

"I've counted them three times, Cortez."

"Very good."

"And I'm quite accurate."

"Please, darling…how much?"

She smiled, drawing the moment out. "There are three hundred thirty-nine bearer bonds. The total value is sixteen point nine five million, U.S."

Cortez Redon's jaw came unhinged.

She moved her hand over his, rubbing it like a lover might. "And I'll split it with you, Cortez, every dollar. But in order to do that, you have to come with me to Luxembourg and use your influence and experience to make certain that the bank will accept the bonds without trouble. That done, you can go your own way, as will I."

Fighting the urge to let his mind race, Redon narrowed his eyes, focusing on the proposal. "Madam, forgive me, but if you're as successful as you say, why would you want to create a problem of such a large amount of excess cash?"

"My money is tied up in real estate. And need I tell you what has happened in real estate?" She finished her water. "There is a beach somewhere in this world with sugary sand, and it's calling my name. I shall sit on that beach, reading good books, dining famously, as I spend that cash over the balance of the ten or twenty years I have left. I've no children or grandchildren," she said wistfully, "so walking away for me is not of any concern. And I shall go someplace where cash is welcome payment."

With such wealth on the table, Redon was easily convinced. His mind began to race. With his adequate state salary and his lifetime of legitimate investments, he'd created a nest egg of over one million euro. That number would be quite a bit higher had he not made a few bad moves prior to the long bull market at the end of the previous century but, nonetheless, it was quite enough to support his overweight wife—provided she lived frugally. He wasn't concerned about his two sons, ungrateful shits they were. Both were well beyond the age of accountability and could fend for themselves as far as he was concerned.

But the jewel of Redon's "retirement package" was the nearly three million euro tucked away in Switzerland at the Banque Hottinger. Nearly all of it had come from his illegal dealings with Navarro and Xavier, along with that one tidy addition he'd made years ago in return for throwing a murder trial (but that was another story). As his secret fund had swelled, he'd found it harder and harder not to leave his wife. She'd grown fatter by the day, now taking painkillers just from the discomfort of holding up her massive girth. It sickened him. Every time Redon mounted a skinny young woman, staring up at him as if he were the lord of creation, he would instantly think about the bliss of his long-awaited escape to the islands.

Unfortunately, Redon had never been able to make the math work with his three million euro. At a conversion of about four million dollars, he'd struggle to make three percent. So, living on dividends only, he'd only generate $120,000 a year. Given the lifestyle he'd come to expect, that wasn't nearly enough money to satisfy him.

But now, after this glorious turn of events, he could walk away with twelve million dollars U.S., which would immediately put him in a different strata with the discreet banking community. He'd be able to assure himself a very safe five percent return, perhaps as much as ten if the economy turned.

At five percent on twelve million dollars, tax-free of course, he was looking at an annual return of nearly $600,000. *That's not private jet money, but it's fine dinners, a damn nice second-row villa on Seven Mile Beach and first-class tickets whenever I feel the need to fly.*

Unable to help his avarice, Redon closed his eyes, thinking of the vacationing women, and how impressed they would be with his shiny sports car, his villa and, of course, his outdoor hot tub. Though he didn't care for drugs, he'd make sure to keep a stash of coke and weed, just to loosen the vacationers up...*and*, he thought with unrestrained glee, *there'll be a whole new batch of them each week. All I need to do now is travel to Luxembourg and Zurich and buy a good established identity.*

Then the realization hit him: *I can be on the beach in a week!*

He opened his eyes, again clasping his hands over Señora Herrero's, unable to contain his jury smile. "Madam, provided you and I can trust each other to keep this to ourselves for as long as we both shall live, I'd say this is the beginning of a lovely, albeit brief, partnership."

"There's one item I'm hesitant to mention."

"Please do," he sang.

"Through some incredibly subtle inquiries, I learned that the authorities believe Ernesto Navarro was killed by a rival gang. Supposedly, they're assuming his operations."

"Go on," he said warily.

"It did occur to me that perhaps I should approach them with these bearer bonds instead. Perhaps they would give me a larger percentage than you."

Cortez Redon nearly fell off his stool. "They would take every last American penny of that money because they would kill you," he spat. "They would kill you viciously."

She touched her hand to her mouth.

"Madam, scrub such thoughts from your mind," he admonished. "You're speaking of Los Leones…savages." He softened his face. "But by working with me, you're assuring yourself of safety, of security and refinement. Do you understand?"

"You're heaven-sent, señor."

"We both are."

He watched as she placed the bottle of mineral water in her purse and used a wet paper napkin to wipe her glass and the table where her arms had rested. Easing herself off the stool, she glanced outside. Bringing her eyes back she said, "Now, Cortez, as you might imagine, I have not used my real name today. And, if I get the remotest inclination that you're following me or trying to find me, I will make this deal with someone else."

Showing his palms, he dipped his head and said, "I'm only interested in working with you, madam—not following you."

"I need your mobile number."

He handed over his card.

"Very well," she replied, dropping it in her purse. "I will call you tomorrow, early. Can you be ready to go at a moment's notice?"

Uncharacteristically showing nervousness, he chewed on his thumbnail, thinking through all the loose ends. He did own a term life insurance policy, one that was purchased long before the euro conversion. It was worth about

800,000 euro and, despite his disdain for his marital partner, would go a long way in making sure she could easily survive without him. If he were to choose an activity, such as sailing alone—something he did on occasion—and were to come up missing, a case could be made that the insurance company should pay even with the absence of a body. It would be a battle for her, but there was precedent and a good team of lawyers would have a solid case, especially with his standing in Catalonia.

"As you might imagine, I have quite a bit to do, but I think, starting tomorrow, I could leave with several hours' notice."

"Fine. You'll hear from me. Make sure you answer when I call."

"I will."

"Please pay the tab," she said with a wink. He watched as she pushed the door open with her rump, still careful not to leave any fingerprints, and headed down the street away from his office.

Mind lurching into overdrive, Redon turned to find the server so he might pay. But, to his great surprise, standing next to the glass counter, her large blue eyes on his, was the tall Polish bombshell from earlier.

Feeling his lips parting uncontrollably, he said, "How long have you been here?"

"When I finished changing my tire, I parked and came in to thank you." She gnawed on her lip, dipping her head. "I guess that was your wife."

"My wife?" he blurted. "No, no, no, dear…that was not my wife. That was a, uh, business meeting."

Redon watched her head come back up, mirth spreading over her face. She took two steps toward him, towering over him.

"Sorry I stopped talking on the street."

"Don't be," he whispered.

"I was feeling…tempted. Sometimes, when I'm lonely, I'm too easy."

His mouth moved but he made no sound.

"Is there someplace we can go?" she asked.

"Go?" he croaked.

Her hand dithered on his lapel, moving behind his head in a massaging motion. "I'd like to be alone with you. I realize that sounds bad but, please understand, my time in Spain has not been good and I'm truly craving the company of a cultured man. I've got all afternoon and no plans tonight, either."

Feeling his jaw muscles fail him again, Redon stared up at her and thought, *Of all days! I've been paying for ass for twenty years now and, on the day my bejeweled ship finally comes in, when I've got more to do than I can fathom, I get propositioned by a Polish girl fit for a Mallorca stripper pole.*

Probably sensing his hesitation, she leaned over, kissing his cheek and whispering in his ear. "I'm sure you have to get back to work and you're probably married. Just think of it as a long lunch and," she said, cupping his head in her hands, "you have to promise me it won't be a one-time thing. Since I turned eighteen I've exclusively dated older men and, while I'm here, I'd like a boyfriend like you...one who can take care of me."

"I should go buy an *El Gordo* ticket today," he mumbled, speaking of the Spanish lottery.

"What?"

"Nothing, darling," he replied, dropping ten euro on the counter and leading her out. "There's a hotel just down the street here—" He froze in the doorway, feeling a stab of stupidity. "That is what you had in mind, isn't it?"

"Cortez," she said, leaning to his ear, "take me to that hotel and make beautiful love to me."

Acusador Cortez Redon nearly lost his balance. But, after recovering quickly, he tugged her hand, unable to keep from skipping down the Carrer de Pau Claris.

STANDING ACROSS the street under the breathing lavender blooms of a Jacaranda tree, Xavier Zambrano watched Acusador Cortez Redon interacting with the tall blonde in the doorway of a place called El Café de Limón. Minutes earlier, Xavier had spotted him in the café, sitting there talking to the dumpy old woman with the beehive hairdo. Having crossed the street to await his exit, Xavier now had watched the entire scene play out, one that reminded him of the types of grifts he and his fellow neighborhood punks had run as teens.

The tall blonde, who for some reason seemed familiar to Xavier, had approached the café from the parking garage down the street. She'd nearly tiptoed in her approach to the café, peering through the large glass front from its edge. Then she eased into the café and watched Redon and the older woman from the far side of the dining area.

After a few minutes the older woman exited and, just when Xavier had been about to follow her, she walked away but quickly came back, peering through the window just as the comely blonde had done. Finally, smiling at what she'd seen, the older woman crossed the perpendicular street and that's when Xavier had followed just to see her get into the passenger seat of a white Volvo parked on the first level of the parking garage. Realizing she wasn't going anywhere, he moved back to his position across the street—where he was now, watching the tender exchange between Redon and the tall blonde. Then, with that familiar inflamed glow of fresh lovers, they hurried down the street hand in hand.

Cortez, you horny idiot. You're too small, too old, and you look like a fairytale elf. Are you gullible enough to think that piece of tail would be interested in you?

Xavier followed from across the street and was able to see the older woman's silhouette in the shadowed garage. She lowered herself in the passenger seat but turned, watching the couple pass by from her furtive position.

This was definitely a hustle of some sort—and Xavier remembered the message he'd seen at Redon's office: a woman claiming to have Ernesto Navarro's money. He looked around, finding no other people who seemed to be interested in the couple's movements.

Why would two women be working such an angle on Acusador Cortez Redon?

He pondered it, not thinking too long about it because, just past the garage, he watched as the couple stopped in front of a Riposo Hotel—one of hundreds spread throughout Europe's larger cities—and devour one another with a kiss. Redon's hands, already lower because of his small stature, roamed up the back of the tall blonde's legs, cupping her rear end with his fingers before they eventually probed underneath her short skirt.

Then, laughing like thieves, they entered the hotel.

His mind warring over which path to take, Xavier turned left, walking back toward the café. He entered the side of the parking garage by jumping a waist-high wall, closing on the rear of the Volvo with great speed and stealth. The light of a mobile phone could be seen in the darkened car—the old woman was typing on it. Unable to discern if the car was locked, he dropped below the window at the back and waited a moment before he lightly tapped on the sheet metal of the rear hatch, rhythmically setting a slow beat, very soft.

Tap, tap, tap, tap—never changing tone or speed.

Nothing happened.

He continued to tap, the sound not unlike an annoying dripping from above.

Still no response from the woman.

Like a patient snake stalking its prey, Xavier continued to tap.

SEÑORA MORENO had just replayed the recording of Cortez Redon. It wasn't as clear as she would have liked—actually undecipherable in spots—but his indictment of Los Leones was clear as a bell, and might come in handy later.

Tap-tap-tap.

She turned her head. *What in the world is that?*

It went on and on. Señora Moreno wondered if it was droplets of drainage water dripping on the car from the level above. But the constant rhythm was irritating and continued on for several minutes while she texted several instructional messages to Justina. Finally, when the noise didn't abate, she unlocked the car and stepped out. She viewed the diminutive spare tire that Justina had installed. It seemed to be on tight. She walked to the rear of the car, where the sound had come from, viewing the roof as best she could and finding no evidence of water droplets. In fact, standing still, she could no longer hear the sound.

Looking out at Carrer de Pau Claris she glanced both directions, seeing nothing but parked scooters, swaying trees, and two businesswomen in smart suits walking with white bags that probably contained their lunch.

Feeling an unnerving shiver travel up her back, she took a steadying breath and walked back to the passenger door. With one final glance around the mostly empty parking garage, Señora Moreno again took her seat in the Volvo.

And, just as she did, the driver's door opened and a man, menacing black blade in his left hand, dropped into the driver's seat. He clamped one hand over her mouth and put the point of the blade to her throat.

Speaking accented Catalan, he told her to close her door.

Feeling the blade puncturing her skin, and unflinchingly realizing this was probably her end, her passageway to reunite with her beloved Mateo, Señora Moreno, queerly excited by this dangerous liaison, found the door handle and pulled the door shut, her mind running through her narrow series of options.

The man, keeping the blade on her throat, reached to the driver's door, mimicking her actions. He wore a beard, neatly trimmed, over his richly tanned face. He had one of those sneering smiles, trashy but handsome, and could have been a famous athlete, an actor or even the sleazy womanizer who barked for the Ferris wheel at the carnival. But most prominent, even in the shadows of the darkened car, was the conspicuous tattoo on the man's neck—it was the tattoo of a smoking revolver.

Los Leones.

The man moved his tongue around his lower teeth, his wet mouth audible with the movement. Suddenly, he pricked her throat, sending a sharp pain through her body before he asked, "Who are you, lady, and why are you working a confidence game with that tall blonde on Cortez Redon?"

"What tall blonde are you talking abo—*ayeee!*" Señora Moreno squealed, unable to control herself as the blade of his knife twisted on the skin of her neck.

"Now *that*, my dear, is just a flesh wound," he murmured, pulling the knife back and sounding completely at ease. "I can honestly tell you I don't get my kicks from harming old women but," he said, moving his right hand behind her neck as the flat black blade of the Smith & Wesson M&P knife was held in front of her eyes, "I won't hesitate if you lie to me. Redon is a gutter-dwelling piece of shit—that I won't argue. So, please, dispense with your lies and tell me about this hustle."

Her mind briefly clouded by pain, Señora Moreno gasped for breath, trying to determine an angle for proceeding. What she came up with was surprisingly lucid. The goal today was to entrap Acusador Redon. And Justina's boyfriend, Gage, was at odds with Los Leones over Navarro's money. This knife-wielding man was with Los Leones, so bringing Navarro's money into it would be the incorrect pathway. It would incense her aggressor and make the situation worse. She'd be better off to put him on the wrong track. She chose the first idea that came to her mind.

"That girl you saw...we work together."

"How?"

"We run schemes against men in public places."

"What kind of schemes?"

"All kinds. It just depends on our target's proclivities."

"Really," he said flatly, clearly not a question.

"As you said, Redon's not a good man...an easy target for a girl like her."

"Then why were you talking to him first, in the café?"

After years of real estate deals, Señora Moreno was an expert at ferreting out liars. She knew the telltale signs, the hesitations, the tonal changes. Rather than appear distressed by his questioning, she tried to make herself look disappointed, like a sullen teenager who'd been caught with cigarettes but was too old, too experienced to be entirely scared of the coming punishment.

"Why?" he asked, shaking her neck and lifting the blade.

"Like I said, we have a process. I approached him, telling him I'm her aunt and her brother is awaiting trial for robbery. Then, after wending my way through the story, I offered her to him, sexually, in exchange for his intervention, so the charges against her brother might be dropped."

"So, there is no brother?" he asked.

"Of course not," she said. "And now we will have pictures of him, naked, in a hotel room."

He smiled with mouth only. "Poor Cortez."

Señora Moreno eyed her captor.

His smile faded. "You know what? You're a magnificent liar."

"Why do you say that?"

"Because I know you called Redon about Ernesto Navarro's money."

Oh no...

Feeling the tension change in his controlling hand, Señora Moreno futilely resisted as the blade ascended, pointing between both of her eyes before he lowered it, pushing it between her lips.

Just before he sliced her face, in his British-accented Catalan, he said, "Time to tell the truth, old lady."

Despite her absence of fear, Señora Moreno was unable to control her screams as he sawed through her flesh.

Chapter Twenty-Nine

GAGE CLOMPED down the prison hallway, shield over his face, baton in his right hand—*this is how the guards walk*, he reminded himself. Swaggering. Arrogant. Uncaring. He recalled first entering through this same hallway, having no idea that he'd be stabbed soon thereafter. And while he could certainly feel the prick of the scabs over his still-healing wounds, it was now his upper buttocks and kidney area that screamed with each step. Gage knew he needed to get a strong antibiotic into his system—once they were free and clear of Berga.

The double doors were just ahead and to the right. According to Angelines, her car was just through the doors, situated behind a screen of boxes. As he pushed through the door, he heard someone calling out from down the hallway—a man's voice. Without hesitating, using the mechanical clicking of the door's metal latch as a reason to not hear the voice, Gage walked straight through.

Damn it!

As soon as he'd passed through the doors, he lurched to the left. With Angelines' car in his peripheral vision, Gage wielded the baton from the shadowy blind spot.

Don't follow. Please, don't follow.

Gage waited, silently cursing their luck. If the guards learned that Angelines was in on this, the game was up.

A droplet of sweat collected on Gage's nose under the mask. Quite a bit of time had passed. Maybe whoever had yelled had dismissed Gage's coming into the warehouse.

The door latch clicked.

The door opened to the inside, beaming antiseptic light into the darkened area. Without any discernible caution, a guard in full armor stepped through. He didn't look left but walked straight ahead, as if he were routinely headed out into the warehouse. He must have been one of the guards who'd been mustered in the main bay. Gage reasoned the guard didn't suspect him; he probably assumed Gage was one of the tower guards.

There was one problem: according to Angelines, the warehouse guard was required to remain at his post at all times. If this guard stepped out into the warehouse, the warehouse guard would see him. They would talk and then this one would ask where the guard who just came through the double doors went. The warehouse guard wouldn't know who he was talking about. Then suspicions would rise and all sorts of bad things would happen.

Gage had no choice. He lunged forward, smacking the guard in the back of his neck, right where his spine met with his skull. It was a dangerous blow but, because of the guard's protective helmet, Gage was limited in his places to strike. As the baton had come whipping across, Gage took a little bit off his swing. The blow itself, even at eighty percent, knocked the guard out cold. He went down in a heap, his helmet clattering on the floor. Gage whipped a thick orange zip tie from his belt and secured his hands behind him.

The door flung open again. Gage whirled, jerking the AutoMag from its unmatched holster, his finger on the trigger.

It was Angelines.

"What happened?" she asked, her hair still dripping as she stared at the downed guard.

"He was behind me in the hallway. The muster that you called must be over. Now we've got to haul ass before someone finds him, or us."

She clicked her key fob and the trunk automatically popped up.

"Let me drive," Gage said. "This jig is about to be up."

"No," she still insisted. "They're going to come after us with the same gusto, regardless. And with me driving, if we can get out peacefully, it might buy us an hour before they figure out what happened."

Gage climbed into the trunk. "If something happens, gun the gas and don't let up." He tapped the piece of plastic leading to the back seat. "Open this pass-through so you can hear me." That done, he held the trunk lid down with one hand and the AutoMag in his other. When she started the car, he asked if she could hear him.

"Yes, clear as a bell."

"Can you tell the trunk is unlatched?"

She peered out her door. "No. Now be quiet."

Faster than he would have liked, she backed from the wall of cardboard boxes as her tires lightly squealed on the painted floor. There was a light chirp from the brakes as she stopped reversing. They drove forward a bit before stopping again. Gage heard the window going down.

"Gotta hurry, Pito," she said, sounding routine yet irritable.

"What happened to you, *capitana*? You're soaked," came the distant voice. "We heard on the radio that there were bottle bombs on the second terrace. Were you up there?"

"That's why I called the muster. I had one thrown at me, too, and I got covered in some sort of acid."

"Are you okay?"

"I will be once you open this door. I tried to wash it off but regular water won't remove it completely."

"But *capitana*, the infirmary…they have something to neutralize acid. Don't waste time driving to—"

"I've already been to the infirmary and their stuff didn't work!" she yelled. "My skin's on fire so I'm driving to the hospital at Manresa and, because I think there could be more to the riot, I didn't want to pull anyone from the infirmary staff to go with me. Now, can you open the damned door? I'll be back as soon as they treat my skin."

"*Sí*, right away."

The mechanical sounds of the motorized door began, followed by her rolling up her window.

"Good girl," Gage whispered. She'd played that well. Then, just as she'd begun to pull forward, he heard a distant sound from the back of the car. It was a clunking sound, like a door being open and shut.

Following that was an urgent yell, in Spanish. *"Alto! Alto!"*

"Alto," of course, meant "stop."

Gage pressed his face to the pass-through, yelling for her to go. No sooner had he gotten the words from his mouth than he heard the alarm, a whooping tone intermingled with a low, menacing buzz. He was thrown to the side as the Opel lurched forward and into a fast turn. He raised the trunk, risking being shot to gage the situation.

Above him, having passed through the threshold, Gage could see the guard Angelines had just been talking to. He was brandishing a rifle, fumbling with it. Aiming to the right of the man, though with the wheeling car his aim would almost certainly be foul, Gage squeezed off a single .44 round, watching the aluminum puncture several feet from the guard's head. Predictably for a poorly paid civil servant who'd probably never been in a firefight, he scurried back inside his guard shack.

"Hold on!" came the warning from the front, followed by a calamitous boom as the car blasted through a gate, sending a shudder through the Opel. Gage heard the crackle of machine gun fire. He yanked the trunk lid back down, latching it, just before they went through a second gate, this one sounding, and feeling, more formidable against the light sheet metal of the car. Then, as the machine gun fire faded, the car accelerated onto a smooth surface. It was only a second or two before he felt the thumping.

"One of my tires is flat," she yelled.

"Ten minutes until response?" he asked through the pass-through, fumbling for the mechanical catch that would fold down the rear seat. He glimpsed the depleted airbag fluttering in her lap.

"At least ten. There will be two police on duty in Berga, and one each in Cercs and Gironella. They'll be called and the Catalonian police from Manresa—they'll send a chopper."

"You're headed towards Cercs."

"That's what you said to do."

Finally the seat released, pushing forward. When Gage climbed through, he crouched in the back seat and pushed the seat back into its original position.

"How's the car driving?" he asked, peering over her shoulder at the gauges.

"Pulling hard to the right."

Gage rolled down the window, putting his head out. "It's your right rear tire."

"What now?" she asked.

He recalled this stretch of two-lane road between Berga and Cercs. It was rural, with scrub land on both sides and not much else. With the flat tire, the car was laboring to do eighty-kilometers per hour.

"Can you go faster?"

"The pedal is in the floor."

He eyed the tachometer, finding it nearing the engine's redline. Then, at once, a cluster of red warning lights came on.

"Shit! They hit more than the tire." Gage glanced back, seeing dark smoke trailing in their vortex. His eyes moved upward, noticing shredded threads hanging from the roof liner. Bullet holes. Then he noticed the cracked hole in the driver's window, and that's when his eyes went to Angelines' left leg.

It was crimson, and her left hand was clamped on it.

"How bad?" he asked.

"The hole feels big but, oddly enough, it doesn't hurt that much."

Gage pushed his hand back through his hair, reckoning that it had been two minutes since their bust-out. Assuming the call to Cercs, which is where they were headed, had just taken place, the policia there were jumping in their car right now.

The turnoff to the lake house was about two kilometers ahead.

Was there time?

"How far from here to the town of Cercs?" he yelled.

"I...I don't know. Maybe six or seven kilometers?"

"Are you sure?" he yelled, shaking her headrest.

"As sure as I can be!" she yelled back over the whining engine.

He glanced at the instrument cluster. The car was now only making forty kilometers per hour while the tachometer was in the redline. The rear wheel, grating on the asphalt, was probably nearly gone and the car was struggling to keep plowing forward.

The engine would seize up soon and they'd be left out here on the barren road, like an ugly red zit on an otherwise clear face.

A small blue car passed them in the opposite direction, the driver peering at them with curiosity. Gage turned. Thankfully the blue car kept going. But Gage could see that the smoke from the Opel had increased, whirling from the vortex created by both cars.

Then, without hesitation, he leaned into the driver's area and yanked the wheel to the right, causing the Opel to career off the road and down a steep embankment. Seeing a tree in their path, Gage whipped the wheel left, causing the car to spin ninety degrees where it came to a smoldering stop.

"Turn off the car and get out. If you see a fire start from the heat, throw dirt on it."

"But my leg is—"

"Just do it!" he yelled. He lurched from the backseat, scrambling back up the hill, twenty feet above the copse where the car sat. The area was wooded and hilly, probably a hundred meters higher in elevation than the lake house which sat on the valley's hillside, north of their current location.

At the road, seeing no cars coming, Gage used his feet and hands to flatten the cuts on the shoulder created by the tires and the one destroyed wheel. There were faint gouges in the asphalt, veering to the right. He used road grit from the very edge of the asphalt, walking back thirty meters and concealing it as best he could. He turned, thankful that the wisps of smoke from the Opel were no longer visible as they had been dissipated by a stiff breeze.

The sound of an engine could be heard, revving high, accompanied by the distinct sound of cutting air. It was a car, and though he couldn't see it yet, he knew it was driving very fast. Gage moved backward, just below the weeds at the edge of the embankment, flattening himself. From his right, from Cercs, came a Mercedes with police markings, hurtling through the mild curve. The police weren't using their siren but the lights on top were on. The car whizzed by, never braking. There were two police officers in the car.

Gage ran back down to the Opel, finding Angelines sitting on the pine-needle-covered earth next to the rear wheel. She was trying to fashion a bandage from a piece of cloth. He moved her hands aside, ripping the pants suit open and probing the wound with his fingers. She'd taken a bullet on the side of her thigh. It had been traveling downward and Gage could feel the exit wound underneath. Fortunately for her the bullet had been jacketed and didn't mushroom as it ripped through her leg. Both holes were the diameter of a pinkie finger but were bleeding profusely.

"Do you have a knife?"

Her eyes searched the area, as if she might find one.

Please don't go into shock, he thought. Grasping her shoulders and noticing that her nose was bleeding—from the airbag—he said, "It's not all that bad, okay? If we can stem that blood, you'll be fine. Wait right here."

As he opened the trunk, he processed the timeline. The Cercs police car would be at Berga Prison in another minute. He'd have to assume by that time the Berga and Gironella police would be there also. Hopefully, coming from such small towns, those police wouldn't be assertive because, surely, the Berga prison guards would tell them Capitana de la Mancha's car had sped to the north. She'd said that the Manresa Police, with the helicopter, would have jurisdiction in representation of the territory known as Comarques Centrals. As he yanked the small first aid kit from the trunk, he looked up at the sparse canopy of pine trees, knowing an air search would reveal the Opel in short order.

They would need to be far away by that time.

Guessing at the timeline with a measure of optimism, he wagered the first cops on the scene were just now hearing the story.

Assume ten more minutes before the Manresa Police arrive in their helicopter, hopefully making the decision to land first. Give them ten more minutes to get their bearings and organize a search, and that's when the chopper lifts off again. This car will be spotted in five more minutes, tops. They'll probably use dogs to trail us. That will take at least five minutes, maybe more. Give the dogs and their handlers two minutes to get the scents, and then the chase is on.

Thirty-two minutes until the dogs are here...let's be pessimistic and call it twenty.

Using the pair of scissors from the first aid kit, Gage pulled the rear seatbelt out as far as he could get it, slicing it from both ends. He hurried back to Angelines, taking the cloth from her and cutting it in two, wadding it into two pieces.

"Hold these directly on top of each wound." He wound the seatbelt around her leg, threading it through the bar on the buckle to create tension. He eyed her. "You ready?"

She nodded.

He yanked.

She gritted her teeth, wincing fiercely.

Gage tugged on the pressure dressing, probing around it with his fingers. Satisfied, he pointed to her wrist, where she wore a fashionable runner's watch. "Give me that watch." He pressed a few buttons, finding the stopwatch feature, starting it.

"The police will be here soon. I know you're in pain, but I also know you're a dedicated runner. Look at me!" he said, lifting her chin, grasping both of her hands. "*Capitana*...Angelines...this is what you've done all that running for. If you want to see your son, give him the life you talked about, then we have to haul some serious ass, okay? They're going to bring dogs in here and we can forget all that bullshit about going through streams. We need to create *distance*. Do you understand?"

Swallowing a few times, she nodded. He helped her to her feet. She pushed his hands away, testing her leg. Though she winced, she gave him a double thumbs-up.

"Head that way," he said, pointing north. When she did, he went back to the car to find her mobile phone. Unfortunately, it had been clipped by one of the bullets and lay in pieces in the passenger seat.

Running, Gage caught up to Angelines. As they negotiated a thicket of briars, she asked where they were going.

"We're going to get the money."

"Then what?"

Gage jerked her through the last section of briars and pushed her out in front. "Hopefully the consulate is working in our favor by now. Otherwise, I've got no frigging idea. Just keep moving and we'll figure it out when we get there."

All things considered, they made good time.

GAGE'S TIME estimate was remarkably accurate. Though the police chopper was actually a civilian helicopter, used only during rare emergencies, it was under the directive of the Policía de Manresa and, just as he'd hoped, they landed just outside the gates of the prison as they listened to the briefing from the shaken guards at Berga.

Six policemen were marshaled in a small circle near the inner gate that Angelines had barreled through. No one questioned the head guard, a man named Pilopes, as he detailed a story that involved an American prisoner armed with a homemade bomb who managed to disarm several guards and gain access to a firearm.

"Injuries?" the senior policeman, a detective from Manresa, asked.

"Yes, several, one of them being a prisoner with smashed testicles."

That drew a host of raised eyebrows.

When they'd first arrived, Pilopes had briefed the policemen on the situation, telling them that they suspected the American prisoner had taken their captain hostage, and that she was under duress as she'd driven the escape.

"About the captain," the senior man said, clearly puzzled. "How did she get her car all the way inside?"

Pilopes nodded, a mirthless smile coming over his face. "This is exactly why I always warned her against such a thing. She insisted her car be allowed inside, for many years, so she wouldn't have to walk from the parking area. She is a prima donna."

The senior policeman eyed the guard towers. "You were shooting from that tower?" he asked, pointing to the one near the busted outer gate.

"Sí, *jefe*, our guard was."

"Even though your captain was in the car and you felt she was being held *hostage*?"

There was a pause as the guards looked at one another. Finally, Pilopes said, "We were shooting at the tires."

"Did you hit any of them?"

"Sí. One tire that we know of."

"Do you have the security video of them leaving?"

Pilopes shook his head. "The bomb damaged our servers which are just outside of the captain's office. The video may be intact but it will be some time before we know."

"Fine, then." The senior man turned to the police. "Until we gain benefit from the *Mossos d'Esquadra*, which could be another hour, I want both cars to head north while we go by air. If we can spot their car, we'll direct you from our view." He pointed to a truck that had stopped outside the fence. "That's Manuel and his dogs. In case the American has bailed out—and it's quite possible since the tire was allegedly shot—you make sure his truck stays with you."

There were only a few questions, which the detective answered as they walked to their respective vehicles. He stopped them as he motioned the pilot to rev up the chopper.

"If you see the American and can get a clean shot, kill him."

Chopper lifting off, the Catalonian posse set out after an American murderer supposedly named Gregory Harris.

FOLLOWING HIS sense of direction and the topography, Gage had plowed straight north to the Baells Reservoir. Though he'd felt inclined to offer Angelines assistance, he made the decision to let fear be her motivator. So, instead of constantly waiting for her, he pressed forward, making her push beyond the boundaries of her pain tolerance.

They arrived at Señora Moreno's lakeside empire nearly a kilometer west of Justina's cabin. Rather than take the gravel road that led around the lake, Gage followed the road from a distance of a hundred meters, finally stopping when the cabin was in sight. Angelines soon moved beside him, sucking great quantities of air and gently massaging her leg above the pressure dressing.

"How's the leg?" he asked, happy to see that her nose had stopped bleeding.

"It hurts like hell," she snapped.

"Well...you're still alive. That's the cabin where the money is," he said, pointing.

"Is that her car?"

"Yeah."

"Can we take it?"

"Let me think about that," he said, peering into the sky through breaks in the trees.

"Or why don't we just get the money, then do something to throw off our scent? Then we could break into one of the other cabins and wait out the search."

"No way," he said. "That wouldn't work. They'd have us inside of an...*shhh!*" he suddenly hissed, raising his hand.

The sound was growing, alternating through the high pines. It was the familiar whomp-whomp-whomp thudding of a helicopter's blades beating the air.

"They found the car. Damn! Come on," he said, crossing the gravel road without reluctance. Gage stepped up the two wooden steps and, hardly slowing, planted his guard's boot on the doorknob, shattering the doorframe as the door thudded inward.

Gage stepped inside, finding a note sitting on top of a sealed cardboard box. As he lifted the note, he heard Angelines let out a scream.

Gage turned, finding an aged man brandishing what looked like an old M14, aimed squarely at his face. Behind the man stood another man, aiming a beautiful side-by-side shotgun at Angelines.

"Qui diables és vostè?" the man with the rifle growled at Gage. It meant, "Who the devil are you?"

THE HOTEL room was consistent with the Riposo chain. Clean and modern, with lots of chrome and angles, it held the faint smell of detergent, probably from the linens. Justina felt repulsed by the little man's rancid coffee breath and obnoxious roaming fingers. At the front desk, as the clerk's eyes were diverted while he prepared the electronic key, Redon had clasped Justina's breast before leading her hand down to his own inadequate rigidity. It had been all she could do to force a smile.

Now, finally in the room, despite the heavy thump of her heart, Justina knew her actions had to be perfect. Tolerating one more kiss as he fumbled with the zipper on her tight skirt, she finally disentangled herself from his hands and, stepping backward, told him to get undressed.

"Where are you going?" he panted.

"I've got to do one little thing in the restroom. When I come out, the fun begins," she said, feigning ecstasy as she watched him kick off his wee loafers while his hands quickly unbuttoned his shirt.

Justina stepped into the restroom and pushed the door shut, pulling out her mobile phone. Señora Moreno had texted her several times. Her first message was one of triumph, informing Justina that Redon had bought the bearer bonds story: hook, line, and sinker.

Then Justina read the following message:

> It's your decision J. R fell hard for my angle. Not sure you should even go thru with plan B with that little perverted weasel. Let me know.

Justina removed one of Gage's silver pistols from her bag, eyeing it. The plan had been, obviously, to entrap the acusador. But, as Señora Moreno had written, this secondary plan was no longer necessary. Just being near Redon disgusted Justina to her soul but, since she had him here, she might consider stringing him along before making an excuse to leave. Then, if things went awry in Plan A, at least she'd have an open line to him.

Sneering at her reflection, repulsed by the thought, Justina made the decision to proceed with caution. Before things got too physical she would stop. She would tell Redon that she felt immoral, and that she knew he was married. That way she could send him back to his office with a set of blue balls and, if Señora Moreno thought it necessary, she could call him later in the day with the excuse that she changed her mind.

Tucking the pistol back in her purse, she gripped the door handle. *Here we go. Yuck.* Sucking in a great breath, she flung the door open, turning to the right, looking for the spritely lawyer.

But there was a problem.

Redon wasn't on the bed.

Justina skittered to a stop, wheeling around, expecting to be tackled.

No one.

She moved beyond the simple bed, which was actually two singles pushed together in the European manner, checking the floor in the blind spot.

Not there.

She jerked at the drapes. Yanked open the closet.

Redon was nowhere to be found.

Feeling panicked, she ran back to the door and flipped the hasp to lock it.

Then, her immediate fear subsiding, she crossed the room and pressed her face to the glass, peering down three stories to the street and sidewalk. After ten seconds Justina watched as Acusador Redon emerged from the hotel, hurrying out of sight, headed in the direction of his office.

Dejected, Justina trudged back to the bathroom, lifting her phone to call Señora Moreno. Just as she began dialing the numbers, the phone beeped. It was a text.

Just saw acusador. Running scared back to his building. Glad you blew him off! Come down and we will get ready for Plan A. :)

Tilting her head back to the ceiling, Justina felt the tension slide away from her body like wet, heavy clothing. At least she'd tried. Who knows, maybe her sudden sexual interest spooked Redon. Although he was crooked, he certainly wasn't stupid. He had to know he wasn't much to look at, and must have come to the realization that this liaison was too good to be true. Once she'd gone into the bathroom, his paranoia had probably spiked—and with good reason.

It's over now.

Justina stretched, working out the tension from her shoulders and back. She took a long swig from the room's three-euro bottle of water, compliments of Cortez Redon's Visa, and exited the room.

Padding down the long hallway, Justina considered how magnanimous a person Señora Moreno was. Here Justina was, a companion of only a few weeks, and this lady was willing to risk a large chunk of her fortune just to help her.

Someday, I will find a way to pay her back.

Life was positively full of wonderful surprises.

Justina waited for the elevator, watching as it lingered at another floor. After a full minute, feeling the sudden craving for a cigarette, she pushed through the steel doorway to the stairwell, eager to get back to the garage where she'd left the Volvo.

She had no idea of the welcome she was about to receive.

Chapter Thirty

THE MAN aiming the rifle at Gage had to have been at least seventy. His eyes were cold and unflinching. He was waiting for Gage's reply.

Calmly and slowly, Gage replied in Spanish. "I do not speak Catalan."

"Who are you?" the old man asked, his Spanish oddly accented.

"The woman who lives here, Justina—I'm her boyfriend. We rented this cabin together."

"Justina's boyfriend is in prison. Señora told me all about it."

"I *was* in prison. I'm here for my money."

The man didn't respond. Gage looked beyond him as Angelines adjusted her position, grunting from the pain.

"This one's shot in the leg," the other man said.

Gage's captor briefly turned his head. He brought his eyes back to Gage. "Tell me what happened."

"My name is Gage Hartline," Gage replied. "I was hired by Ernesto Navarro to protect his son in Berga Prison. He used people in the government to insert me, and paid me a great deal of money. Once there, I was double-crossed by a host of collaborators and this morning I escaped with this lady's help."

The old man licked his leathery lips, lowering the rifle which was, indeed, a beautifully maintained M14 with a shiny walnut stock. "And who is this lady?" he asked.

"That's the prison's captain, sir."

"She helped you escape, or did you bring her captive?"

"A little of both, sir." Gage kept his hands up despite the fact the gentleman had allowed the M14 to hang down by his side. "I don't want to get either of you in trouble, sir, so if you're inclined to let us continue with our escape, I'd appreciate it. But our time is pressing. The police have a helicopter and I'm pretty sure the dogs will be on our scent soon, if they aren't already."

The man narrowed his eyes at Gage. "Where will you go from here?"

"Don't know yet."

"You're sure they'll bring hounds?"

"Still the best method, sir."

There was a bit of silence in the cabin, marked by the ticking of the mantel clock.

"May we move?" Gage asked.

"Señora Moreno, who is our boss by the way, accompanied your girlfriend to Barcelona."

Gage closed his eyes and slumped. "Thank God. Maybe the consul general can get the ambassador to intervene."

"They changed that plan. Didn't go to the consulate."

"What?" Gage asked, searching each person's eyes.

"Against our advice, they went to Barcelona to entrap someone, so they could get a confession out of him."

"Who?"

"All Señora said was that they were going to perform a little magic trick on someone she called the *acusador*."

Gage whipped his head to Angelines. Her eyes were wide. "Oh, *madre mía!*"

"May I move?" Gage asked.

"Anywhere you like."

Gage checked the time. "We've got about ten minutes. Do you have a first-aid kit and do you know where Justina left the keys to the car?"

"You can use the car if you like," the man answered, "but I have a better idea. Amancio, while I tell Mister Hartline about my idea, would you please go fetch the first-aid box?"

As Amancio took his leave, Sven led Gage across the room, pointing down the hill. "That, my friend, is your best ticket out of here."

Gage stared at his new transportation, optimism descending upon him.

Ask and ye shall receive.

JUSTINA'S PLATFORM sandals made the narrow staircase tricky. She still managed the flights of stairs with good speed, hoping some light physical activity would shuttle the disturbing memories of that little man's probing fingers far, far away. She burst through the steel fire door at the bottom of the stairs, ignoring the simpering smile from the clerk at the counter. He probably thought she'd just turned a fast trick.

Especially in this tight getup.

Outside on the Carrer de Pau Claris, still fighting the craving for a cigarette, she couldn't help but take in the beauty of the breathing blooms on the Jacaranda trees. The flowers made her think of Paris, and that caused her to wonder how Gage was doing. Surely he was sending for the money in an effort to pay his way out of Berga—that's why he'd asked her to leave the money.

Right?

But why did he want her to leave one of the pistols?

Please, let him be okay.

Justina remembered Señora's words: "Even if your Gage tries to escape, they catch people who escape from prison, dear. The best way we can help your man is by proving he wasn't supposed to be in prison in the first place."

As Justina turned to head toward the parking garage, she considered Señora Moreno's stance on how to leave things with the acusador: "While you'll certainly want Redon to have to pay for what he's done to Gage, we need to leave him a way out. Believe me, corrupt men like him cooperate best when they've got options. Corner them, and that's when they get dangerous."

Justina entered the cool shadows of the garage, walking toward the Volvo. As she neared, she could see Señora Moreno's darkened profile in the passenger seat.

I guess I'm driving.

When Justina came around to the driver's side, she looked through the window. Señora Moreno was leaning back against the headrest. Her mouth was hanging slack, like a person sleeping in an upright seat on an airliner. As Justina narrowed her eyes, peering closely, she could see that Señora Moreno's neck and mouth were crimson with blood.

Feeling her pulse spike as alarms shrieked in her mind, Justina straightened, whirling, looking around the garage as her hand fumbled for the pistol in her purse.

Just as her hands gripped the pistol, she heard a quick scrape of footsteps, then felt a mighty, thudding blow on the crown of her head.

The last sensation Justina had was her chin striking the concrete.

ONCE GAGE and the man called Sven had quickly outlined their plan—a very good plan, in Gage's eyes—Amancio arrived back at the cabin with the first aid box, handing it to Gage.

"Are you sure you're willing to do this?" Gage asked Sven.

"What can they do to me?"

"Put you in jail," Gage replied with a firm nod. "Or kill you."

"Well, Mister Hartline, I've already lived a full life. And with Señora Moreno's help and influence on my side, I'm willing to take my chances."

"Any other time I might try to talk you out of it, sir, but there's simply no time." Gage rushed Angelines to the only bathroom in the cabin. Carrying the large first-aid box, he led her inside and closed the door.

"No time for modesty. Take off all your clothes, and I mean everything."

She eyed him for a moment before she complied, removing her blouse and bra as he released the pressure dressing. Gage heard her let out a small cry but that was all.

"You okay?" he asked, keeping his eyes diverted as he turned on the shower.

"Just don't look at my ass."

"What?"

"I hate it."

He shook his head, having no clue what she was talking about.

"I feel lightheaded," she said, grasping the counter.

"And you probably will for a while. Trust me, I've had a similar injury before and I know it's no picnic." He pointed to the shower. "Put all your clothes beside the toilet in that corner and get in the shower. We're going to have to soap each other's backs because we have to get every trace of our current scent off of our bodies." Glanced at her watch. "We need to leave here in about three minutes. Get in *now*."

Keeping his eyes on her leg wound as she removed all of her clothes, he viewed both the entry and exit wound, thankful the wound was as clean as it was. The exit portion was slightly larger and marked by a few strings of shredded skin and muscle fiber. The deep red of early clotting surrounded both wounds. The shower would wash much of the clotting away, but Gage would fix that afterward.

Angelines stepped into the water. She made a sharp hissing sound as the water coursed over her leg wound.

"That'll pass," Gage said, quickly stripping down and climbing in with her. He grabbed Justina's shampoo and dumped half the bottle over

Angelines' head, then his own. "Rub that in good, then take that soap and get it everywhere on your body, even on your wound."

Gage turned the other way, hurriedly soaping his hair, his face, his ears, his chest, his stomach, legs, feet—every piece of his body he could reach. "You okay?" he asked, working soap under his arms.

"It still burns, but, yeah," came her reply. He then felt her hands on his back, soaping his shoulder blades and the center of his back, moving downward. Eyes burning, he told her to turn around, following her lead as he soaped her backside. After sticking his face and head under the stream of water, Gage took one step out of the shower and grabbed the mouthwash from the counter, taking a massive mouthful from it and swishing. He suffered a brief coughing fit before handing the bottle to Angelines.

"Swish that around and go so far as to actually drink a little bit," he said, eyes watering. As she did, he rinsed himself, climbing over the tub wall and quickly drying himself. Angelines exited next.

"Whatever you do, do not touch our old clothes. Stay clear of them."

Angelines' leg was marked by diluted blood streaming down her leg after the clots had given way. Gage opened the door and tugged in the stack of clean clothes, segregating them into two piles. Once she'd dried herself, he ripped open a bag of clotting powder, just like he'd used in prison, and pushed globs of the powder into her entry and exit wounds. Again she hissed as she closed her eyes, tilting her head back to the ceiling. Gage then wrapped her leg with an elastic bandage and told her to get dressed as fast as she could.

The woman's clothes were Justina's, taken from the bedroom. The shirt was from Eastern Bloc, a t-shirt, along with a pair of athletic shorts. Señora Moreno's men had also provided her with a pair of women's running shoes, although Gage was pretty sure they weren't Justina's based on the size. As Gage handed the shoes over, Angelines, sitting on the closed toilet, grabbed Gage's arms, pulling him to her as she locked her mouth on his. Instinctively, Gage let it happen for just a moment—one or two seconds—as her tongue probed his mouth. He pulled back, stunned, knowing nothing else to do but look at her watch and inform her they had only thirty seconds.

He donned his own clothes that, thankfully, Justina had laundered and kept for him: old blue jeans, his favorite black utility shirt, and his running shoes. With both of them dressed, he yanked the door open, finding Sven and Amancio standing to the side.

"Are you sure about this?" Gage asked.

Sven dangled a set of keys attached to a miniature orange lifebuoy. "She's already full of fuel. There's a compass onboard. Just follow the reservoir due east. With the spring rains the dam has been on full release, and the river is swollen so you shouldn't have any impassable areas clear to the Llobregat." He handed Gage a cell phone. "Señora Moreno's number is first on the speed dial. I've been calling," he said with a worried shake of his head.

"No answer?"

"No."

"We'll keep trying."

"You won't have coverage on the river. And there's one other thing."

"We've really got to go," Gage protested.

Sven told Gage about the bearer bonds. "They're in a cardboard box, already on the boat."

Gage was speechless.

"Señora Moreno insisted that, if you showed up, you take those bonds."

"Why?"

"She said they would be yours to use if need be. I honestly don't know more than that."

"Thank you for everything." Gage grabbed Angelines by the hand and burst from the rear door of the cabin. She was moving better with the tight leg wrap—the jog to the waiting boat took less than a minute.

Gage helped her onboard before climbing behind the controls of the combo fishing and recreational boat. As he turned the key and powered up the Yamaha 115, he estimated the boat as a 17-footer with a low draft due to the tri-hull design. After carving a tight turn on the turquoise water, he headed due east under the cover of the shore trees. Gage spoke over the engine, telling Angelines to stand behind him and keep an eye out for the chopper.

She lingered beside him for a few seconds, grasping his left hand and squeezing it. "I'm sorry for kissing you earlier, Gage. I...I..."

"Let me know if you see that helicopter," he said abruptly, easing around a protruding dock. "The farther we get from here, the better. And guzzle some water. With all that blood you've lost, you need fluid. Give me one, too," he said, motioning to the sack of cold bottled water Sven had placed in the boat.

She handed him a bottle. "Gage, look at me."

There were a pair of mirrored aviator sunglasses wedged into the nook of the console—a nice pair of Smith's. Gage wiped them on his shirt and donned them, staring forward as he kept the bow ten feet from the water's edge.

"Gage," she persisted.

"Pretty busy here," he said, eyes still ahead as he swigged the water.

As was her habit with him, especially when having a serious conversation, she switched to English. "Gage, I haven't been treated well by a man in years. It's partly my own fault. Years ago, after another failed relationship, I became bitter, and that's when I began to let things occur around me. Illegal things."

He turned his head and hitched his thumb backward. "I really need your eyes scanning the sky for that helicopter."

"I'm going to say this, *damn it*, whether you like it or not."

Gage edged the throttle back slightly, lowering the speed to twenty kilometers per hour as the waterway began to narrow, giving way to a wide, flat river.

"I told you that the things I allowed to happen in Berga would have happened anyway and, even though I know what I did was wrong, I still do believe that."

He kept his eyes ahead.

"I came up through the ranks in the prison system doing things the right way, and outworking everyone else. That's how I became a captain at such an early age." She quickly scanned the sky. "I was in a relationship and I had a child just after I was awarded Berga." Her chest rose and fell as she took a large breath. "One afternoon, while I thought my mother was watching my son, a prisoner went through all the proper channels by requesting to see me."

Gage turned for a moment.

"They had Jordi, Gage. They had my son. The prisoner didn't prove it, didn't show me pictures…he just told me, and I knew by that man's dead, soulless eyes that he was telling the truth."

"What happened?" Gage asked flatly, maneuvering the boat to the left around a bifurcation buoy, choosing the secondary channel due to the boat's light draft.

As the massive looming hills slid by, Angelines dropped into the seat next to him, rubbing her leg above the bandage. "Their demand was simple. If I allowed them free reign in Berga, they'd leave my son alone and they'd begin to compensate me."

"If you didn't?"

She covered her mouth, shaking her head as if she couldn't say it.

"So, if you didn't comply, their people on the outside would kill him?"

She nodded.

"But over time, your guards became corrupt, too, and all that extra money Los Leones afforded you became far too rewarding to throw away by reporting them."

Eyes glistening, she looked up at him. "I kissed you, Gage, because I desperately want to be normal again, and that's how you've treated me. Though I don't expect you to understand, just a week ago I was fine with being a corrupt prison official. But when you made that suggestion about the money, it was as if the sun came up on the black night that's my life." She wiped her eyes. "It all came clear."

"Well, that may be clear, but our situation here isn't."

"Thank you, Gage, for treating me the way you have."

He nodded, then checked the sky behind the boat. "If you really want to be normal again, *capitana*, sit your ass—which looks fine to me, by the way— on the rear deck and keep your eyes out for that helicopter."

She stood, pulling his head to the side and giving him a wet kiss on the cheek.

While pleased with her seemingly genuine transformation, Gage's mind was occupied with two things: escaping, and wondering what sort of stunt Justina and Señora Moreno had tried to pull on Cortez Redon.

THE HOUNDS followed the scent straight to the cabin, howling indignant protests at the locked front door. After several bangs on the door and no answer, the trailing police knocked the door in, tactically entering with pistols outstretched. The two hounds followed, slobbering and wailing, momentarily confused by the sudden change in environment. One took considerable notice of the bathroom. A policeman checked the shower, yelling that it was wet. The other hound pawed at the back door as its handler yelled that they needed to keep going.

Behind the cabin, both dogs quickly picked up on the scent, headed west, past the dam and toward the town of Cercs. As the posse pressed on, they radioed to their rapidly gathering brethren, telling them to continue setting their roadblocks, but to keep a keen eye out in the direction of Cercs.

After scanning the lake, the police in the chopper raced ahead of the hounds, trying to spot the two runners before they acquired transportation.

Nearly the entire posse, guided by the sensitive noses of the two hounds, focused their attention westward.

While Gage and Angelines were now fifteen kilometers in the opposite direction, headed to the east.

Chapter Thirty-One

Lloret de Mar, Spain

MUSIC.

It was classical, heavy on the piano, an orchestra following a virtuoso pianist of some sort. A concerto...

Justina blinked her eyes, seeing blobs of blurred nothingness as she worked her mouth, running her tongue over her upper and lower teeth, taking inventory, finally finding the one that was broken. It was one of her top rear teeth, second from the back if her tongue's probing was accurate. She wanted to touch it but her hands seemed to be restrained behind her, though she didn't feel like her tugging was generating much in the way of force.

The pain on top of her head was easily matched by the pain of her chin and jaw. Fortunately the broken tooth didn't seem to be affecting any nerves. But her headache and an impending feeling of nausea began to come to the forefront with every beat of her heart.

Thump-thump, went her heart.

A hitched breath and several swallows.

Thump-thump.

More swallows, mouth all wet.

Thump-thump.

Vomitus—explosive vomitus.

Justina retched for a full minute, ending with dry heaves. She leaned back in the chair, sucking in great quantities of air as the blue of the sky began to come clear. Suddenly, cold water splashed all over her legs as what felt like a hose squirted around her feet. She looked to her left, seeing a tall man, the hose in one hand, a beer dangling casually in the other. He was aiming the hose's spray around her feet.

"I knew that would be coming," he said in Spanish. "Your friend woke up ten minutes ago and did the same thing, although yours was much more impressive. A triple dose of painkillers, unless you're used to it, will make anyone sick." He curled his finger. "Come on...come with me."

The man walked to Justina, gently helping her up. Dreamily, she looked around, realizing she was on an elevated deck and could see the deep blue of the ocean, nearly melding into the monochromatic azure sky. He led her inside. The sudden cool upon passing through the threshold meant the home she was entering was air-conditioned—the mark of excess wealth in temperate northern Spain.

Realizing that her faculties were returning, Justina resisted and began to scream. The man chuckled, easily turning her and pushing her onto a sofa. Sitting across from her, holding a pink towel to her face, was Señora Moreno. She looked much older and lowered the towel long enough to curse the man.

What Justina saw took her breath.

Señora Moreno had been sliced open from the left opening of her mouth to her earlobe. It was a ghastly image. Justina covered her own mouth with her hand, stifling a scream. The man, still casually swigging his beer, moved a plastic pail across the floor with his foot.

"If you feel sick again, precious, I'd suggest you use that bucket."

"Why did you do that to her face?"

After considering Señora Moreno for a moment, he shrugged and spoke mildly. "Not my finest moment, for sure. I don't like harming women, even old ones, but I *won't* hesitate to do so when it comes to my own ascension."

He moved to Señora Moreno, touching her hand and lowering the towel. "She'll need to be sewn up soon. I've never seen this wound having been done on only one side—it's usually done on both sides. Though I've never known someone to die from the full wound—it's known, among other things, as a Glasgow grin—I've heard that dehydration can be a problem." He moved Señora Moreno's now unkempt hair back, like a loving caregiver might. "Would you like to try some water, m'lady?"

"*Que te jodan,*" she whispered in an injury-modulated voice.

"Suit yourself." His amusement faded when he looked at Justina. "I'm going to give you a few more minutes to wake up. By that time, one of my friends should be here and we're all going to have a little chat."

As he spoke, Justina got a better look at him. Tall and lean, yet muscular, he had an angular, chiseled face. His beard was black, flecked by only a few hairs of gray, and his tan was rich and fresh. His odd, pleasant accent and his expensive casual clothing would typically make such a man seem harmless, and even refined—but she sensed an underlying trashiness to him. It bubbled just under his surface, escaping his polished veneer here and there. When he turned away, Justina glimpsed a brief flash of a tattoo on the man's neck as his long hair swept to the side.

It was the tattoo of a smoking revolver.

Los Leones.

The man walked away, tossing the beer into a garbage can and retrieving another. He walked to the stereo, increasing the volume to a blaring level.

Justina knew she couldn't yell above the music without alerting the man. Making her mouth movements pronounced, she mimed the words to Señora Moreno: "Is he after the money?"

Señora Moreno nodded.

"Your money?"

She shook her head.

"Navarro's money?"

A pronounced nod.

Just as Justina was preparing her next question—had Gage escaped?—a deep bell could be heard over the music. She watched as the man turned down the volume, crossing the room. "That must be my friend. You'll like her, I promise."

Turning around on the sofa, Justina watched as the man opened the door, admitting a small, thin woman with very short hair. He closed the door behind her, then passionately kissed her as his hands freely roamed her body.

Justina could see that the woman carried a small leather bag.

When their fervent kiss was finished, the man led her into the sitting area by her hand. Now that Justina could see her well, she realized with an odd spike of recognizance that she'd seen this woman before—on numerous occasions at Eastern Bloc. The woman was probably in her late twenties with a striking narrow face and full lips. Her head was shaved on the sides though the top was somewhat sculpted, giving her a trendy appearance, as if she were a pop star. Emerging from the woman's black t-shirt Justina could see numerous tattoos. She was obviously going for the anarchistic look.

More important, however, were her numerous visits to Eastern Bloc.

Who had she typically come with? Justina thought, her mind muddled by whatever drug she'd been given.

"Lower the towel," the tattooed woman said in a distinctive alto voice. After a moment, Señora Moreno removed the towel from her face, at which time the woman nodded and spoke rapid, indecipherable Catalan to the man. Then the woman turned to Justina, narrowing her eyes.

"Where have I seen you before?" she asked, switching to Spanish.

Justina made sure to look puzzled yet indignant when she shrugged.

"Is she from Lloret?" the woman asked the man.

"Don't know where she lives. I think she's Polish."

"I know I've seen her before."

"Have you been to Lloret?" the man asked Justina.

"No," Justina answered with a sneer.

The woman walked to Justina, touching her forehead, running her fingers back through her hair, making a humming sound as she said, "She's really beautiful."

"D'acord," the man replied, pressing himself behind the woman, licking the back of her neck, leaving a slick trail.

The woman turned and they kissed again, their tongues entwining like impassioned asps. After the moment passed, he gestured to Señora Moreno's wound. "Can you manage?"

The woman moved next to Señora and viewed the incision. "It may not be pretty." From the bag she removed a bottle, a small syringe, a small pair of scissors and a plastic container with what appeared to be needles and surgical suture.

After preparing a needle, she touched Señora Moreno's shoulder. "You'll be glad to know that I'm going to numb your face." She injected Señora Moreno's face in four locations, setting the needle aside and resuming her necking with her beau.

Several minutes later, needle in hand, she went to work.

MORE THAN a half hour after departing the cabin, the posse, led by the dogs, followed the upper lake to its river source. After continuing on, they crossed at a foot bridge, the hounds picking up the scent on the other side. They knew the prisoner and the prison's captain had to be close. On the far side of the river, soaked from slogging through a bog, the posse rushed to the south, each man satisfied that the hounds seemed to be growing excited as the scent grew more powerful.

But, to everyone's surprise, the scent halted around a jutting headland. There they found an older gentleman on a stump, placidly fishing with an improvised pole. In one hand was a flask—it contained Swedish vodka. He took a swig and lowered his fishing pole.

"You folks looking for a man and a woman?" he asked in his oddly-accented Catalan.

When the handler quieted the hounds, the Manresan police chief stepped forward. "Yes. Did you see them?"

"Sure did. Just know I'm well-oiled this afternoon. And unless I was seeing things, I'm pretty sure they went in right here and started swimming." He pointed straight out over the water.

It took ten minutes to find the clothing that had been sunk by the heavy stones.

Sven was arrested on the spot, but the posse was nearly an hour behind Gage and Angelines.

They would not catch up.

FORTUNATELY, THERE had been no epic chase on the river. Gage had navigated by Garmin, never really having to rely on it since the river's path was obvious and marked. But after some time, when the available fuel was well below half a tank, he began to see markers denoting a major confluence.

When he zoomed out on the Garmin, the confluence was distinct—the Llobregat River loomed just ahead. This was good, meaning they were now forty kilometers away from where they'd ditched the car. But the bad news was the controlled locks on the Llobregat as the river descended toward the Mediterranean. According to Señora Moreno's man Sven, once the rivers converged, Gage and Angelines would need to find other transport since the first locks were only a few kilometers downstream—and operated by workers from the government. Those workers could easily be on the lookout for two fugitives.

As they floated into a town at the confluence, Angelines turned to Gage. "This is Ripoll."

"Do you know it?"

"Not really. It's about like Berga. Just another hill town."

"We've got to trade this boat for some other type of ride, and we need to do it very quietly." Gage pulled the throttle back, checking the current as the boat idled. Although close to the confluence, the current was still mild. Not knowing the depth near the shore, he tilted the prop up, keeping it submerged just enough for thrust. He reversed a few times, easing the boat to the shore, a slight thud announcing their impact.

Gage leapt from the front, holding the bow while he found two steel stakes under the bow hatch. When he turned, he saw an older woman on her knees, peering at him from behind a clump of yellow meadow buttercup. She was on a knee-pad, a small shovel in her hand. Wearing a straw hat held down by a filmy kerchief, Gage could see a smile on her kindly face.

"Hola!" he said cheerily, just any recreational boater happy to have a day off. Continuing in his American-accented Spanish, he said, "My girlfriend and I are hungry and looking for a bite. Is it okay if we leave our boat here for a bit?"

"But of course," the woman replied, standing. When Angelines babied herself from the boat, wincing from the impact, the woman's face clouded as she gestured to the bandage. "You seem to be in a bit of pain."

Angelines smiled and dismissed it. "I cut myself earlier—just a surface wound."

"So, you're from around here?" the older woman asked in Catalan upon hearing Angelines' accent.

"Sí, sóc de Barcelona."

Seeming unfazed by their presence, the woman resumed her position on the kneepad and continued her weeding. "Please, leave the boat as long as you like."

Gage leapt from the boat, carrying the cardboard box before making the line fast. "We'll be an hour or two, madam," Gage said, backing away. Under his breath he said, "Now we've just got to hope she doesn't go inside and turn on the television."

"Where are we going?"

"No clue," he said, looking both directions as they reached the narrow road in front of the woman's cottage.

"Esperi!" the woman called out after them.

"No," Gage groaned. "You talk to her since she's speaking Catalan."

Angelines turned, cupping her hand to her ear. *"Sí, senyora?"*

"If you're looking for a meal with a good view, you should go to the Restaurante Panorámico…it's just south of town, on the right. An easy walk from here."

"Thank you!" Angelines called out, while Gage grumbled from the continued attention.

"And make sure you sit on the back patio where you can look at the towering mountains and watch the parasailers and parachutists," the woman continued. "It's a well-kept secret among the locals."

Gage asked for a translation and received it. His grin grew from fake to genuine as he waved his thanks.

When the restaurant was in sight, he moved to the side of the road and lowered the cardboard box to the flowery weeds.

"What are you doing?"

"Sven mentioned something earlier." Gage tore the box open, finding a letter on top. He read it, his hand absently rubbing his sweaty hair.

"My God," he breathed.

"What?"

Taking loud breaths, Gage lifted the sheaf of greenish paper from the top of the box. Underneath the thick sheaf were stacks of euros. He thumbed the sheaf several times, shaking his head.

"What are those?"

He handed her the top sheet of linen paper.

"Bearer bonds?" she asked, holding the paper close to her face.

"Along with the money I was paid, Señora Moreno has left me nearly seventeen-million dollars in these bonds."

"Why?"

"She said they didn't know if I would even show up today. But in case I did, she left these for me to negotiate with, if necessary."

"Whose bonds are they?"

"Hers."

"Señora Moreno's?"

Taking the bond back from Angelines, Gage nodded.

"She's that wealthy?"

"Apparently so."

He handed her the note, explaining as she read.

"So they went to Redon," Angelines said, "pretending to have access to Ernesto Navarro's money."

"As I told you earlier, last night I called Justina but I could only speak for a minute." He put everything back into the box, looking up at Angelines. "And based on what I told her, she had no idea I was escaping. So, she told Señora Moreno about my instructions that she go to the U.S. Consulate. Señora Moreno said that was not a good plan and, instead, they hatched a plan to go and entrap Cortez Redon."

"Using these bearer bonds."

"Correct, acting like they'd found Navarro's fortune. Señora Moreno wrote that she took one with her to use as proof. Since I asked Justina to leave the money *and* the pistol, they thought maybe I was somehow coming to retrieve it, hence her leaving the rest of the bearer bonds."

Angelines shook her head. "But that plan is reckless. What if you'd sent me, or a guard, or Los Leones for the money?"

"That's why she left the bonds, and the money, *with* her armed men." Tugging on his bottom lip, Gage said, "The plan's not all that bad. But it's dangerous."

Gage removed Sven's phone and battery from his pocket, mating them and waiting for the power to come on. He held down the first speed dial, listening to the rings followed by Señora Moreno's voicemail message.

"Damn!"

"No answer?"

He shook his head and stared at the phone. "I assume this phone belonged to that man called Sven."

"Yeah?"

"I'm debating whether or not to disconnect the battery. My training tells me to leave it disconnected."

She shrugged.

"But instinct tells me to keep it on."

"Instinct," Angelines said.

"C'mon," he said, dropping the still-operating mobile phone into the cardboard box.

Bruised and battered, the fugitive couple headed south.

WHEN THEY reached the Restaurante Panorámico, a rustic establishment constructed from what appeared to be local timber, Angelines waited for their order in a vacant corner. In the meantime, Gage hiked across the rolling meadow behind the restaurant. Across the meadow, about a kilometer away, was a small metal hangar and short asphalt airstrip, both nestled at the base of a rocky peak. As he closed in on the hangar, he watched several parasailers, so much more common in Europe, soaring gracefully, using the updrafts created by the rapidly warming day and the arching towers of rock. Added to the updrafts caused by radiational heating, Gage mused, was the upward air effect when gusts of wind were forced to move up and over the mountain. With a light breeze at the mountain's southern face, Gage assumed that today was the perfect day for soaring.

He also heard the droning of an aircraft somewhere high above, most likely the jump plane. Gage shielded his eyes, hearing the pitch change as he walked. The aircraft had just turned on what's known as "jump run", the slow pass when the jumpers exit. He spotted the plane's T-silhouette high above. The airplane was a single engine, but Gage could tell no more from his position approximately 10,000 feet below. Rather than strain his eyes, he kept walking.

When he reached the hangar, receiving a few polite nods, he saw the normal goings on one would expect to see at a skydiving center. Even though this dropzone was smaller than Raeford—it seemed like years ago when Gage met Hunter there—there were still a number of similarities.

On the grass, staked down near the hangar, were several blue packing mats. An instructor stood on one of the mats, speaking Spanish, teaching several students the "flat pack" with what appeared to be a large student canopy. Behind her were diagrams of the proper skydiving "arch," a basic body technique that makes a jumper fall face to earth.

With a flash of melancholy, Gage recalled his first free-fall instructions two decades before, his Alabaman green beret instructor spitting tobacco juice as he yelled, "Just aim your dick for the dirt!"

Long time.

While Gage was looking for an unoccupied "up-jumper," meaning a non-student, to ask a few questions, he heard the familiar rip-popping of parachutes opening in the skies above. Thankful for Sven's sunglasses, Gage looked up to see four parachutes, spread apart but at roughly the same altitude, open and flying quickly. They'd opened at what Gage estimated to be between 2,000 and 2,500 feet above ground level, indicating the foursome were experienced jumpers. Added to that fact was the rapid forward speed of each of the canopies. He could tell the chutes were zero-porosity, and small, meaning they didn't bleed air and truly acted as a wing. The fact that the canopies were small in relation to the body and gear they supported denoted them as high-performance, allowing the operator of the parachute to generate high forward speed. While more dangerous, the landing result was often breathtaking and, to some skydivers, as great a rush as the freefall itself.

Gage watched the canopies setting up like F-16s preparing for high speed landings.

The first canopy, marked by the familiar Performance Design logo, a Stiletto, turned sharply from its blazing fast downwind leg, swinging the parachutist face-to-ground at several hundred feet. This was by design and was a method known as "swooping," something only experienced jumpers should attempt. Like an aircraft racing straight toward the ground, the parachutist applied pressure to the steering toggles, generating lift. Then, as pretty as Gage had ever seen, the parachutist leveled out with the ground, moving at least fifty miles per hour, lifting his legs to prevent further drag. The effect was breathtaking, and allowed the jumper to "turf surf" nearly the length of a football field.

Each of the other jumpers followed suit, with the last one misjudging things slightly, but recovering enough to wind up in a harmless low-speed tumble on the ground. This generated good-natured laughter from his fellow jumpers while the parachutist, after brushing himself off, took a self-deprecating bow. Something about the tumble reminded Gage of his old Army buddy, Chuck. Chuck was a natural skydiver when it came to relative work—maneuvers while free-falling—but had never been known for his pretty landings.

As the quartet removed their helmets, Gage realized two of the jumpers were women. While the first one daisy-chained her lines, he walked over and asked who the owner of the skydiving center was.

The woman, with an open and friendly face, tilted her head upon hearing his accent. Then, with her gloved hand, she pointed up and made a circling motion. "You're looking for Arturo, he's also the pilot. His aircraft isn't a turbine—it takes him a while to get down so he doesn't over-cool the engine."

"Are you a pilot?" Gage asked.

"Student pilot," she said. "You're a jumper?"

"I am."

"Novice?" she asked, switching to English.

"Not a novice, but not exactly current either."

"How many jumps do you have?" she asked, gathering her chute in her arms.

"I haven't kept a strict count in a long time, but probably five, six...maybe seven thousand."

Her eyes went wide. He was being truthful and, while large, such a high number certainly isn't unheard of. In the U.S., especially at large drop-zones like Raeford, a person can find dozens, maybe hundreds, of skydivers with over seven thousand jumps. But in Spain, where jumping is far more expensive, and tougher to accumulate with a small piston aircraft, it would take a skydiver decades to accumulate such a total. Plus, most of Gage's jumps were military, often coming during training when they would make ten to twelve practice jumps in a day.

"What's in the box?" the woman asked.

"Ah...just some of my old gear."

They chatted a bit more before they saw the single-engine airplane, a Cessna 182, turn in on a short final. Arturo landed on the asphalt airstrip expertly, flaring at the last moment, resulting in a very short landing roll. When he killed the engine in the grass, a small pickup truck with a large fuel drum on the bed drove to the aircraft. Gage watched as Arturo exited.

"Do you know Arturo well?" he asked the woman.

The woman was shading her eyes, waving and smiling. "I'll say," she replied with obvious affection. "I've dated him for eight years."

Arturo returned her wave, crossing the wide field.

"He wasn't military, was he?" Gage asked.

She turned to Gage. "How did you know?"

"This is a skydiving center. I'd have put the odds at one-in-three."

As he approached, Arturo spoke Spanish to his girlfriend at such a rapid rate Gage couldn't keep up. Arturo hitched his thumb back to his aircraft and was saying something about the exit door and its latch. Then he asked her about her jump.

"We almost flushed and only got five stinking points," she said, shaking her head in disgust. "I wasn't very focused." Quickly brightening, she motioned to Gage. "Arturo, this is our guest, but I didn't get his name."

"Hola, amigo," Arturo said with a genuine smile, removing his sunglasses and tucking them into his shirt pocket. He was a few inches shorter than Gage, but probably the same age. His hair was black and streaked with gray, bushy with natural curls. His well-tanned face was notable due to its deep, natural lines and affable dimples. The man had keen, light brown eyes and shook Gage's hand firmly. Gage instantly liked him.

"I'm Greg," Gage said.

"And he has about seven thousand jumps," the woman said proudly.

"Somewhere in that range," Gage corrected. "And many were hop-and-pops. Nothing to get excited over."

Arturo poked out his lips, briefly surveying Gage with narrowed eyes. "Still…that's a huge number around here. You're here to jump?"

"Uh, yeah, I think I'd like to jump…me and my, uh, friend. Especially if we can rent some rigs."

"You are licensed?"

"Yes, but I don't have it on me." Gage licked his lips. "I'm in the USPA database."

Arturo nodded. "No problem, but it may be a while. My door isn't latching the way it should and, until my mechanic can get it working smoothly, I'm grounding her. I called a pilot friend north of Barcelona. He's going to fly up and take our loads for the rest of the day."

"I'm going to go pack," the girlfriend said. She turned to Gage, giving him a firm handshake. "Pleasure to meet you, Greg."

Arturo motioned to the hangar. "You want to come look around, check out our rigs?"

Gage turned, looking back the way he'd come. He could see Angelines walking from the distant restaurant. Her limp seemed about the same and she was carrying two paper sacks, one darkened, presumably, by the bottles of cold water.

Gage turned to Arturo. "I understand you were in the military?"

"Twenty-three years."

"What branch, may I ask?"

"I was in the Spanish Army."

"Were you a jumper?"

"I was, airborne initially. Then I attended HALO school."

"Where?"

"We came to the U.S., actually. Fort Bragg."

Gage nodded knowingly. "You were special operations." It wasn't a question.

"Indeed," Arturo replied. "Grupo Valencia."

Maintaining eye contact, Gage said, "I was in special ops, too, my friend...and I *desperately* need a favor."

The affability slid from Arturo and, behind it, Gage saw the cold, calculating mask of a warrior. The two men stood there in a gulf of silence.

As Angelines approached, her face splotchy, her breathing a bit ragged, Arturo turned to her. Gage watched as the Spaniard's eye moved down to the bandage on her leg. Despite the clotting powder, it had begun to weep wine-colored blood in its center.

Arturo turned back to Gage. "Tell me everything. No lies. And that guarantees you nothing."

Gage took a bottle of water from Angelines, drinking half in one pull. He wiped his mouth with the back of his hand and started talking.

Forty-five minutes later, wearing yellow student jumpsuits and parachute rigs, Gage and Angelines followed Arturo and his girlfriend to the Cessna. Arturo placed the cardboard box inside before turning and walking back to the manifest table, telling the manifest manager what to do when his friend arrived with the backup aircraft.

"But I thought the Cessna was dead-lined," the woman said, pointing to the trio boarding Arturo's airplane.

"That was all just a cover story," Arturo replied, putting a finger over his lips. "But keep that quiet, okay?"

"What's the deal?"

"I'm going to put those two out over the beach near L'escala," Arturo said in a low voice. "They're on their honeymoon and he's paying me a great deal of cash, but it's an illegal jump, so keep that to yourself, okay?"

The manager shrugged. Moments later, the Cessna strained against its brakes as Arturo did his run-up. Seconds later, they were aloft.

GAGE AND Arturo chatted over the headset while Angelines and Marina, Arturo's girlfriend, rewrapped Angelines' leg in the rear. There was only one seat, the pilot's, so Gage knelt in the jumpmaster's position, normally where the seat next to the pilot would be.

"Here's the way we're going to play this," Arturo said. "Right now we're about three thousand feet AGL. In a few minutes we're going to enter El Prat's airspace and they're going to call me. I've got my transponder on so they know who and where we are. If I don't respond, it will send up red flags. So I *will* respond, and I'll tell them we're a jump plane and we're landing at a private grass strip at La Rabassada to pick up a part for my door."

"Will that concern them?"

Arturo shook his head. "Not a bit. They might vector me a little bit but they shouldn't care about us that far from El Prat, especially to the west. They'll probably bring me low and just keep an eye on us."

"And once we land?"

Arturo looked at Gage and smiled. "You're going to 'steal' my friend's car. And if I get questioned about this, I will say that an American madman hijacked me at gunpoint."

Gage nodded approvingly then asked, "And if they ask why you didn't report it immediately?"

"I'll tell them you threatened revenge if I ever talked. What choice did I have other than to keep my mouth shut? Don't worry, my friend, I'll play it off if necessary."

As the sprawling metropolis of Barcelona slid into view, pinks and whites and tans, Gage checked the time. It was growing quite late in the afternoon. He gritted his teeth, hoping he could get to Acusador Redon before he left for the day.

Just then, the radio squawked and Barcelona's Approach Control called Arturo's aircraft. Arturo went with the same story he'd told Gage. There was a brief pause before Approach Control advised him to continue at 3,000 AGL and to call out his downwind, base, and final legs.

Arturo gave Gage a thumbs up. "If they thought you were aboard this aircraft, they'd have delayed me."

Ignoring the searing pain from his kidney, Gage turned to Angelines, yelling over the prop and rushing wind. "We're landing in five minutes. Be ready to haul ass."

Angelines leaned back, covering her eyes with her hand. "Believe me," she replied. "I'm ready to be done with all of this."

Chapter Thirty-Two

JUSTINA HAD watched in horror as the tattooed woman sewed Señora Moreno's face back together. While the woman worked, speaking in a surprisingly clinical tone, she told Señora she was a registered nurse. Taking her time and occasionally snipping away minute pieces of ragged flesh from Señora's narcotic-deadened face, the woman added what amounted to about thirty well-done, tight stitches from Señora's ear to mouth. Finished, she coated both sides with antibiotic ointment before covering it with an adhesive bandage and securing it with a wrap that traveled over the top of Señora's head.

"I've never sewn up that type of wound before." The nurse glanced at the man for a moment, lowering her voice. "You'll still need to have it looked at soon. While I trust my stitches will take, there may be other considerations when sewing a cheek back together."

The man had been lounging in a chair opposite Justina during the medical procedure. He'd fiddled with his iPhone for a bit, afterward thumbing through a magazine. When the nurse finished, he beckoned her, whispering something in her ear. She nodded, walking into another room while the man stood before Justina and Señora Moreno. "Now that the unpleasantness has been repaired, it's time to have a bit of frank discussion."

With rapid footsteps, the tattooed woman rushed back into view with a large hypodermic needle in her hand. The man moved quickly, clamping Justina's upper arms, pulling them behind her. The nurse wasted no time administering the shot in Justina's shoulder. It stung, burning afterward as the fluid dissipated in her body.

"Relax," the nurse smiled. "You've never felt so good when that hits your bloodstream."

"Her, too," he said, nudging Señora Moreno's foot. "Full dosage, if not a little bit more."

"The dosage chart is specific. We don't want to kill her."

"Not yet," the man laughed, the sounds modulating. What had been sharp, exultant laughter from the man suddenly drew out like a recording run at a quarter-speed.

Justina's vision was altered. Movements began to appear like streaked neon. The smallest of sounds became clinging cymbals and bellowing bass tones. As the woman walked away from Señora Moreno, Justina watched as the nurse's tattoos stretched out, melding with the background, becoming a canvas of inky blur. *And my headache is gone*, Justina blissfully realized, quickly scolding herself for her suddenly contented demeanor but soon after forgetting why exactly she needed to maintain focus.

What is happening?

"How long?" she heard him ask, bringing Justina back to the situation at hand.

"It'll be best in ten or fifteen minutes, when it's had time to marinate into all recesses of her brain."

"How long until it dissipates?"

"At least an hour. Maybe an hour-and-a-half."

There were three of them, each. Three bearded men to her left, three tattooed nurses to the right, spinning like a twisted kaleidoscope. They kissed again, their tongues doing the dance of the snakes.

Then they were gone, all six of them.

Justina blinked rapidly.

Time began to slow, or did it speed up? As Justina turned her twenty kilo head to Señora Moreno, whose head had tilted backward, eyes partially shut, lolling, Justina suddenly heard the moans and what must have been the rhythmic bumping of a headboard.

They're in there doing it. While we sit here like two heroin addicts, slaves to the narcotics in our veins, that sicko is in there satisfying his sexual urges.

In one of the more peculiar situations of her life, Justina discovered that certain parts of her brain wanted to function normally while the remainder of her brain, and her body, were falling further and further under the drug's spell. It reminded her of those miserable dreams where she wanted something that was clearly in reach: the clichéd expanding hallway, a tarry surface that trapped her feet, or (her least favorite) a prancing demon that tied her up and flayed her while a crowd cheered from the sidelines.

As she slid to the floor, she realized the arrogance of the bearded man. While he'd handcuffed her, he'd done nothing to prevent her escape. And as she slid across the floor like some terminal drunkard in her last moments of consciousness, Justina briefly forgot what it was she was hoping to do.

There was a smacking sound from the bedroom followed by the woman's cackling laughter. Then another smack. She could hear their voices, inflamed, speaking Catalan. Justina didn't know the language well, but had been propositioned enough to know the vulgar words when she heard them.

Coming back up to her knees, first banging her head on the stucco wall, Justina, using her mouth, rooted into Señora's purse like a gluttonous sow into a feeding trough. Aware of the slobber she couldn't contain, she used her mouth to clamp Señora Moreno's iPhone, holding it as best she could.

It was nearly hopeless. Her motor skills were quickly deteriorating. She tried to wake the iPhone with her nose, realizing that it had been turned off. In a movement that took a full minute, Justina rolled her body over, fumbling with her fingers until she eventually felt the trademark Apple oval slide switch at the top—the sleep button. Following two missed tries, she finally wedged her thumbnail under the rubberized phone protector, holding the switch on for what felt like ten seconds. She let the phone drop and tried to roll over.

Her body failed her. The motor skills she'd possessed thirty seconds ago were gone.

Do not accept that as fact. Just do it! Twist your body and roll!

If allowed an out-of-body experience, Justina would love to slap herself across the face. Twice. Half of the usable cells in her brain screamed for her body to move, but her muscles would no longer comply.

Her plan was simple: roll over, tap the phone with her nose, and redial Sven's phone, or Señora's lawyer, or whatever number that happened to pop up. It would take only two touches of her nose.

Can I even speak?

"Kkkkannn I eeefffennn thhhpppeeekkk?" she mumbled in English, drooling again as she tested her ability to articulate.

Get it together, Justina commanded herself, her Polish inner voice authoritarian and demanding. *You can do this! Roll over. Tap the phone twice. Give whomever the critical information or just leave the damned phone on. Maybe the authorities can home in on the signal. This will be the difference between your living and your dying.*

Justina heard the tattooed woman crying out in ecstasy, yelling for the man to do something harder. Her screams sounded like the overdone, ridiculous noises from the actresses in an adult video Justina had laughingly, and embarrassingly, viewed once with a curious friend back in Poland.

With a renewed burst of effort, Justina managed to twist herself, hearing her own involuntary grunts. The phone was mercifully face-up, the home screen shining brightly. Coiling herself like an inchworm, Justina brought her face down on the iPhone, stabbing the phone icon. There, the second number of the oversize digits (*thank you Señora Moreno for setting your phone to the hard-of-viewing setting!*) was Sven's number, just below Redon's office number.

Touch it, Justina. Touch it and tell your story, no matter if he answers or not. You can leave a message if you have to.

With a jerk of her head she successfully touched the number, her satisfied chirp foreign to her as the screen changed to a phone image, shaking back and forth as it rang. One ring, two rings, three rings.

The phone screen changed. It had been answered!

MOMENTS EARLIER, the Cessna 182 had roared back into the sky. Arturo wagged the wings back and forth, a pilot's goodbye but probably in this case intended to symbolize good luck. After waving back to him through the rolled-down window, Gage shifted gears on the old, compact Toyota pickup, bouncing away from the private airport when an alarm-style ringing startled them both from the cardboard box.

"Phone!" Gage shouted, watching as Angelines tore the box open, reaching below the sheaf of bonds, into the stacks of money, and pulling the mobile phone out.

The caller ID read "Lydia Moreno."

"Give it!" he yelled, snatching the phone away and pressing the green button.

"Hello! Justina! Señora Moreno! Señora Moreno! Justina?"

The connection went dead.

THE BARE heel smashed down on the iPhone, destroying it despite the rubberized protective case. Justina was too immobilized to even lift her head. She simply laid there, a line of saliva flowing from the side of her mouth, numbly eyeing the tanned foot, marked by sun-bleached hair running from the ankle onto the top of the arched foot. Shards of glass penetrated the heel and, with each minute movement, she watched the prism-effect of the glass, gouging the thick cutaneous tissue. Then she was lifted, face-to-face, with the bearded man. He smirked at her, like a parent secretly proud of their mischievous child.

"Naughty girl," he admonished, his tongue slithering over his curled lip.

When she was dumped back into her chair, pain briefly spiking through her shoulders due to her cuffed wrists taking the brunt of her weight, she watched as the naked man, his excitement visibly abating, picked the glass from his heel, licking his own blood from his fingers afterward. The tattooed girl appeared, cinching a short robe around her waist, frowning at his foot as he relayed what had just happened.

The nurse listened before she turned and nodded approvingly at Justina. Though much of her body was currently useless, Justina's eyes went wide at the sudden recollection.

Gennady!

The nurse was one of Gennady's girlfriends.

Gennady was the manager of Eastern Bloc.

"Our little fun time is over," the bearded man said, walking away. Seconds later he was back, wearing loose athletic pants and nothing else. "It's time to get some answers." He walked in front of Justina, looking down at her.

"I'm going to ask you some questions. Will you answer them, and answer them truthfully?"

This moment was, unfortunately, the worst few seconds of the entire drug-induced episode. Despite the bellowing of her inner good judgment, telling her, of course, to mislead him or outright lie, and despite some deep-seeded gut knowledge of what she needed to do, to her utter horror, she felt her chin dip, followed by a tightening in the rear of her neck.

It was a nodding movement. She was unwillingly cooperating.

The man touched her cheek affectionately, murmuring, "*Bona noia.*"

Chapter Thirty-Three

STARING WESTWARD through the floor-to-ceiling glass of his office, Cortez Redon sipped the icy whiskey, allowing it to sear his throat. Earlier, his assistant, Mara, visibly puzzled by the events of the day, had come in to ask him if it was okay for her to leave. Having irritably dismissed her, he now chain smoked, strictly forbidden in government buildings, not that he cared. His loafers off, Redon rubbed his feet on the tight Berber-style carpet, and on one another, watching the blaze of tangerine sun as it slowly descended in the western sky, overheating the office since his blinds were pulled to the top.

Cortez Redon was scared.

Earlier, when he'd been down the street in the hotel room with that tall siren, his cell phone had buzzed just as he was disrobing.

"You're being set up, you stupid little bastard," was all Xavier Zambrano had said.

And for a moment, Redon's heart had ceased to beat.

He'd immediately asked for clarification, but Xavier had already hung up.

Xavier Zambrano...

...not who you want such a phone call from.

Xavier Zambrano, head of Los Leones. Xavier Zambrano, a man who'd probably ordered at least a thousand kills in the past decade. Xavier Zambrano, the man who Redon feared more than any other man on earth.

Redon stared at the handsome blue bank book on the desk. Ruefully, he pondered his earlier excitement, when that older woman had told him of the Navarro fortune, followed by the beautiful young woman who'd seemingly desired him in bed. What a heady moment it had been.

You're being set up...

Redon dragged on his cigarette, an ultra-mild German Auslese de Luxe, and pressed it into the notch of his ashtray. Lifting the bank book, he thumbed the pages, eyeing each of the entries, still intoxicated by what the old woman had told him earlier.

Xavier's words rang in his mind: *You're being set up. You're being set up. You're being set up.*

Tossing the bank book back on his desk, Redon lifted the cigarette, pulling fiercely on it before he finished his drink, three full shots' worth, allowing it to sear his mouth and throat and burn like a hot coal in his belly.

Leaving his coat in the office, Redon slipped the bank book in his back pocket, buttoning it. From one of his desk drawers, underneath a cream folder, he produced the diminutive pistol, known as a "Baby Browning." At .25 caliber, and small enough to be concealed in the palm of one's hand, pistols like this had long since been made illegal. He tipped the slide, making certain it was loaded.

Wishing for another whiskey, but thinking better of it, Redon slipped his feet back into his loafers, taking the keys to his Mercedes and easing into the hallway from his direct door. Springs of sweat erupted on the back of his neck as he tuned his ears for noises. When he heard none, he moved into the stairwell, a concrete and metal affair, heading downward, peering around the railing to check each landing before making the turn. With each step he wondered, "Where the hell is Xavier Zambrano?"

Earlier, after evacuating the hotel room, Redon had called Xavier back no less than six times. The mobster had not once answered. Clearing his calendar, because there was no way he might have focused, Redon spent the afternoon trying to decide if the old woman's offer had been genuine. Did Xavier intervene because he knew the money he so desperately sought was slipping from his grip? But, if so, then who was the girl? Was she somehow working with the old woman? And how did Xavier know about any of it?

"If only that prick would explain things," Redon whispered at the bottom of the stairs, pausing to gather himself. Xavier's silence was the worst omen. When a man like him goes silent, it often means one thing.

Or, maybe he's just occupied, Redon reasoned.

He knew he'd find out very soon. The door to the stairs opened into the narrow alleyway that fed into the Carrer de Pau Claris. If it was going to happen, Redon didn't think Xavier would suspect that he might take the stairs.

Do not underestimate him!

Regardless, Redon would bet eighty percent of the money represented in his bank book that the killing would take place at his Mercedes, parked in the reserved space on the street garage's second floor.

But that won't happen, because I'm going to take a taxi.

Or maybe he's waiting outside.

This was the critical moment.

Redon removed the Baby Browning, easing the door open, metal on metal, stepping into the grit of the shaded alleyway that ran northeast to southwest. Other than a feral cat, staring at him with indignation as his *caza de ratas* had been rudely interrupted, there was no one.

Relieved, but still concealing the pistol by his side, Redon tiptoed to the Carrer de Pau Claris, looking both ways. He angled his head, peering across the street into the dark second level of the garage, trying to make out his car. He spotted it. There seemed to be no abnormal activity there, or here on the street.

As they had done earlier, the beautiful Jacaranda trees swayed and undulated. The weather was warm and pleasant. The smell of the blooms, and of calamari, soothed his nostrils. The afternoon was quite agreeable. Optimism descended upon Cortez Redon.

Despite the sudden feelings of positivity, until he was able to gain some clarity from Xavier, Redon did not plan on driving his car, nor did he plan to go home. Instead, he would take a taxi, unannounced, to Sofia's apartment over on Barcelona's famed Bogatell Beach. Sofia was Italian, in her early twenties, an incredibly expensive prostitute. Her apartment was sumptuous, her services exclusive—and exquisite. Even with the five-thousand euro price for a full evening, plus another thousand if she had to break an appointment that was already set, Redon could release his tension from earlier and sleep safe with the knowledge that his location was unknown.

He'd brought his phone with him, but had turned it off and removed the battery. And now, stepping up the sidewalk of Carrer de Pau Claris, his office slowly disappearing behind him, Redon relaxed because, ahead of him on Barcelona's busy Avinguda Diagonal, he would find solace in a taxi, and would be relieving himself inside the leggy young Italian within the hour.

Tomorrow he could revisit this unpleasantness. And, perhaps, he might hear from the older woman again. *A tedious tightrope navigation, but that's my specialty.* Having escaped the area of likely ambush, Redon allowed himself the tiniest of smiles.

All this worry over nothing. Xavier knows I'm close to the money, the greedy bastard. He's just trying to spook me.

Redon's smile disappeared when, just before the intersection at Carrer de Mallorca, a large man burst from a dilapidated pickup truck and, before Redon could lift the mini Browning, punched him square in his face. Rather than watch Redon tumble to the ground, the man grasped the diminutive attorney and tossed him into the truck's floorboard.

When the man crammed himself into the passenger seat, crushing Redon's petite body further into the uncomfortable floor space, Redon spied a woman he recognized, driving the truck. She was cursing like a Marseilles sailor, complaining about vicious motherfucking pain in her leg.

The man above him, somehow, had the Baby Browning in his hand, now aiming it at Redon's face. "Remember me?" he asked in English.

Due to the circumstances, it took Redon a moment to make the connection. Had he been able to properly breathe, he might have sucked in a sharp breath. Despite his contorted predicament, it all came to him. She was the captain—the very crooked captain—from Berga Prison. And the man was the American hired by Ernesto Navarro to protect his shit of a son.

Redon recalled the American's limited dossier—he was a highly-trained killer.

Joder!

All the worry over Xavier had made Redon forget his numerous other adversaries.

Contorted like an unwilling gymnast in Le Cirque, he clenched his eyes shut, dealing with numerous discomforts over the balance of a twenty-minute ride.

IT WAS obvious the drug—its trade name was Amylobarbitone, known on the street as "parlador"—was beginning to lose its effectiveness with the Polish girl. She'd spoken to Xavier for thirty full minutes, answering his questions in a zombie-like monotone, but with palpable frankness. Now, however, he could see minor tells as he continued to question her, although he felt he'd already learned all he could.

In summary, she told him the prisoner at Berga, Gage Hartline, had contacted her last night. He was somehow escaping the bonds of the prison and needed Navarro's fee money for a payoff of some sort. The Polish girl had said she'd left the money in a cabin near the Baells Reservoir. Upon hearing this, Xavier checked his messages. There was one message and six missed calls from that little shit Redon. There were three additional messages from Luis, the wily old lieutenant who oversaw the Contratos end of his business. Each of the messages dealt with the prison break. The second message informed Xavier that El Toro had been gravely wounded in the bust-out. But it was Luis's third message that sent a shiver of rage through Xavier's body. Luis had learned more about the prison break, discovering that the federal police were looking for the American, Hartline. He'd escaped with the captain of the prison, Angelines de la Mancha.

While the police first thought her to be a hostage, they now believed that she was complicit.

That insolent whore.

Xavier recalled what he knew about de la Mancha. He knew that his associates had blackmailed her at first, but she'd become a willing accomplice over time. She'd allowed Los Leones the run of that prison and, in return, had taken hundreds of thousands of euro in exchange for her cooperation.

She also knew where all the bodies were buried, certainly possessing the knowledge to sink two dozen ranking Leones.

And maybe me along with them.

Xavier turned his mind to Cesar Navarro. Once he'd been killed, the American would have felt urgency to get out of Berga. He'd have soon found out that Redon was in on things, so that avenue of release was no good. Then, with nowhere else to turn, he'd go to the money-grubbing captain.

I've got a deal for you, capitana. I'll pay you a million euro of Navarro's money and, in return, you bust me out.

Xavier grudgingly admitted that it was a good plan.

But that's my damned money! As is the rest of Navarro's money, whenever I find it.

While Xavier was a criminal and not classically educated, he was remarkably prescient. Mind racing, he studied the drugged Polish woman, weighing his options. His first inclination—one of anger—was to gut both her and the old bat.

But they had more to give. He didn't know what it was, but his senses told him he'd missed something. He eyed the pretty woman for a moment. Then he turned to the old woman.

"Why are you helping her?"

"She's my daughter," the old woman answered, slurring.

"What?"

"Not my real daughter, but my daughter just the same."

Xavier processed this. "What else have I missed?"

"Missed?"

"What facts should I know?"

"My head is too muddled."

"How much money is in the box?" the nurse suddenly asked. Xavier, irritated, glared at her.

The older woman twisted her head to the Polish woman. "Gage spent some...wasn't it about a million euro less what he'd spent?"

The Polish woman nodded.

Xavier rolled his eyes. He knew how much money he was after. But just as he prepared a query along a much different line of questioning, the old woman said something that nearly caused his heart to seize.

"Don't forget...the million is just what's in *cash*."

Xavier lifted his hand, preventing the nurse from responding. He was aware of his own pulse in three different zones of his body. After a few steadying breaths, he spoke. "What other monies are in that box?"

"I wanted to help Justina's beau. So I went into my safe and I removed my entire sheaf of bearer bonds."

"Bearer bonds?"

"Yes. I've been saving them for years."

Xavier wasted no time. "What are they worth?"

"As you know, they're negotiable," the older woman slurred, her tone matter-of-fact. "Their full face value is nearly seventeen million...U.S."

Time stopped. The world ceased its rotation. All the years of Xavier's life flashed before his knowing eyes. His time as a grubby child, fighting his own siblings for an extra helping of rice in their filthy hovel. His early onset of puberty. The first girl he'd had, an eighteen year-old tramp who'd taken him all the way at Xavier's ripe old age of twelve. He recalled his first gang initiation, when a street hood named Lupo had held Xavier's head in a filthy toilet. Lupo had died for that only a week later. And after that, since that time, Xavier had climbed the Pyrenees of the underworld. All leading to this, the summit. Then, just as a flurry of white doves flittered out the open door, time started again.

And, blaringly, joyously loud, the Vienna Philharmonic suddenly played *Exultate Jubilate*.

Oh, what a moment!

It took him a moment to regain his composure.

"And these bearer bonds are with the cash her boyfriend was paid?" he asked.

"Yes. A plain cardboard box. It has money, bonds, a gun and a note."

Xavier closed his eyes. "Tell me about the note."

The older woman blinked several times, tilting her head as the memory came to her. "We told him to use the money and bonds if need be, but to try to wait through today because we were going to Barcelona to trap Cortez Redon."

He turned to his nurse friend. "How much more of that parlador do you have?" he sang.

"A large vial."

"If I give them another shot, will it be harmful?"

She shrugged. "At that dose I don't think it will harm them, per se. But it might make them lose consciousness."

"What if I administer that amount every hour?"

She shook her head. "You'll have to be careful stacking it like that. If it doesn't wear all the way off and you continue to add more, they might stop breathing."

Xavier chewed on the inside of his cheek as he walked to the older woman, stroking her hair. "You're sure about the bearer bonds?"

"Quite."

"And how much money are you worth?" Xavier said, the notion suddenly occurring to him.

"I don't ever add it up."

"Then guess."

"Liquid?"

"Altogether."

She made a humming sound, finally shrugging. "My mind is awash. With tied-up real estate, perhaps a hundred million. Liquid…about double the bearer bonds. Thirty million or so."

"Euro?"

"Sí, querida."

"Does that include the bonds?" he asked.

She nodded.

"Given her condition, who knows if she's accurate or not? But if she is, she's got access to more than double the amount of those bearer bonds," Xavier said, turning to the nurse and winking. "Worth keeping her alive over, for sure. And the girl is the ticket to the American."

Theo Garcia, you little worm, I may have just hit the mother lode.

Xavier jabbed a finger past the kitchen. "The interior storeroom is where I want to keep them. We'll handcuff them and bind their legs and feet."

"They'll need to lie down. Parlador makes a person unsteady and tired."

"Go get some things from one of the bedrooms. And bring the parlador and syringes."

Ten minutes later, after situating each wobbly woman on the pallet created by the nurse, Xavier checked their cuffs before tethering their arms together by a third set of cuffs. He instructed the nurse to give them another injection, agreeing that it be only three-quarters the amount from earlier.

"Gennady," Justina whispered as the nurse prepared her shot.

Xavier was on the phone.

The nurse leaned close. "What about Gennady?"

"You're his girlfriend."

The nurse glanced at Xavier before looking back. "So?"

"I remember you."

"From Eastern Bloc?"

"Yeah," Justina breathed. "Help me."

The nurse checked Xavier again. "The best thing you can do is just do what he says. He's not a bad person."

"He is," Justina countered. "He's going to kill us, and you too."

"What the hell are you talking about?" Xavier thundered. "Give her the damned shot."

The nurse plunged the needle into Justina's arm. Unbeknownst to Xavier, she only gave her half of the parlador.

"Now the old woman," he said.

Moments later, Xavier watched as the drug slowly went to work on both women. The older woman lay on her side, cradling the good side of her face on her arm, as if she were settling in for a pleasant slumber. Once both of his prisoners seemed fully sedated, he lifted a third needle from the plastic bag, handing it to the nurse.

"Prepare one for yourself."

She laughed. "Yeah, right."

Xavier stared at her.

The nurse straightened, her expression changing to worry. "You're serious."

"Indeed, lover girl. I've a number of things to do here, and they're not for your eyes to see. When my associates arrive—very powerful men from the government—if you were to see them, they would want me to eliminate you." He touched her face. "I don't want that. I'm not that type of guy."

Rubbing his arm, she pressed her crotch over his thigh and said, "But you already know I don't care about the things you do. The same goes for anyone you work with. I want to be trusted."

"I'm not going to hurt you," Xavier said soothingly. "But you need to comply immediately."

"Why can't I just leave?"

"I may need you later."

"For what?"

He smiled reassuringly. "Your skills are invaluable and, before this night is over, additional injuries are possible. And the injuries may occur to people who I don't want to die. So, please, fill a clean syringe so you can take a nice nap. You love drugs anyway, so I don't see why you're so concerned."

Worry still blanketing her face, the nurse pressed a new needle into the vial, extracting the same dosage she'd just drawn for the other two. "More," he said coldly. "That was their second dose."

She complied and slid the robe aside, rubbing an alcohol wipe on her buttocks. "I'm too skinny for a shoulder injection," she said, handing him the syringe and lying prone on the cushions next to the two drugged women. When he prepared to make the injection, she stopped him. "You saw me give them their shots...it was purposefully injected into the muscle. To heroin addicts it's known as *muscling*, and it's very important. When you stick the needle in, pull the plunger back to make sure no blood comes through. This much parlador given in a vein or artery would kill me if given all at once."

"But in the muscle it dissipates more slowly?"

"Yes."

Xavier viewed her shapely rear-end, marked by a lower back tattoo of roses twirling around her delicious Venus dimples. Setting the syringe aside, he massaged her buttocks, briefly flirting with the idea of a quick denouement to their earlier copulation.

"Mmmmm," she moaned as he kneaded.

He halted himself as the urgency of the situation came to the forefront. *Seventeen million dollars in bearer bonds, plus a million euro in loose cash!* Wanting to get this entire situation over with and get his money, Xavier straddled the nurse, watching as she toyed with his toes while he eyed the spot she'd wiped the alcohol on. Just to the inside of that area was a deep purple line—a thick vein.

"Are you ready?"

"If I have a headache later, I expect you to pamper me."

"Have no fear, my dear."

He held the needle above the dark vein line, pressing it in only a few millimeters.

"Ow," she said, turning her head but not enough to see. "I hope you're doing that where I cleaned."

"Just relax." He dropped the needle a fraction, changing the angle and pulling back on the plunger to see the rush of bright red blood, signifying the needle's presence in the vein.

"It doesn't feel like you went deep enough."

"It's all the way in," he said.

"Then just push the plunger in really slow, okay? If you go too fast it'll leave a mouse that'll hurt like hell."

Xavier had already depressed the plunger to the hilt. He slid the needle from the vein, pressing his thumb on the tiny dome of blood that emerged from the hole.

"How's that feel?" he asked, rolling her over.

"It didn't hurt a bit," she answered, opening her legs around him, pulling him forward with her feet. She took his hands, placing them on her breasts. "It'll take a few minutes. Want to finish as I start floating?"

Massaging her small breasts, he leaned over and brushed one kiss on her lips. As he pulled back, her expression changed.

"Xavier," she said in a breathy voice, blinking her eyes rapidly. "It's hitting too fast." She licked her lips and took several ragged breaths. "Oh shit. Oh shit. I'm scared, baby."

"Don't be, precious," he said, taking her hand.

"Oh-oh-oh-oh." Her voice came in hitches, softer each time.

The nurse's pupils began to bounce up and down. He allowed her limp hand to drop. Her chest rose and fell a dozen more times until it finally stopped. A rattling sound emanated from her mouth as her final breath modulated her vocal cords.

Then she was gone.

Xavier slapped her thigh affectionately, coming to a standing position. As he lifted the nurse's light body from the floor, he noticed the Polish woman, Justina, eyeing him through slit eyes.

"Go to sleep," Xavier commanded, flipping off the light in the cupboard and pulling the door shut.

He carried the slight nurse to the hall closet, stuffing her inside, thoroughly disgusted when her bowels released due to the pressure of her contortion. Hoping to contain the smell, Xavier wet a towel and jammed it against the outer base of the door. Then, from the kitchen, he looped a piece of string around the resident dinner bell, hanging it on the doorknob of the storeroom.

Using his cell phone, Xavier touched redial for Acusador Cortez Redon.

"That little shit better use every bit of his influence to find Gage Hartline."

Cocked an eyebrow. "And my money."

SOMETHING HAPPENED while Angelines drove the small pickup truck westward across the sunset-splashed city of Barcelona. Though it had been hitting him in waves over the past day, Gage's fear for Justina uncorked, constricting his optical nerves in a cousin to his old PTSD headaches. This headache wasn't completely debilitating—but it was quite painful. And while Barcelona was streaked with the low afternoon sun, to Gage it flamed red, worsening his headache with every second.

Redon was still in the floorboard, his protestations having quieted after Gage stomped on him a few times. Now the lawyer was curled into a modified fetal position, whimpering occasionally, surrendered to his fate. Unable to speak with a great deal of coherence, Gage motioned Angelines to follow the road by the Llobregat River. She followed the river inland for ten kilometers, as the city abruptly gave way to a pastoral setting, with rows and rows of plantings beside the curving waterway.

At a rural bridge crossing, Gage asked Angelines to slow, having her turn down a dusty access road that led to the river's edge. There, at the base of a low bridge, a good ten feet below the road and completely hidden, Gage held his left hand up to stop her.

"What are we going to—"

Her query was cut off because Gage was already out of the truck. He thrust both hands back in, grasping Redon's lapels and yanking him from the truck so hard that Redon's forehead snagged on a protruding screw head at the bottom of the dashboard, ripping it open and leaving the acusador squealing like a pig.

"My kidney's about to rupture! My head is splitting! I've got stab wounds! Acid burns!" Gage's rant continued as he dragged the howling little man down to the coffee-colored water, his actions concealed by the looming bridge. Above them, the radial sound of car and truck tires on the steel grate-work drowned out the acusador's screamed protests and impassioned cries for help.

Dropping down into the knee-deep water just below the bank, Gage twisted the acusador so his back was against the grass and mud, and then he began to beat the man.

First blow: straight right to the mouth. Finger-width gash on the upper lip and two teeth knocked loose.

Second blow: left hook into Redon's right ear. No visible damage other than a stunned reaction.

Third blow: another straight right, directly into the acusador's pristine Gallic nose. Nose visibly broken afterward, replete with running blood and red snot bubbles.

Fourth, and final, blow: left cross to left eyebrow. Deep fissure of a cut on the sharp brow line, matching the lip cut in severity.

Through it all, the acusador had blubbered legal protestations, as if a bailiff might rush in to save him. Finished punching him, Gage dunked the lawyer into the waters of the Llobregat, silencing the acusador's remonstrations. Now, other than the traffic, all that could be heard was bubbling and thrashing.

As he held the crooked little man under, Gage turned to Angelines, who was watching him in horror.

"Let him up!" she screamed. "You'll kill him."

Gage continued the hold for ten more seconds, then lifted Redon, his bloody, split maw a rictus of sucking air. "He's alive," Gage said monotone, thrusting him under again.

The thrashing continued. Foaming water. Churning. It had all the frenzy of a crocodile attack.

Defeating the car sounds, the splashing, and Angelines' objections, was a smooth female voice from the recesses of Gage's mind. The accent wasn't American; it was indistinct. It could have been Justina, could have been Monika, he couldn't tell—but the words, and their meaning, were clear enough:

Let him up, Gage. No more killing.

It might have been the only thing that saved the acusador, and since the voice belonged to a woman Gage loved, though he didn't know which one, he obeyed.

Still holding the lawyer's soaked lapels, Gage jerked him from the river's silt. He hoisted Redon onto the dusty bank, leaving him flat on his back. Once the acusador had his breath, he began to cry, wailing loudly. Redon reminded Gage of the proverbial neighborhood bully once he'd finally met his match, taking a vicious and humiliating ass-whipping from the new kid on the block and not having a clue of how to react to total defeat with some measure of decorum.

Gage pulled himself up, staggering to Angelines as his fury melted away. "Get ready to leave."

"Don't kill him, Gage," she pleaded.

He pointed to the truck. She complied.

By the time Gage took a knee by the acusador, the Spaniard's cries had reduced to whimpers. *"No mas,"* the pathetic man sniveled. *"No mas, por favor!"*

"Stop your crying," Gage said, curling his lip.

"Wh-wh-what are you going to do to me?"

"Before you tell me what I want to know, I'm going to make you a promise."

Redon began to gingerly touch his facial cuts.

"Look at me," Gage said. When Redon did, Gage spoke calmly but firmly. "If you cooperate with me, Redon, I *will* allow you to live. If you lie to me, or clam up, you're going back in that river and you're not coming up." Raising his eyebrows, Gage waited for acknowledgement.

"I will do anything you say. Anything."

"Later, Redon, when your little pains and fears subside, if you try to take legal action against me, or try to tip off your gangster buddies, I swear to you above all I hold sacred, that the piss-ant beating you just took will seem enjoyable next to what I will do to you. I will make it my life's final mission to pay you back, and to do it as painfully as I can dream." Gage gripped the man's jaw, squeezing it. "Because, *Acusador* Cortez Redon, in my eyes there's nothing worse than a man who is supposed to serve the people that, instead, steals from them and makes their lives collectively more dangerous. It would give me great joy to kill your ass over the most tortuous week imaginable."

Gage let that sink in for a moment. "Do you believe me?"

Redon nodded, vigorously. And Gage was sure he smelled fresh piss. He stood, placing his hands on his hips.

"Did you receive a visit from a tall Polish girl and an older Spanish woman today?"

Redon's eyes grew wide. "Yes."

"Where did you see them?"

"Near where you grabbed me, in a café."

"What happened?"

Despite the stress of the situation, Redon concisely exposited the story about Señora Moreno and Navarro's money. Then he explained that he didn't know they were together, and told Gage about going to the hotel with the Polish girl.

Trying to make sense of what he'd just heard, and guessing correctly that it was a two-pronged setup, Gage grasped Redon's wet tie and dirty-water-stained white shirt, twisting it. "Where are they now?"

"I truly don't know."

"Tell me what happened."

"When we got up to the hotel room, when the girl was in the bathroom, I received a call."

"Who called?"

A visible swallow. "A man named Xavier, the head of Los Leones."

"The same man who you were secretly working for when you double-crossed Navarro?"

"Sí."

"And what did he tell you?"

"He said I was being set up, so I ran away."

"And he snatched the girl and the woman?"

"I don't know that but, if you're unable to reach them, I would presume he did."

"Where would he take them?"

"I don't know," Redon answered immediately. Making a fist, Gage pulled his right arm back as Redon cowered, whimpering that he'd been calling Xavier all day long.

Angelines, having been sitting in the passenger seat with the window open, stepped out with Redon's phone, an Android. "What's the password?" she asked, wagging the phone.

"George Town." He said it in English.

She typed. "Not working."

Gage pulled back again.

"It's two words!" Redon screamed. "Upper-case 'G' and 'T': George-space-Town."

She tapped the words in, nodding as the screen lit up. "You've received two calls," she said, handing Redon the phone.

Squinting his eyes, Redon nodded enthusiastically. "They were from him."

"Message?" Gage asked.

"No. Never. He expects me to answer. He doesn't leave messages."

"If I let you call him…"

"I will behave as if my very life depends on my cooperation."

"It does."

Chapter Thirty-Four

XAVIER STOOD on the balcony, eyeing the distant, darkening Mediterranean. He knew that many people of varying authority could possibly be looking for his three "houseguests." A plan in mind, he went inside, methodically searching all their clothing, finding no cellular phones or anything that could be emitting a signal. That done, he searched the nurse's purse, discovering an older Blackberry, which he disabled by removing the battery.

Satisfied that the most recent parlador injection had at least thirty more minutes of effectiveness, he took the inner stairs down to the enclosed garage, inspecting the Volvo. Right away he noticed a large, purple handbag and, inside, a wallet and a cell phone. The phone was cheap, of the prepaid variety. Since he couldn't determine a way to eliminate its signal, he removed the battery. Xavier set it aside, eyeing the dormant GPS on the dash of the Volvo.

Could this still be sending out a signal?

He recalled something about a radio advertisement, describing a person whose car had been stolen, and the overly-cheery operator finding it due to the car's global positioning system. Of course, the advertisement failed to mention the car-jacker's vow for revenge against the car owner, or the crooked judge, or the beating the car-jacker put on the engine and transmission while trying to escape. No matter, Xavier located an adjustable wrench and, after popping the hood, disconnected the grease-coated red cable leading to the battery.

Ascending the stairs, Xavier checked the door to the storeroom. It was closed and he could hear no movement. As he pondered his next move, his own phone buzzed on the counter. He eyed the phone number, recognizing it as Cortez Redon's cell phone.

"Where the hell have you been?" Xavier snapped.

"I'm sorry, but it's been a very interesting afternoon."

Knowing he had no room to talk, Xavier admonished Redon anyway. "How could you be so stupid, so cock-driven to get lured to a hotel room by some slut you don't even know, with all you and I have on the line?"

"I realize that now," Redon said in a contrite voice.

337

"And what did the old woman talk to you about in the café?"

"That's why I'm calling. She offered money."

"I know about the bearer bonds. Do you have them?"

"No, Xavier. The man who *kidnapped* me has the bonds."

Xavier didn't respond for a moment. He padded through the house, walking outside, collapsing into one of the patio chairs as Redon repeated his name.

"Xavier, are you still there?"

Leaning his head back to the growing dusk, Xavier calculated the situation and said, "If he kidnapped you, and now you're calling me, it can only mean that he wants his women."

"That is exactly what he wants."

"Wait a moment," Xavier said, concentrating. With Navarro's organization at his disposal, despite the current cash crunch, Xavier felt confident Los Leones could pull through in their current state. Rather than bargain with this American prick, he could order his entire organization to hunt this man—hunt him and kill him. Xavier gave himself a one-in-three chance of finding him before the dawn.

Besides, the old woman in that storeroom was loaded. With a deft hand, Xavier might be able to extract her wealth instead. He lifted the phone.

"Tell your American I said to fuck off. And he can gut you for all I care, Cortez."

"There's more to it than that," Redon said, his voice shaking.

"I told you I know about the money *and* the bearer bonds."

"Not that."

"What then?"

"Angelines de la Mancha, from Berga, is with him. If you don't bargain with him, he said they're going to the American Embassy. They're going to expose Berga, and expose you." Redon lowered his voice. "And they're going to take me with them. It will be bad for you, Xavier. While you may rule Catalonia, such pressure from the United States would force Spain to crush Los Leones, despite all the government officials on your payroll."

"You would turn on me?"

"Yes. I will."

Xavier stood and walked inside, trembling in his rage. *Breathe, Xavier, breathe.* He took another beer from the refrigerator, biting off the top and taking a long draught.

"Are you still there?" Redon asked.

"I think the American is a desperate liar. And that cunt from Berga, too. There's no way in hell they'll admit what they've done. They'll go to jail."

"No. They'll be cutting a deal to bring down Spain's most brutal gang. We all will. And we'll get immunity, Xavier. While you'll get hunted down."

"You're somewhere with this American's pistol aimed at your nose, *mariquita*. Like I should believe you."

"It's the truth and it will make for great news and publicity for a country that makes its living from tourism."

From somewhere in the corner of his mind, Theo Garcia demanded that Xavier cut a deal and get that damned money. Xavier rubbed his temples...

Swallow your pride, Xavier. Swallow your pride and meet the American. You can make the deal and still deceive him. You'll get your money, thereby satisfying Garcia and solidifying Los Leones. Then you can kill the American, de la Mancha, and that little prick, Redon.

Then, when the coffers are full, rent another yacht and head to Italy.

It made sense.

Xavier idly glanced at the supply closet, wishing he hadn't overdosed his nurse friend. After this call he was going to require an intense release.

"Fine," Xavier finally said. "Tell the American we can make the trade. The two women for the money. If anyone tries to go to the embassy or the authorities, I promise a blood war that Spain has never before seen."

"Wait a moment." It sounded as if Redon covered the phone. When he came back he said, "He wants proof the two people are alive."

"To hell with him," Xavier laughed. "He will never, *ever*, make demands to—"

"You better not hurt them, you sonofabitch!"

The voice that had just yelled was different, and in English.

It was the American, Hartline.

Although momentarily surprised, Xavier was experienced in making, and dealing with, threats. Rather than let it sound as if it affected him, he made his voice silky as he said, "Your two conniving friends are just fine and both resting comfortably."

"Hear me," Hartline said, his voice suddenly calm. "If you hurt those two women, I will destroy you."

Xavier thought he might keep going but he didn't. That was the sum total of his threats. And the conciseness and tone actually made Xavier believe the American—or, believe that he would die trying. In some small way, he respected the man. Unfortunately for the American, he wouldn't be alive to mete out any destruction. Nevertheless, Xavier appreciated such economy and coolness. It made the threat seem far more ominous.

"Mister Hartline, I am a businessman. You have my attorney, and my money. And I have your women. Let's don't take the dark road. Let's figure this out, and be done with it."

"The captain keeps the cash."

"Pardon?"

"The captain, de la Mancha, keeps the cash. You get the bonds. I get my women. Redon goes back to work. I could give a shit what you and him do afterward."

"How much cash is there for her to—"

"Doesn't matter," Hartline barked. "She keeps the cash. Not negotiable. And in about eight hours, at zero-four-hundred on the button, you will stand on the beach of Tossa de Mar, near where you killed our friend, Ernesto Navarro."

"Whoa, whoa, whoa," Xavier said. "Don't think you're going to set the meeting for—"

There was a click. The line went dead.

Xavier's testicles lurched to the back of his throat.

He was motionless for a moment, eventually swigging the remainder of the Heineken.

He'll call back.

Five minutes passed. No call.

Closing his eyes, Xavier redialed. The phone was answered and he could hear Acusador Redon pleading in the background. After a moment Redon came on line. "Do not push him! He's ready to walk."

"Even without his women?" Xavier said, angry at himself for his entreating tone but unable to contain it as it left his mouth.

There was a shuffling sound before the American came back on, his voice steely. "I know all about leverage, you piece of trash."

"You'd be willing to let your women die?"

"And you'd be willing to live every day of your life in fear of me slitting your throat?" the American countered.

Wide-eyed, Xavier stared at the phone. He truly despised this Hartline. Somehow, Xavier had to flip the odds while managing to ensnare Navarro's fortune. For now, however, Xavier knew he had to pretend to be complicit. Gritting his teeth, he said, "I apologize. Please proceed."

"Zero-four-hundred, you walk out on Tossa de Mar beach, all the way to the water's edge, directly in front of the long boardwalk. Know where I mean?"

"Yes."

"Be right there, ankles in the water, or I walk. You will wear no shoes and no shirt, and you'd better not have a weapon on you or you'll wind up feeding the sharks as the sun comes up. Bring both women and I'll give you the bonds."

"Please, may I ask a question?"

"What?"

"What's to prevent you from killing me?"

"That's the point. It keeps you honest."

"I will not do an exchange this way because I trust you no more than you trust me."

"Then I guess you won't get your money, you prick."

Xavier squeezed his eyes shut, expecting the American to hang up again. But he didn't. Slowly, Xavier opened his eyes, feeling the pendulum swinging his way. Was the American blustering?

After clearing his throat, Xavier said, "You're aware of mutually assured destruction?"

Silence.

"Because, if I show up unarmed, you can knife me quietly and leave with everything."

"That's right."

Recalling a Monaco poker game he'd once participated in, one with a one-million euro buy-in for each player, Xavier still regretted what had caused him to lose. He'd made it to the final two but lost his chip advantage before losing everything two hands later. Xavier had found out the next morning (after beating the winner with a cricket bat) that, on the critical hand, the man had been bluffing with only a pair of fives. But, because such cash was at stake, Xavier had been wound too tight. Although he'd simply stolen the man's winnings (and left him for dead,) Xavier vowed to never be bluffed again.

"So, these conditions are the only way you will meet?" Xavier asked.

"That's right," the American replied.

Xavier hung up the phone.

GAGE HEARD the click.

Xavier Zambrano had hung up.

"Shit."

"You pushed him too hard!" Redon said, lowering his bloody t-shirt from his mouth.

Gage glared at the dishonest attorney until Redon lowered his eyes. Angelines was sitting in the passenger seat of the pickup truck, her hand on her wounded leg. Gage walked to her. "Think he'll call back?"

"I don't know how he operates. But he has so much power that I can't imagine it's worth it to him to meet you straight up if he thinks he might die—even for that much money."

"I negotiate for a living and he was dying to meet you!" Redon chastised. "But your demand was unreasonable. And now he will *not* call back, and those two women are dead due to your stubbornness."

Gage tilted his head back, massaging the bridge of his nose. The sun had just dipped below the western mountains, dragging behind it a blanket of cool air from the Mediterranean. As he looked up, watching the line of aircraft on their downwind leg into El Prat airport over by the coast, Gage saw one small aircraft in the pattern, a Cessna Caravan. Larger than the plane they had flown on earlier, the single-engine aircraft was still diminutive in comparison to the other jet aircraft setting up in the pattern.

The brilliant bloom of a distant idea burst from a corner of Gage's mind. He continued to eye the Caravan, flying quickly to keep up with the commercial traffic.

This could work.

Gage turned to Redon. "Get in the truck between her and me." He looked at Angelines. "If he twitches, shoot him in the stomach with the AutoMag."

Stepping away from the noise of the bridge, Gage dug into his pocket, retrieving the business card given to him by Arturo the jump pilot. Using Redon's phone, Gage dialed Arturo, initially thanking him for the ride and the use of the truck before asking Arturo a detailed set of questions. He listened to all of Arturo's responses, satisfied with all of them but the final objection.

"With your transponder off, assuming you drop from radar afterward, how would they know?"

"They probably wouldn't," Arturo admitted.

"Would you reconsider if I offered you one-hundred-thousand euro in unmarked bills?"

Arturo chortled a rueful laugh. "My friend…"

"If you do your part correctly, I will *not* get you burned. You have that on my word as a fellow soldier. I will die before I give up your name."

The speaker crackled as Arturo blew out a hard breath. "You're serious?"

"I am. I can't go to the authorities on this one, my friend…but if I don't act now, innocent people will die."

"*Entiendo.* When can you be here?"

"Tonight, but I'm not exactly sure what time yet. We'll call you when we're on the way. I'm still in Barcelona and I need to make a very important stop on the way to your D.Z."

"I can't get caught," Arturo said. "My life's been nothing but clean living since I retired from *El Grupo.*"

"Just drop below radar until you land. No one will know and I will *never* tell."

Arturo grew silent for a moment. "I'm in."

"Thank you. Call you in a bit." Gage hung up and jogged to the truck, praying that Zambrano hadn't harmed the women. He wheeled the pickup into a spinning turn on the dusty access road.

"Where are we going?" Angelines asked.

"I have a plan," Gage said, wheeling the old truck into a 180-turn.

Chapter Thirty-Five

Gage motored to the north, following the signs to the AP-7, known as the *Autopista del Mediterráneo*, running the length of Spain's eastern shore. He merged onto the busy highway, headed to the northeast.

"What's the plan?" Angelines asked.

"We're headed to Lloret de Mar, first. There's a pharmacy next to where we're going, unless my brain is playing tricks on me. I'll get something for your pain."

"What about Xavier?"

"I'm getting ready to call him." Gage took a number of deep breaths.

This was the big moment.

He touched Xavier's number. Predictably, Xavier didn't answer the first time. Without hesitation, Gage called again. And again.

"What?" Xavier yelled after picking up on Gage's third try.

Breathing a sigh of relief, Gage said, "You apologized earlier, now it's my turn. I'm sorry and, as a tactician, you're correct to refuse my demand. You shouldn't be expected to agree to an unprotected meeting."

"I'm pleased that you're at least intelligent enough to realize that," Xavier stated coldly.

"Are the ladies still alive?"

"For the moment."

"Don't hurt them."

"Then don't make stupid demands."

"Understood. How about this? We meet in the same place, at Tossa. You bring the women—I bring the bonds."

"Go on."

"I'll have someone with me. A woman."

"De la Mancha."

"And she's wounded, Xavier. A threat to no one."

"I want a backup man, also."

"No."

344

"No deal," Xavier said.

Gage relented. "One backup man, standing at a distance, and he better not have a rifle."

"Have no fear."

Gage knew Xavier wouldn't honor these terms. But he had to act as if he trusted the man for this situation to come off.

"So, we're clear?" Gage asked. "Zero-four-hundred, at the water, armed but not carrying, one man in the distance."

"Yes. And I will bring your women."

"I will have the bonds and the lawyer."

Xavier clicked off.

Gage rubbed his face with his free hand before handing the phone to Angelines. "Turn off the phone's radio."

As she did, she asked, "Why are we going to Lloret, of all places?"

Gage was silent.

"Did you hear me? Why Lloret?"

Gage jarred, turning to her. "There's someone there I need to see."

As night fell, and the blackness of the Mediterranean to the east beckoned their rendezvous with Xavier, the old pickup puttered on, growing closer to Lloret de Mar.

XAVIER HELD the phone in his hand, his mind racing. What was he not seeing? What was the angle?

Because Tossa was perfect, absolutely perfect—for Xavier.

A crescent beach. Several hundred meters of flat sand with no obstructions. Plenty of beachside buildings to place a sniper.

And, since Tossa wasn't a party town, the entire population would be asleep.

This was going to be too easy.

Xavier began thumbing through his contacts. He knew just who to call.

Lloret de Mar, Spain

THE ANXIOUS crowd numbered at least fifty people, packed five-deep inside the velvet ropes. Confined like sheep in a pen, they breathed the universal scent of urban center dance clubs: the overblown aroma of cologne and perfume, mingled with liquor, cigarettes, and pheromones. The revelers shared a common agenda: drink, have fun, and get raucously laid by daybreak.

Gage visited the pharmacy first. Thankful that he didn't need a prescription in Spain, he purchased over-the-counter antibiotics for his kidney, taking a dry double dose in front of the cashier. He then carried a large bottle of *Espidifen*, Spanish Advil, power bars and water bottles to the pickup truck parked on a dark street behind the rows of brightly lit buildings. Angelines was doing fine, holding the acusador at bay. Gage told her to wait an hour.

"If I'm not back by then, take the money and disappear."

"How?"

"No idea," he answered honestly, walking back to the lights of the main thoroughfare.

Gage knew getting in was going to take some effort once he saw the mob outside of the club Eastern Bloc. Typical of clubs like this one, a large bouncer stood on the small elevated stoop, meaty hands clasped in front of him, ready to unleash an ass-whipping on anyone who got out of line.

As Gage lingered in the distance, he watched as two women finally exited the club. The man inside spoke by radio to the large bouncer who then perused the waiting crowd. Rather than accept the three cheesy club-maven males at the front of the horde, the bouncer called a couple forward, both of them striking—especially the woman. As the crowd jeered his choice, the couple waited as red bands were taped around their wrists by the man just inside the door. That done, the other bouncer, this one outside the ropes, admitted two more people inside the ropes.

Moving to his left, Gage could see inside the doors to the bright red stairwell. Sitting where he had been when Gage first met him was his Russian friend in the gaudy burgundy suit. This was Gage's "*priyatel*," the one he'd relieved of the two pistols.

There was no way to get to the stairwell without going through the crowd and, to do that, Gage would have to increase his odds somehow. He turned, watching the people on the busy sidewalk until he noticed two women who certainly had the assets to pull off his plan. Gage stopped them, not surprised at the way they recoiled. Today had been a very long day and he had no illusions about his appearance. His forehead was still bruised. There were cuts on his face and, worst of all, he could smell himself. The old

Army saying was, "If you can smell yourself, everyone else smelled you two days ago."

"We have no money," one of the girls immediately said in broken Spanish.

They think I'm a panhandler.

Gage smiled, hoping he could later share this story with Justina. In the time he'd known her, he found her sense of humor irresistible.

"I don't want your money," Gage said to the young women, speaking English as he produced a crisp hundred euro bill from his back pocket, taken from the stash in the cardboard box. "I want to pay you for a favor."

"We're not like that," the other girl said, screwing up her face.

"This money is yours if you simply get me into that club," he said, pointing to the Eastern Bloc.

The taller of the two eyed him narrowly. "What do we have to do inside?"

"Nothing," Gage said openly. "I just need to get in. You can take the money and leave if you like."

The girls, Irish if Gage heard their accents correctly, looked at one another and shrugged.

Putting his arms around both girls' trim waistlines, Gage led them to the outer rope, pushing his way through the crowd of men, ignoring protests and threats directed at him in at least five languages. The massive bouncer, charged with letting people into the inner circle, cocked a bushy eyebrow at the trio, nodding once as he unclipped the rope, allowing them access to the inner circle.

Once in, Gage leaned to the one on his right, the taller one, a striking redhead with expressive blue eyes. "Now you walk up and get the big bouncer at the door to let us in. Stick this in his palm," Gage said, handing her a folded fifty euro bill. He stood with her friend, keeping her close to prevent her from getting crushed by the energetic mob as he viewed the other Irish woman push her way forward, in the way only beautiful women can get away with. At the door, she stood next to the bouncer, speaking in his ear while she pressed the money in his hand.

The bouncer looked at his palm, a grin forming on his face as he nodded.

C'mon Igor, do it. That's got to be a night's pay for you.

"Igor" wagged his finger at the crowd, saying something to Gage's new friend. She pointed directly at Gage and her friend. Breathing a sigh of relief, combing his ragged hair with his fingers, Gage allowed the other Irish woman to push forward, walking behind her to conceal his filthy clothing.

Finally, upon reaching the platform, the bouncer instructed them to stand next to him. He spoke English, saying, "Next three people come out, you go in, yes?"

The girls stood by the bouncer as Gage stood behind them, concealing himself.

He dreaded what was coming.

THE RUSSIAN in the burgundy suit was named Dmitry, a former prisoner in Moscow and now just another thug in the globally-mushrooming *Ispanskiy* crime syndicate. Things had not been going very well for Dmitry in Spain, especially after the beating he'd taken at the hands of a stranger several weeks before. His boss, a ruthless sort named Gennady, had beaten him further over the incident, citing his own embarrassment at his top club man being so easily taken down by what he called a "pussy westerner." The two pistols that were stolen had been issued to Dmitry upon his arrival to Spain. Due to their loss, Dmitry had to pay Gennady back from his own paycheck, and Gennady's appraisal of the Star pistols was at least six times what they were really worth.

Though he was a lowly soldier in the Ispanskiy syndicate, Dmitry had aspirations, too. Toward the end of his stretch in the infamous Butyrka prison, he'd been told about the position here in Spain, eagerly seeking it after hearing of its glorious nature, endearing himself to one of the mob bosses by beating collections and obscene interest out of several other prisoners.

Like so many things in life, Dmitry later learned this Spain-based job wasn't near as glamorous as they'd made it sound. He'd had no idea that he would wind up a glorified babysitter for a dozen Polish swine. He was also never told he would work seven days a week, fourteen hours a day, for six months out of the year. Sure, since arriving, he'd had his share of women, but one gets tired of vacationing club girls with their disgusting white-crusted nostrils.

Dmitry dreamed of his own club, operated by his own decisions. He'd have an office just above the dance floor, hidden behind a strip of mirrored windows. He would arrive each evening around nine, greeting his regulars warmly and going straight upstairs to read the numbers on yesterday's take. By midnight he would choose the girl he wanted, having his bouncers retrieve her and bring her to his well-appointed office, full of chrome and leather. Then, once he'd had his fill, Dmitry would finish off the night by walking the floor, thanking the biggest spenders with a free round on the house.

Anything but this, sitting here in a stuffy, stinking stairwell, putting on wrist bands and using a hand-counter to satisfy the corrupt Lloret de Mar fire marshal.

His droning thoughts were interrupted as two couples ascended the stairs, speaking in British accents as they made fun of the "trashy Russkie crowd" in the club. A year ago Dmitry might have threatened them; now he simply didn't have the energy and, honestly, could give a shit what they thought.

Working the button on his hand-counter with one hand, Dmitry depressed the button on his Motorola handset with his other, saying, *"Otpravit' v chetyrekh lyudey."* It meant, "Send in four more."

In seconds, two leggy beauties strode through the door, turning and saying something to their friend before heading down the stairs. Then, suddenly, Dmitry's cold, gray world brightened considerably. Because standing in the door of the Eastern Bloc, his bruised face illuminated in a gothic red shadow by the CCCP neon light, was the man who'd beaten Dmitry and taken his pistols.

Filthy and stinking, the man immediately placed both of his hands behind his head and, speaking English, said, "I come in peace and mean you no harm. In fact, I'm here to tell you something you and your associates will certainly want to hear."

Dmitry hardly heard the words. Instead, he lurched from behind his small stand with a leather-wrapped sap. Though the American partially blocked the blow to his head, it was enough to knock him down.

And that made Dmitry happy.

GAGE SAT in an office chair, his hands still behind his head. His fall had been faked. The blow from the Russian had hurt, all right—hurt his left forearm, which is what Gage used to parry the blow. But, knowing he needed to let the suited ape be the hero, Gage had fallen, throwing his hands up as if asking for mercy. With the assistance of one of the colossal bouncers, the Russian had wrenched Gage's arm behind his back, walking him down the stairs and, after striking the double doors with Gage's face and body, into the pulsating disco.

As Gage had been shoved over the length of the long club, he looked to his left, to the bar where, just weeks before, Justina had poured him a beer.

The thought of her clamped on his heart.

He had been led through a brightly-lit rear hallway, then into a darkened office outfitted with cheap furniture and one laptop computer. That's where he now sat. There was a floor safe in the corner and, on each wall, cheaply framed photographs of nude women, obviously taken by an amateur who thought he was a professional.

The big bouncer, after listening to Gage's friend's instructions, had taken his leave. Now it was just Gage and his Russian buddy, Dmitry, who happened to be aiming a Walther PP, made conspicuous by the curved ribbon logo, at Gage's head.

"I had to buy gun after you steal my other two guns, you piece shit!" the Russian said, spitting on Gage's face.

Wishing he could wipe the spittle from his nose and mouth, Gage pressed on. "I'm here today to pay you for those pistols."

"Pay me?"

"I brought you the money for them. It's in my back pocket," Gage said, slowly lowering his right hand.

The Russian twisted the pistol gangster style. "Wait for Gennady!" he growled.

As if on cue, the office door banged open and in walked the one who must be Gennady. Gage recalled having seen him behind the club on the night he'd liberated Justina. Not overly tall, the man had a shaved head and his face, other than a lantern jaw, was unremarkable. It was his steroid-enhanced muscles, however, that were the man's most noticeable asset. He wore a custom gray suit with a wide-collared, powder blue shirt, unbuttoned halfway down his stomach to reveal his numerous gold chains floating over his prison tattoos and rippling abs.

"This is man who robbed me of guns!" Dmitry yelled. "The one who kidnapped Justina from us!"

After murmuring something to Dmitry with what Gage felt was a note of disdain, the man named Gennady sneered at Gage.

"*Vy govorite na russkom?*" he asked.

Gage knew enough Russian phrases to know he'd just been asked if he spoke Russian. Keeping his unchallenging eyes down, Gage replied, "Only English, German, or Spanish."

Gennady rubbed the stubble on his broad chin, poking his lips out as he nodded. Then, with that same hand, he open-handed Gage across his face. Having seen it coming, Gage turned his cheek as the blow struck. It hurt, but Gage had been prepared for some pain when he'd come up with this foolhardy scheme.

"That, *pindos*, was for first stepping foot in my club." From his pocket he retrieved a chrome switchblade, flicking it open to reveal a long blade. "And the scar I'm going to leave across your face is for what you took from Dmitry, and me." Gennady hitched his head to Dmitry. Dmitry moved behind Gage, grasping his wrists and tugging downward. It was an awkward position and one Gage would have a tough time resisting from.

"Wait, Gennady," Gage grunted through the pain. "Just listen to me for one minute."

The Russian was pulling down so hard on Gage's arms that Gage feared his shoulders might dislocate. Gennady jabbed Gage's already sore forehead above his temple, obviously getting ready to give Gage a diagonal face slash—a mark of a thief in Russia.

"Why would I have come back?" Gage yelled as the blade pierced his thick hide of skin on his forehead, beginning to slowly scrape downward. "I've brought you something!"

The sound of the blade grinding against skull was worse than fingers on a chalkboard.

"Millions of euro!" Gage added.

Though Gage couldn't tell from his wrenched-backward position, Gennady had only cut a few centimeters of Gage's forehead. The Russian stopped cutting, straightening and telling Dmitry to ease up.

With the tip of the blade aimed at Gage's eye, Gennady said, "You've got ten seconds, *pindos*."

"Have you heard of Los Leones?" Gage asked, a steady trickle of blood running through his right eyebrow.

"What about Los Leones?"

"I'm meeting their top man tonight, in an isolated spot."

No response.

"Don't you get it?" Gage asked. "Their man, Xavier Zambrano, could easily be taken down or even captured at this meeting."

Gennday listened to this impassively, shrugging afterward as he curled his lip. "So?"

"Xavier Zambrano is everything to Los Leones. They're struggling to take over Los Soldados, Ernesto Navarro's operation." Gage arched his eyebrows. "Navarro was just killed. You know that, right?"

"What is meaning of this?"

Gage spaced out his words. "Los Leones is shaky and has poor leadership. If you take Zambrano down, assuming you import enough muscle, you could potentially assume Los Leones' position in Spain."

"Why you telling me this?"

"Because I have a problem with Los Leones and Xavier Zambrano. But I have *no* problem with you."

Gennady lowered the switchblade and rubbed his whiskers. "You think killing Zambrano will end Los Leones? I knew you were stupid for robbing from the *brotherhood*—now I think you're just crazy." Again he hitched his head at Dmitry, who yanked down on Gage's wrists.

"Argh!" Gage grunted, recalling what Ernesto Navarro had initially told him. "Listen to me! Los Leones are broke! They have no money!"

"So what?" Gennady asked, holding the knife over Gage's forehead.

"They can't go on without the money I *have* in my possession. If *you* have the money, you can demand Los Leones fall in behind you."

Gennady was straddling Gage on the chair, having touched the blade of the knife into the wound again. "What money?"

The pressure on his wrists eased slightly. "Told you...*argh*...I've got damn near a million in euro, in loose cash. That's why I am meeting Xavier tonight. He thinks the money is his."

Gennady pressed down on the blade as if he were trying to bore a hole in Gage's skull. "Why he thinks it's his?"

"Because Zambrano has something I want," Gage growled through clenched teeth.

"What he has?"

"Justina, the Polish woman who used to work for you!"

Gennady pulled back, cocking his eyebrow. Amusement darted over his face. "This cannot be true."

After a few deep breaths Gage said, "Well, it is."

"You came here today, knowing you'd be beaten, for poor Polish girl?"

"Yes," Gage answered earnestly. "I came for her, and her alone."

Still amused, as if he were listening to a child spinning fantastic lies, Gennady's iron chest hitched in a chuckle as he glanced back at Dmitry. "A million euro?"

"Reach down and get a wad of it from my back pocket."

Gennady lifted his chin. As the pressure on his right hand was released, Gage leaned forward so Dmitry could retrieve the wad from his back pocket. He slid the money out, handing it to Gennady. It was still banded, though Gage had used a few bills earlier.

"That's payment for the guns."

"Where is rest of money?" Gennady asked, moving forward.

"The cash I have is not for you. I'm offering you Xavier Zambrano. And, just so you know, Ernesto Navarro's fortune is still hidden out there somewhere. If you can take the mantle in Spain, the spoils are yours."

"I don't believe you. This is trap."

"Again I ask you, why would I come here otherwise?" Gage asked. "I didn't come here to die. I came to make a deal with you."

Gennady said something in Russian to Dmitry, who released Gage's arms. Gennady eyed Gage. "You want us to kill Zambrano."

"I don't care what you do to him," Gage answered. "But, in return for me delivering him to you, you must agree to do things my way. Because I just want to get my girls and leave."

"Girls?"

"Yeah."

Gennady depressed the button on his knife, and stashed his blade. "Explain, *pindos*."

The three men met for twenty minutes.

Chapter Thirty-Six

Tossa de Mar, Spain

IT WAS 3:47 A.M. The breeze that had at first seemed cool now whipped with chilly fervor, combining with the dampness of the Mediterranean to seep into a person's bones in minutes. Few lights burned in windows. Most of the illumination came from street lamps with the balance being cast down in electric blue by the waxing gibbous moon.

The seaside town's lone night patrol idled by the beach strip, turning up the curving road that led back into the hills. Angelines watched this from the alleyway very near where Gage had first met Ernesto Navarro. When the car had passed, she lifted the cigarette to her mouth, the dangerous excitement of the situation making her tingle in her loins.

"Shouldn't we be the first ones out there?" she asked.

"Unless they have sniper on rooftop."

"I hope this goes to plan."

He held his fingers scissored open for her cigarette, which he accepted and dragged deeply from. "Nothing ever goes like plan," he replied, exhaling smoke and dropping the cigarette to the ground, twisting his boot on it. "But we'll chance sniper. We don't have choice."

As he carried the cardboard box loaded with money and the alleged bearer bonds, Angelines led the way out onto the beach, limping heavily. She turned as she walked down the boardwalk, their feet scratching over scattered sand on the wooden planks. Her nervous perspiration added to her chill.

And the filmy, oversize white blouse she wore unbuttoned over her camisole was doing absolutely nothing to keep her warm.

It was, however, serving its purpose as it popped and furled with the southwesterly breeze.

MOMENTS EARLIER, Xavier had parked the Mercedes on Passeig del Mar, between the Club Hotel Giverola and the Mediterranean Sea. Passeig del Mar was typically brightly lit, teeming with cheery restaurants and bars, each covered with the massive beer or cigarette umbrellas so typical of European cafés. But at this time of night the beachside resort was deserted, spooky even, except for the lights approaching from Xavier's rear. He could see the reflection of dormant blue lights on top of the car and the *policia* markings on the hood.

"Don't move," he commanded the man beside him. His rear passengers were slumped down and sleeping, so Xavier and his partner sat perfectly still as the police car idled past, never once slowing. The car turned up the hill into the town, disappearing and marked only by the glow of its taillights, slowly fading to darkness.

Then, from the black rectangle of one of the pedestrian streets, two figures emerged. One was large and well-muscled, lugging a cardboard box. He fit the bill for the American, although he wore a dark watch cap pulled down over his hair. The other, wearing a bright white shirt, was female. She was limping. Xavier lifted the binoculars to his eyes, watching as the couple strode under the decorative street lamp that marked the strip. He wasn't at all surprised to see Angelines de la Mancha, the captain from Berga. That's who he thought it would be. Xavier couldn't help but briefly recall the stories he'd heard about her, sexual stories, involving his prison chief, El Toro.

Why is she still with the American? What is there to gain? Is he screwing her? And, if so, what would he want with this Polish girl and the old woman?

He glanced back. The Polish girl, despite her haggard appearance, was beautiful. He could see why the American might want *her*. But why the old lady?

And what is Angelines de la Mancha's angle?

"Do you see your friend?" Xavier asked the man in his passenger seat.

"He's there."

"You two better be as good as advertised."

The man snapped his fingers and held out his hand. Xavier placed two banded stacks of money in his hand. "Stay by the beach wall until the shooting goes down, then clean it up."

"I heard you earlier," the mercenary said.

"Well, hear me again."

The man exited the car, gently closing the door and low-crawling into a covered doorway next to the car. He'd come by earlier, smashing the light above the door. Now, standing there in the blackness, protected from above, the mercenary was virtually invisible.

Once he was in place, Xavier turned to the backseat. "Wake up!" he yelled, watching in the mirror as the two women started. Before leaving his rental home he'd injected them again, this time with only a half-dose of parlador. In fact, he'd kept them drugged all night, having given each woman a total of four injections since his nurse friend had perished.

Their arms were behind their backs, handcuffed. He turned around, watching as the two women blinked their eyes, the confusion of their drug-induced haze far too much to quickly blink away.

"You," he said to Justina. "Sit up." He pointed to the pair walking on the boardwalk. "Is that your boyfriend, Hartline, carrying the box?"

She leaned forward, her eyes dilated, a line of drool spilling from her open mouth. He again pointed to the boardwalk leading out to the beach, where the two darkening shadows walked.

"Tak," was all she said, the answer coming in her native Polish as her head fell forward onto the seat.

Xavier lifted the small radio the mercenaries had given him and pressed the button. "How does the shot look?"

"Clean and easy," the sniper answered.

"See anything unusual?"

"Only that the woman is limping."

"He said she was wounded. Could be bullshit. See any weapons?"

"The man is very muscular and is packing under his shirt, backside. Amateur hour."

"Have you seen anyone else?"

"Just the cop that just did a drive-by."

"You're sure?"

"I've peered at every nook and cranny with the thermal scope. There's no one."

"You're sure about the shot?"

A momentary pause. "There's a stiff breeze, about fifteen kilometers an hour and my range is a hundred and forty meters."

"I don't want statistics," Xavier snapped. "Can you hit them?"

"Easy, pal…I'm explaining myself," the second mercenary said. "Now, I'm confident I can be inside of a half-meter on my first shot. So, when you signal me, just make sure you take a step back. If I don't kill him on the first shot, I will on the second, even if he runs."

"Get the woman, too."

"She'll be the fun one, scrambling around while her boyfriend's brains are all over her face." The radio crackled. "But why not just shoot now?"

Xavier cursed. "I've got to *verify* that they have the bonds. Got it? Do—*not*—shoot until I touch my head."

"Just know, when your right hand touches anything north of your neck, I'm sending lead downrange."

"Make sure you finish these two women before the both of you disappear. You'll get the balance of your money in the morning while the media converges on this slaughter."

"Just remember," one of the American mercenaries warned, "if you fuck us, you'll be the one in our crosshairs."

"How frightening," Xavier said, monotone. "Just don't miss." He hung up and stepped from his Mercedes, opening the rear door and dragging the old woman out. After situating her on the adjacent park bench, looking out over the blackness of the ocean, he pulled Justina from the car, shushing her as she stirred.

When both women were safely situated on the bench, he stood beside them until they slumped into each other, unconscious again. Xavier nudged the rear door shut with his hip, checking the pistol in the right pocket of his charcoal gray Burberry waistcoat.

The couple had walked past the end of the boardwalk, out to the foamy edge of the surf.

"Seventeen million," he privately sang as he strode forward. "Seventeen million followed by a decadent month in Mallorca."

AS THE members of the treacherous liaison converged upon one another, Cortez Redon cried in the pickup truck. Wrapped around his head were several layers of thick duct tape, covering his mouth. It had restricted his breathing and, once the tears began, his nose began to get stuffy. Now, with each exhalation, pink snot bubbles burst outside his shattered nose as he struggled for breath.

A sturdy pair of Russian handcuffs bound Redon to the steering wheel of the battered pickup. Once Redon had begun laboring to breathe, he'd decided to try to be constructive rather than give up. Upon sliding his loafers off, he lowered himself into the floorboard, probing under the seats with his bare feet. Using his feet as pincers, he removed all manner of items. But the most important item was the tool he'd just transferred to his hindered hands.

A screwdriver.

After popping the horn cover off with the screwdriver, he had just enough slack in the cuffs to turn the screws that held the steering wheel fast.

It was a tedious job, but Redon was highly motivated. He had no desire to be around when the beach meeting ended. Though, if pressed, he hoped

Xavier Zambrano prevailed. But, after all that had transpired, neither party was very palatable to Redon. If it were up to him, they all should die.

But what motivated Cortez Redon the most was what was hidden behind the seat of the old truck.

That item, a sheaf of A4 linen paper, was his nirvana.

"HERE HE comes," Angelines said.

"Alone."

"Yeah, so it appears." Her tone changed. "Gage, are you reading me over all this wind and surf?"

"I've had you the entire time," he replied. "We're banking hard, circling so I can use the scope. Do you hear the airplane?"

"The surf and wind are way too loud."

"Good. I can see the body moving in your direction. Is it Xavier?"

"Yes," Angelines answered.

"Good," Gage replied. "Make sure you stand to the south, facing the north."

"That's how we're set up," Angelines said.

"Almost show time," Gage said. "Once I pop this door, communication is over. Dmitry, do you hear me?"

"Yes."

"Straight back from the boardwalk they walked out on, directly across the street, is a restaurant with four umbrellas out front. I cannot make out colors on the scope, but if you walked straight off the boardwalk, you'd eventually walk into the restaurant."

"I've got it," Dmitry answered.

"On top of that building, pressed up against the façade, is a nice warm body. I'm guessing he's holding a three-oh-eight, or something similar. Stay back because I bet that sniper has a thermal scope like this one and as soon as your warm body is exposed he's got you."

"He not see me," Dmitry said. "Anyone else?"

"Xavier put two live bodies on the bench by his car. I hope to God that's my two girls. Otherwise, there's not another warm soul that I can find," Gage answered. "Keep in mind, he could have others out there."

"But you don't see any?" Dmitry asked.

"If they're under cover, I won't."

"He's about to reach the boardwalk," Angelines interjected.

"Turn in," Gage could be heard saying to Arturo. "Okay, gang, I'm outta here. E.T.A. on the beach is about two to three minutes. Dmitry, wait until you see whether I make contact or not, then take your man out. You should have time because Xavier is going to want confirmation of the bearer bonds. Angelines, did you bring them?"

"We brought one on top of a stack of plain paper. The rest are in the truck with the cash."

"Where's Redon?"

"Handcuffed to the truck."

There was a pause.

"Did you hear me?" she asked.

"Yeah."

"Problem?"

"Doesn't matter. There's no time. I'm on my way."

"Be careful, Gage," Angelines said. She was greeted with a burst of static followed by silence. As she turned her head, deftly slipping the Bluetooth device into her pocket, Xavier turned left on the boardwalk, holding both arms out to his side to demonstrate that he wasn't carrying a weapon in his hand.

Chapter Thirty-Seven

ARTURO'S REPAIRED jump door worked as designed. Gage climbed out and stepped down to the diamond-plate section of steel affixed to the wheel strut of the Cessna 182. He glanced inside, seeing his fellow soldier, Arturo, faintly illuminated by the Cessna's blue cockpit lights. Arturo saluted Gage, following it with a thumbs-up. Gage nodded his thanks, then let go of the wing strut, falling to the earth as he arched his back.

Knees in the breeze...

As Gage arched, he came face to earth as the relative wind—somewhat slow during the Cessna's mild 80 knot "jump run"—decreased. Coming face to earth, going through an altitude of 6,000 feet above sea level, Gage oriented himself as his body reached terminal velocity. He reached back to his harness, his hand immediately finding the hacky sack. With a solid tug he liberated the attached pilot chute and tossed it to his right, feeling a series of jerks as the collapsible preliminary chute yanked the high-performance, zero-porosity main chute from the form-fitting Javelin Odyssey container. After a planned "snivel," the parachute, a Stiletto 150, fully opened. Gage collapsed the slider and re-oriented himself, grasping both steering toggles.

Regarding his position over the earth, he was approximately 500 meters northeast of the Tossa de Mar boardwalk. There was plenty of light to see what was happening on the beach. And the tall, lean figure of Xavier Zambrano was just reaching Angelines and Gennady. Gage checked his altitude—just above 4,000 feet—he was right on schedule.

Thinking about the one practice jump he'd made ninety minutes earlier, and his numerous mistakes, Gage began to S-turn his way to the rendezvous site, reminding himself to leave sufficient altitude for the high-performance turn he planned.

As the Stiletto rocketed forward, managing plenty of forward speed under Gage's "suited" 220 pounds, he went through his final preparations, setting aside his worry over Señora Moreno and, of course, Justina.

When he turned to the north, to do a penetration check into the wind, Gage estimated fifty seconds to impact.

"ANGELINES DE la Mancha," Xavier sang out as he approached through the sugary portion of the sand. "Fancy seeing you here." His tone was one of long lost friends.

Feeling the need to respond, even though she knew he was trying to put her on the defensive, and knowing she needed to buy some time for Gage, Angelines made her reply cutting. "I'm finished, Zambrano. Finished with you. Finished with that animal, El Toro. Finished with Berga. When I saw what you did to Navarro's son, and learned that you were behind a dozen other killings in my prison, I washed my hands of it."

"Just blind all those years," he sang.

Xavier stopped a few meters away, standing west of their position. He surveyed Gennady, who he thought was Gage. "And look at this big fellow. You've no doubt been enjoying him, Angelines, but I hope he knows how many of my Leones you've spread those legs of yours for. That's quite a busy crotch you have."

Feeling her cheeks flush, Angelines looked down at her blouse, making sure her arms weren't preventing its loose tails from whipping with the wind. Before she could stop herself, she looked up into the sky, wondering where Gage was.

Xavier followed her eyes, his own going up into the sky as he smiled broadly. "A beautiful evening, isn't it?" He looked at Gennady. "I understand you didn't care for Berga, or my men."

"Correct," Gennady answered mechanically. He put his foot behind the cardboard box, sliding it toward Xavier.

"I take it that's my bonds," Xavier said.

"Before you get the bonds," Angelines said, "you've got to turn over the two women."

Xavier's smile still broad, he turned to Gennady. "Do you always let this cunt do your talking for you, *gilipollas*?"

Gennady stepped over the cardboard box, walking toward Xavier.

"Stop!" Angelines yelled.

Xavier stood his ground, his arms open wide as if he welcomed the challenge.

"Come back over here," she said. "Fighting will get us nowhere tonight." Then, from the corner of her eye, she was aware of a quick flashing, not unlike a bat passing in front of a floodlight. But it had been heading away from her. With a slight turn of her head, she could see the black shadow of the parachute zipping to the north.

"Show me the bonds," Xavier commanded.

Angelines knelt down, putting her hand on the box.

"Do it slowly," Xavier warned, licking his lips.

GAGE HAD no time to check his tritium-based altimeter. From this point on, it was all about instinct and snap judgment as he raced past the threshold over which the three people stood. He was pulling down on both front risers, making the canopy's angle of attack even steeper, creating highway-like forward speed for the canopy as the buildings to the left, especially a tall hotel, began to rise up to his level.

And in a moment, the real fun would begin.

Just before initiating his riser turn, he remembered the location of the two bodies next to the car Xavier had exited. Gage looked in that direction, his ten o'clock, momentarily surprised to see the distinctly tall silhouette of Justina staggering down the street, toward the boardwalk.

Oh, no! Justina...please, just stay put.

But, by this point, there was no turning back. Gage released the right front riser and pulled the left riser down further. This snapped the Stiletto into a left turn, swinging Gage out in a straight plunge to the sands of Tossa de Mar. Then, with the toggles, as his speed neared that of free fall, Gage began to plane out.

His target was facing away from him, staring down at Angelines and the cardboard box.

As Gage was on his final approach, he heard a loud pop to his right. Something was wrong. It was too early for Dmitry to excise the shooter on top of the building.

Had Justina been shot?

Whatever had happened, it caused Xavier to turn and take a few steps to the side, meaning Gage had to adjust his approach.

Five seconds...

FIFTEEN SECONDS earlier, Angelines lifted the one genuine bearer bond from the prop sheaf in the cardboard box. "There," she said. "Satisfied? Now let the two women go."

Xavier eyed the bond as she held it up for him to view its authenticity. His grin was genuine, but grew malevolent. Then, he raised his hand to his hair. It was an odd, out-of-place gesture.

Several things happened in short order. Angelines saw a flash of light up at the main road. Then, behind her, where Gennady stood, came a wet, plunking sound. It sounded the way a mallet does when hitting a piece of meat.

Then she heard the rifle's report.

Angelines turned, watching Gennady's massive form tumble to the sand. He held both hands over his neck.

She turned back around, her mouth readying a protest, just as she heard the ripping of air. Almost instantly, a flash of black appeared and collided with Xavier. Xavier, as if tethered to a speeding truck, was immediately thrust fifty feet down the beach in a tumbling, Vitruvian man pose of flinging limbs and sand.

JUSTINA DIDN'T know where she was going. She simply knew that she needed to move. As she'd staggered down the sidewalk, having no idea where she was, she witnessed a man lurch from an alcove and shoot another man on the sidewalk. In her muddy drug haze, she wasn't even certain sure what she'd seen.

Am I dreaming?

Her mind was still muddled with swimmy visions of her captor...Xavier...and his tattooed nurse friend.

Did he kill her?

Yes...he injected her. Her breathing stopped.

My God, what has happened to me?

Her head slowly clearing, Justina stepped to her right, into a café's courtyard, kneeling behind a fence. On all fours, she lifted her head, peering down the sidewalk.

The man that had been shot lay there, fifty feet away. He wasn't moving. She lifted her head higher. A cold spike of recognition came to Justina, especially when she noticed the dead man's ruby earrings.

Dmitry from Eastern Bloc.

"Get your head down," came a whispered voice from behind her.

Had Justina not been drugged, she would have certainly screamed. Instead, she obeyed and turned. Directly behind her was a man in an athletic wheelchair. He had large, powerful arms and a bushy moustache. His hair was curly and long, held up by a sweatband, reminiscent of many soccer stars decades before.

"I remember you," Justina whispered, her own voice sounding foreign to her. Despite all that had happened, she distinctly remembered having met this man when she and Gage had been in Tossa before. Before Gage accepted the job. Before the insanity.

"Why the hell are you out here, pretty lady?" the man whispered, ducking his head. "People are killing each other."

"I don't really know," she murmured, slurring. "I was kidnapped."

He adjusted his wheels to get a better look. "There's one down on the sidewalk. Looks like he dropped a grenade, too. The guy who shot him moved up behind the sea wall. And I saw a shooter on the roof, up behind the facade. Do you know who's who?"

"The man who was shot...I know him."

Then, from the beach came a muffled thud followed by several distant yells. Both Justina and the man in the wheelchair whipped their heads to the sounds, seeing a rolling mass tumbling inside of what looked like a large, black sheet.

From the beach, a woman screamed Gage's name.

"Gage is with me," Justina whispered.

As commotion reigned on the beach, the sniper and the man who'd shot Dmitry began speaking urgently, doing nothing to conceal their voices. The man in the wheelchair cupped his ear, listening to them.

"They're trying to kill your friend."

"Can you help?" Justina cried.

The man who'd been hiding behind the sea wall began running for the beach.

"Stay here," the man in the wheelchair commanded. Then, keeping himself in the dark shadows, and making sure the umbrellas were between him and the sniper, he began rolling to where Dmitry had fallen.

GAGE HAD purposefully landed downwind for greater speed and had impacted Xavier with both of his feet extended out in front of him. He'd kept his knees slightly bent but his closing speed had been tremendous, probably around fifty miles per hour. Thankfully the tall Spaniard was a moveable object. But, despite that fact, as Gage now clung to the man through the black of the crumpled Stiletto parachute, he could feel his own left leg, below the knee, popping and grinding.

It was a sensation known well to Gage—the grating of splintered bone against splintered bone.

After a few seconds—it felt like minutes—of scrambling in the murkiness of the parachute, Gage found the head of the gangster, still covered by the fabric. Gage wrapped the parachute's low-profile lines around Xavier's neck, choking him with one hand while hitting him with his other.

"Someone's shooting!" Angelines yelled.

"Then get down!" Gage yelled back, struggling to maintain his hold.

In Gage's weakened condition, and with his freshly broken leg, he didn't have the strength or leverage to control Xavier. The Spaniard yanked Gage to the side, spinning him, giving Gage an unfortunate glimpse of his grotesquely broken leg—the one that appeared to have a new knee at mid-shin.

As Gage tumbled to the sand, Xavier burst from an opening in the parachute, a glinting blade in his hand.

"Gage!" Angelines screamed, grasping Xavier's right hand before it could plunge downward. Holding the mobster's arm, Angelines lurched forward, her mouth opened wide. Like a vampire, her clamping mouth found his neck, eliciting a screech from Xavier.

A hundred and fifty meters away, the sniper angled for a shot.

Worse, however, was the man on the ground, racing forward with an outstretched pistol.

THEY MUST be communicating by an open radio line, the man in the wheelchair realized. He knew this because the man on the roof was openly speaking English, telling the one that had just jumped over the wall what he was seeing through his scope.

The man in the wheelchair reached down with his massive arm, finding the object that had rolled away from the dead Russian.

As he'd thought it was, indeed, a hand grenade. He took a quick glance at the grenade, appraising it as the same NATO variety grenade he'd been armed with in the Gulf.

After crossing himself, the man in the wheelchair, feeling as alive as he had since losing his legs in the Persian Gulf War, gripped the grenade in his right hand and pulled the pin. He let the spoon fall into his lap and counted to two. Then he lobbed the grenade over the massive umbrellas, listening with satisfaction as the half-kilo hand-bomb plunked on the roof.

There was a chirp of a shout—it was cut off by the explosion.

The man in the wheelchair watched with fascination as the sniper vaulted forward, briefly illuminated by the flash, tumbling onto the umbrellas below him. The man fell to the patio, his torn body silent and unmoving.

But more important to the man in the wheelchair was the rifle that tumbled down to the patio.

IT WAS a primal scene. Angelines remained connected to Xavier like a snapping turtle. Despite his writhing, thankfully, she never let go. Back up at the street, a flash of light was soon followed by a calamitous boom. Gage instantly recognized it as a grenade report. Though his heart briefly sank as he feared for Justina, he saw the oncoming silhouette of a man, a pistol held out in front of him, zig-zagging in a fast crouch.

Gage tapped his chest, unaware of what had happened to the AutoMag in the collision. To his left, in the low surf, was Gennady. Blood bubbling from his mouth, Gennady unsteadily held a pistol outstretched. Despite the agony of his leg twisting over its splintered fracture, Gage propelled himself to Gennady's outstretched hand by clawing the wet sand. He jerked the pistol from the Russian, whipping it around and firing the semi-automatic as fast as he could pull the trigger, unleashing four rounds at the rushing person. The man had been approaching in the manner of a person who wasn't expecting to be fired upon. He was wrong.

The jacketed rounds struck the man in his torso, cutting through him like a sharp pencil puncturing a thin sheet of paper.

Though the rest of the onrushing man had stopped working, curiously his legs managed a few more wobbly strides. But that soon ended as the man fell facedown, his face burrowing to a stop in the sand.

Gage turned back to the fray, watching as Angelines opened her mouth and finally released the screaming Xavier. The mobster's hand, having long since released the blade, shot to his neck. Unfortunately, for him, his trademark tattoo was now missing a chunk of skin the size of a muffin top.

Angelines struggled to a standing position while Gage checked his rounds and surveyed the beach for threats. The lights at the road showed twin shadows, one tall and one short. Gage squinted at the images, watching as the tall shadow dropped to its knees, burying its head in its hands.

Justina…

Refocusing, Gage dragged himself to Xavier. The impact from his parachute had left the Spanish gangster in bad shape, made worse by Angelines' bite.

Gage didn't care.

Reminiscent of what Xavier had done to Camilo, his narcotics lieutenant, Gage grabbed the gangster's hand, twisting it and pulling the pinkie finger all the way back.

"Who else is out there?"

Xavier spit at Gage, clawing at his eyes. Despite his leg's twisting, Gage fell flat on the parachute with Xavier, striking him with the pistol.

Xavier cursed Gage in three languages.

Both men greatly weakened, chests heaving, Gage resumed his grip on Xavier's hand, pulling his pinkie all the way back to his wrist.

It sounded like a hard pretzel snapping.

"Who else is out there?" Gage growled.

"No one!"

Gage pulled the Spaniard's ring finger back, snapping it also.

"Who else?"

"I swear on my mother it was only the two gunmen," Xavier blubbered.

"He wanted to kill us, Gage!" Angelines yelled, her mouth still dripping with Xavier's blood.

Still holding Xavier's arm, Gage twisted it so the Spaniard would have to roll to his stomach. Keeping the arm in the center of Xavier's back, Gage positioned himself on top, so he could control the man without much effort.

"Yeah, he was going to kill us," Gage agreed. He turned his eyes to the road now seeing Justina and Señora Moreno staggering toward the boardwalk. With them was—

"Do it, you twat!"

Gage turned, seeing that Angelines had moved to the right and had found the AutoMag. She gripped it in both her hands, aiming it at the Spaniard's head.

"Angelines, wait!" Gage yelled.

"I don't care what the repercussions are," she said, her glinting red smile broad and scary. "This man is pure toxin."

"Go ahead!" Xavier yelled, jerking his battered body under Gage. He twisted his head back to Gage, maniacal. "You better letter her do it, *coño*, because I've killed a million men and I'll kill a million more and I'm starting with your ass. I'm the law in Spain! You got that?"

Gage slid back off the man.

Xavier rolled over, opening his arms wide, beating his own chest, still ranting in a demented monologue as he sat up.

"Just today, I proved what kind of man I am, *coño*, when I resisted my urge and I spared your two women but destroyed a woman I was close to. I didn't want to kill her but I went through with it." Using sticky blood from his neck, he swept his hair back, smiling proudly. "You know why I killed her? You know why? For preservation of my kingdom, *capullo*!" he yelled, gesturing his arms all around. "That's right! Not Navarro's kingdom. Not King Juan Carlos' and damn sure not your kingdom, motherfucker! This bitch is all mine! Every house—every business—every man, woman, and child! And unless you kill me now, I'll be walking these streets by sundown tomorrow with you and your fat whore first on my—"

A long tongue of flame emerged from the wide barrel of the powerful handgun, sending with it the death shot that struck the mobster in the back of his head and exploded from his right eye. Xavier twitched before falling backward, his body benignly accepting two more of Angelines' gunshots squarely in his crotch.

She spit on him afterward.

Having seen, and acted upon, such rage before, Gage understood.

He turned to Gennady, now lying still as a trickle of blood exited his mouth in the low surf. There was no rise and fall of his chest. Gennady's pistol, Gage realized, had saved them. Still uncertain of what other threats were out there, Gage clawed his way back to Gennady and found another full magazine in the Russian's pocket.

Growling in pain, Gage again reset his leg. Sitting there with the Mediterranean's tide rushing in around him, he held the pistol at the ready as his mind replayed all that had happened. Xavier had surreptitiously positioned a sniper on the roof to kill all involved once he had the bearer bonds. Gennady and Gage had anticipated something of the sort—that's why they had stationed Dmitry at beach center, hiding him back behind the first row of buildings.

Gage assumed Dmitry had killed the sniper with the grenade.

But, Gage reasoned, if that were the case, then where was Dmitry? Perhaps Xavier's backup man, the one Gage had just shot, wounded or killed Dmitry. Gage hoped not. Certainly these Russians knew they were getting into a dangerous situation, but it was not Gage's intention to lead them both to their death.

"You okay?" Gage grunted.

Angelines had fallen to the sand next to Xavier, her again-bleeding leg outstretched, her body shuddering with tears. She was covering her face with her hands and, through her tears, nodded.

"You can take that cash and go, Angelines. The cops are going to be here any second and I can delay my explanation under a shroud of shock."

She lowered her hands, wiping her eyes. "No, Gage. I'm staying."

"Thank you for your help. You saved me."

"No…you saved me," she said. "Because no matter what happens, I'm free now."

As she spoke, Justina and Señora Moreno approached, trudging to the end of the boardwalk behind a man in a wheelchair.

Even through his considerable pain, Gage remembered the man. He was another soldier, Gage's worldwide brotherhood.

Justina stepped around the wheelchair, staggering to where Gage sat. She knelt beside him, lowering him to the sand and finger-depth surf. And, as was her habit, she ran her fingers through Gage's hair.

Their smiles turned to relieved, warm laughter.

She's still alive, Gage thought, the joy overriding any agony his physical body was enduring. *Thank God, she's still alive.*

"Are you okay?" he asked.

"I am now."

Angelines and Señora Moreno staggered up to the man in the wheelchair while Gage and Justina remained in the water.

"Is Dmitry dead?" Gage whispered.

"We thought so but—"

Movement catching his eye, Gage lifted the pistol, aiming it at the brawny man staggering around the trio, his hand clamped over his shoulder.

Dmitry.

He trudged forward, eyeing the scene, focusing on Gennady. When Gage realized Dmitry meant no harm, he lowered the pistol. "Gennady's dead."

Dmitry just stood there, seemingly in shock.

"Spain's yours for the taking, *priyatel*. I'd suggest you haul ass and get busy."

Recognition flooded Dmitry's face as a weak smile appeared. Bolstered, he turned and hurried away.

Gage fell back and closed his eyes, his hand again finding Justina's face. "I just want to hold you," he said, pulling her on top of him.

"Together again," Justina said, pressing her lips to his.

When she pulled back, Gage whispered, "We made it."

Then he passed out.

TWELVE MINUTES later, after the beach was sealed off by a Catalonian state police SWAT team, each of the individuals involved were loaded into a line of ambulances. Gage, under the influence of heavy morphine, and accompanied by two armed police officers, mumbled questions to his accompanying police.

Most puzzling to the police were Gage's repeated, out of place questions about the well-known Catalonian Acusador Cortez Redon.

Gage Hartline would have surgery in two hours and not awaken until the following day.

And somewhere, well up the beach, clinging to a wet rock, was the single bearer bond Xavier Zambrano had held when Gage collided with him.

It was the only one of Señora Moreno's bearer bonds still unaccounted for.

Chapter Thirty-Eight

Barcelona, Spain

NINE DAYS later, Gage and Justina held hands as they waited for the closed-door meeting to end.

Gage, having refused a wheelchair for this, his first trip away from the hospital, sat in a desk chair, his leg propped on another chair.

Justina, sitting to his right and looking vibrant in cheap, off-the-sale-rack clothes provided to her by someone at the Polish Consul General, winked at Gage as they waited.

Señora Moreno, flanked by three of her own attorneys, spoke. Though her voice was slightly modulated by her redone stitches, it was still quite clear. She proudly remarked about what a dashing couple Gage and Justina made. She asked each of her attorneys—gray-haired, scowling, overstuffed men—if they agreed. After much throat clearing and collar adjusting, each of the men, as if she were the only person on earth who might somehow cow them, mumbled undecipherable yet obsequious agreements.

Finally, after nearly an hour, the closed-door session ended. All of the officials exited the office, returning to the well-appointed ante-room. Among others were the United States Consul General from Barcelona, her counterpart from Poland, Colonel Hunter (who had been with Gage for nearly a week now), numerous officials from the Spanish State Department, and a host of suited, yet shadowy, men whose presence was never explained.

The chief man from the Spanish State Department, another whose name and position were never given to Gage, stood in the center of the group, continuing in English as they had done prior to the private session. He looked at Señora Moreno, smiling in a suddenly unctuous manner.

"Señora Moreno, after reviewing your involvement in this…well, this regrettable and astonishing set of circumstances…it is our position that, provided you vow your continued silence and sign agreements to that end, you shall be free to go. Your employees who intervened in the escape will also be free of any charges. Additionally, due to the hazard created by the alleged criminal activity that occurred, you will—"

"Alleged?" one of her attorneys roared.

The man next to the state department representative spoke up. "Let's not split hairs, Molina," he whispered forcefully.

Molina.

"Pardon me, Señora Moreno," Molina said, recovering smoothly. "Due to what you endured, the Catalonian government, through an agreement that will accompany your vow of silence, will compensate you for all future medical treatment, and we agree to work vigorously with your representation to finalize a pain-and-suffering settlement within thirty days," he cut his eyes to her attorneys, "as *demanded* by your battery of representation."

Despite the hidden stitches in her face, Señora Moreno looked around, crossing her hands on her lap and smiling as if her pie just won the contest at a county fair.

"You may go, madam," Molina said, gesturing to the door.

"No."

Molina stiffened, looking to the man to his right. That man, probably also an attorney, said, "Señora Moreno, what we have to discuss with the others is confidential."

Ignoring him, Señora Moreno huddled with her attorneys. Anyone in the room could hear that she was doing one hundred percent of the talking. Finished, one of her attorneys spoke for her. "Señora Moreno wants to stay. It's her right to hear all that is said."

"That wasn't part of our agreement," Molina said, his ears glowing red while his clasped hands fidgeted with one another.

"Let her stay," Gage remarked in a soft voice. "The rest involves Justina and me—we have no secrets at all from this fine lady. Her intervention saved our lives."

The state department's attorney again massaged the bridge of his nose as he seemed to whisper something acquiescent. The only truly audible portion was a well-known English curse word.

"Fine, then," Molina murmured. He turned to Gage, his tone turning to one of distaste. "Mister Hartline, in a similar accord, we are going to suspend prosecution against you provided you also vow silence, through an airtight non-disclosure agreement, and leave this country immediately with an agreement to *never* return."

Gage turned to Colonel Hunter. Hunter, in that way of his, where he smiled with only his eyes, gave a slight nod of his head.

"And?" Gage asked, adjusting himself in his chair.

"Provided you sign the agreement, that is all."

"My injuries?"

"Your medical bills will be forgiven," the lawyer next to Molina said, his lip curled. "We'll see to that."

"And Miss Kaminski, what about her?"

The state department attorney's words cracked like three well-aimed bullets. "Same—exact—agreement."

"And?" Gage asked.

"And, what? Were you hoping for something else?" Molina asked, his accent overdone, emphasizing "else," making it sound like the nastiest of words.

"Before you went into that room, I had several requirements." Gage rose, supporting himself with his crutches. "Were they met?"

"They will be when the agreement is signed."

Again, Gage turned to Hunter, who spoke in that soft steel voice of his, sounding like a Montanan rancher talking about his cattle. "In return for you not talking about all the damned corruption they got in this government"— his eyes surveyed the room as he said this—"they'll compensate you to the tune of five grand, U.S., for each week you've been here, rounded up."

Gage let out a relieved breath. "And what about Angelines de la Mancha?"

Hunter shook his head. "They're going to take care of the mother and son, and they've agreed to transparency to our state department so we can monitor the situation."

"What about Angelines?" Gage asked.

"Short stint in prison," Hunter said flatly. "Club-Fed type…nothing like that animal farm where you were."

"The laws she broke were egregious," Molina said, lifting his pointy nose.

"You mean, the laws she broke along with your government officials?" Gage asked.

Molina and the attorney joined eyes then looked away.

No one said anything for several moments until Justina broke the silence. "What about my friend, the man in the wheelchair in Tossa de Mar?"

"He doesn't want his name revealed," Molina replied, his tone much different when speaking to Justina. "He's under a full pension due to his war injuries and he told us to tell those involved that he was 'just doing his duty,' whatever that means."

As the meeting was ending, Gage brought up a subject he'd brought up every day since the incident at Tossa de Mar. "What about Cortez Redon?"

Molina let out an exasperated breath. "He's missing. If we had found him, we would tell you."

"Perhaps someone killed him," the attorney said, staring at Gage with an arched brow. "Perhaps that person who killed him keeps asking about Redon in an effort to throw the investigators off his trail."

Before Gage could speak, Hunter spoke for him. "Begging your pardon, buddy, but if my boy here had killed that little pecker he'd proudly let us all know how the rubbin' out went down."

"What about the money?" Justina asked.

"No one recovered any money other than a single bearer bond. It was found nearly a kilometer away," the attorney said. "We've been over this."

Justina and Gage eyed Señora Moreno. She'd insisted the bearer bonds not be mentioned and, once again, shook her head.

Gage rubbed his face and said, "Let's just end this."

A battery of papers was produced for Gage, Justina, and Señora Moreno. Gage and Justina's agreements were carefully explained by attorneys from the U.S. and Polish consulates. Colonel Hunter sat in the corner, leaning back against the wall, quietly nibbling sunflower seeds, depositing the hulls in a paper cup.

After the meeting, before they were led from the nondescript federal building, Gage asked to see Molina in private. When he was told that Molina was busy, Gage steadied himself on his crutches, telling the Spanish officials that he would wait.

Their escorting envoy, a young Spanish man with little diplomatic ability, rolled his eyes in irritation before stalking away. Minutes later, Señor Molina and his attorney—attached to his hip like a Siamese twin—reappeared.

"I'd rather hoped you were on an airplane by this time, Mister Hartline," Molina said, pursing his lips afterward.

"I'll be gone by sundown," Gage said, glancing at the clock that showed it to be nearly five in the afternoon. "But I'd like to see Angelines de la Mancha for just a few minutes before I leave."

"Absolutely not!" Molina snapped, shaking his head while clamping his eyes shut. It was the gesture of a man who'd been terribly spoiled as a child.

Gage made his own expression earnest. "Why not, sir? She's going to prison. What's ten minutes?"

"I'm sorry," he said, using the tone of a man who is anything but sorry. "I can't allow it."

Gage eyed the man, softening his own voice as he said, "Please."

Molina's eyes were bleary. Tired. He looked at his attorney, who shrugged. Finally, Molina threw his hands up. "If you're not in the air by sundown, that agreement is considered breached and we will prosecute you." He pointed to the toadying envoy. "Take them to the hospital and call my cell if you don't witness them board their aircraft before nine tonight."

"HEY THERE, *Capitana*," Gage said.

Her head was slightly tilted to the side as she slept, her hands resting on a clean white sheet that covered most of her body. From across the room she looked fine but, as Gage stepped closer, her skin still showed lingering scratches from their marathon day. All things considered, other than her leg that was held in traction, Angelines de la Mancha looked damn good.

"I'm no longer *la capitana*," she murmured, her large eyes fluttering open. She extended her left hand and Gage took it. Justina's footsteps could be heard walking away.

Angelines motioned to the door. "Does she think you and I...?"

"No," Gage replied. "I assured her."

She gave his hand a little tug. "Well, there's still time and this bed is very soft."

Gage couldn't help but enjoy her bawdy humor, finding her similar to many of the people he'd been in service with. His smile quickly faded. "So, will you stand trial?"

"My attorney knew they wouldn't want that."

"And?"

"Provided I agree to all their conditions, which mainly revolve around silence, he thinks I'll only do a year. And there will be a stipend for my son and my mother, plus tuition and expenses for his university."

"You can do a year standing on your head," Gage repeated.

"Yeah," she laughed weakly. "Supposedly, I'll get my own little suite, an *aposento*, and can even have male visitors on the weekends." She squeezed his hand. "You remember that if you and your lady don't make it."

They chatted for a few minutes, with Gage telling her all he knew.

"So, who were the men with Xavier?"

"Mercs."

"What?"

"Mercenaries. Americans. Hell, I knew one of them."

She covered her mouth.

"Some people will do anything for money."

"How'd you find out?"

"Colonel Hunter told me."

"And what about Justina? Is she okay?"

"Luckily, yes. She's lucky that sicko didn't O.D. her, though." Gage tapped his Timex. "Unfortunately, I have to leave in a few minutes."

She looked away for a moment before refocusing on Gage. "If there had been no Justina, would you have had interest in me?"

"Yes."

"You're just saying that."

"I'm not. But I don't think we'd make it long-term."

"Why's that?"

He smiled as he patted the back of her hand. "Of the few women I've dated for any length of time, none of them were anything like you."

She cocked her eyebrow. "That doesn't sound good."

"You're type-A, Angelines. We'd have fun for a week or two before we killed each other."

She smiled with him. "But what a fun week or two that would be."

He nearly responded but instead averted his eyes.

"Where will you go?" she asked.

"Back to the States."

"Why the rush?"

"My agreement provides that I will never set foot in Spain again."

"Right. And you always follow the rules, don't you?"

A period of silence ensued. It was the uninhibited type, when both people had other things to say but they knew there was no real point in saying them. The entire time, Angelines continued to massage his hand with hers.

Finally, Gage said two words. "Cortez Redon."

He watched as she nestled her head back into the pillow, eyeing the ceiling as her nostrils flared. "I'm trying not to dwell on it."

"What happened?"

Her large eyes flashed to his. "You've heard nothing?"

"I've asked about him a dozen times but they've stonewalled me."

She nodded. "And they've questioned me about him a number of times but won't tell me anything."

"Did you see him again on the beach?"

She shook her head. "After you were taken away, I'd told the policemen about Cortez being handcuffed in the truck and, a few minutes later, one of the cops came back and said the steering wheel was gone from the truck."

"And you left the bonds in the truck?" he asked.

"Yes. Because he was handcuffed securely." She shook her head. "You should have killed him when you had a chance."

"Thought you were done with that kind of life."

"He's an exception." She gave his hand a final squeeze, letting it go and giving him a little shove. "Go on now; live up to your agreement."

Gage stood above her, making a fist. "Be strong, Angelines. And do it right from here on out."

An impish grin came over her face. "Did you meet Fabian Molina?"

"My buddy," Gage said monotone.

"He's my ace in the hole."

"What do you mean?"

"I have a few things on Señor Molina. Very, very bad things from what I remember. But I haven't decided, yet, if I want to play the angle."

"Has your agreement been finalized?"

Still grinning, she shook her head.

"Do I even want to know?" Gage asked.

"No," she laughed. "Just know that, if I decide to make a few calls, there's a video of him 'cavorting' that he will not want getting out."

"*Bona sort*," Gage said, kissing her on her forehead.

An hour later, after making numerous promises to Señora Moreno, Gage, Justina and Colonel Hunter departed Spain on a well-appointed Dassault Falcon 7X.

Chapter Thirty-Nine

Grand Cayman, Cayman Islands - Eight months later

THE INCOMING guard force arrived through the back of the compound, mustering per S.O.P. in the maintenance garage. Leaving his own force in place until each station was relieved, Gage Hartline, limping ever so slightly, came around the corner, walking to the rear of the garage, away from the guards. Standing there was his counterpart. Gage handed him the small hand radio and the binder containing all guests, vendors, possible threats and contingency plans.

"Nothing to report?" the night commander, a former Sayeret Matkal commando—a part of Israel's special forces—asked.

Gage leaned against the Bentley, rubbing the shin of his still-healing left leg. "Just after we came on this morning, we had a perimeter motion detector flash on us. Turns out it was a huge bird. She was circling around later and then we saw her working on a nest in the tallest royal palm beside the home."

"Great. We may have to adjust the sensitivity if she keeps landing."

"Other than that, nothing out of the ordinary."

"What's his mood today?"

"Didn't say too much, but seemed happy about something."

"The missus?"

"Same old tricks. As soon as he left for meetings in town, she went out to the pool and dropped all her clothes, parading around for everyone to see before she sunbathed for three straight hours. Later she asked Trillio if he could come inside and help her 'adjust the shower head'."

"You didn't let him?"

Gage straightened and made sure he hadn't left a mark on the Bentley. "I called in a plumber, a very obese plumber."

Once the positions had been assumed, Gage handed his counterpart a letter.

"What's this?"

"My resignation," Gage breathed. "I'm sorry I couldn't give a notice."

"Shit."

"Yeah. My forwarding address is in there, too. Will you pass it on to the boss?"

"Sure will." The night commander eyed Gage. "Where you headed?"

"Someplace I've been waiting to go, to see someone I've been waiting to see." Gage winked. "I'm going to serve someone a very cold dish."

It took a moment, but the night commander soon connected the dots. He shook Gage's hand and wished him luck.

Gage found his small guard force waiting for him and, together, they walked down the rear drive. There, in a concealed strong box, they each deposited their weapons. Outside the gate, Gage bade the group farewell, not telling them that he was leaving for good.

Gage didn't like goodbyes.

The group of capable men, happy to be done for the day, ambled down the hill, toward Bodden Town, where they would collectively catch the 6:15 bus back into George Town. Gage, however, ascended, cresting the hill in the exclusive, Beverly Hills-styled enclave, finding Justina just over the other side in their tiny red Ford.

Sitting in the passenger seat, he leaned over and kissed her, removing his tie and tucking it into the pocket of his jacket. Gage wouldn't wear another tie for some time.

"Good day?"

"Yes," Justina answered. "I spoke to my mother and my brother is doing very well. They have him on an experimental medicine and it's helping." She smiled.

"Outstanding," Gage said, kissing her again.

"How was your day?"

"Uneventful, thankfully. With what we've got planned, I couldn't focus and definitely did not earn my pay."

"Where was the aging pop star?"

"He was in town managing his fortune, or so he told us. Fortunately he didn't want me to go with him."

"And did *she* take off her clothes?"

Silence.

"Did she?"

"Yeah," Gage breathed.

"*Dziwka*," Justina snapped. "Did you look?"

"Of course not." He pushed Justina's sun-bleached blonde hair back, rubbing the backs of his fingers on her cheek. "How about your day?"

"I ran this morning. Ran again this afternoon."

"If I ever fully heal up, it's gonna be hell catching up to you."

"I had to keep my mind occupied. Like you, I'm anxious about tonight. This has been six months of planning and waiting."

"Waiting comprises nine-tenths of my job."

"Why did we wait so long, Gage?"

"I wanted to heal up. Work for a few months. Clear my head."

"And is it clear?"

He kissed her for his answer. "You ready?"

"*Tak*," she answered in her native tongue. "Oh, and are we eventually going after that Air Force man that tracked the satellite phone?"

"Yes."

"Why not now?"

"Colonel Hunter will let me know. That asshole's still in Spain."

"Does the asshole know that you know?"

"He has no idea. That payback is going to be dessert."

"And tonight is the main course?"

"Are you positive you want to do this?" he asked. "I could go in alone."

"Hell no."

Gage ran through the threats, trying to find even one that would give him enough pause to delay this operation. He couldn't. Instead, he slapped the dashboard and said, "Let's go do it."

They drove for about a half-hour, to the area at the north end of the island informally known as Turtle Beach. They talked about the operation the entire way.

"What happens afterward?" she asked.

"It'll be a fluid situation."

"That's one of those colloquial-whatevers," she said, twirling her hand as she couldn't find the word. "I have no idea what 'fluid situation' means."

"It means that we'll make it up as we go along."

"Like you typically do," she said, smiling.

"Correct."

Just like they had planned, they parked in the rear lot of a charming condominium complex. The condos were similar to those found in the United States, especially beachside, painted gray and two stories, the units side by side. There were lots of slanted angles and accents of shaker shingles. Massive clumps of pampas grass grew at the walkup to each unit and, across from them, right where he expected it to be, the nearly new cherry red BMW 335i gleamed in the setting sun.

"What now?" Justina asked.

Gage lifted his sleeve, glancing at his Timex. "We wait. And if he doesn't make the call, then we wait for another night."

"Doesn't he call every Monday?"

"Yep."

"Did you call our friend today?"

"She's waiting by her phone." Gage placed a special cellular phone of his own on the dash of the Ford. They settled in.

People came and went. Gage and Justina watched with amusement as a long-haired couple in their sixties furtively smoked what must have been at least two joints on their balcony. Then, after night had fallen, the cell phone finally chirped. Gage opened the third-party phone he'd paid a small mint for, holding his finger over his mouth as he listened. After a minute, he turned off the phone.

"Are you ready?" he asked.

"Yes."

"It'll be a half-hour. Finish up your getup."

"Why do you have to intercept the hooker?"

"I don't want her stumbling into what we've got planned."

While they waited, Justina applied heavy makeup and donned a wig. Thirty-five minutes later, a George Town taxi appeared, a mini-van. It stopped near the BMW.

"Stay here and wait," Gage commanded.

When the woman exited the taxi, Gage spoke to her. There was a brief conversation before she walked with him over to the Ford.

"And all you have to do is take my money and call another cab," Gage said.

The woman, a striking ebony escort, stared at the thick wad of bills in Gage's hand. "And this is only because your girl here wants to hook up with him?" she asked in what sounded like a Jamaican accent.

Justina exited, holding her hands over her heart. "I've wanted him for so long."

"Him?" the escort asked, having obviously come here before. "We are talking about the same man?"

"He's the man of my dreams."

The escort finally shrugged, snatching the money away. "The longer I live, the less surprised I am by what people are into."

Gage had stepped a few feet away. He ended his call and said, "I called you a taxi. It'll be right over there by the entrance in about five minutes."

The escort lit a long cigarette, winking at Gage. She tucked the money down into her moon-lit décolletage. "Thank you, sweetie."

Before the escort ambled away, Justina asked her for a cigarette, accepting a light but not inhaling. When they were alone, Gage cocked an eyebrow at her.

"To help obscure my face," she said. Justina slid on her aviator-style sunglasses, strutting up the walkway as Gage entered the breezeway from the rear of the building, concealing himself just out of sight.

"I'm nervous," she whispered as she stared at the red door.

"Don't be," Gage said. "This will be nothing but sheer fun."

After a final deep breath, Justina rang the doorbell. She held the cigarette to her lips, standing back to give the condo owner a full view. The bolt shot. As the door opened, the man was already talking, his voice dripping with disgust.

"...going to quit using your damned service. I was very clear about wanting an African woman tonight."

"Hello, Cortez," Justina said, lowering the cigarette and pulling her sunglasses off.

Cortez Redon, living under the alias of Julian Cirrosa, gaped at her. Though he probably looked vibrant on a normal day, with his deep tan, an open silk shirt, linen shorts and expensive flip-flops, right now he was the picture of terror.

"My name is Julian," he mumbled.

"Don't you remember your real name?" she asked, tugging the wig off.

Just then, Gage stormed around the corner and grabbed Redon by his neck.

The two men ended up on the sofa with Gage straddling the little man. The barrel of Gage's pistol, a handsome Ruger P95, was inside Redon's mouth. Behind Gage, Justina locked the door, striding in and sitting demurely across from the scene.

Gage eased the pistol out of the Spaniard's mouth and spoke over his shoulder. "Make the call."

Justina dialed a long number on her mobile phone. "Hola, Señora. I know it's late there but I assume you've been waiting up for us." She listened for a moment, smiling. "Yes, we're inside and little Cortez is here, right here in front of me. Do you have a message for him?" She nodded. "Let me put you on speaker." Justina touched the screen of her phone.

"Cortez?" came the voice over the speaker.

Redon was wide-eyed but silent. Gage rapped him on top of his head with the pistol. "Answer her."

"Y-y-yes?" Redon said, rubbing his head.

"Cortez, Mister Hartline and Miss Kaminski are under my employment now. They're there to retrieve something of mine."

The famous painting known as "The Scream" was a good representation of Redon's face at that moment.

"Gage, dear?"

"Yes, Señora Moreno?"

"Help Cortez remember where he put my money. I'll hold the line and listen."

Gage handed the pistol to Justina. He then shed his suit coat and cracked his knuckles as he stared at Redon with balled fists. "You ready, *hombrecito?*"

Cortez Redon soiled himself.

THE END

To The Lions is my first effort at writing a series. I hope you enjoyed it. After reading *The Diaries*, so many readers requested a series built around Gage Hartline. Honestly, creating a series was never something that appealed to me but, after writing this "sequel", I now know it was enjoyable—at least from my end. Please let me know if you want more of Gage.

As always, my books are highly-contrived and not to be taken seriously. Factual and grammatical errors surely exist, and all of them lie solely with me.

About the Spanish man in the wheelchair: he was inspired by two very brave people I'm fortunate enough to call friends. The first, Jamie Spears, lost his legs in a silage cutter. The second, Andrew Kinard, lost his legs in an IED explosion while serving as a Marine officer in Iraq. Both men are as capable as any human beings I know. They are heroes for inspiring so many others and they define the essence of human spirit.

Before I go on a jag of gratitude, the ultimate thanks belongs to my readers. To know that people want to share my thoughts is one of the warmest feelings I've ever experienced. It keeps me going and inspires me to give you more. I cannot thank you enough.

To my beta readers: John Humphries, Phillip Day, Scott Hortis, Jack Wright, and Lauren Knight—thank you! Your insights helped me make this book better. I wouldn't be able to produce anything worthwhile without people like you.

To Elizabeth Brazeal, editor extraordinaire, you're a well-oiled machine. I appreciate your hard work and your hunger for my books. It's a perfect combination.

Sarah Humphries, your Spanish knowledge is greatly appreciated. *Mi español es todavía muy mal!*

For my eagle-eyed proofers: AJ Norris, Curt "Courtis" von Berg, Kelley Norris, and Laura Hortis—I'm grateful that you spotted those niggling little errors that I'm simply unable to see.

Nat Shane, you're a wizard with cover art! Thanks for lending your talent and for your willingness to always help.

A portion of the proceeds of this book will be donated to The Wounded Warrior Project. Learn more at **http://www.woundedwarriorproject.org**.

Until next time, when I may take you either to Berlin or to South America (I'm still struggling to decide), I wish you all the best.

God bless,
C.

About the Author

Chuck Driskell is a United States Army veteran who now makes his living as an advertising executive. He lives in South Carolina with his wife and two children. *To The Lions* is Chuck's fifth novel.